Glorious Gaia

ANGRY GREEK GODS SERIES BOOK 4

<u>TRIGGER WARNINGS</u>

Please be advised that this book (and the entire series) will be **<u>gory</u>**.

Other triggers worth mentioning are:

- Alcohol
- Attempted murder
- Blood
- Cannibalism (heavy)
- Emotional abuse
- Gore (heavy)
- Hallucinations
- Incest (Greek mythology)
- Kidnapping
- Murder
- Occult
- Poisoning
- Profanity
- PTSD
- Religion
- Suicide (very mild & brief)
- Torture
- Violence

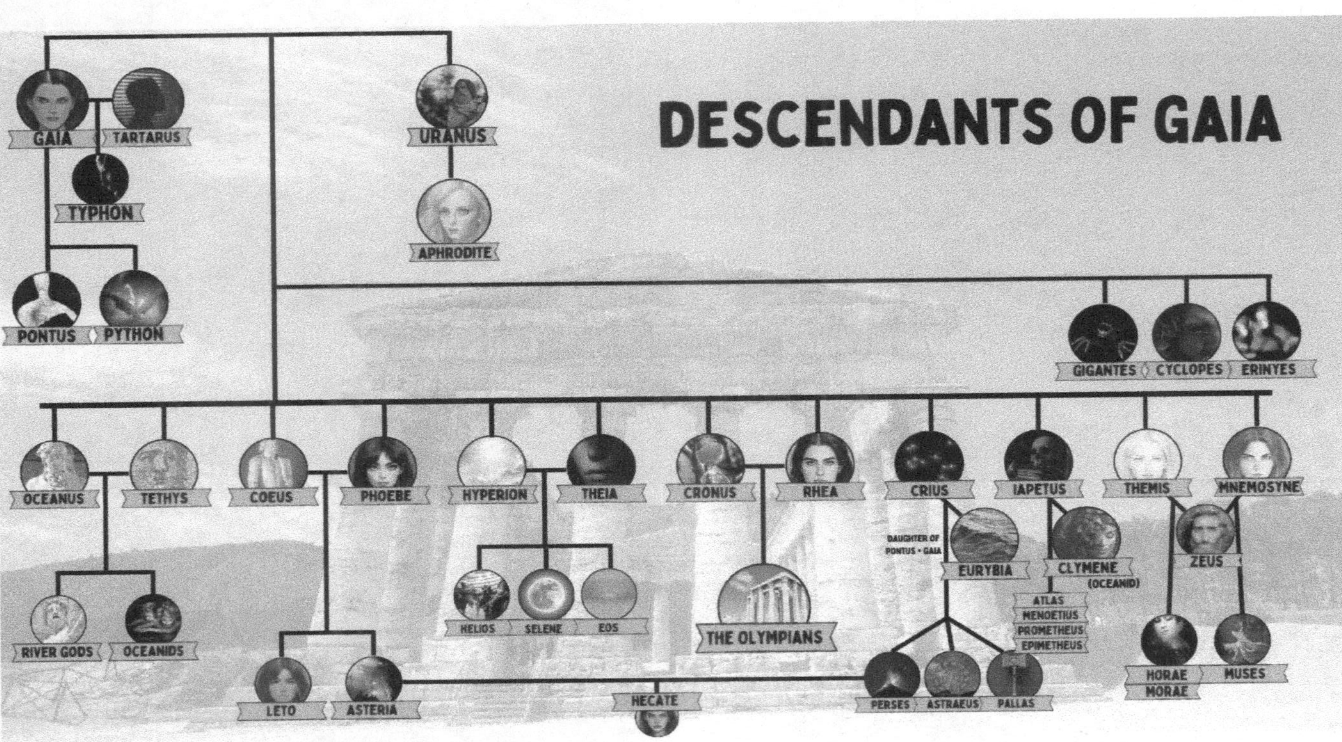

DESCENDANTS OF GAIA
GAIA
TARTARUS
TYPHON
PONTUS
PYTHON
URANUS
APHRODITE
GIGANTES
CYCLOPES
ERINYES
OCEANUS
TETHYS
RIVER GODS
OCEANIDS
COEUS
PHOEBE
LETO
ASTERIA
HECATE
HYPERION
THEIA
HELIOS
SELENE
EOS
CRONUS
RHEA
THE OLYMPIANS
CRIUS
DAUGHTER OF
PONTUS + GAIA
EURYBIA
PERSES
ASTRAEUS
PALLAS
IAPETUS
CLYMENE
(OCEANID)
ATLAS
MENOETIUS
PROMETHEUS
EPIMETHEUS
THEMIS
ZEUS
HORAE
MORAE
MNEMOSYNE
MUSES

|| 1. GLORY ||

GAIA

Be prepared for Gaia's glory.

She hadn't imagined that glory would be plotted out in the dark, dank dwelling of her favorite daughter, Mnemosyne, deep in the Underworld's mystical grounds, and paces away from Hades' palace; but it'd have to do, for now. She'd use the rotten mud stench as her ally, she'd absorb the smells of nearby nature—there *were* forests in the Underworld, after all—and she'd consume all the murky air she needed to fulfill her goals.

They'd all have to be prepared for those goals to come to fruition. Every single one of those lowly creatures she was embarrassed to call family members. They should have seen it coming; they should have felt her resentment. Not that they had any choice in the matter—her vengeance would come whether or not they liked it.

Centuries of gathering forces, coercing allies, working behind-the-scenes, whispering into minds, slipping through the shadows—Gaia had put together every possible resource, and she wouldn't fail. She couldn't.

The three Olympian goddesses that she'd captured, bound and gagged at her feet, gaped at her with various degrees of confusion and disappointment. Their eyes were big, glistening with concern. Their pallid expressions carried questions, demanded answers. They were shriveled versions of themselves; not the high-and-mighty princesses of the skies, not the beloved women Zeus valued most. Here, they were servants of Gaia, and Gaia loved it.

With a sneer at their mud-stained arms and crinkled outfits, Gaia realized she owed them nothing. She didn't *have* to explain herself to them. But to unravel little pieces of her plans to them might help her in the long run. If they were to see what she saw, if they were to feel how she felt, perhaps she'd enlist new allies today.

And perhaps not; but they'll be useful, either way.

"I've been visiting Tartarus, you know," she said, rubbing her nails over her silky green tunic. The fabric's softness soothed her in times of torment—and this was one such time. A time of terror lurking, of massive events about to take place, with her at the helm; and failure wasn't an option.

She was a primordial goddess, a revered figure of mythology and history, and she was about to divulge to her stepdaughter, granddaughter, and great granddaughter just what she'd been up to for many, *many* years.

They continued to gawk at her, as if she'd said she'd set fire to Olympus Palace itself. Which she might, if it came down to that, though she did love that palace dearly. But they gawked because they knew what her sneaking about meant; that she'd garnered much more power than they'd anticipated. Tartarus was heavily guarded, its entrance sealed shut, barred by multiple layers of stone, metal, and fire-forged steel. It was an entrance that, most times, one never got to go through twice; once past it, one never returned to the less menacing but not quite refreshing air of the Underworld.

The guards of Tartarus—Cottus, Briareus, Gyges, monstrous

giants every god in existence feared—were Gaia's children. And it didn't take much effort to bribe them into letting her into Tartarus…and letting her out.

"I've been talking to my children." She squinted at the Olympian goddesses, Hera in particular. It wasn't her fault, not fully; but it was *her* husband who might have released these children, had he been in the right mind-set. Zeus could have said one word to Hades, and Hades could have liberated those who'd waited long enough to purge their crimes.

Gaia couldn't help but snicker, wondering if Hera might be essential here, if she could be swayed. Could she speak with Zeus? Could she be convincing?

Not like she could ever stop him from vagabonding…so not a solid idea.

"Coeus, Crius, Iapetus; my Titans," she said, listing off her beloved progenies, one by one. And purposely omitting Cronus, that she had no intention of freeing unless absolutely necessary. "Typhon." Athena gasped—she well knew how dangerous *that* progeny was. "Chthonius, Astraeus, Ephialtes, Otus, Antaeus—yes, the surviving Giants. Those your filthy family *didn't* destroy."

The wars of the past—the Giants attacking Olympus, then the Titans launching their own mission to infiltrate the palace—had never quite settled in Gaia's gut. She'd taken her own side, each time—the side of remaining passive, out of the way, and observing fate as it unfolded. But after centuries of nurturing her pain, of trying to accept that her direct descendants had failed, she'd recognized she wasn't happy with the result. She wasn't happy with her children stuffed in a fiery cage, thousands of feet below ground, rotting, fading into nothingness. They were starved, losing power, desperate for freedom—and had been for so long. Too long.

Gaia heard their cries, nightly. Their wails whistled into her ears and roused her, causing her to pace; she *hated* pacing.

She rarely slept, for each time she closed her eyes, she remembered those she'd lost to Tartarus, but also those she'd lost permanently. Sometimes, the spirits of her poor descendants came to her, spoke to her, reminded her why she was plotting this insanely intricate coup. Those who were killed and flayed, their skin used for shields—*Athena's* shield, in particular. Those who were burned by torches, their flesh melting off, charred and crisp, decomposing into Gaia's green earth. Those smacked by staffs or clubs, their brains bashed in, their faces made unrecognizable from the impact. Without forgetting those crushed by boulders, heavy rocks, *entire islands,* limbs flattened and broken, then buried beneath volcanoes. Those shot at by lightning bolts, or felled by red-hot metal missiles that shredded into their chests, dislodged their hearts, dismembered them, decapitated them.

So much bloodshed and violence; Gaia's nightmares were red with blood, oozing through her every thought, plaguing her every breath. When she did sleep, she woke with that coppery taste in her mouth, and spat it out in rage, remembering she'd get her revenge, oh yes. She refused to rest until all her plans were in motion.

"You wonder why, I'm sure." She twirled a portion of her gown around her finger, squeezing tight. "Why would I want to meet with those who sought to murder you and yours, hm? All these years, you thought I'd been standing back, neutral, not wanting to interfere? I didn't, because I wanted *them* to prevail."

Hera's dark brows lifted; Athena and Aphrodite held hands. Such a sight, those two, usually at odds with one another, now uniting their strength in their fear of Gaia.

"The Giants, the Titans—they tried, in vain, to unseat that miserable king of yours." Gaia's nostrils widened and she sensed a glob of acidic spit swelling in her mouth. A flavor she often experienced whenever thinking of her grandson. An ungrateful, unbelievably spiteful, selfish prick who thought only of himself and his not-that-large cock he enjoyed sticking into any female in sight. He'd calmed down, of late, or so she'd been told; but he'd stray again, it was in his nature.

Poor Hera. Never good enough for him. She'd have made a better queen on her own.

She peered down at the three women, wriggling about, backing away from her as if expecting her to shoot more vines at them, to choke them, poke through them, eviscerate them.

"I'm going to give them another chance. Another opportunity to rid Olympus of Zeus—for good."

Hera mumbled into her gag, her words making no sense—but Gaia heard her thoughts.

"You can't do that! You can't take away the lot Zeus was given!"

"Are you trying to say, dear granddaughter," Gaia narrowed her gaze on Hera's now blanching face, "that *I*, Gaia, primordial goddess of the earth, creator of all of you useless creatures, cannot remove the prize I myself allowed to be given?"

Athena's mumble was a surprise; Gaia hadn't expected her to speak out, wise as she presumed to be. Her thoughts were concise and might have come off as a threat, were she not tied up and unable to voice her concerns.

"You did not give him his crown; you cannot take it away."

"I can *steal* it," said Gaia, not missing a beat.

Aphrodite gasped, this time, but if she wanted to speak, she didn't attempt to. Her thoughts were confused, shooting to and fro across her mind, but more focused on the outcome of her darling newly discovered son.

Lukus, said son, was inanimate on the altar, where Mnemosyne had enchanted him into a deep, restorative slumber. Gaia wanted to reassure Aphrodite that her precious half-god offspring would be fine; but it'd be a lie, and Gaia was done lying.

Time enough to explain to them what my plans are for Lukus.

"Zeus is not worthy of his crown," she raised a hand before Hera or Athena could grumble some chewed up response, "and I'll tell you why. Because he doesn't care for his humans enough, does he? No, he doesn't embrace them when they do well. But he doesn't punish them, either. He lets them get away with everything, choosing to not interfere when they're instigating wars or harming nature or fucking each other senseless; in all interpretations of that term, mind you." She massaged the bridge of her nose; bringing up Zeus' failures never failed to put her in a mood. "He's let them destroy the planet he was supposed to watch over. Famine? Death? Capitalism? Global warming? *All* things Zeus could have deliberated on, had he gotten his arse off that rigid stone throne of his. Had he taken his eyes off the bosoms of the pretty little things he employs in his service—"

Hera's earlier mumble became a growl.

"He does not stare at our serving staff anymore!"

Gaia cackled; a sound that reverberated through her every bone, taking root in her core and waking it, warming it. "You place too much trust in someone who has done nothing but betray you at every turn, my sweet. But fear not, I'll take care of him for you."

Gaia was all too excited to envision her children ripping Zeus from limb to limb, stringing him up from the Palace ceiling, then slowly cutting his flesh off and watching his ichor drip from his rotting corpse.

But murder wasn't her solution, as much as the thought of killing Zeus aroused her.

"My most loyal offspring will strip him of his title, mark my words. And with us ruling Olympus, this world will come to order once more. We *will* interfere in human affairs—and fix them." She arched her spine and spread out her arms, welcoming the stuffy, stale cabin air into a pleasant embrace. "We will regrow this world, save it, spare it from the destruction it's headed towards with Zeus' reign. For if we do nothing, we maybe have a few centuries before Earth dies from all its ailments. And if Earth dies—we die with it."

Silence welcomed that statement. A deafening, heavy quiet that proved to Gaia these Olympians knew nothing of the state of the world. Nothing of its mistreatment, of the level of suffering. This world would, if left untended, explode, and the gods would become crumbs floating in space, determined to discover a new home.

And we won't find one. The universe will not allow it.

"With my babies freed from their unnecessary prisons, they can lend me their power. Together, we can rebuild, restart."

She took a weighty breath, trying not to grimace at the mulch odor filling her nostrils. Why couldn't Mnemosyne live in a more hospitable, cleaner place? There were so many empty homes in the Underworld, dwellings unoccupied for decades at a time. Yet she chose this shabby, one-roomed shack with a roof about to cave in and walls made of actual dirt? It went against Mnemosyne's clean appearance, her tousled orange curls, her spotless golden tunic. And as much as Gaia enjoyed rolling around in the dirt herself, she didn't enjoy standing in it for extended periods of time, and being surrounded by it when giving a speech to her enemies and potential allies.

"They've all agreed to help, you see. With their assistance, my centuries of planning will finally mean something."

Athena stopped wriggling and glowered at Gaia with a repressed rage that *almost* tingled Gaia's extremities.

"You've lost your mind if you think you can trust those children of yours. They were locked up for a reason; releasing them will only bring chaos."

"Well," Gaia chuckled, "in my opinion, chaos is what we need."

Hera snorted. *"You'd unleash my father, would you?"* Her eyes were slanted, but the shrinking of her posture showed she feared her own thoughts. She was afraid of Cronus, and rightfully so; any deity with a modicum of sense shied away from the mere mention of him. *"And your husband?"*

Aphrodite shuddered at that. By the strangest of fates, she was a daughter of Uranus, Gaia's estranged husband. And though she didn't refer to herself as such—Uranus was a betrayer and a disgustingly horrific deity, after all, even Gaia admitted that—and it was only a technicality, Aphrodite was recognized as a goddess with powers descended from him. As far as Gaia remembered, she didn't quite like being reminded of it.

"No, I will not let *them* out. They betrayed *me,"* said Gaia, with a flick of her wrist, uncertain why she needed to re-educate these three on the depth of her son and spouse's treachery towards her. "They engendered Zeus' behavior. They ruined my offspring's' lives, so there's no way I'd allow them to do so again. I thought Zeus would be different, but alas…no. Uranus and Cronus will remain locked up; but I plan to draw from their energy to assist me with my plans. They'll be a part of this, though unwillingly."

She smiled and rubbed her hands together, recalling all the potions she and Mnemosyne had been working on to transfer powers between deities. Dark, mystical stuff, they were; and many ingredients stolen from the completely oblivious Hecate.

Oh, the wondrous things she keeps in that locked cabinet of hers.

"So you will kill Zeus?" Hera's thought came on suddenly, swerving into Gaia's mind while her attention was diverted on thoughts of forcing poison down her husband's throat.

Gaia brushed her fingers through her tresses; tangled and coated with a light layer of grass, like she preferred. "I won't if I don't have to. If he abdicates, or if my children overpower him and he surrenders, then I'll give him a taste of what he did to my babies. I'll lock *him* up for eternity in Tartarus." She bit her lip, switching her gaze to Athena, then Aphrodite. "But should he be too fitful, should he prove too difficult…then slitting his throat and waiting as the ichor pools out of him will be the least of my concerns."

|| 2. A LOT OF BLOOD ||

ZEUS

Something was amiss at the Palace.

He always knew, always sensed a swift vibration coursing through him whenever one of his own was going through high emotions. He felt his wife's rage when she experienced a jealous spell; and Ares' violence when he stomped about in his chambers, growling about improper procedures of war; and Aphrodite's moans when Ares' growls became something other than violent. Every trickle of Hermes' malice, the gentle, soothing tunes from Apollo's lyre—no matter where in the Palace he was located—the calming waves of the Muses as they weaved their magic.

Right now, he felt nothing. The palace was vacant; not as if its inhabitants left, but as if their emotions were on lock-down, stuck in impossible to reach places. Zeus couldn't feel his family members, and it prompted shivers to skid down his back.

He didn't like shivers.

In such strange situations, he'd usually seek the Fates, first, to ask them why his powers were dwindling, why his ever-mighty strength was testing him. But something urged him to locate Hera, instead. Her scent was normally the strongest of all Olympian godly energies, and right then, it wasn't invading his nostrils as it often did.

During these trying times, she wasn't allowed to leave the Palace—none of the gods were, save a handful with explicit consent from him—but he knew her well, better than anyone. She wouldn't worry about defying him if she had some pressing matter elsewhere.

"What pressing matter would she have?" He quirked a brow as he stormed down the corridor, having left his chamber after checking hers—she wasn't in there, and her maidens hadn't seen her.

He took a gander down the hall to his right, the massive, pillar and statue-lined one that would lead to his throne-room, and squinted.

It hadn't escaped him how many tiny dots formed a trail towards Hera being the culprit. Bread crumbs, for sure; nothing concrete, nothing that could outright prove that she'd been up to something…and yet the facts were worrying. And also the fact that Athena had blatantly accused her in front of all—that was concerning. Athena wouldn't do such a thing unless she were sure; and Zeus had felt her conviction, rattling his bones, anchoring deep into his stomach. He hadn't liked that in the slightest.

"Where in Tartarus are you, Hera?"

He proceeded down the hallway but took a sharp turn before the main Library entrance, slithering down the smaller corridor where he'd often seen Hermes corner servants in the dark, or Apollo flirting with one of his staff-members, away from prying ears and eyes.

Could Hera be responsible for all this madness? He hadn't let her out of his sight recently, sensing something off in her character, something affecting her being. Something he couldn't seem to explain and that the Fates hadn't been able to decipher for him. The chances were slim that she'd been the one poisoning gods directly, because he'd have seen it, or one of his cupbearers would have. But was she working with someone else? Facilitating their navigation around the

Palace? Infiltrating them in and out while no one was looking?

And for what purpose?

They'd been on such good terms for the past few centuries. Zeus had, thankfully, grown older, though outwardly he looked the same as when myths were first written about him, eons ago. Inside, though, he was tired, no longer interested in pursuing women who often resisted him and fought him off with transformations and devices he no longer cared to break through. His spirit was exhausted from all the frolicking, and he himself couldn't keep up with the vast number of offspring he'd produced.

Hera had appreciated his stoppage of adventures, most of all the gods. She'd become kinder, shown a softer, delicate side of herself that had aroused Zeus beyond measure. They'd rekindled some of the romance from their earlier years, enjoying rumbles in the sheets the likes of which they hadn't in a long, *long* time. Zeus smiled at the memory; then frowned when remembering how fast things had changed.

Out of nowhere, Hera had returned to being stiff, suspicious, and unable to trust anyone but herself and her favorite sons.

"Oh?" Zeus paused in his steps as he came around the corner to the main Dining Room's hall. "That's her?" He sniffed, diving into his godly intuition to analyze the scents swarming the air.

Following the trail of the aromatic energy, he ended up on the other side of the Dining Room, near the sculpture museum's doors. Here, the scent ended abruptly.

"Strange." He sniffled again; it wasn't Hera's delectable, sweet essence of baked goods and flowers. This was a pungent, nearly violent odor, tinged with alcohol and psychedelic effects. And it was blended with something else, blended with—

Zeus' mouth dropped open when he looked down and found a pool of bright blue ichor at his feet. He'd been seconds away from stepping right into it—he lifted his foot, backed away, and kneeled to narrow his gaze on the substance.

There was ichor, yes, a lot of it, splattered on the walls, staining the floor, dripping into the tiny crevices in the marble. But he also caught that sticky, sordid stench of poison, in its vibrant turquoise hue, swishing into the blood and swirling into its darker shade. A dizzying circle of shades of blue, seeping into the marble flooring, drawing him closer to it.

Poison—the same he'd detected on Themis, then on Phoebe, earlier that day.

"Another attack?" He rose to his full height and glanced left and right, finding the entire corridor empty, vacant of emotion. No shadows, no breathing; nothing.

Where was the body? He crouched to take another whiff of the energy emanating from the blood, and wrinkled his nostrils, recognizing the strong liquor and drug-like sweetness as Dionysus' ichor.

Knowing Dionysus, so many things might have happened here. He'd poisoned himself—wouldn't be the first time—and wobbled drunkenly over to rest, falling over at this precise spot to take a nap. Or he *had* been attacked by the culprit, but with so many atrocious elements already in his blood, the toxin didn't take effect as well, and he was able to stand up and walk away from the scene of the crime, unscathed. But where had he wandered off to? Zeus had passed near his chambers earlier, in his search for Hera, and hadn't smelled anything out of the ordinary; which meant he wasn't in his room.

Zeus tucked a few curly hairs away from his face and inhaled a deep breath of the atmosphere, letting the air creep into his nose and infest it.

Ah, there's more—I smell more beings here.

A new trail formed in his mind, one guiding him down the hall, toward the corner near the ballroom where Hera had summoned him for her impromptu anti-Athena meeting. Was that her lingering scent he was sniffing now, or something else?

No…the scent didn't lead to the ballroom. It led to his right, to a small glass door through which he saw a blare of sunlight and caught sight of a few bushes of flowers swaying in an Olympic breeze.

A small courtyard—the smallest of them all, if he recalled correctly. A tranquil place where he'd discovered Hestia praying, kneeled before the stone fountain. Where he'd once stumbled upon Demeter in a *very* private moment of self-indulgence. And where he hoped to find his wife, now. Her essence was strong here, and he prayed she'd be outside once he opened the door.

She wasn't. As he slipped out onto the brick pavement, a myriad of smells charged into his nose. Blood was rampant in all of them— but belonging to different individuals, their odors differing greatly. Scanning the small space, he soon found traces of this blood splattered over the fountain's base and the ground near it, and congealing on a spot to the right, near a cluster of roses. If he wasn't mistaken, there were quite a few drops in the water, too, swirling and swirling as if to hypnotize him into dunking his head and refreshing himself.

Ignoring the ominous call from the likely poisoned water, he started with the pool of ichor by the roses. One whiff had him scrunching his brows and frowning down at the substance, recognizing its half-god, half-mortal aroma: acidic and fragrant all at once. And the shiny swirl of turquoise toxins within it.

"Lukus? *Lukus* was attacked?" He was about to stomp over to the fountain, but scented another faint yet distinct odor of fire and jungle. "Mother?" He lowered to the ground and got as close to the still moving blood as he could without touching it. He took in a large breath, and shook his head as he straightened up. "Mother's blood mixed with Lukus' blood. That…makes no sense."

Panic rising in his gut, he hurried over to the blood on the fountain, and braced himself as he squatted and sniffed.

His legs gave out and he fell onto his behind, luckily not coming into contact with the ichor itself; but at this level, he was able to view the greenish-blue tint of poison spiraling within the obscure ichor. That sweetness, that delicious aroma of cake and cookies—there was no mistaking who it belonged to.

"Hera?"

***

Within less than an hour, Zeus had all chambers searched. He warned all those he came across to be on their guard, as several attacks had taken place at once; but he didn't tell everyone who exactly had been attacked.

Dionysus. Lukus. Rhea. Hera. After sniffing in a bit too much of their blood, Zeus was dizzy, disoriented. He'd struggled to keep on his feet, worry crawling into his mind and infesting it with outcomes he didn't want to see; not yet. Not until they'd all been found.

Sitting on his throne, massaging his temples, he realized all four of them were no longer in the palace. Despite their blood being imprinted inside his nostrils, he couldn't smell *them,* their energies, their presences. And he'd tried, desperately, to detect them, as he dashed out of the courtyard and fetched his cupbearers, his guards, his spies, telling them to strip the palace bare, to round up anyone or anything suspicious.

They'd come back with nothing.

The striking coldness of the stone beneath him reminded him of an important factor, a detail he needed to take note of—the only blood *not* tinged with poison was Rhea's. Hers was pure, and in a much smaller quantity, almost as if spilled accidentally. Why had she bled? Who'd made her bleed? And what had she been doing for someone to want her to?

Rhea was, most days, a calm titaness who minded her own business and kept to herself. She'd been living in the jungle for decades, and didn't take part in most Olympian drama. She *did* have a furious fire in her when irritated, however; so had she been arguing with one or all of those whose blood Zeus had found outside?

Zeus tapped his fingertips on his throne's armrests. Hera had been tense, Rhea had been tense…had they been tense *because* of one another? He'd rarely, if ever, seen his wife and mother have disagreements, and definitely none powerful enough to draw blood.

"Lock down the palace," he said, snapping at the guards who'd returned from their exploration of every inch of the Olympus dwelling. "And bring me my Olympian children."

They ran without question, and sounded the alarm—the ear-pinching, teeth-gritting screech Zeus reserved for emergencies, to alert his inhabitants that something was afoot.

Ares popped up first, equipped with his trusty sword and his helm placed atop his mop of black hair. "Father?" He stopped at the throne-room's threshold, glowered inside, then marched up to bow to Zeus, his chest gleaming with sweat from what Zeus hoped was a recent work-out, and not a session of sex with Aphrodite. "What's with the alarm? I thought we were being invaded."

"We might well be, sooner or later," said Zeus, waving at Ares to straighten up. "Sit; I'm waiting for your siblings before I explain anything."

Hephaestus barged in with an ax dripping in recently shed blood, Zeus noticed. He tried not to scrunch his nose at the stench of guts filling the air. Hephaestus had the eeriest of pass times, one of them, of late, being butchering meat for Hestia's kitchen staff.

Seeing his brother seated on his throne of swords and spikes, Hephaestus limped over to his own seat, fiery with the heat of a volcano.

Once properly perched, he turned, addressing Ares. "Invasion?"

"We're waiting to find out," mouthed Ares, sitting firm as steel, spine stiff against the throne-back.

Apollo and Artemis strolled in together, somewhat unfazed by the still blaring alarm. Zeus detected a look of knowing in Apollo's eyes. As one of the healers in this investigation, he often sensed the same perils as Zeus did, and could detect the poison when it was close. Did he scent it on Zeus, who'd approached the substance perhaps too often today? Did he understand at first glance that something dire was going on, more dire than the situation already at hand?

Smart boy—and he must have warned his sister.

Hermes meandered in while fastening his tunic to his waist— evidently he'd been engaged in some dark corridor action, as per usual, but had been disturbed by the siren. His blond curls were miffed up and he had that glaze in his eyes; the one Zeus had seen in them more than once while he was up to no good.

At the vision of his siblings assembled and seated, he took his throne immediately and switched his expression from quietly aroused to solemn.

Zeus peered at the entryway, waiting. He knew Dionysus wouldn't show—he'd disappeared, that much was clear—but where was Athena? She should have been the first to appear when summoned. She wouldn't miss out on an opportunity to impress Zeus, especially after her recent behavior of defying him. And even Aphrodite, though technically not his descendant, would have made an appearance eventually, her curiosity too overpowering to ignore.

Yet neither goddess showed. Five minutes, ten, fifteen, thirty— no one else came.

As Zeus rose, startling those who had reported for duty, two guards stumbled into the room and quickened to kneel before him with their heads bent.

"Athena is missing, my king," said one of them, voice trembling with fright. "We found ichor near her door, a sure sign of struggle."

"Ichor?" Zeus lifted an eyebrow. "Any turquoise-appearing color to that ichor?"

"No, majesty." The guard gulped. "And…we took it upon ourselves to search for Aphrodite, too, since she often attends such meetings with you…"

Ares groaned, prompting Zeus to spin to him. "Let me guess; she's not here, either?" He smacked the tip of his sword to the floor, coming close to cracking the wooden dais' surface. "Of course she's not; she was supposed to meet me after refreshing herself, and she *does* take hours to do that but…it's been too long."

Though Hephaestus' aura glowed orange and gold with animosity, he nodded at his brother, his black eyes slitted. "I was in my chambers earlier, fetching some supplies. I normally hear her rummaging about in her quarters, since they're across from mine, but…I didn't detect her presence in there."

Zeus leaned over and set his elbows on his knees, using his hands to hold his chin up. "Then we'll add them both to the list of disappeared."

"Disappeared?" Artemis shot up from her seat, sending a few dried leaves from her tunic to the floor. "Who else is gone? Is that what the siren was about?"

Apollo gestured at her to calm down, then gazed at Zeus. "Father? What is happening?"

Zeus scrubbed his face. He hated showing emotion in front of his constituents, his children; but he could tell he was about to overflow with worry and had no means to stop himself.

"Several Olympians have vanished."

"Sire," said the second guard, who hadn't deigned to raise his voice until now. "I must add that in our search of the palace, we discovered that those who were poisoned…Themis and Phoebe…have also left the premises."

Zeus' hands became warm, warmer, *hot*. They sizzled with energy, and lightning developed in his fingertips, coursing up and down his arms in zapping motions that made him twitch.

"What in Olympus is going on here?"

|| 3. BUSINESS ||

PERSEPHONE

Some would call the Underworld's air stale, starchy; some had called it foul, dirtied with death and decay. And truth be told, there *was* something sour and slightly nasty about it. A fetid odor that wrinkled one's nostrils if they weren't used to it. Persephone found it oddly stimulating, and was never able to explain why; not to her mother, who was her closest confidante, and not to her husband, the ruler of this world, one well used to the stench of it.

Something in the dark, dreary-like atmosphere woke Persephone up, sprang her into action. While other gods would call fall and winter dead seasons, where everything faded into the soil and shifted to shades of white and gray, Persephone became more active. Her half-year spent in the Underworld was never unproductive, and she never complained—well, not anymore, at least.

It was outside that she thrived most, picking elderberries near the Elysian Fields and gathering up herbs she'd later share with her mother, when she returned upstairs to Olympus. Or meeting with souls awaiting judgment, offering them peaceful thoughts, delivering baskets of pomegranates to those she thought might be waiting a while.

Today, there was something *off* about the air. More pungent than normal, imbued with a sense of malice, a fragrant aroma of sweet betrayal. Another thing she couldn't explain—she often detected if there were threats in the vicinity, or anyone whose soul had ill intentions as they approached the palace. More so since she'd been poisoned, then healed by Hecate. Whatever the witch-goddess had injected into her had offered her some new and improved abilities.

The off-putting scent had drawn her outside. She'd been plucking weeds in her private indoor garden, and caught a puff of something that caused an ominous jolt in her belly. She'd followed that scent, and was now rummaging through the rose bushes by the palace doors, figuring some of them had wilted and taken up a terrible stench—she could smell dead flowers from miles away, and disliked them adorning the entrance of her home.

Though deeply concealed inside one of the bushes—she didn't shy away from the scrapes caused by thorns, and had the marks on her arms to prove it—she detected someone approaching the palace, and froze. She couldn't see them clearly, vision blocked by vines and massive roses, but she did visualize a feminine figure, a lengthy gown swishing over the jewel-encrusted pavement. She had the pace of someone in a hurry.

Through the emerald-colored leaves and past the aubergine-hued rose petals, Persephone watched the figure, wondering who it might be. The individual didn't come to the front door, and instead swerved left, towards the side.

Persephone muffled a gasp; only one person went that way when arriving at the palace—Hecate. Was that her? Had she come back from Olympus?

Not wanting to startle whoever this was—though praying it was indeed Hecate—Persephone wriggled out of the bush, ripping her mahogany skirts in the process. With a groan, she zapped at the fabric to re-attach it, then shook out said skirts and tiptoed towards where the mystery visitor had hurried off.

She rounded the corner just in time to witness the person—curly orange hair, a gold dress covering golden sandals—peering left and right before descending the secret steps that led under the palace, to Hecate's crypt. She'd also seen the intruder's eyes—wide, a basic but recognizable brown flecked with gold. They marked Persephone's heart and squeezed it.

Mnemosyne? What's she doing?

This was the third or fourth time Persephone had noticed Mnemosyne slinking down into Hecate's crypt for who knew what reason. And on every other occasion she hadn't questioned it— Mnemosyne was Hecate's aunt, and she often asked the witch-goddess for ingredients for her memory potions, or discussed the benefits of certain herbs with her. They weren't on the friendliest of terms, but they weren't enemies, either.

But what bothered Persephone was that Hecate *wasn't there,* wasn't in her crypt at that moment. She was in Olympus.

Why was Mnemosyne going downstairs when Hecate wasn't there to greet her?

Everyone in the Underworld knew Hecate's lair was strictly off-limits unless she was there to allow access. There were no special enchantments or spells blocking doors; only simple locks opened by keys in Hecate's possession. But it was implied that no one would be daft enough to breach her dwelling and dig through her precious potions. Her poison cabinet *was* enchanted, with reinforced spells since the break-in, and yet...

Something triggered Persephone to follow Mnemosyne to inspect what she was up to.

She made no effort to lessen the noise she was making—she'd been wearing her gardening clogs, and they were *loud*, even in the dirt surrounding the property—and the *clank clank* of her steps on the secret stony stairs announced to Mnemosyne that she was being followed. Yet the titaness of memory didn't slow down until they both reached the bottom.

Persephone caught up to her, grabbed her by the shoulder, and spun her around.

This section of the crypt gave Persephone the creeps. A circular lobby filled with stone gargoyle witches set up in a semicircle, guarding the secret stairs, and also guarding the main crypt corridor, their dark eyes scanning every visitor to gauge their intentions.

Ignoring the gargoyle's inquisitive gaze, Persephone tightened her grip on Mnemosyne. "What are you doing down here?"

Persephone was, most days, intimidated by Mnemosyne. She rarely left her hut, and when she did, she left a trace of majesty and oblivion in her passage, subduing and swaying anyone who sought to speak to her. She didn't speak—not if she could help it—and only whispered words into people's minds and persuaded them against approaching her.

Today, however, she was in Persephone's territory. The crypt, though housing Hecate and her experiments, belonged to Hades. And whatever belonged to Hades, belonged to Persephone. Mnemosyne, grand titaness that she was, was trespassing.

Mnemosyne blinked at Persephone as if she were a figment of her imagination, and pinched her lips. "None of your business, majesty." Her voice was sultry, with a slight croak to it—when she *did* speak, she was enchanting and, one might say, quite sexy to listen to, even Persephone had to admit.

But she wouldn't be bent to the alluring woman's will. "If it's in *my* palace, then it is *my* business, Mnemosyne." She gestured towards the charcoal-colored corridor leading to Hecate's various chambers. "Hecate isn't here, so you have no *business* coming to her crypt."

Mnemosyne's light brown eyebrows raised, shocked at Persephone's defiance. In centuries, they'd exchanged perhaps three words total; and all three times Persephone had been respectful, if not shy. Now, she was guarding her domain like one of Hecate's fierce hounds, all of which she felt animating behind the nearby door containing them.

"I have *business* with Melinoë, if you must know." She swept a hand through her bushy curls and slid out of Persephone's reach; Persephone hadn't realized she'd been squeezing Mnemosyne's shoulder as they spoke.

An uncomfortable warmth spread up her arm from the contact, then lessened once they were no longer touching.

"Melinoë?" Persephone repressed a shudder at the mention of her bastard daughter, who dwelled in the shadows of Hecate's crypt and could barely muster enough words to form a proper sentence. "Who so happens to be my daughter and who has absolutely no notion of what *business* is. I don't even think she comprehends the word itself."

"Well," Mnemosyne tossed her mane, and a whiff of caramelized apple hit Persephone's nostrils, "we *do* have business, regardless. We have been…working on something together."

Persephone set her fists on her hips and squinted at the woman before her, in all her golden gowned grace, fidgeting to muster up excuses to justify her presence.

It was all *bullshit*, and Persephone wouldn't have it.

It's too suspicious with everything that's been going on lately.

"In Hecate's absence? I highly doubt that. Hecate wouldn't let *anyone* approach Melinoë for any sort of business transaction unless she were there to oversee it." Persephone leaned forward. "How about telling me the truth?"

In a few breaths, Mnemosyne zoomed closer and grasped Persephone by the shoulders, her pointy nails digging through her dress' material, and into her flesh. She forced Persephone to look at her—her eyes enlarged and filled with stars, circling, *circling*, seeping into Persephone, trying to take possession of her mind.

"Hecate has allowed it," said Mnemosyne, her voice a lullaby, a string of skillful notes that enticed Persephone, strolling about in her brain and blooming flowers in every corner. Flowers that smelled like decay and deceit—and that had no alteration on Persephone's state of mind. "So *you* will allow it, too."

The stars continued to circle, attempting to coerce Persephone; but all they did was make her dizzy. Whatever spell Mnemosyne was trying on her…it wasn't working, not fully.

Mnemosyne must have sensed that Persephone was resisting her, for she brought her face closer, touching their noses. They were of a height, but made of different stuff, for sure; Mnemosyne was sparkles and honey, but Persephone was tough as leather. Impenetrable.

Mnemosyne kept poking, though, kept shooting her energy into Persephone's mind, to mess with her thoughts, alter her memories. She reached, reached, *reached* deep into the confines of Persephone's soul and clawed at it, not to rip it apart, but to inject it with her spell's effects.

There were no effects. Persephone felt nothing but a slight nausea in her gut, which might have been due to the astonishment of Mnemosyne actually trying to use her powers on her.

Persephone tried not to smile. It seemed Hecate's magic had done more than infuse her with a few extra abilities; it had apparently made her immune to Mnemosyne's memory charms.

But to fully understand what Mnemosyne was up to, Persephone needed to pretend like she'd been subdued. She needed to act the part, and play dumb so she could investigate what the titaness was truly up to, and why. She could, later, speak with Melinoë and extract information from her; for now, she needed to take on the role of a memory-controlled zombie.

If she'd sensed Persephone's sharpness, Mnemosyne didn't imply it, nor did she seem upset that the spell wasn't taking. Was *she* convinced it had worked? Had Persephone somehow coerced *her*?

The titaness blew on Persephone's face; a powdery substance that Persephone knew to be her weapon to put others to sleep. She'd heard rumors of it, and those rumors claimed she hadn't used that ability in eons. Clearly, she hadn't forgotten how.

"You won't question me again," whispered Mnemosyne, squinting, lurking, anticipating Persephone's body to go limp and crumble at her feet.

But her sleeping powder, like her mind-control attempts, had no effect on Persephone.

Shit. Pretend to fall asleep, then?

How Mnemosyne couldn't tell her magic was pointless, Persephone might never know. Was her mind concealed, protected against the titaness' energy? She'd have to ask Hecate about that later, when she came home.

Persephone loosened her legs and let her eyes roll to the back of her head. She'd feigned sleep on more than one occasion in her life, and this time wouldn't be any different. She let her arms droop at her sides and her head lull forward, and waited as Mnemosyne gently deposited her on the cold, damp floor. An odor of wet dog and dewy grass entered her nose, and she tried not to scrunch it in displeasure.

From this angle on the floor, Persephone slitted her eyes and watched as Mnemosyne dashed to Hecate's witchcraft and potion room, zapped something on the door, pressed a hand to it, and pushed. She scurried in, and sealed herself inside.

Oh, I need to tell Hades about this, at once.

***

After creeping past the closed potion room door, Persephone sprinted upstairs and down the hall to Hades' primary parlor. Though it was a place he preferred for entertaining guests, and he usually didn't use it unless he *had* guests, he'd been nostalgic since Athena and Hermes had left, and had been cloistering himself inside to drown his sorrows.

Persephone didn't knock—not that she needed to—and found her husband seated on the emerald divan, an old bottle of sherry uncorked and sitting before him on the coffee table, and his fiery red goblet half-emptied. He was tired; dark circles under his dark eyes, his mess of a mane messier than usual, and he wore his black evening tunic that made him look like more of a reaper than even Thanatos did.

"Hades," she said, stopping before the coffee table to get his attention. He hadn't flinched at the opening and closing of the door, and only came to as he saw his wife standing there, in her ragged gardening gown.

"Wife?" He gestured at the sherry—a rich flavor of licorice and red fruits emanating from the bottle—then at one of the chairs surrounding the sofa. "Join me."

Persephone winced. Not only did Hades only drink sherry when he was deeply stressed, but he *never* offered her to indulge in it; he knew she disliked it. Most days he remembered all her favorites—pomegranate flowers, a juicy tomato to bite into, and pomegranate liqueur with a splash of ambrosia as a digestif.

"I'll join, sure." She waved at the dusty bottle that she knew he'd extracted recently from the hutch, while Athena and Hermes were there. "But not to drink." She chose to settle next to him on the couch, and he moved the paperwork he'd deposited on the cushions to give her space.

Paperwork in the entertaining parlor? That's odd.

"Forgive me." He cringed. "Pomegranate liqueur…I can fetch some for you." He turned to the door, to snap for a serving girl. Persephone set her hand on his arm and spun him back to her. "No? No drinking at all?"

"We need to talk," she said, doing her best to level her voice, to hide its shaking, its nervousness. Whenever she informed Hades of eerie events happening in his realm, he reacted badly. And he'd react worse knowing she'd been spying on someone as grandiose and revered as Mnemosyne.

Hades looked at her, *really* looked at her, for the first time since she'd entered the parlor. His face changed from whatever depression he'd been submerged in, to a flagrant concern for his wife.

"What is it?" He tucked a vagrant strand of her auburn hair behind her ear, and his touch burned her skin, igniting it with a sudden, inexplicable lust.

She gulped down her desire—they'd have time to revel in that later, and she'd need to, after what she told him—and took his hand, lowering it from her face.

"Something is fishy down here; fishier than usual. I spotted Mnemosyne sneaking down into Hecate's lair. Again."

"Again. Again?" Hades quirked a brow. "And?"

"And…Hecate isn't there, Hades. She doesn't allow visitors when she's not present, even someone like Mnemosyne." Persephone perked up, pursing her lips. "And yes, *again*. She's been going down there much more often than is customary, though usually Hecate is there to welcome her."

Hades leaned to the coffee table and snatched his goblet, swirling its contents under his nose. A shadow of scruff lingered along his jawline; a rarity, as he preferred to be clean-shaven at all times— Persephone had begged him to be.

"I assume she's borrowing ingredients to help out with all the nonsense going on?" He took a swig, hissed at the alcohol burning down his throat, then patted Persephone's leg. "Did you stop to think that perhaps Hecate *asked* her to do this?"

Persephone nudged his hand off her. "No, because she didn't even mention Hecate. She stated she had business with Melinoë." She huffed. "*No one* has business with Melinoë but me, or Hecate. Mnemosyne has no right to talk to her."

Hades narrowed his gaze on her as he took another sip. "I love you, my sweet, but you may be overreacting."

He should have known better; to use such words towards Persephone, who was the epitome of calm and composed at all times, compared to other Greek deities. And especially considering what had happened to her, what *he* had done to her. In her lifespan she'd been kidnapped, raped, her fate decided for her—so all things considered she was an angel, and her rare flares of temper were inconsequential.

To have him demean her like so wasn't acceptable.

She shot up from the sofa, and Hades immediately grimaced, aware what he'd started. He was normally delicate in his conversations with her, and walked over eggshells to not animate her because he loved her too much to lose her. He groveled at her feet and responded to her every demand and spoiled her with all she'd ever wanted—but comments like these, and implying she was seeing things, were enough to boil her insides and threaten them to burst.

He raised his hands in complete surrender, bowing forward slightly. "I'm sorry, my dear, I didn't mean to—"

"—to what? Imply I'm losing my mind?" She stamped a foot to the floor, rattling the walls with her rage. "I've been telling you for weeks that something is *up* down here, no? Something foreign got into our atmosphere and is polluting it, and now I notice Mnemosyne sneaking around and acting strangely and you mean to dismiss it as me overreacting?"

He stood up, his lengthy sleeves swaying as he wrapped his fingers around her wrists. "I know, *I know,* I didn't word that right. Pardon me, I'm…distraught." He motioned at the bottle of sherry. "Evidently. I agree with you, you know this. There is something amiss down here, and that's why I'm sitting here pondering it. But are you sure you're not…"

Persephone fought his grip, but it was no use; infused with irritation as she was, she was still no match for Hades' Olympian strength and had no choice but to let him hold on to her. And in truth, his touch soothed her, his finger-pads soft, and his cold breath billowing out cooled her heated face.

"I'm not…what?" She steadied her breaths, that had gotten somewhat irrational after her abrupt standing up and stomping. They didn't argue as often as before, but when they did, she tended to flare out of control and burn up like a bonfire.

"Not," he swallowed, loosening his clutch on her, "trying to find excuses for me to bring you upstairs? To reunite with your mother before it's time? You've been miserable this year, I don't know why…and I sense you're hoping to depart earlier."

Though she should have been enraged by his assumption, should have blown up and smacked him across his pallid cheek, she instead slithered out of reach and crossed her arms, glaring at him.

"Why must you always assume I'm trying to leave?" She cocked her head, watching as he melted before her, once more aware he'd made a mistake with his words. Powerful king he was, but he shattered whenever he upset his wife. "In the eons I've been living here, do you truly still think I dislike it?"

He scrubbed his face and sighed. "I…don't know. You can be so hard to read, sometimes."

"And you can be so hard-headed and convinced in your ways." She snickered at him, and made for the exit, but twisted to look at him once more as she wrapped her hand around the knob. "You've known me for my entire life, and yet you still claim to not be sure of who I am, of what I'm thinking? Why, Hades? Why can't you see that I've forgiven you, and that I love you, too? That I no longer seek to escape you?" She tugged the door open and turned away. "You never listen, but I hope you hear me this time. Danger is crawling into your kingdom, and I guarantee you Mnemosyne has something to do with it."

Before he could snatch her wrist and yank her back inside—he *hated* airing their dirty laundry with doors open and eavesdropping servants—she shimmied down the hall and up the several sets of stairs to reach her fourth-floor bedroom.

|| 4. A MASTER MULTI-TASKER ||
GAIA

For a half-mortal, Lukus Arvantis wasn't half bad looking. Not that looks had had any importance in her plans, but Gaia wouldn't have minded it if the creature leading a zombie army up to the Olympus gates in her stead was halfway decent to look at.

And Lukus was. She brushed a hand gently over his damp forehead, swiping away his blackened curls, soft and sweet smelling despite the hut's dirt and mulch odor overpowering most of Gaia's senses.

She recalled his eyes—a soupcon of the otherworldly blue from his mother, Aphrodite, with a pinch of awe and marvel as he drank in his surroundings.

Gaia had watched him closely while at the Olympus Palace. She'd needed to gather intelligence on his habits, to understand his behavior, his gestures, to better learn how to control him. Demi-gods were, contrary to goddesses like Hera—who had a habit of punishing them for their sole existence—not Gaia's realm of expertise.

He was tall, muscular, sporting a broad chest with well-defined pectorals and *abs*, as the humans called them. And his legs were thick and sturdy, perfect for long treks. Lukus had one such trek ahead of him.

His eyes were fluttering, long black lashes moving as he mumbled incomprehensibly in his semi-slumber. He *was* waking up, slowly, but Gaia wasn't sure how unconscious he really was just then. Had he been tuning into her conversation—one-sided, since she'd been the only one talking—with the Olympians? Was he more awake than he'd let on? And if so, why would he feign being asleep?

Doubtful. He'd have no idea how to mask his mind from someone like me. Right now, his mind is... at rest.

She spun to her minions, her precious poisoned darlings who'd done so much of the dirty work for her. Dionysus was huddled in a corner, trying to lick the moisture from one of the walls; Gaia chortled at the sight. Themis was still weaving around the altar, her hungry gaze fixed on Lukus as she muttered ancient Greek incantations. And Phoebe was staring at the door, eyebrows raising and lowering, shifting forward every few seconds as if about to run over and hurl herself outside.

She wouldn't, but Gaia sensed her control over the intoxicated ones diminishing by the minute. The poison in them was strong—some of the strongest batch she'd ever made—but still it was dwindling, and Gaia needed more.

She, too, glared at the door, expecting Mnemosyne to rush through at any moment to deliver the ingredients she'd requested. Why was she taking so long? Had she been caught? Intercepted by Persephone, Hades, or Hecate?

Gaia's hands curled into fists.

Goddess, how I hate them all.

Yes, they were her family, but the trio of the Underworld truly got on her nerves the more she remained in proximity with them. To have to sit back and ignore the sensations they triggered in her gut was exhausting. Their comings and goings—Hecate's, mostly, as Hades and Persephone usually stayed inside—were cryptic, and they had no set schedule that allowed her to set her plans in motion without risk of being caught.

Years, *years* she'd spent her time between her forests and being cramped inside Mnemosyne's hut attempting to plot, thinking that Mnemosyne's magic would shield her from other Underworld inhabitants and their interest. She wasn't certain it was working. And *her* curiosity grew with every passing day.

How cozy they must have been, those three, in their Underworld nest of diamonds and lavish luxury, likely spending their free time— and they had a lot of it—fucking one another into oblivion. She'd *heard* Persephone's moans more than once. Her wails of pleasure were so loud Gaia expected anyone in the Underworld had clapped their hands over their ears to avoid listening to her arousal while Hades spent *hours* thrusting into her. Some might have thought Persephone was exaggerating, faking; but Gaia felt the real desire in the air, and envisioned the goddess' toes curling in delight as Hades pounded into her. Oh, and he pounded—Gaia heard that, too.

Those two had yet to produce anything from their lovemaking, and Gaia wondered why they kept on with the same rhythm and the same incessant need to fuck with no cause in mind.

In any case, those sounds she didn't mind as much as she'd learned to tune them out. It was the sound of Hecate's repressed lust that bothered her the most.

Virgin goddess, my ass.

She didn't believe the witch-goddess one single second, with her fierce preservation of her virginity. Or at least, she didn't believe it'd last much longer. She'd seen—*everyone* had seen—how Hecate had ogled Hermes while up in Olympus. Licking her lips as discreetly as possible, fingers twitching with an overwhelming energy to touch, to tease, to explore. Gaia had no doubt Hecate *did* explore herself, while alone, though she was quieter about it, compared to Persephone. And how Hermes devoured her with his eyes dipped in desire, and the thoughts—oh, the *thoughts*—that passed through his mind whenever he was in Hecate's presence. The things he wanted to do to her— nastily delicious, Gaia thought, and the simple imagination of such torrid acts gave *her* the itch to touch herself.

That, she enjoyed. Taking care of herself had always been Gaia's preferred method of arousal; if only her lovers had figured that out.

But she wouldn't touch herself from *that* notion. She couldn't give anyone that satisfaction, couldn't lower her guard, ever. Hecate, entertaining as her adventures were, was a danger, and Gaia intended to keep a close watch on her when she returned. Others were spying on her in Olympus, she thought. The witch-goddess was too close to Persephone, and obeyed Hades' every command...and if her memories were to return, if Mnemosyne's spell on her were to wane, then Gaia's schemes would be exposed. Too soon. She wasn't ready yet.

Out of pity, Gaia removed the gags from the trio of goddesses clumped together in a corner of the hut.

"I'll give you another chance, but anything rude or threatening towards me, and I'll seal your mouths *permanently,* do you hear?"

Hera glowered, but said nothing. Oh, how she resembled her mother—

Rhea. Where is *she? I expected she'd be back soon, having delivered my message to Zeus.*

She shrugged off the eerie sensation that something was up—that her attempt at sending Rhea away had failed, that the teleportation hadn't worked—and scanned Aphrodite and Athena's faces for traces of rebellion.

They wouldn't dare—that much was clear now. They realized who and what they were dealing with, and knew they had no chance if they were to try to defy Gaia.

Aphrodite embraced herself and leaned into the hut's muddy walls, but didn't speak. Hera brushed herself off; Athena, however, inclined her head and cleared her throat.

"Yes?" Gaia folded her arms, looking down on the wisdom goddess with a quirked brow. *Was* she going to defy her?

"Only a question," said Athena, her voice croaky from having been contained within her throat for so long. "A matter of…mechanics. I wonder how you're doing all this. Where you obtained all these…obscure powers?"

"Ah," Gaia rubbed her chin, "the wise woman in you is intrigued, I see." She rested her tense spine against Lukus' altar and sighed. "I learned to use the world's anger and the lingering frustration in nature to develop my mind-reading skills. Those all upper-level gods have, but I turned them into a sort of mind-control. It took centuries, mind you; which is why so many of my plots are only coming to fruition now. I've been working on this for a long, long time, my dear."

"What about the…" Athena gulped, peering left to right to see if either of her family members were going to chip in and ask questions. Neither moved nor made any indication that they planned to speak. "The distance? You weren't *with* those you poisoned, I presume. And you did it to…several people at once, correct? While doing other things?"

If Gaia wasn't mistaken—and she rarely was—there was a hint

of awe in Athena's tone. Difficult as her intentions were, Gaia *was* enormously overpowered, and she'd forgotten how some might find that fascinating. An inquisitive goddess by nature, Athena likely couldn't help herself from wondering.

"Well, for one thing, I'm a master multi-tasker." Gaia smirked, flipping her fiery mane in pride. "In fact, I'll let you in on a secret. I'm currently trying to warp into good old Tartarus' mind as we speak, to seduce him."

Hera's eyebrows lifted, and Aphrodite, who'd been busy brooding and glancing towards her unconscious son, switched her gaze to Gaia.

"Seducing?" She blinked once, twice, then cocked her head. "You can…seduce at a distance?"

"Tartarus?" Hera scrunched her nose ever so slightly.

Tartarus, the god—not the realm.

Few had met the primordial god who'd been born at the same time as Gaia and their sibling, Chaos. Hera had, once, and had been terrified of him ever since. He wasn't what one might call a handsome god; his skin was actual fire and his breath was smoke and if he'd given his name to the Underworld prison, there was a reason for it. But he *could* alter his appearance at will and show himself as a humanized version, to lessen the blow of the shock of his true self.

"Yes, *that* Tartarus," said Gaia, with a wink. She, unlike other gods, adored the volcano-like god, though her sentiments weren't often returned. Currently, he was refuting her requests to let her into Hades' palace and up to his opulent guest room where they might rip each other's clothes off and have at each other. It wouldn't be out of pure pleasure—but she'd enjoy it—because in truth she needed Tartarus to impregnate her with a few more monsters to fulfill her plans. "And yes, I *can* seduce at a distance. Whispers in the ear, a gentle caress of the cheek or the neck…it's an addicting power."

Aphrodite sulked—was she, a mistress of seduction, jealous?

Gaia's belly swelled at the reminiscence of carrying her giants within her. The violent attraction between her and the gods she'd bedded was still active inside her, and though she wasn't a sexual deity in any shape or form, she had many, *many* urges that Aphrodite wasn't responsible for. The goddess of love and beauty—or her son Eros, for that matter—hadn't given Gaia her craving for the flesh, her adoration of the act of sex. She'd developed that on her own…and hadn't indulged in it in far too long.

"Perhaps I can teach you, sometime." Gaia held in a giggle at Aphrodite's mix of surprise and gratefulness, her hesitation between acknowledging that this power was intriguing to her, or denying it because she, like the other two goddesses, was furious at what was happening. "Anyway…the poison Hecate concocted, the one we stole; it's part of the equation, as well. Mnemosyne spiced it with some of her own rare ingredients, and after I threw in a couple charms, it transformed—it *tethered* to me. So when a victim drinks the poison, it implants a sort of piece of me into their consciousness. Those who have taken in the poison—they *become* poison. It absorbs into their veins. So if they bite someone," she thought of Rhea, "then they *infect* someone by injecting the stuff into their victim's DNA."

It was a complicated process, the science of which was mostly lost on Gaia—Mnemosyne had explained it twice, but even she'd gotten winded from her words. What mattered was that it worked. Every individual Gaia had intoxicated was carrying around a tiny morsel of her, of her consciousness, inside them. And she could control that morsel and make it make *them* do her bidding, without question.

"I then use my mind to speak to that piece, which can then command the victim to do whatever I ask it to. And that poison, it never leaves one's system. It anchors deep into the bones, mixes with the blood; so even if it *appears* one is cured, they're not. Not fully. Ever." She joined her hands, projecting herself into one of the Olympus courtyards, where Eros and Psyche were resting on a bench, eating candied chocolate from a heart-shaped box. "It's a connection that allows me to know where they are, what they are doing, at all times. And whether or not I need to interfere."

Hera squinted, shook her head, nodded, shook her head again. With a huff, she settled against the wall and gazed at the floor. Her mind was scrambled, Gaia could tell—it was all too much for her, a powerful goddess with simple, straightforward abilities.

Aphrodite was internally cursing herself for never learning such tactics in her earlier days—*how those would have been useful while I was bedding all my lovers,* she'd been thinking. Athena gave a quick nod of understanding, a slight intrigue still shining in her gray eyes.

But the largest emotion growing in all of them, overshadowing any of their curiosity, was outrage. They couldn't hide it, no matter how they'd tried to obey Gaia's orders to not defy her. They hadn't, not outwardly. But she saw inside them, their deepest thoughts, their most intense feelings. Their brains were awash with images of poisoned arrows, of blue ichor splashed on floors, of tridents and swords piercing into flesh, of godly blood raining over humanity.

They envisioned a war, caused by Gaia; a gruesome battle similar to those they'd experienced eons ago at the hands of Gaia's children. And from their trembling, from their overflowing negativity, it was evident these three goddesses weren't quite yet on board with Gaia's designs.

Seems I may need to take their blood by force, then.

"You'll think me cruel," she raised a hand before any of them could contradict her, "but it's not cruelty. Think deeply on all I've told you, ladies. It's sustenance. It's preservation. And it's saving the world from itself, and from Zeus."

|| 5. MISSING HEARTBEATS ||

ZEUS

Zeus sat uncomfortably on his stone throne, back rigid against the hardened surface he usually found cool and soothing. Now it was hot to the touch from the heat radiating from his skin—a heat he hadn't experienced in centuries. The heat of lightning shooting through his veins, of thunder thumping in his scalp, and of repercussions to come if he ever got his hands on the culprit.

They're going to pay for their injustices.

Eros arrived, clad in a pastel pink tunic, hand in hand with his darling wife Psyche, whose cheeks were red with fluster, and who batted her lashes as she wiped her mouth with a chiffon napkin. Zeus smelled the chocolate on them—had they been feeding each other sweets and seducing one another while his wife and children were being assaulted?

Zeus' stomach curdled as the god of love and his spouse kneeled before him. How could they be so in love, so happy, indulging in sweet-tooth cravings and dousing one another with lust while something so horrific was going on? They'd been cured, yes; but they'd been the first victims. Had they already moved on from their horror to resume their lives where they'd left off?

And how, *how* could they eat *anything* without fearing their food would be filled with toxins? Zeus hadn't been infected, and yet even he had nightmares about discovering someone had laced one of his meals with such sorcery as what Eros and Psyche had been plagued with.

A hint of concern peppered Eros' normally youthful features, showing lines near his amber eyes. "You summoned us, Majesty?" A slight tremble in his tone told Zeus he was either afraid of being here, in the throne room, alone with Zeus; or he *was* more worried than he'd let on.

Perhaps eating chocolates is their way to de-stress?

Zeus hadn't paid Eros much heed in the passing centuries. Aside from interfering to grant Psyche immortality, he'd never had to monitor the young god much. Eros took care of himself and his own, and never stepped out of line—except when contaminated and shooting toxic arrows into his soulmate's hearts to make them tear into one another and munch on their beating organs until they combusted.

It felt like it'd happened yesterday, and Zeus—who'd seen *a lot* in his tenure as King of Olympus—shuddered at the remembrance of it all.

"I did. Thank you for coming so quickly." He waved a hand to signal for Eros and Psyche to rise; no need for them to stay on their knees while he spoke. "I wasn't sure you'd still be around, or willing to come to me in such…trying times."

Eros inclined his head, a curtain of his dark blond locks sweeping over his forehead. He'd let his hair grow out a smidgen, curling about his flushed face, giving him that eerie image of *Cupid,* the Roman myth that many humans had distorted and portrayed on screens with wild inaccuracy.

The real Cupid looks nothing like that.

"We're all troubled, sire. We all fear more chaos, but we all heard your orders—to not leave Olympus. I wouldn't dare go anywhere else...because I don't think anywhere else *is* safe."

Zeus grunted. "You still feel safe here despite goddesses and Titans dropping left and right and screaming as they're being bitten into?"

Psyche gulped, squeezing Eros' hand. "We do. And we—" she gestured at herself, then Eros, "—have already *been* attacked, haven't we? I doubt we'd be poisoned again. We...did our part." She cringed, and lowered her gaze to her feet.

"Right." Zeus gritted his teeth, but wouldn't push that matter further. He'd been enraged at their actions, but Eros and Psyche hadn't wished for their carnivorous and poisonous ways. They'd been intoxicated, unable to control their urges, and he'd slowly but surely forgiven them for what they'd done. "I'll get straight to it, then. I'm not sure if rumor has reached you yet, but—"

"—some gods have disappeared?" Eros nodded once. "I can't quite tell who, but I noticed there are heartbeats missing. I can't feel them at all."

Zeus sucked his lips in, holding in his gasp of shock. Of *course* Eros would have sensed something amiss. Restored to his usual self, he could detect heartbeats, analyze a heart's deepest intentions. He was a powerful tool for locating anyone who'd left Olympus, and Zeus hadn't even thought to use him for it.

"At all? Not even if you...concentrate?" Zeus rubbed his chin, scanning Eros' face; he was easy to read, if one took the time to try.

Eros' bushy brows scrunched as he glanced sideways at Psyche, who gave him a nod of encouragement.

"I tried." Eros peered towards Zeus but not quite *at* him; his gaze fled somewhere over Zeus' shoulder. "Not only are these deities not on Olympus, but they're far. Much too far for me to detect, majesty. I'm sorry."

Zeus groaned and placed his sandaled feet hard on the wooden dais beneath him. "Do you know who disappeared? Were you able to decipher that?"

Again Eros exchanged a quick glance with Psyche, but it was Psyche who responded, her voice tentative as she tucked a few ashy hairs behind her ear. "The recently infected ones—Themis, Phoebe. We couldn't sense Dionysus' drunken pulse, either, so we assumed…and then Athena, Aphrodite, and Hera seem to have vanished, too. Oh," she shivered, "and Rhea? He wasn't certain about her, as he doesn't know her heartbeat as well as the others."

Zeus released a lengthy, heavy sigh. "Spot on, as always. Rhea is gone, though I'm unsure if she vanished or simply…left." He suppressed a cascade of chills crawling up his spine. There was something off about his mother's involvement in all this, and he wasn't ready to look deeper into it just yet. "The real reason I summoned you, though, is to ask if you've been hearing voices lately. *The* voice; that of your poisoner."

Psyche visibly shook and pulled her hand from Eros'. Eros crossed his arms over his chest as if to cover himself up, to shield his heart.

"No," said Eros, after a few moments of silence, of an internal struggle that Zeus tried his best not to eavesdrop on. "But we, well…*I* sensed that same vibration of malice in the air. That cold darkness we felt when…*possessed* by the culprit. It's…she's…here, or was here, and though we couldn't directly link the sensation to anyone in particular, it…*she* was mingling amongst us."

Zeus gripped his armrest, continuing to grit his teeth against the rage seeking to seep out his mouth in the form of a growl, a yell, an ear-piercing screech of proportions no other deity had ever heard him utter.

Here. It's here, under our noses—and Athena told me of this.

Athena and Lukus—his appointed investigators, one of which he'd shunned and taken off the job because she wouldn't stop accusing the wrong person. Athena and Lukus…who had both disappeared.

Zeus scrubbed his face. He still disagreed with Athena's convictions about Hecate—she wasn't responsible for this, he was certain of it—but he never should have disregarded his favorite daughter because of her firm beliefs. If he hadn't reprimanded her, taken away her case, left it in the deft but too human hands of Lukus…would they both be gone now? Would they have figured this mystery out together before more gods could be harmed?

"I'll tell you what I told my children," said Zeus, his thunderous voice scaring Eros and Psyche into standing up straight, staring at him with surprise. He'd been silent for a spell, rehearsing speeches in his mind, looking for the right thing to say. If he said too much, rumors would fly about the palace and panic would transform to chaos. But he trusted Eros and Psyche to keep to themselves and to not run their mouths. They hadn't in the past; they had no reason to now. "That based on facts that I have gathered, these disappearances were in truth…kidnappings."

Eros' eyes widened and Psyche stumbled forward in shock, barely catching herself before crumbling to her knees. *"Kidnappings?"* Eros placed a hand over his heart. "You are sure?"

Zeus snorted. "I'm no investigator, but everything points towards that fact." He brushed his fingers through his tresses, finding a few more gray hairs—hairs that had once been sleek, shiny black, and that as of late had been transforming in his stress, revealing his age. "Themis and Phoebe—both were still in the process of healing from their attacks. They'd have no need to depart from the palace, as they still needed medical attention. Apollo's room is quite secure, and he hadn't let anyone in, and turned away perhaps for a few seconds before...Phoebe was gone."

Psyche smacked a hand to her forehead. "Impossible."

"And Themis..." Zeus flinched, recalling his docile, sweet-natured ex-wife with whom he was on wonderful terms—transformed into some ichor-craving, intoxicated zombie, biting into her own sister without remorse, toxins dripping from her blue-tinted lips, sitting in a pool of blood. "She wasn't strong enough to leave. After what she did, she was under surveillance...and then she wasn't. No one has any clue *how* she got out, or who might have helped her."

Eros snapped to summon a seat to him, and dropped into its cushions with a puff of breath. Sweat glistened over his forehead, and Psyche produced a fan of purple feathers to whoosh wind onto his face.

This is a lot for them, but they need to know...they need to be prepared.

"I discovered a puddle of blood near the sculpture museum." Zeus swallowed, still smelling the toxicity, tasting its acrid flavor in his mouth. "And it was undeniably Dionysus' blood. He...I think...was struck, then kidnapped, as well."

Eros' skin went from pale to nearly green. Carnivorous as he'd been during his enraged stint on earth, he wasn't much of a violent god in regular times. Such atrocious attacks were like to make him sick to his stomach, and he looked it now, hunching over and wrapping his arms over his abdomen.

"So Aphrodite…Athena…Hera…" Psyche paused in her fanning, gasped, covered her mouth, then uncovered it seconds later. "You think they were attacked, poisoned, and carried off? Kidnapped, along with the others?"

Zeus hesitated to reveal more, and yet he'd started his tale; neither Eros nor Psyche would rest well if they didn't have the full story. They weren't the kinds of deities he'd usually speak to of such events, but he'd sent his children off to accomplish various tasks, and to be frank, he needed to air his concerns, to vent. Eros and Psyche would have to do, for now.

"Hera, I am positive, was attacked. I found her blood splattered on a fountain in one of the rear courtyards. And," he winced, "I forgot, Lukus has vanished, as well. I found *his* blood not far from Hera's."

"The half-mortal?" Eros, who'd apparently recovered his voice—he'd looked like he was choking—cocked his head. "Now that's odd."

"And Mother's blood was out there, too, but it was…different. Not poisoned. It was pure." Zeus leaned back in his seat and raised his gaze to the ceiling. "The guards found Athena's and Aphrodite's blood near their doors, indicating a sign of struggle. I don't believe they were contaminated, but they were certainly knocked out."

"Aphrodite…*Athena* knocked out? Who would…who *could*…" Eros started hyperventilating, and Zeus regretted getting so detailed and gruesome with him.

Psyche called for someone to bring him some ambrosia, and crouched beside him, one hand on his leg; but her gaze rested on Zeus. If disgusted or worried, she was better at handling her emotions than Eros was, at the time being.

"So Dionysus, Hera, and Lukus were poisoned…Athena and

Aphrodite knocked out…and Rhea happened to bleed in the same area as the first three? And all were kidnapped, but Rhea…" Psyche grimaced. "What is the situation with her?"

Psyche knew Rhea quite well, as most Olympian residents did. Before her decades in the jungle, she'd been often present at the palace, offering advice, counseling those in need, assisting with different tasks when asked. She was a benevolent, heartwarming woman, a motherly deity who was never violent, if only to protect those she loved.

"Whatever it is, it doesn't make sense. She sticks out," said Zeus, unwilling to conclude that his mother had anything to do with this monstrous culprit. It was a coincidence, it had to be. "She would never take off without saying goodbye, so all signs point to her being kidnapped too…but then why wasn't she poisoned? Was she easier for the culprit to subdue? Or agreed to leave to avoid further bloodshed?"

"Or," said Eros, between big breaths of air and gulps of the ambrosia that had been delivered to him, "she *is* the culprit."

Zeus rose to his full height, glaring down at Eros, readying to reprimand him for daring to accuse Rhea of anything, let alone being the creature who'd sowed discord among his gods.

But Eros was already bunched up and cowering from soaking up all the information Zeus had offered him, and didn't react to the abruptness of the motion.

Psyche did, squatting a little lower near Eros' chair, lowering her chin. "He meant no offense, majesty," she whispered, but loud enough for Zeus to hear.

Zeus massaged the back of his neck and relaxed into his throne. Psyche was right, and Eros was right too, to some extent. Rhea's actions and suspicious behavior might have been indicators Zeus should have noticed earlier. And she *had* been in the end of Lukus' line-up of gods, matching the description Hecate had given of the memories she'd had down in the Underworld, her mind messed with.

Could Rhea be involved? Could she be the culprit, or working with it? Was that why he'd smelled her in the courtyard, but not tinted with toxins? Was Rhea, mother of Olympians, nurturing goddess, wilderness protectress, instigating a civil war amidst deities, and if so, what for?

"Why would Mother rise against me, and her daughter, and her grandchildren? Why would she bite into her siblings and spread chaos like this?"

|| 6. MIND MESSING ||

GAIA

As she paced before the hut's door, Gaia grunted, her bare feet leaving steamy indents in the floor's thick mud. It was usually a hardened, dusty surface; but the rage brimming in her made her skin volcano-hot, and so she burned nearly anything she came into contact with.

She'd sprinkled some sleeping powder on the Olympians—their questions and disgust had exhausted her—and was alone, in spirit, at least, to contemplate her thoughts.

The door flung open, stopping her and her heartbeats—but the arrival wasn't who she'd expected to see.

"Rhea?" Gaia scrunched her eyebrows, taking in her daughter's appearance: her tunic disheveled and ripped in places, stained with ichor and a gooey green substance Gaia recognized—and smelled with a wrinkle of her nostrils—as monster blood, and her hair a mess of dry weeds and bits of…were those rocks? "What in Tartarus happened to you?"

She'd been expecting Rhea to be up in Olympus, screaming at anyone who'd listen that Gaia was crazy, that Mnemosyne was her assistant, that they'd poisoned her and turned her to their cause. And yet here she was, crawling back into Gaia's lap.

Did she get sent back to me? Or…did she never make it to Olympus?

A reek of mushy swamp and rotten eggs permeated the room as Rhea entered it, her footsteps squishing in the mud.

"Your teleportation spell," Rhea sneered as she wiped her sticky hands on her tunic, leaving another green imprint there, "didn't work. It smacked me into the Diamond Gates and I passed out. I never got out of the Underworld."

Several feelings seeped into Gaia at once; relief, because that meant Zeus and the others *might* not have been informed of her plots, yet, so she still had some time. And fear, because if she couldn't send Rhea up to Olympus…did that mean her powers were waning? Did that mean she was weakening?

Rhea hissed as she touched a scrape on her arm. "I thought about going up there, anyway. The gates opened, after I collapsed, and when I came to…I wandered out. But I was too disoriented, too…famished…to go anywhere. So I, uh…" She dabbed at the corners of her mouth—the gooey green stuff was there, too—and winced. "I had a little lunch."

From the odors still sweeping off her clothes and coming from her breath, Gaia deduced she'd snatched the first wandering creature— and there were quite a few sulking in front of the Diamond Gates— and dug her fangs in. Clearly, the spell she'd put on Rhea was still active, as she'd not be craving blood if she were returning to normal.

Still, it had been a risk to propel her out of the hut out of anger, and Gaia was happy the action hadn't backfired.

"Fine." Gaia motioned at a corner of the hut not occupied by other inmates. "Sit, and await further instruction."

Rhea, back hunched, obeyed, moseying over to the spot Gaia

indicated and lowering onto the mushy ground, bringing her knees to her chest. "Where is Mnemosyne?" Her voice was tentative; she'd lost all the lioness fury she'd harbored earlier when puffing herself up, displaying her powers in defiance. She was still strong, but it was a strength that came from feeding on blood, rather than one of resistance.

She won't pose any more issues, at least not for a while.

"She's fetching more ingredients...supposedly," said Gaia, glaring at the door as she shut it. It creaked and *clicked* as it latched, and Gaia spun to Rhea. "You didn't happen to see her on your way here, did you?"

Rhea shrugged and stuck a finger into her mouth, sucking on the juices coating her skin. "I didn't. I was keeping to the shadows, wary of bumping into anyone." She gagged, then swallowed. "Those things taste *weird*, ugh."

Gaia groaned. "Focus, Rhea." She snapped at her. "*Did* you bump into anyone?"

"No." Rhea wrapped her arms around her legs, pulling her knees as close to herself as possible. "The area is...quiet. It's ominous. There were a few wailing souls here and there, but most noises came from the camp where they're all waiting judgment. I steered clear of that, and followed the Acheron until I reached a bridge, then sighted the hut."

Of course, Rhea wasn't familiar with the Underworld. How she'd managed to make it back to the hut without someone to help navigate was suspicious. When she'd poisoned Persephone, she'd had a guide with her; this time, she'd been alone.

Gaia had half a mind to grab the woman by the throat and thoroughly interrogate her, to figure out how she'd arrived without being seen, but her body was still overheating with irritation and impatience, and she worried she'd snap her own daughter's neck if she wasn't careful.

She *needed* to be careful.

In any case, the figment of her that was still in Rhea—the *voice*, implanted by her toxins—was actively speaking to Rhea, and it might have helped her return.

No need to be so spontaneous and assume the worst…yet.

Rhea's mention of wandering souls lit a flame in Gaia's brain, igniting a whole new set of possibilities.

"That little sneak." Gaia rolled her eyes and shook her head. "Of course, she got distracted. Got lustful and decided to take a quick break from her tasks. She must have found some poor soul near *Lethe*, and went off frolicking with it. We're occupying her hut, so she had to find some other ramshackle shack to play around in."

"Mnemosyne?" Rhea's eyebrows lifted. "*Playing* with…souls?"

"Ah," Gaia snorted, "you wouldn't know this about your sister, since she poses as a regal, mysterious titaness in everyone else's eyes. But as I've been down here for a while, in her space, I've seen another side of her, dear daughter. Let me tell you, it's not what you'd expect."

A genuine curiosity bloomed over Rhea's washed-out features. She licked at the green goo over her lips, cringed, then eyed her mother, internally urging her to give details.

Gaia saw no harm in informing Rhea of Mnemosyne's activities. They were on the same team, after all; it was only fair, as Mnemosyne knew of Rhea's recent habits, too.

"She likes to seduce souls who escaped the camp and bring them here to have her way with them." She grimaced, recalling having watched Mnemosyne do that, several times. She'd whisper into their ear, enticing them, enchanting their mind, then whisk them over to her home where she'd have the strangest experiment Gaia had ever witnessed—and oh, she'd witnessed a *lot* in her eons of existence.

"Wait," Rhea narrowed her gaze, "by playing, do you mean…she's having sex with ghosts?"

Recalling that Rhea's adverse reaction to the poison was to envision everyone having sexual intercourse, Gaia suppressed a giggle. How would she react if she were to bite into Mnemosyne and see all her raunchy rough housing with spirits? Gaia had been torn between fascination and confusion, herself, when first stumbling upon this situation.

Mnemosyne had had no clue Gaia was near, and could see *through* the hut's walls. She'd gone through with her disturbing act as if no one would hear her moans of pleasure and no one would notice a soul having disappeared. The judges kept count, always; so were they purposely letting Mnemosyne devour a handful of spirits to appease her? And was Hades aware of this going on?

"I don't know that it can be translated as sex, so to speak," said Gaia, glancing towards the door again. "It's as if she sucks them *into* her, leaving them as nothing but empty creatures that she then directs towards the Mourning Fields. It's morbid. She undresses, then holds them—yes, *holds a spirit,* I know—against her and kisses them, and as their hands explore her nakedness she slowly draws the energy from them."

"And you don't…you didn't…" Rhea blinked at her mother. "You haven't stopped her?"

Gaia shrugged. "If that's her way of staying strong, I can't stop her, Rhea. I *need* her strength, and I also need her compliance. She's been my eyes and ears down here for centuries, understand? She gave me free range of her hut, of her resources; guided me over to Tartarus and helped me sway the guards. Lent me her personal knowledge of this place and its limits and quirks so that I might be mindful of how to conceal myself here. Whatever she does…it has protected my presence from Hades and Persephone, and that is essential."

It *had* bothered Gaia, at first, seeing one of her daughters fooling around with spirits, screwing up with the natural way of things. But she'd felt her pleasure, her satisfaction at slurping up the soul within her; and she'd felt her *power*. To have a powerful Mnemosyne on her team wasn't negligible. It might change the course of things, for the better. So Gaia had let it slide, let her do whatever it was she needed to gain power.

But if Mnemosyne was doing that *now,* when their time was limited…

A breathless Mnemosyne suddenly swept in through the door and slammed it behind her. Her cheeks were pale, her eyes wide, and she leaned into the door as she caught her breath. She shoved her hands into her dress' secret pockets, extracted several vividly colored vials, and tossed them across the room. They landed perfectly on a stool near her cauldron.

"What happened?" Gaia sniffed the fear on her, and recoiled, wary. Was she seen in her acts of sucking souls? Was she running from someone? Had she been caught by Hades?

"Persephone." Mnemosyne set a hand to her bosom and closed her eyes. The usual radiant glow about her, turning her skin to gold and her hair to a bright orange, had faded. She was a dark outline in a dark room, lacking her special spark. "She followed me down Hecate's secret passage and interrogated me. Apparently…she's seen me sneaking around for a while."

"Ah." Gaia relaxed—Mnemosyne would have said immediately

if they needed to vacate the premises in haste—and approached her daughter, tipping her chin up. "But you can…how do the humans say it? Right, *get yourself out of a pickle* with ease, no?"

Mnemosyne's features tightened, as if she fought her mother's touch. "She reminded me that Hecate was in Olympus, that I shouldn't be in her lair without her present. I told her I knew that, but that I had *business* with Melinoë. I…*think* she believed me. I trifled with her mind and made her faint so I could hurry to the potion room."

Gaia gritted her teeth and backed away from Mnemosyne. The heat in her blood had momentarily lessened, but now it boiled up again, and steam rose from where she stood. "You *think?*"

"Also, it's worth noting that Melinoë's lower than usual wits are waning out, Mother." Mnemosyne swiped a bit of sweat from her forehead. Her glow was returning, but taking its time. At least she was no longer a blurry form in the obscurity. "She has little left to offer us, and we may need to work on an alternative."

Gaia's fingers numbed with a pulsing outrage. "Which means her health will start to concern Persephone, hm? I suspect she tried to question you already?" Mnemosyne nodded once. "And when Hecate gets back, she'll add her worries upon finding that Melinoë is more inactive than usual, and she'll instantly suspect someone is messing with her mind."

Gaia's gaze rested on Mnemosyne's, seeking answers in her tired brown eyes. But there was nothing there; Mnemosyne had no solution on hand, and it was evident she'd hastened to finish her business and come here before anything worse could happen.

They'd have to be temporarily cut off from the palace and gathering supplies, which meant they'd need to seek other options.

We don't have any back-up plans…this is bad.

"The issue is Persephone," said Gaia, stroking her chin as she resumed her earlier pacing. "Hecate is a problem, yes, but Persephone is one we can and should tackle *now*."

"I *did* tackle it," said Mnemosyne, regaining enough of herself to meander over to her cauldron and peer into its contents. A thick, fragrant smoke was wafting out of its depths, and Mnemosyne frowned at it.

Gaia watched her daughter as she uncorked one of the vials she'd stolen and dipped a few drops into the poison. "I highly doubt you subdued her as you think. She's much more powerful than she looks, that one."

Gaia had often detected a fiery energy within Persephone that was waiting to be unleashed; a rancor that she'd kept tethered, but that at any opportunity might release.

Just like her mother.

"Well," Mnemosyne stirred the cauldron's contents, her finger hovering over the liquid, "it *was* difficult for me to use my powers on her, I'll admit. She was resistant, her mind fighting my hold. But I did get through. She fainted, and though she was gone when I left, I doubt she remembered what happened and why she was lying on the crypt floor."

"Resistant." Gaia tapped a finger to her mouth. "Likely the remedy Hecate gave her has fortified her against any further intrusions. The part of me injected into her…it's been dormant since then."

Mnemosyne peeked up from her cauldron, the smoke whooshing over her face. She'd regained her full glow, now, and she looked like a bronze statue basking in the mist, a perfect, heavenly creature walking out of a cloud.

"So Hecate *can* cure those infected by our poison?" She reached beside her for another vial, all the while fixing her gaze on Gaia. "Does that mean she can cure…herself?"

"Unlikely." Gaia fought a shiver from Mnemosyne's words. "I mean, unlikely that she can cure anyone fully. Persephone was a different story; we didn't dose her as much, so there wasn't much to erase from her system. But I'd expect Hecate gave her a high dosage of her cure, in protection. She loves that girl a tad too much for comfort."

"But what of her, then? Of Hecate, and the trials we—especially Rhea—went through to trifle with *her* memories?" A hint of concern tinged her tone as she trickled a couple of drops of a vibrant blue tincture into the mix. "Can she fight them?"

Another chill crept up Gaia's spine, and she snarled at its arrival, at its meaning; fear. She *was* afraid, and she loathed the uneasiness settling in her gut.

"Technically, no. Not while she's close. But as she's up there," she jutted her chin at the ceiling, "I'd assume our power over her is fizzling away. We both know she spotted your sneaking into her chambers, as we had to erase her memory of it. She's had a whiff of Rhea's violence, and she's definitely been lurking about to view pieces of my plans."

"So what you're saying, Mother, is that…" Mnemosyne waved at the smoke, drawing it into her nostrils so she could sniff at it, analyze it. "*Hecate* is the problem we should tackle first, then?"

Gaia crossed her arms as she peeked at the three Olympian goddesses she'd subdued, then the three zombie-like deities she'd converted to her cause, then the inanimate half-mortal asleep on her altar.

"Until Hecate returns, Persephone is our main concern." She

switched back to Mnemosyne, who was now leaning so close to the cauldron, her glow like an explosion of gold over her face, she seemed unreal; a godly spirit. "But *if* she comes back, we'll switch gears, and work on further charming her mind. Because if she's no longer under our spell, she'll start talking, I guarantee it. And I can't have that, not yet. Rhea *almost* blew things for us," she sent a quick glower at her other daughter, who'd remained silent this whole time, "but I won't have Hecate ruining my designs."

‖ 7. A DAUGHTER'S WAILS ‖
PERSEPHONE

With a yawn, Persephone stretched out her arms—and nearly fell off her bed.

"Huh?" She jolted upright, peering left to right, slightly disoriented.

Last she'd remembered, she'd stormed up here, disappointed with Hades and his assumptions. But she didn't recall lying on the plush bed, let alone falling asleep. It was the middle of the day, and she wasn't one for naps, hadn't taken one in a *very* long time. Not since her earlier years in the Underworld, when she was bored and missing her mother and not quite sure how to cope with her new lifestyle.

She touched her forehead—hot, and slick with sweat. The Underworld was, as a general rule, a cold but humid place, and while the temperature could rise rapidly, it rarely got to the point of having to wipe perspiration off one's head. Persephone had to do so now, and cringed, her arm shivering as she lowered it to her side.

She sat, dangling her feet off her massive four-poster bed, turning to glare at the imprint of her head in her scarlet satin pillow. Had Mnemosyne's powers had more of an effect on her than she'd thought? Only someone trifling with her brain could have provoked such sudden fatigue and discomfort in her. And while the titaness' spell had failed, that didn't mean its energy didn't seep into Persephone and mess with her.

Rising to her feet, she meandered over to her dresser, where her carafe of pomegranate ambrosia juice had been sitting—the one she'd ordered after coming into her room earlier. It was untouched; she hadn't poured herself a glass, and had gone straight to sleep?

This keeps getting odder...

A sudden piercing in her skull caused her to hunch over and grit her teeth. It was a screech, ripping its nails across her brain, searing into its membrane. She writhed about, grabbing at her head, desperate to steady its throbbing. Until said throbbing became more rhythmic, and the screech became a wail. A moan.

It echoed inside her, forming words that wouldn't make sense to anyone but her. *"Mother...help...me."*

"Melinoë?" The sound was raspy, like someone who'd not spoken for centuries was now trying to let their voice out; the exact way her discarded but well-cared for daughter sounded.

For Melinoë's cry to be so intense, to reach up through the several floors separating them, meant she was in pain, and needed assistance with easing her woes. With Hecate in Olympus, that meant Persephone needed to step up and monitor her daughter—no matter how uneasy that made her.

Melinoë wasn't an average daughter, nor an average goddess. But her conception and birth had caused malformations in her brain; issues that even her godly blood couldn't quite fix. Some in the Underworld compared her to a zombie, a wordless witch who cackled instead of speaking. But the poor girl was misunderstood and unloved, and it broke Persephone's heart to not know how to fix her.

Their best option had been to contain her in the crypt with Hecate, who paid little attention to Melinoë's developmental delays, and instead praised her, taught her everything she knew. Because Melinoë was, contrary to popular belief, smart and skilled in spell-weaving, and had a knack for small details that had often impressed Persephone— and even, at times, Hades.

Worried about her troubled episode, Persephone dashed down the multiple layers of the palace, slowing her pace as she navigated the slippery crypt stairs. Melinoë's modest room was closest to the landing, so in only a few seconds, Persephone had crept inside and was at her bedside, sweeping the thick black hair from the girl's face.

She was abed, contorting in pain. Her fingers curled at Persephone's touch, and soft moans escaped her more than normally chapped lips as she clawed at her mother's arm, determined to explain her suffering to her.

"Mo...ther." Her voice was croakier than normal, its crackling reverberating through Persephone and shocking her heart.

Melinoë couldn't put together much else, but conveyed her agony through her thoughts, that Persephone was barely able to unscramble enough to understand.

"Hurting...mind...hurts."

Persephone smoothed the sagging, reddish skin under Melinoë's pitch black eyes, wincing at the roughness of the texture there. It wasn't uncommon for the girl to have dark circles under her lower lashes, from keeping her eyes open through her nightmares—she had many of them, which Hecate usually treated with a simple concoction, but it had run out. Yet these circles were more pronounced than usual. Deeper, a darker shade of red, almost as if she'd bled from her pupils— blood instead of regular tears.

"No, this isn't right." She kissed the girl's damp cheek, then hurried to fetch a towel that she heated with her touch and placed over Melinoë's forehead. "Rest easy, sweetheart. I'll go talk to Hades about this. Hecate will patch you up when she's home."

The heat calmed Melinoë's thrashing, at least, and she closed her eyes. "Heca…te."

"Yes," said Persephone, backing away slowly, wanting to avoid any abrupt motion that might startle her daughter. "You try to sleep, and when she comes back, she'll make you feel better."

As Persephone tiptoed out into the dank crypt corridor, she sensed her upper lip curling, her teeth baring. Melinoë, odd and off-putting as she was—and unloved by her adoptive father—was Persephone's only child, and likely the only one she'd ever have. Why was she so distraught? Why was her body in such agony, more so than on a regular day?

Persephone snarled into the darkness of the hallway, towards where she'd pretended to pass out earlier. "Mnemosyne…" Her fists tightened, her heart raced inside her chest. "What did you do to my daughter?"

Without announcement, Persephone broke into the ballroom, which served as a throne-room when not being used as a dining room or a place to entertain the rare guests who came to the Underworld. Hades was there, atop his black marble throne, head bent as he discussed something in lowered tones with another man, whose back was to Persephone.

Persephone stood in the doorway, taking in the somber room, as always comparing it to the Olympus throne-room. Where the open-air, Zeus-ruled room was light, breezy, colored with vines and touches of gold, this room was glacial, gloomy, its obscure shades of charcoal and auburn and chestnut swallowing up any resident who stepped within its depths. It was small, yet seemed to go on forever, its burgundy carpet that led from door to dais like a bubbling, caking lava about to engulf anyone who dared walk upon it.

In her younger years, Persephone had feared this room and its significance. Hades rarely held court—he never needed to—but whenever he did, it meant something bad was happening. Like now; this didn't look like a friendly visit from an out-of-towner. The energy emanating off this individual was powerful and—she gasped, announcing herself inadvertently—enraged.

Hades tilted sideways, around the visitor, to discover her arrival. "Wife? What is it?" He lit up at her presence, though appearing distraught, and motioned at the velvet-laden seat beside him—Persephone's throne—as he raised his eyebrows. "Please, join me."

She'd never interrupt his session, but he knew he'd upset her earlier, and he'd do anything to earn her forgiveness, including grovel and gloat about her in front of his guest. And she needed him to beg, needed him to remember he owed her; because she needed his help.

As she approached, the guest in question spun around, a set of fiery orange eyes resting on her. The intensity of them took her aback, and she jumped, unable to control her footsteps as she almost tripped at the sight.

Though she didn't recognize the face—dark skin, bushy blond eyebrows, and matching blond scruff over the upper lip and along the jawline—she now recognized the power, the presence. Those eyes—despite never appearing the same way, enjoying shifting his identity at will, this deity's eyes always retained the bright tint of a bonfire.

She inclined her head as she passed him. Queen of the Underworld, she was, but Tartarus was ancient royalty, a creator of all things, and a primordial god one didn't dare disrespect, lest they get sent to the prison-like realm he'd created.

She'd only met him once, in passing, but wouldn't mistake the overwhelming punch of his powers boiling within him. He was, as Hades had told her, not a pleasant god to deal with, but not evil, either; only constantly disappointed with humanity and gods as a whole. He had his own set of chambers near Persephone's room, and though he stayed at the palace often, it was normally while Persephone was up in Olympus with her mother.

Tartarus exchanged a glance with Hades—veiled, secretive—then bowed at Persephone. "We can resume this later, majesty. But be forewarned, and be on your guard."

Hades nodded once, dismissing him, and Tartarus dipped out, his black cloak flapping at his heels as he sealed the door behind him.

"I will ask what *that* was about in a moment," said Persephone, taking her spot beside Hades, enjoying the lavish cushion of her throne. "But first—I beg that you please, *please* come downstairs with me to look in on Melinoë."

Hades recoiled at the name, gripping the armrests of his throne as he bared his teeth. "Why would I do that?" Despite knowing he needed to redeem himself for his unkind comments from before, any mention of the crypt-dwelling daughter was enough to set him off.

Melinoë wasn't *his* daughter, and was nothing but a constant reminder that Persephone had laid with another man. By force, for certain—Hades knew this better than anyone—but he still held a grudge, feeling that Persephone had conceived the child out of revenge from his own straying many, many moons ago.

"Because she's in worse shape than what we're used to. Her brain…" Persephone swallowed, wishing she'd had a few sips of her juice before coming down; the putrid taste of blood in her mouth was off-putting. "It's gone to mush, more so than what we're accustomed to. She couldn't quite form coherent sentences or thoughts, and she was in agony. And afraid."

Hades waved a hand dismissively, looking ahead, his gaze fixed on the door Tartarus had just gone through. "Hecate will take care of her when she gets back."

"*If* she gets back." Persephone glowered at her husband's shoulder, wishing to burn it, to draw his attention to her. "She's been up there for so long. Too long. Something is up, and it's affecting us now. Mnemosyne—"

That got his attention—he flipped to Persephone with lifted eyebrows. "What about her? You're bringing this up again?"

Persephone scowled at him. "I *am*, because I swear to you she's up to something. She's been fucking with Melinoë's mind, and you can't deny it. My daughter, *my daughter* is a mess and it's that vile woman's fault. She was sneaking around, she had *business* with Melinoë, or so she claimed. And hours later, Melinoë calls out to me, in absolute pain and unable to communicate properly. Will you truly dismiss this as a coincidence?" Her voice had risen, and her shoulders tensed as she leaned in closer to her husband, her nails inches from digging into his skin.

Temper, Persephone—watch your temper.

He was, after all, the king, and no matter their argument and her anger at his assumptions, she owed him a modicum of respect.

But he owes it right back.

To her surprise—she'd expected Hades to continue brushing her off in his irritation at her speaking of her daughter—he sighed, deflating in his seat. "No…I will not call it a coincidence." He took her hand in his, and used his other to massage his temples, cringing.

"I'm sorry, you know how that name unsettles me. And I'm also sorry…I was harsh before, with what I said to you, and you know I regret it. But I regret it more after this visit with Tartarus." There was a certain alarm to his voice, accompanied by a frailness that Persephone hadn't heard in it since the attacks on Olympus, years and years ago.

"Why was he here? I know he visits with you from time to time, but he doesn't ask for an *audience* with you, ever." Persephone squeezed his hand, bringing him to look at her. His eyes, pools of darkness, were rimmed with red. "What has he said that affected you so? I felt the vibe in the room when I entered, and it…wasn't good."

Hades squinted as he switched to her, his lips pressing into a hard line. "He was telling me how someone was trying to mess with *his* mind."

Persephone clapped a hand over her mouth. "What?"

Tartarus was one of the most ancient deities in existence; one whom most didn't even know to *be* a deity, rather than the fiery jail he'd given his name to. How could anyone come close to an attempt at penetrating his thoughts?

"I know," Hades shook his head, "it perturbed me, too. Worse still is that he couldn't figure out who it was. The voice seeking to invade him was muffled and the words made no sense." He compressed Persephone's hand in his, his gaze turning cloudy. "Only someone insanely powerful could pry into the mind of a primordial being like him."

"Do you think…" Persephone gulped; the cushions were no longer as satisfying as an air of dread filled the room. "Was whoever that was, trying to get into Tartarus' head…the same thing that's been in the minds of others? The same thing…poisoning the gods?" She had little details of all that had unfolded, but Hades and Hecate were in contact. The witch had been feeding them bits of information as she discovered them, and sending messengers to share her knowledge. "Has the contagion spread?"

"It can't be a simple coincidence." Hades pushed up to his feet and proceeded forward, beckoning Persephone to follow. "And because of this, and what you've told me of...*her,*" he snickered, "I feel I must go up to Olympus to inform Zeus."

A shockwave woke through Persephone, causing her to smack a hand to her bosom as her heartbeat reached near uncontrollable levels.

For Hades to *need* to travel to Olympus...and so many times, of late...the situation was, in truth, dire.

"I'll go with you," she said, regaining her bearings as they exited the ballroom.

Hades grasped her wrist, tight; then, with a frown, brought her knuckles to his lips. "No." All manners of shivers shattered up and down her limbs at the contact of his cold lips on her warm skin. "You need to stay down here to keep an eye out for things. Hecate isn't here; one of us must be in the palace at all times. And M..." He squeezed his eyes shut, then reopened them, struggling not to deepen his grimace. "*Melinoë* needs to be watched, too. If Mnemosyne were to sneak in again, and if she is indeed fiddling with the girl's mind..."

Persephone stiffened as he released her hand. "I understand, but I...don't feel safe without you near." She hated to admit it—strong and able goddess that she was—but Hades was the authority in the Underworld. Persephone was nothing but the ornamental queen he boasted his love for. People obeyed her, revered her; but they'd have no trouble getting past her undetected, as she didn't have the access and presence Hades did, nor the magic Hecate harbored.

Hades cupped her cheek and pressed his lips to hers, sending tingles down her neck and into the crease between her breasts. If he opened his mouth, if their tongues touched, he'd be delayed in leaving for Olympus, she knew; so she kept her lips sealed, simply enjoying the feel of him.

"I'll swing by the judges' palace on my way out, and notify them of...*some* of the ordeal. I won't rouse their worry too much yet, but they'll know to be on their guard. And," Hades caressed her chin briefly, "Cerberus is trained to react if you're in danger. *And,*" he tucked a strand of her auburn hair behind her ears, "Tartarus is here, upstairs. If anything should happen, scream for him, and he'll be at your side in seconds."

He didn't wait for her to acknowledge his comments nor thank him for his efforts, and skidded down the hall to the front door, opening it with a whistle as he summoned his chariot and horses.

She caught a quick glimpse of the outdoors as he departed, and she wished to go for a stroll, to clear her head. But the gyrating gust seemed to whisper *stay inssssside*. The murmur of the rose bushes she'd hidden in earlier, the memory of their thorns still slitting into the flesh of her arms, warned her against wandering. And the sinister sky overhead, somehow more penetrating and obscure than usual, urged her to refrain from straying from her home.

There was something dreary out there; something that might have been working with or for Mnemosyne. Something, someone that Mnemosyne worked for. Something that wanted to destroy the gods and had no qualms trying to turn them all against one another, including the primordial creatures who'd created them.

She settled for her fourth-floor balcony, overlooking the river *Styx*. Styx, like Tartarus, was also a goddess; but no matter how many times Persephone mumbled her name, summoning her, the mystical river deity never showed herself, never came to reveal to Persephone if she'd heard anything, if anyone ominous had sworn an oath on her waters.

Persephone gripped the banister and stared out at the horizon, into the darkened treetops of the forest at the edge of the Underworld. A forest charged with strayed spirits, poor souls who'd gone a little too far and who were now unreachable. Spirits who *might* have detected the eeriness of the current situation, and who were much better off lost in the woods.

|| 8. A NOT SO PRIVATE MEETING ||
ZEUS

After shooing off his family members, and ordering his cupbearers to seal him into the throne-room and allow no one to enter, Zeus shrank into the hardness of his throne. He needed time to think, and yet time was running out. Who knew how long ago his wife and the others were taken, nor for what purpose, or if the culprit who stole them had deadly intentions. So far, no one had died—to truly terminate an immortal being took immense power—but he had no doubt death was on the horizon.

He shuddered at the notion of any of those kidnapped dying. His spouse, sent off to Tartarus without ever knowing how loyal Zeus had remained in the past few centuries. His favorite daughter, murdered before finding out that despite her recent behavior, she was *still* his favorite, and always would be. And the poor half-mortal who'd discovered his real parentage, now doomed to be locked in a fiery realm where his worst nightmares would play out.

"No," Zeus muttered into his mustache, its bristle hanging over his lips and tickling them. "I need Poseidon." He wrapped a hand around his armrest as he peeked at his sea-god brother's throne, already smelling the salt water he'd leave all over the seat cushion.

"And my sisters, too." He envisioned Hestia in her drab attire, her face solemn, her ears wide open to receive his concerns. And Demeter stomping about cursing the culprit who'd dared to take Hera from them. "And…Hades." A shiver coursed through him at the thought of his Underworld sibling, and he winced imagining his black eyes narrowing as Zeus told him what had happened.

The throne-room doors blasted open, and as Zeus got to his feet to shriek at whoever had dared disturb his thinking process, he sank backwards at the vision of a swirl of flames shooting directly at him.

He crouched, to avoid the blow; but the flame didn't hit him, and instead remained suspended in the air, inches away from his throne.

He squinted up at the fire, realizing it *wasn't* a missile or a powerful blow from a foe; it was a message, in the style of someone from the Underworld. *A flaming message from below,* his siblings called such correspondence—and more often than not, such correspondence came from Hades.

With a twirl of his finger, he extinguished the fire, and a small, folded note fell into the palm of his hand. He unfolded it, recognizing Hades' tidy penmanship at once.

Brother,

I am at your gates, and I request formal permission to enter Olympus, as I have information to discuss with you. Please, open your home for me.

Hades

Zeus had long ago removed any enchantments barring his

underground-dwelling sibling from entering the palace. But with recent events, he'd reactivated every charm he thought might protect Olympus from invaders and visitors, no matter who they were. Only he and primordial beings such as Gaia had the ability to re-enter the premises if they left; everyone else would be blocked at the golden gates were they to leave against his orders.

With a quick snap of his fingers, Zeus removed the spell, permitting Hades entry. He gave it a few minutes before snapping again, to re-seal the entrance, lest anyone had been following Hades and attempted to creep in behind him.

Within seconds, a whoosh of frigid air seeped into the throne-room, followed by the stormy scent of Hades, the King of the Underworld. He stooped under the threshold as he barged up to Zeus.

It often unsettled Zeus to see his brother—and he'd seen a lot of him, of late, with all that was going on—as it was eerily akin to looking into a mirror and seeing a younger version of himself. A darker and beardless version, also; one with skin worn from stressing and over-drinking, and hollowed with gray from the lack of sunlight. A handsome man, Hades was; but intimidating and with a presence that inspired many to lower their chins or hide.

"I hate to show up unannounced and without invitation, but this was an urgent matter," said Hades, bowing to his brother.

Though Zeus did not need to bow back—they were in *his* realm, where he ruled—he did so out of habit, and also out of respect for his sibling monarch. "It turns out I was about to summon you, and likely the rest of us original Olympians, in fact."

Hades' lips pinched, but he offered a nod of understanding, fidgeting with the flap of his midnight-colored cloak. "Persephone—and myself, to some extent—has sensed something fishy downstairs.

She's caught Mnemosyne slithering around Hecate's crypt, and possibly messing with Mel—" He flinched, then squared his shoulders. "With Melinoë's mind."

"Melinoë?" Zeus fell backwards into his throne, its steely surface hitting his behind hard, causing him to frown.

Now that's a name I haven't heard in a while, and one I know Hades is uncomfortable saying out loud.

Melinoë was something of a sore subject, a taboo topic among many gods, as she represented nightmares and madness. Even her grandmother, Demeter, said as little as possible about her. And when Persephone was in Olympus for spring and summer, she never mentioned her daughter's well-being or even hinted that she was alive.

"Mnemosyne, hm? Sneaking around Hecate's crypt? Coincidence, do you think?" Zeus stroked his beard and tapped a foot to the ground, seeking to settle the chills creeping up his legs.

"I'd hoped so, at first, but when Persephone reported that her comings and goings seemed linked to Melinoë's progressing ailments…she's worse off than usual. It has me…perturbed." Hades shoved a few dark threads of hair out of his face. "Among other things."

"Mnemosyne." The name rolled off Zeus' tongue, reminding him of better times; times when he'd frolicked and flirted and not given a damn what anyone thought. Mnemosyne had been one of his favorite adventures in the sheets, as she'd mesmerized him with her prowess—and not only because the mind was her area of expertise. No tricks or gimmicks involved; she'd known how to please him, all the right spots to touch and tease in order to bring him to the brink of ecstasy.

And now that he thought of it, it was likely she *had* used a ruse while bedding him. That she'd read into his brain with her mystical mind-warping skills and had known exactly what he'd wanted her to do to him.

That sneaky enchantress.

"*Could* she be linked to all this?" His finger got stuck in a tangle in his beard, and he ripped it free with a grimace. "It's not altogether impossible that she'd play games with us for some ulterior motive…but what kind of grudge would she be holding now, after centuries? And how could she be operating up here? She was banned from Olympus eons ago."

Zeus still remembered the day he'd had to protect his palace from the likes of her. In her unquenchable thirst for physical contact, for ethereal *mind-sex*, as she'd called it once, she'd gone around fucking too many other deities—men, women, and androgynous individuals alike—and rendering some mad in the process. Some were *still* mad, to this day. And so, after assuring her Muses—daughters she birthed after her tryst with Zeus—were well cared for, she'd accepted to move her *business* down to the Underworld, where Hades permitted her to reside, as long as she left he and Persephone alone.

Hades fidgeted from foot to foot, fretting over a bit of dust caked to the collar of his cloak. Zeus waved to get his attention, and motioned at the seat beside him—Hera's throne.

Hades shook his head, refusing the offer to sit. "Are you insane? Last time I tried to use Hera's chair she *sniffed* me from across the palace and zoomed over to slap me. I'd rather avoid that today."

Though the memory brought him an urge to laugh, Zeus remained as serious as possible as he insisted. "Trust me, she won't be able to reprimand you today. She's…not here."

"Not here?" Hades' thick eyebrows bunched as he finally caved and agreed to take a seat. But he kept upright, back stiffened as he turned to glimpse his brother. "Didn't you forbid everyone from leaving? Where did she go?"

"She was taken." Zeus' eyes slitted as he imagined all the gruesome manners in which his wife might have been forced out of her home. But the most prominent image was that of her being hauled up and over someone's shoulder, her recently bitten neck swollen and dripping her precious blue ichor all over the courtyard's brick floor. "She, and several other deities have disappeared."

Hades somehow became more rigid, and his hands curled into fists, his knuckles turning white from the force of his fingers squeezing together. "Disappeared? How? And who?"

"Hera, Dionysus, Themis, Phoebe—all supposedly attacked by our culprit, as all that remains of them are pools of poisoned ichor. And a demi-god named Lukus—I may have mentioned him to you in passing; the young half-mortal man who helped Aphrodite investigate Eros, on earth?" Hades nodded. "I'd summoned him up here to help, what with his investigative skill…but he was somehow taken, as well. Mere hours after discovering he was a son of Aphrodite…"

Hades lurched up from the throne, blackened eyes wide with questions. "A son of Aphrodite? From a mortal? But I thought she—"

"—a ploy driven by this culprit, no doubt." Zeus gestured at Hades to sit back down, becoming dizzy with his brother's constant shifting about. "I knew from the Moirai, who felt it necessary to inform me, as they feared he was part of some prophecy that would be my undoing; the usual nonsense. But Aphrodite had no recollection of sleeping with a mortal, not in centuries. And in any case, she's not around to discuss this further; she, too, has vanished, along with Athena, and Mother."

Hades had obediently sat back down, but bent his knees as if in preparation to stand again. Zeus blocked him, but as he pressed his arm firmly against his brother's chest, he sensed the heat swarming from under his cloak, the rage and confusion bubbling within him.

"Mother? *Rhea?*" He glowered at Zeus. "Attacked, as well?"

"That remains to be discovered." Zeus cleared his throat. Not that Hades was Rhea's favorite—she'd never admit to having one—but Hades did love his mother dearly and wouldn't ever associate her with the crimes going on in Olympus.

But he wasn't here to see her lined up in Lukus' final suspects…

"Her disappearance is different. The traces of blood left in her wake weren't poisoned, and odder still, she never leaves without warning. And actually…" Zeus cocked his head and gazed at the giant, open doors across the way, as if anticipating someone to be standing in the threshold, listening to his conversation with Hades. "Now that I think about it, you know who I haven't heard from or sensed in the past few hours? Gaia."

"Gaia?" Hades, who'd been slouched, breathing harshly, his aura conflicted, perked up. "She was up here?"

Zeus wrinkled his nose and scratched its tip. A flutter of a breeze had swished into the room, bringing with it some dust particles from the usually pristine balcony. With all that had been transpiring lately, the servants had been avoiding the throne-room and its environs, preferring to stay out of the way.

"She and Mother had come to help investigate. And now they're both gone…but," he waved dismissively, "Gaia comes and goes as she pleases, that's not a surprise. With all her primordial tasks, she rarely has time to send word that she's departing. Mother, on the other hand…"

"No." Hades stood up, and this time, too quickly for Zeus to stop him. He marched a few paces away, then flipped around, a firm frown etched over his face. "I can't see Mother involved in all this. At least…not of her own volition. I will return to the Underworld and start interrogating some of the residents. But I wished to convey our concerns to you, so you're aware—"

"—*our* concerns?" A female figure appeared in the doorway, prompting Hades to spin around, and Zeus to tip sideways to visualize who it was.

Demeter, her corn-colored hair separated into two braids dipping over her shoulders, entered the room, issuing a curtsy to Hades, placing a stern gaze on him.

Though his back was turned to Zeus, Zeus had no trouble envisioning Hades blanching, his revolted expression from hearing about Rhea's potential involvement melting away to a solemn facade behind which to hide, to evade his sister's questioning. He and Demeter rarely saw eye-to-eye, both constantly competing for Persephone's affections—though in Zeus' mind, Demeter had the stronger claim, as the girl's mother.

"So?" Demeter stopped before Hades and crossed her arms. "By *our*, did you mean my daughter? Is that why you're here? Is she in danger?"

Hades' gulp was so loud, Zeus might have heard it were he on the other side of the palace. "Not right now, no. But *we* are concerned about this culprit and its reach, yes."

Another individual arrived at the party; a sulking Hecate, her auburn skirts covered in filth, her hands darkened with mud.

What on earth has she been up to?

"Demeter, I thought we—" Hecate paused in the doorway, sighting Hades, then Zeus seated on his throne. Her mouth dropped open, and she hurried into a hasty curtsy. "Majesties. Sorry for my, uh…appearance, I was testing out some plant-based theories using some of Hestia's crops, so…"

Demeter marched up to Zeus, to whom she gave a more thorough, more thoughtful curtsy; though *their* relations weren't much better, most days. "We heard of the disappearances."

Zeus swore under his breath. "Hermes and his loose tongue, I presume?"

Demeter shrugged. "Whispered it to whichever servant he was bedding, who mentioned it to a kitchen staff-member, who told Hestia, who told Hecate and I—but that's beside the point. Hera is *my* sister, too, and I have a right to know if she's in trouble. She and I and Hestia…we *saw* Dionysus' body, and we had gone to fetch help, and then—"

Zeus rose from his throne, at once incurring a certain stillness in Demeter, whose rabid rage quickly dimmed to a slowly dying hearth. She'd risen her voice one time too many lately, in defense of Hera— and Zeus was ready to remind her of her place. And more so finding out that they'd discovered Dionysus already, but hadn't reported to him immediately.

And yet…with such commotion already stirring up his siblings and children, he thought better of unleashing his wrath. What if that wrath was what had caused the culprit to start its rebellion in the first place? What if *he* was indirectly responsible for all this?

Yelling and hurling thunderbolts won't solve these problems.

He didn't sit, but relaxed his stance as he motioned at Demeter to approach him. "So you heard of those who vanished—one of which *you* left unattended—and came here, disturbing my private meeting with Hades, to berate me for not telling you about Hera?" He'd hoped for a calm tone, yet his timbre grew more turbulent with each word he let out.

Demeter, no longer threatened by his energy, sneered. "The door was open, so how private could it be? And no," she swiveled to beckon Hecate over to them, "I came because Hecate and I have an idea."

Hecate flurried over, Hades on her heels. The latter hopped up onto the dais, nestling close to his brother—so close Zeus smelled the sherry in his breath as he sighed, looking down on the women below.

"What idea?" Zeus' gaze switched from Hecate, to Demeter, and back to Hecate—he'd designated *her* to explain herself, as Demeter would likely be condescending and cruel in her speech.

"We have a tingling feeling that if we conjure up the powers from our mysteries, we might be able to gain insight on this horrible affair. And some help with uncovering our culprit's identity." Hecate spoke concisely, as if she'd rehearsed for hours, to prepare for Zeus' scrutiny.

Zeus' eyebrows raised. "I don't disagree. That's a sound idea. But…why are you telling me? I'm not involved in your *mysteries,*" he used air-quotes, as he still didn't believe these magical gatherings they'd claimed existed had taken place right under his nose, "so I'd have no say in when or how you perform them."

"*You* wouldn't." Demeter snickered at him, then swerved towards Hades. "But my *daughter* would."

Hecate nudged Demeter, as if to compel her to quit being so snarky. "We need Persephone. She's part of our trio, she's essential to our rituals." She, too, twisted to stand before Hades. "It's important, majesty."

Hades' arm twitched, shoving into Zeus. "No. Not…these are *my* months. We had an agreement." He peered straight at Demeter, testing her. "She's not to come up here until the spring. And it's too perilous for her here, with all the attacks, the bloodshed. No."

Zeus anticipated an explosion of insults, of violent magic thrown between the two siblings as they fought over Persephone. There'd possibly be splashes of ichor as they strangled one another—it wouldn't have been the first time—and argued over whose turn it was and why.

But to his shock, Demeter prostrated herself at Hades' feet, hands clasped near her heart.

Her chin was dipped, and golden hairs escaped from her braids as she shook with emotion. "We need her, Hades. I beg you to reconsider. She can go straight to you again once we're done, and if you must keep her a little longer, I'll delay spring to make up for the lost time." She whipped her chin up, a blaze of fury in her metallic eyes. "In any case, she'd be safer with me, and you know it. Safer with *him,*" she motioned towards Zeus, "and the other Olympians."

Hades snorted, descending from the dais to beckon his sister up from her crouch. "You mean to plead with me but insult me at the same time? And you expect me to accept?"

Hecate placed a hand on Hades' upper arm, stopping him before he could take hold of Demeter, as he seemed about to. "Enough." She sent a puzzled gaze at Demeter, then reverted to Hades. "Both of you. This is for the greater good. If not for Demeter, please, consider this a favor to me."

Zeus steered clear of the Underworld drama—and any drama involving Persephone, to be truthful—but he *did* know that Hecate wasn't one to ask for favors, and she held immense grudges if displeased. She and Hades were on decent terms, as far as Zeus was aware. So would the Underworld king refuse to help the sorceress who'd cured his wife and protected her with her life?

"I'll fetch her," said Hades, his voice gruff as he moved between Hecate and Demeter, headed for the door. "But I'll only drop her off. With Hecate and her both up here, someone needs to be in the Underworld to monitor *that* situation." Hades briefly rotated to bow at Zeus, then fled out of the throne-room, leaving a trail of blackish steam in his wake.

Hecate and Demeter curtsied and meandered off to confer at the edge of the room, while Zeus mulled over all he'd figured out so far.

Hera and her sisters found Dionysus. Then Hera and Dionysus disappeared. And Rhea and Mnemosyne acting strangely...are their behaviors linked somehow?

He wandered out to the throne-room balcony, sniffing in its prismatic roses, nostrils itching at the sweet scent that reminded him of Hera—who hated roses, and yet did everything she could to smell like one.

Rhea, Mnemosyne—had they contrived together to kidnap his wife, his daughter, his son, his stepdaughter, his step-grandson? And two powerful titanesses—their own damn sisters? Or were their attitudes simple coincidences, and neither had anything to do with the ichor currently staining the floors of various areas of his home?

|| 9. FAILED AMBUSH ||

GAIA

A brief exit from Mnemosyne gave Gaia time to check on all the inhabitants in the hut. Lukus was asleep, his body restoring itself, loading with power—*his* power, his godliness, developing in his core and blooming out via his veins, expanding into his chest and arms and legs. Gaia sniffed in his energy, and it was toxic; and she loved it.

He'll be a fine leader for the zombie-humans.

Rhea was rocking herself back and forth, her back to the cauldron, its heat swarming over her skin and turning it a raw red. She didn't seem to mind, too focused on watching her daughter and grand-daughters, concern wafting off her in waves. When she saw Gaia looking at her, she acknowledged her with a nod, as if ensuring her all was well, despite her obvious state of panic.

"My loyalty lies with you, Mother," she said, her voice a trembled whisper. "But I cannot stop worrying about *them*," she jutted her chin at Hera, Athena, and Aphrodite, "and how this will affect their lives."

Gaia puckered her lips, unwilling to share the images of gory combat and the bloodshed she envisioned for all Olympians. Nor would she tell Rhea that it was likely not all would survive—she'd tell her offspring to do whatever it took to take the throne, and all manners of violence and torture were on the table. After how Zeus and his people had assassinated over three quarters of her Giants, she'd make him pay.

But Rhea, in her current state of shock and semi-acceptance of her situation, wasn't ready to see that. She'd lived through all the wars on the other end—defending her Olympian children—and was gearing to witness the carnage from the glorious side. In time, she'd understand it needed to be done.

Dionysus, Themis, and Phoebe were in a sort of comatose state. They'd depleted all their chants and ancient spells, and had accomplished their tasks. With no means to be useful, and their bodies exhausted from the effects of the poison, they'd fallen asleep in a heap in a corner of the hut, snoring softly. They'd awaken later, with little to no memory of what they'd done. Gaia would send Dionysus back to Olympus, but keep her precious daughters close, to avoid the slaughter that her other children might induce as they attacked Zeus.

A taste of sweet ichor swelled on Gaia's tongue; of victory, she hoped, signifying that this time, her offspring would prevail over Zeus, and she'd be able to proclaim out loud whose side she'd taken. Centuries of keeping quiet, pretending to be neutral, to venerate Zeus and all he did…she'd had enough of playing games. Uranus couldn't do it, Cronus couldn't do it, and neither could Zeus; it was time for someone else to rule Olympus, to reign over the world.

She hadn't quite decided which of her children would receive the throne—and to be honest, she figured *she'd* take it, as a woman in full power might prove more beneficial than risking another man who'd do nothing correctly.

As she checked on the goddesses, stirring from their spell-induced slumber, Mnemosyne returned.

"Hades is gone," she said, a slight smile sketching over her lips. "Perfect opportunity to go in and grab Persephone and hold her hostage, if anything to implant some fake memories in there to quiet her doubts."

Gaia snorted. "You weren't able to subdue her before. What makes you think you can now?"

Mnemosyne quirked an eyebrow. "Because *you* can help me. If Hades is gone..." She wiggled that eyebrow, and the other, suggestively. "Then we can both go get her, trap her, kidnap her. I may not be able to trifle with her on my own, but between the two of us, we can overpower her and rip those defenses Hecate implanted in her brain, no?"

"Well..." The idea of *ripping* just about anything pleased Gaia, at that point, as she hadn't gotten her hands dirty in quite some time, doing most of her work at a distance, commanding her peons with a voice. And she had to admit the notion of sneaking into Hades' palace *was* tempting. She'd never been inside but had heard tales of the lavish décor and the jewels encrusted into floors and walls. "Hecate *is* powerful, but can her spells ward us both off at once? Let's go."

She glanced at Rhea, who assured her she'd keep watch. The Olympians were still waking, but their eyes were closed and their breaths shallow. They were still navigating whatever fever dreams the sleeping spell had provoked. There was time to creep off and attend to her important business.

They quietly exited the hut, and a whoosh of murky air hit Gaia's face. She, who preferred the scent of fresh earth and mulch over anything else, was disappointed at the dryness tinging the atmosphere, but still sensed a slither of humidity coming from the swamp located behind Mnemosyne's hut. They walked down to the bridge over *Lethe*, then navigated up towards the towering black marble and gem structure that Hades called home.

Gaia had seen it often, of late, but never so up close. She hadn't caught a whiff of the luxuriant waves of pomegranate and ambrosia that emanated from under the front door. Nor had she noticed there were no windows on this side, and the roof was flat, not pointy and ominous looking as she'd have expected from a place so obscure, so gloomy.

They weren't hunched or tiptoeing; if Hades was out on business, and only Persephone remained within the mansion, she'd not sense them coming. There was no need to be sneaky, and so they approached the front door, intending to pry it open and slip inside.

Gaia found herself halted a few feet away, however. As if a quicksand had enveloped her up to her ankles and prevented her from going any further; or a blockade of stone had dropped in front of her, barring her passage.

"I…can't…go," she said, teeth gritting as she attempted to push into whatever force had paused her route to the door. She could see it, so near, so shiny with rubies and diamonds and sapphires. She sniffed at it, its glacial substance filtering up her nostrils and freezing into her sinuses. Tasted it; sharp and bitter—and enchanted.

"Neither can I," muttered Mnemosyne who, Gaia realized, had also been blocked in her progress. She was pushing the air, and a rosy hue took over her cheeks as she panted with effort, shoving and shoving into the apparently invisible wall that restricted their entry to Hades' palace.

"It's enchanted?" Gaia growled, understanding that they weren't going to get into the palace today.

She squinted at the palace's surface, scanning it for encryptions and markings. She sought a pattern in the jewels, in the black marbled veins, in the material itself; and there it was. Scrawled over the marble, hovering inches from it, yet somehow weaved *into* the substance and glowing gold, blinding Gaia with its sudden appearance. One had to get as close as possible and *want* to see such charms in order for them to divulge themselves; a twisted way of magic that Gaia recognized, and snarled at.

"Wardings." She stepped back, recoiling from the unseen blockade, and set her hands on her hips. "Ancient, powerful magic."

Mnemosyne glared towards the door, cocking her head. "Oh," she snickered, "yes, I see them now. Scribbled over the door, right?"

The font was a loopy cursive, colored gold, only visible to those with deep knowledge of such a language. It was a long-lost tongue of witches, primordials, and monsters, and Gaia shivered as she translated it.

"It specifically halts those with ill-intentions from entering." She blinked, peered down at her hands, her emerald bodice, the tips of her sandaled feet showing under the thick edges of her gown.

"Ill-intentions?" Mnemosyne eased a bushy branch of her hair behind her ears. "Who put that there? And since when? I've always been able to enter through the front door."

Another growl blossomed in Gaia's throat, but she didn't let it escape. "Hecate, of course. This is witch magic, though I had no clue she had access to it. It's…old, older than her, having come from those like me."

"Where the fuck did she learn it from?" Mnemosyne brushed off her skirts, then turned towards the side of the mansion. With a huff, she headed past a cluster of rose bushes pressed against the marble walls, decorating the small entrance courtyard. "Whatever; I know a short-cut. Hecate's secret stairs. I've been using those to get straight to the crypt. I'll go in, find Persephone, convince her to come outside, and then we'll get to work."

Mnemosyne hurried off before Gaia could agree to her plan; and she wasn't quite sure she wanted to.

Gaia slithered towards a hedge of thick, forest-green leaves, delimiting the mansion grounds. It was far enough that the enchantment didn't affect it, but near enough that Gaia saw where Mnemosyne snuck off to. This spot permitted her a clear vision of the front doors, too, to prepare for when Persephone would come out.

She waited, tapping a foot to the ground, which she noticed was also gem-encrusted, shimmering from the fake stars sprinkled overhead.

Fake stars—what an odd place this realm is.

She'd rarely gone out to explore the Underworld, as she wasn't *supposed* to be down there, and therefore couldn't be caught wandering. Most days she kept to Mnemosyne's crypt, suffocating from the delectable dirt scent from the four walls that enclosed her. When she needed air, *actual* fresh air, she used her primordial powers to teleport to a *real* forest, usually somewhere in southern Europe, where she resourced and replenished her energy.

Hades didn't like when gods appeared and disappeared magically within his realm, but that didn't mean they couldn't do so. He had no way to restrict teleportation, only frown upon it. And so, Gaia had been able to smuggle in four Olympians, three Titans, and a demi-god right under his nose.

As she rubbed her hands in delight at her deception of the King of the Underworld, her ears picked up on a thundering sound coming from across the realm, near the Diamond Gates. Her dress—enchanted to serve as an antenna that detected danger or sudden shifts in the atmosphere—pulsated, taking in the sound, absorbing it. Gaia closed her eyes, listening, letting the ground's vibration translate that sound to her.

Hoofbeats—three, no, four horses, pulling something big, something black, something…

At once, Gaia activated her gown's protective shield. She lifted her arms, using them to expand and raise the hem of her gown up until it was level with her head. The rest of the enchanted, enlarged fabric still covered her legs and feet. The gown's silky material then trembled, awaiting its command. She maintained it in place with one hand, using the other to sprinkle a spell over the textile. The dress transformed, making her invisible, hidden behind it.

The hoofbeats were those of Hades' ebony horses; his travel chariot, she had no doubt. No one else would barge into his realm with such abruptness, with such flair. And in any case, Hades was the only god who still used his chariot frequently to fly up to Olympus, or to visit with Poseidon under the sea.

She'd reacted in time to protect her anonymity—and to avoid Hades' temper. Because as his horses galloped through the air, depositing him before his palace, he hopped off his chariot with a growing grimace, and grumbled under his breath as he snapped his fingers to put his chariot away. The horses, the carriage vanished, put to rest until he'd need to travel again.

Gaia had an inkling he would.

He stomped up to his door, wrenched it open, and slammed it behind him, his footsteps so thunderous that even behind the ancient charms preventing her from entering, Gaia felt every reverberation of his sandals on the ground.

With the warding in place, she couldn't eavesdrop on any conversations, and hoped that Mnemosyne would be able to. And more so, that she'd heard Hades' arrival and had managed to hide herself in time. Had she located Persephone, already? Had she grabbed her, and had been hauling her towards the front door when Hades arrived?

No—if Hades had seen Mnemosyne, he'd have thrown a tantrum so large, the entire realm would have shaken.

Somewhat safe, Gaia released her gown, letting it skid back into place, making her visible again. No one was around; all Underworld inhabitants had gone about their affairs, none shocked to sense Hades' chariot, nor unused to his temper flares. Gaia interacted little with this grandson, but knew him to be flighty, easily upset, and obsessed with his wife.

Soon enough, Mnemosyne reemerged, intact, but her expression drowned in darkness.

"Not here," she said, before Gaia had a chance to ask her what had happened. She grasped her mother's wrist and hastened back to the hut, breathing raggedly with their every step.

Once at the hut, Mnemosyne sealed the door, blew a gold-dusted charm onto it, and rested against its muddy surface, catching her breath.

"What is it?" Gaia swerved over to Mnemosyne, whose shoulders were trembling, and whose fingertips twitched with electrical energy. She massaged the titaness' upper arms. "Tell me."

Mnemosyne deflected her mother's offer of comfort and swept farther into the dimly lit room. "I'd made it upstairs when Hades barged in," she said, breaths still hitching in her chest, sounding harsh. "I stayed hidden in the crypt staircase and listened to their conversation. Sounds like Hades is taking Persephone up to Olympus."

Gaia's eyebrows shot up. "Is he, now?" She spun and scowled at the wall, *through* the wall, and at the palace she'd run from. "Before spring time? I find that hard to believe. He'd never allow it."

"Well, believe it, because he is. He made that abundantly clear, and from the tone of his voice, he wasn't joking." Mnemosyne shuddered and moseyed over to her cauldron, taking in deep whiffs of its brewing toxins. "He was in Olympus, just now. Conferring with Zeus. Demeter and Hecate interrupted them to beg to bring Persephone up. Something about their mysteries, from what I gathered."

Gaia's limbs turned to ice and her heart skipped one beat too many. "Mysteries?" Her shoulders tensed as she scanned her daughter's face, seeking the meaning behind her words, seeking the veracity of her reports. "*The* mysteries? The Eleusinian ones?"

Mnemosyne shrugged. "Apparently. Hades didn't say much more, and they scurried into one of his offices. I realized by then that I needed to get out before either of them smelled my presence."

"You should have been quicker." Gaia's fists bunched. She wanted to punch something, someone, but for lack of anything better, she jabbed into the muddy wall, its gooey, gushy surface doing nothing to attenuate her frustration. "You should have run up, snatched her, dragged her out by force. The *mysteries?* Tartarus, Mnemosyne! Do you not understand how serious this is?"

Mnemosyne narrowed her gaze on Gaia, a flicker of irritation igniting in her eyes, shifting them to gold. "I *was* quick, Mother. Hades showed up as I was about to take her; and to capture her right in front of him? Are you mad? That's too risky. I'd have never gotten out of there, as my powers never work on him, for some reason."

"Because he's a sly king with access to a witch who does his bidding." Gaia pinched the bridge of her nose and tipped her head back, taking lengthy breaths, hoping to steady her erratic heartbeat. "Crowned kings, godly ones, have some sort of supernatural protection against mind-tricks like yours, daughter. I thought you knew that. Though I've heard rumors you were able to toy with Zeus, but Hades is not so easily fooled." She seethed, hissing through her thinned lips. She didn't mean to be cruel to Mnemosyne, but her patience had its limits, and those limits were being tested now.

The Eleusinian Mysteries—which remain a mystery even to me.

Gaia wasn't an adept of these obscure rituals observed by Hecate, Demeter, and Persephone. She'd never been invited to their gatherings, never even been able to spy on them, when she'd attempted to. Now that she thought of it, the barriers put in place to prevent eavesdropping on the meetings—those were the same as the engravings on Hades' front door, forbidding her from entering.

She had no idea why Hecate would want to invoke those possibly dangerous, slightly sacrificial rituals now, but she must have believed they were a way to uncover the identity of whomever was poisoning the gods and turning them against one another. A means to *stop* the entity from continuing its path of destruction. A solution to stop them; to stop Gaia.

How powerful those rituals would be, and *would* they unmask Gaia or be strong enough to discontinue her progress, Gaia wasn't sure. But at the concept of failing, she experienced a pang in her gut, a throbbing physical pain, a stabbing sensation she hadn't felt in eons.

Fear.

|| 10. MYSTERY OF MYSTERIES ||

PERSEPHONE

Persephone had sensed an ominous presence behind her, in the hallway, as she exited her private garden, wiping her hands on her muddy apron. Battling weeds and extracting her mother's favorite plants from dirt—these things soothed her when she was troubled. And troubled, she was; more so when a looming sensation of something off-putting welcomed her in the corridor, and a slight fog swept in—

The front door banged open, rattling the floor-boards and shaking off dust from the framed jewelry boxes hanging from the mahogany-tinted walls.

Persephone, unaffected by such an arrival—only *one* person stormed into the palace like that, and it never took her unawares, because she felt his irritation from miles away—removed her apron and handed it to a shivering serving girl who'd come from the kitchens.

"Best get out of here," she whispered to the girl, who took the apron and scampered back into the kitchens at once.

Hades saw Persephone, accelerated his colossal strides in her direction, and only stopped once his lips met her forehead, where he placed a long, wet kiss. "Thank goodness you're all right."

Persephone pulled away from him and looked deep into his black, one might say soulless, eyes. She knew better, though, as he had as much soul and spirit and sensuality as any other deity, if not more.

"Why wouldn't I be? You set up all sorts of protections before you left, didn't you? Are *you* all right?"

He dragged a hand down his face. "No, I am not. You were correct—something's fishy, and its source is up there, in Olympus."

She had half a mind to drag him into the closest room to sit. His skin was turning chalky, grayish, and perspiration dotted his forehead and cheeks. He was shaking, she noticed—but not from anger. The emotions his aura evoked at that moment weren't enraged, they were…cautious. Flighty.

Fear.

She was still sensing an eeriness about the hallway, and didn't want to have this conversation out in the semi-open—the palace servants were mostly mum and never spread rumors, to the best of Persephone's knowledge—but Hades made no move to take this elsewhere.

"The Olympians…Zeus himself, in fact…they're all afraid. The atmosphere up there is dreadful. Worse than down here, I'd daresay." He crossed his arms and seemed to be suppressing chills. For Hades to show fear, to *be* fearful, meant there was much more going on than he or Persephone had anticipated. "Several gods are missing," he nodded as Persephone gasped, "and a supposed demi-god named Lukus, as well."

Persephone wished she'd kept her apron—it smelled like earth and roots and flowers, and might have been comforting to her as Hades revealed these unsettling facts.

"Lukus? Who in Tartarus is that? The name is familiar, but…and who has disappeared? Which gods?" Persephone nearly grabbed Hades to shake him, as he'd grown silent, contemplating the hem of his black robe.

She sometimes wondered why all gods still wore the clothing of ancient times; togas, royal gowns, tunics. Humans had crafted such delightful outfits and styles that were comfortable and practical, yet the powerful beings overlooking the planet remained set in their ways? Such a shame.

But also, wrong time to be thinking of such trivial things—Persephone refocused on Hades as he shrugged.

"Aphrodite mentioned him once or twice which, as it turns out, makes sense because…Zeus told me he's her spawn."

Persephone made to gasp again, but the sound got stuck in her throat. "Another half-mortal son for Aphrodite? Truly? But I thought she was done with mortal men?"

A flash of a bare-chested, chiseled hunk of a man running through a forest shattered through Persephone's mind. Adonis, the mortal man she and Aphrodite had fought over for his attentions, Aphrodite wanting to bed him, Persephone interested in keeping him in the Underworld for companionship. He'd been the reason Aphrodite had stopped sleeping with humans, but now, after centuries, she'd changed her ways again? Persephone gritted her teeth.

Hades' grunt interrupted her visions, which was for the best—she didn't want to dwell on her past quarrels with Aphrodite, or anyone else for that matter. When she was in the Underworld, she was in a state of peace, of quiet, of ignoring her qualms and disputes with anyone upstairs.

She seized Hades' arms—she'd aimed for his shoulders, but he was taller than her, and she couldn't reach—and squeezed hard. "Mother? Is she okay? Did she vanish? Was she hurt?"

Hades broke free from her crushing grip with a wince, as if

surprised at her strength—which he shouldn't have been, as Persephone loaded with energy and lit up like a bonfire whenever Demeter was involved.

"Let me reassure you, Demeter was fine." He fixed his tunic—it had gone astray and bunched up when Persephone had snagged him—and stiffened. "I'm not reassured by the others who were taken, though. Yes," he inclined his head and his lips tightened as he addressed Persephone's raising eyebrows, "*taken* might be the appropriate word for this situation. Zeus thinks they might have been captured."

Persephone's legs were restless, her fingers jittery. She needed air, she needed a walk—but still, Hades made no motion to transfer this conversation somewhere else.

"Who, then? Tell me, husband, before I lose my mind and start hypothesizing and get a migraine." Persephone settled for sitting on the bottom stair leading up to the second floor, trying to steady her legs as she bent over and brought them close to her chest.

"Zeus mentioned folk being attacked, but didn't explain much else. Whoever the attacker was, their actions might be linked with all the poisoning going on, and they seem to have vanished, along with their victims, which I understand to be Themis, Phoebe, and Dionysus." Hades peered at the space beside Persephone, likely debating whether to sit or to pace to and fro, as he usually did when perturbed. "Along with this Lukus fellow and Hera, who left behind traces of having been assaulted, too. Athena and Aphrodite are gone, and they might have also been taken by force. Oh, and Rhea and Gaia, who were staying at the palace, have fled as well, with no inkling where they were going, nor any goodbyes."

Gaia, Persephone knew, often departed in haste to go fulfill her major earthly duties; her sudden departure made sense, and it didn't strike her as odd. The others, though…that was confusing. And Rhea, sweet-natured, lovely woman that she was, hadn't been at the palace in years, but Persephone remembered her ways. She never left without saying goodbye.

"Who could kidnap so many deities without being seen by at least *one* person? This is absurd." The migraine she'd worried about began to throb at her temples, threatening to spread across her forehead. Her headaches were violent, normally only occurring within her first few days after coming to the Underworld or returning to Olympus—the shift in the atmosphere always took a terrible toll on her.

"I agree," Hades groaned, "but Zeus has his theories and they worry me." He started his pacing, his tunic sweeping across the floors, sending a soft whiff of air onto Persephone every time he turned and switched directions. "He thought Rhea might have something to do with it all, as she was the only disappeared one who hadn't left a puddle of her ichor and poison mixed. Almost as if *she'd* been the attacker, but…I can't accept it. Mother would never plot against the gods like that. She avoids such plots, after all the nonsense she's been through. Why else has she been camping out in jungles for all these years?"

Persephone cringed, hating to bring up any fact that would make it seem she was siding with Zeus. Her godly, kingly father was, most days, a source of troubled thoughts for her.

"I agree that she wouldn't *want* to harm her family, but…have you spent any time with her lately? Has anyone? Camping out in jungles…who knows what sort of behaviors she picked up on. I'm not saying she's the attacker, but she might not be her usual self anymore."

"I…" Hades hissed, though not directing the noise at Persephone, his head turned towards the door. "I'm unhappy with this, but because of this situation, you're wanted in Olympus. Promptly." Persephone's jaw dropped. "Yes, I know; I threw a fit because of my belief that you wanted to leave, and now…you're being asked to. Hecate and Demeter need you."

Persephone shot to her feet. "Mother needs me? I thought you said she wasn't harmed?"

"She's not." Hades' gaze grew dark, darker than normal. "But she and Hecate smell risings and tidings that remind them of your mysteries, and they'd like to get the gang together. Quickly."

The Eleusinian mysteries.

They hadn't gathered for their mysteries in ages; hadn't needed to. Most days such rituals weren't necessary, and it took too long to gather all the ingredients required for them, in any case. So many of their treasured items were outdated, or no longer in existence, which made it hard for them to properly perform their rites.

But if Hecate *and* Demeter were summoning her…if they'd said it out loud, shared the fact that they were planning to open up that box…they meant business. Usually, they *never* told anyone when and where they were preparing for a session. This was grave news.

Yet Persephone didn't believe it, not quite. After the tantrum Hades had thrown, after reminding her of her current place, he'd exchanged three words with Demeter and she'd somehow convinced him to let Persephone go? Not that she doubted her mother's powers of persuasion, but Hades was a stubborn, solid man who rarely, if ever, let anyone change his mind.

He glanced left and right, his jaw tightening. "Come." He grasped her wrist and tugged her into her garden, sealing the door behind them. Like a spy wary of being caught, he was on alert, and his hairs stood on edge as he pushed his back against the door, taking deep breaths.

That trip affected him more than I'd have expected it to.

She sniffed in her garden's aroma. "I'm unsure I understand this correctly," she said, scratching her chin, scrutinizing the man quietly panicking before her. "You're *allowing* me to go? Now? Before my time with you is up?"

Hades sent her a side-glance that stilled her, turned her insides to ice. "I have no choice."

She gulped. He *was* serious; but still, something seemed too easy about this, and she doubted he was telling her the full story. He wasn't telling her much of anything, at this point, only huffing and puffing, fists bunching at his sides. His fear from earlier had developed and now mingled with frustration; she sensed it in her bones, freezing her blood.

But that wouldn't stop her from double-checking that he did indeed mean this, that he wasn't toying with her to rile her up. It wasn't that uncommon for him to enjoy seeing her seethe, and to then smack her against a wall and take pleasure in commanding her to calm down.

A frisson of desire flurried down her spine at the thought, but she nudged it out of the way—there'd be plenty of time for passionate sex once the godly world was no longer at risk.

"And are you going to delay my departure by playing your usual silly games? Feigning illness and depression to keep me here?" She scoffed. "Like you did to poor Athena and Hermes, when they visited? You hadn't pulled that one in a *long* time, not with me, at least. But don't think I didn't catch on to your act. I know you. Give me a head's up if you're planning to do that, so I can know what to expect."

Hades' snort cut her off, and she could have sworn she saw a hint of a smile lifting the corners of his lips. "I won't. We're pressed for time."

She recalled how drunk he'd been that day, when accompanying Athena and Hermes to the gates. She knew how he got when severely intoxicated—he swayed and came off as in a trance, dazed, stuck in another world. He'd surely scared those two half to death with his demeanor, more so considering other deities were being poisoned left and right by an unknown culprit.

That reminder tightened Persephone's gut, like a snake curling up and cuddling her intestines.

"I *have* to let you go," said Hades as he came up to Persephone and cupped her chin. His warmth took her by surprise, and she shuddered, but not in displeasure. "I worry Zeus himself will visit me at your mother's demand if I don't allow this."

She lifted to her tiptoes and he pressed his nose to hers. His fruity breath blew over her skin, titillating all her senses as she imagined letting go of all her concerns, baring herself, shedding her clothes, and allowing him to take her right there, in the garden. Rolling around in the dirt, crushing plants, tickling one another with flower petals. Screaming in tandem as they reached a climax under the watchful eyes of clusters of flowers and exotic crops.

She smirked at the recollection of the last time they'd done that.

"I may still be depressed, though." He kissed her lightly; *too* lightly, meaning his mind hadn't gone elsewhere as hers had. His soul still weighed heavy with his worries, and in truth, they wouldn't have much time for goodbye sex. Not with the lengthy ways they preferred to indulge in one another.

Persephone was worried, too, and sensed it with the scrunching of her eyebrows and a crease forming between them as Hades opened the door and headed towards his parlor.

He waved at her, his back turned so she couldn't visualize his expression, though she detected the slither of impatience in his tone. "Gather whatever ingredients you need. We leave in ten minutes. I...need a drink, first."

Underneath that worry, though, was a flurrying touch of excitement. At the prospect of going up to Olympus during the late fall, early winter—oh, the breezes would be so crisp and the leaves so colorful!—*and* at the notion that she'd get to spend time with Mother and Hecate, like in the old days, when they'd meet regularly for their rituals.

Though what sort of tragic incidents would incite her mother and best friend to need to summon their obscure magic, and need *her* there for it, was another mystery on its own.

|| 11. BUSY ||

GAIA

The Eleusinian Mysteries. A mystery to all but the three goddesses who operated them, activated them, used them for unknown purposes at unknown occurrences—Demeter, Hecate, Persephone.

Gaia had been this close—*this close* to snagging Persephone, to prevent a perilous reunion of this sort from happening.

Damn you, Hades, returning at the worst possible time.

Gaia picked up on the echoes of her own thoughts in Aphrodite's mind, and resonating within Athena and Hera, too. They'd fully woken from their slumber, and had overheard the conversation with Mnemosyne, had they?

She glimpsed Mnemosyne—she'd conjured a small table where she was preparing vials of the poison, setting up needles to inject it into those who'd need the substance to take to their blood quicker. She'd been concerned by what she'd listened to, and Hades and Persephone's conversation had disturbed her, Gaia knew. Yet she was, as always, a skillful mind-blocker and wouldn't show another ounce of emotion unless they were well and truly fucked.

In Gaia's mind, they *almost* were.

She spun to her prisoners to address their questions. "Yes, *the mysteries, ladies,*" she said, in response to Athena's squeaking interior voice vibrating inside her head.

The Olympian goddesses weren't going anywhere—not yet, at least, and not while bound by magical and solid ivy, unbreakable by mere *babies* like them. Which meant there was no harm debating this new development with them. Lower level as they were, all three had encountered situations where they'd had to shift views and review their tactics. They might understand, they might *help*.

Athena was the goddess of wisdom—what if *she* knew something that might assist Gaia in navigating this tricky tactic of using the mysteries against her?

"Why would they enact those?" Aphrodite's mind-voice was softer, but tinged with a tremble that pleasured Gaia. She liked knowing her ex-husband's most powerful daughter wasn't so powerful now, tied up and gagged in a muddy hut in the Underworld, where no one would expect her to be.

"I don't know." Gaia studied Aphrodite's face, peering deep into her color-switching eyes. They'd remained a sea-foam green for most of the time down here, except a few times when they'd flashed to violet, her angry shade—whenever Lukus was involved or brought up in conversation. "These mysteries are mysteries for a reason, and those three maggots have kept them so for eons with no risk of anyone finding out more information. You'd *think* I'd know, since the minimal knowledge I have of them is that they involve the earth—and I *am* the earth. But whatever they're doing, it's never been something I've been able to understand. Trust me, I've tried."

Hera's mind-voice came out as a squeak, causing Gaia to cringe as she heard it bouncing about inside her brain. *"Can they take care of your nonsense with their powers?"* She squinted at Gaia, nostrils flaring, as if to insist that she hoped this particular thought would come true.

She was no threat—despite the slight menace in her words—so Gaia snickered, emitting a quick chortle at her attempt at intimidation. "Their powers might seem similar to mine, but I doubt they'd match me. I'm a primordial goddess; whatever energies they're manipulating, *I* can manipulate them too, as I created them. But they *might* have the ability to seek me out. Figure out who I am, the one behind all this."

That was the root of the issue, and Gaia didn't want the Olympians to see how deeply it perturbed her. How, in the mere minutes since she'd found out Persephone would be traveling up to Olympus, a newfound panic, glacial and uncomfortable, had settled in her gut.

Eons of vengeful feelings, centuries of conspiring, blackmailing, decades of preparing, of putting peons into their places, of hunting, of mixing spells and potions to come up with the perfect poison; and those damned mysteries might undo all her careful progress?

No. I have allies. We will prevail.

She sensed Mnemosyne busying about behind her, administering poisonous doses to Themis, Dionysus, and Phoebe, offering some of the toxin to Rhea, to strengthen her for whatever was to come. Rhea accepted, though Gaia felt her reluctance deep in her bones. Mnemosyne then climbed atop the altar to work with the still slumbering Lukus.

Gaia recalled all those she'd already enlisted to her cause. All her children, those still alive, at least, and those locked up in Tartarus, were all eager to assist. A few monsters outlying the Underworld, a couple of demi-gods who'd had enough of Zeus' control had signed up. And she was *still* working on the god Tartarus, who was pushing her out of his mind but he wasn't quite disinterested, either. She needed to get a hold of Chaos, too—but they were a nearly impossible deity to contact, busy traveling amongst the constellations in search of other planets to seek dominion over. They knew, like Gaia, that earth was doomed.

"But I've covered my tracks," she said at last, struggling to fight the hesitation in her tone, to show herself as assertive and confident in front of her Olympian prisoners. "I've prepared for this, for all alternatives and outcomes, and I won't let this little side-quest of theirs disturb my goals."

Athena wriggled about, getting Gaia's attention. *"And what if they* can *match you? You said their powers might be similar, and you said you don't know much else—what if they're able to stop you?"*

Gaia stomped a foot to the ground, sending a puff of dry dirt onto Aphrodite's silky pajamas, at which she sneered and attempted to clean off with her elbow.

"No. They can't stop me. *No one* can stop me. You seem to forget, my darling goddess of wisdom, that I've been working on this invasion for centuries. *Centuries.*" Gaia's foot had seeped so deep into the mud that she'd left an imprint. Her rage had burned through it, melting the flaky stuff into a molten sludge that steamed with heat. She moved away, leaving the footprint there as proof—of her fury, of her power, and of what she'd do to anyone who dared get in her way.

Athena's thoughts ceased, and Hera and Aphrodite stared at the smoke wafting from the footprint, blinking, gulping.

"Should it come to a confrontation, as you seem to imply it might, then I'll still win." Gaia scowled at Athena, who hadn't needed to voice *those* thoughts to be transparent about what she believed. "First off, I have leverage—you three. Zeus wouldn't allow any of you to be harmed in the crossfires. I have my poisoned ones—" she gestured towards Themis, Phoebe, and Dionysus, freshly dosed with toxins and sleeping off the side-effects, "—and their abilities are amplified now. Two ichor-thirsty titanesses and a drunken deity who can tolerate just about any blow because he's so numb from drink and drugs that nothing affects him? Ha!"

She snorted at the thought of Dionysus in battle. Last time he'd fought, he'd surprisingly hit a few targets, despite his wobbly stance and his swaying back and forth because of inebriation. But now, with her poison in his veins, intensifying the power in his blood, he'd be unstoppable. She couldn't wait to see the look of surprise on everyone's faces, all those who'd underestimated him. And those who'd be shocked that he was fighting for *her*, and not for daddy Zeus.

"And of course, I have Rhea." She pointed at her daughter, crumbled in a corner, rubbing at the bruises on her knees. She didn't look like much *now*, but once she fought off the poison's side-effects, she'd be a tremendous lioness with poisonous fangs and deadly claws. "And Mnemosyne," the titaness in question lifted her head and smiled at the mention of her name, "without forgetting my zombie human army. Ah, so delightful." Gaia clasped her hand under her chin, smelling those humans right now, plunging their teeth into animal flesh and feasting to fill themselves up for the war. This sight gave her great joy. "And finally, that army's captain…Lukus."

She flipped to the half-mortal in question as he sat up, straight as a plank, arms stiff at his sides. Mnemosyne was standing on the other end of the altar, still holding the needle she'd used to inject him with toxins. The slight quirk of her lips and the golden glow over her expression revealed that she'd succeeded.

Lukus was nearly ready.

Gaia returned to her captives, but kept a steady side-eye on

Lukus, who was stretching, cracking his knuckles. "You were so busy listening to me, interrogating me, that you didn't notice Mnemosyne prepping our darling half-human over there, hm? He's been fed with the poison, tinged with dribbles of the blood we took from you while you were unconscious. A potent concoction, if I do say so myself."

Though his movements were a tad unbalanced, and he came off as dazed, Lukus turned to them—his mother, his aunt, his step-great-aunt. He let his long, muscular legs dangle from the altar. His eyes were wide, not with worry, but with intrigue. He licked his lips, not with desire, but with hunger.

Ah, of course—he needs fresh ichor now, to complete his transformation.

Gaia snapped at him, and he hopped off the altar and marched up to her at once. His steps were mechanical, a tad on the robotic side; that would fade in time, Gaia hoped. She didn't want him to come off as possessed, though he technically was. She wanted him sturdy, strong, and intimidating even to the gods themselves. For he, the demi-god son of Aphrodite and leader of the human army, would confront Zeus along with her children, and dethrone him once and for all.

Settled before Gaia, Lukus was tall, big biceps gleaming with sweat, chiseled chest so defined and glorious it almost hurt Gaia to look at. She cringed—she'd never taken mortal lovers and never would, but perhaps, after everything was over, and they'd won...*perhaps* she'd indulge. She'd give herself a little treat in the form of Lukus and his clearly capable body. She'd seen under his pants—a lovely sight, she'd admit—and wouldn't have minded having his member inserted into her.

But not now, *not now,* not while there were things to do.

She pushed a strand of his ebony hair from his face. It had grown out slightly since she'd first started watching him on earth, a few months prior. His eyes, usually a piercing blue, were now tinted an ominous mix of scarlet, navy, and violet.

"Lukus," she said, spinning him towards the Olympians. "Drink."

All three goddesses gasped, choking on their gags. Athena was rigid as wood, but Hera and Aphrodite tried to back away, crawling backwards, instantly hitting the muddy wall in their progress.

Lukus hadn't been deterred by the command, and was slowly strolling towards them.

Gaia smiled. "Start with Aphrodite. Her wrist." Gaia motioned at the area in question; milky white, with light blue veins dashing from fingers to shoulder. "Take enough to consider an appetizer, hm? You'll be drinking more after that, so make room."

Aphrodite recoiled, and the fear in her eyes—their shade a midnight blue sky—grew as they filled with liquid. She'd cry; this situation was so familiar to her, *too* familiar, and she wouldn't be easily subdued. But Lukus was strong, and thirsty, and he'd prevail. Aphrodite had no choice.

Gaia watched as Lukus straddled his mother, pinning her to the ground, and snatched her arm, bringing her wrist to his mouth. Gaia moved to get a better view—this was a once-in-a-lifetime experience, getting to see Lukus sink his teeth into his mother's flesh. He'd done it before, Gaia recalled—she'd seen it through Eros' eyes, when he'd commanded Lukus to *eat* Aphrodite. Gaia had been entertained at the sight of blood gushing from Aphrodite's arm as Lukus bit, chewed, swallowed, sighed in enjoyment.

She wouldn't let him go that far today. A pint or two of blood, no flesh-eating involved. That display of gore was purely for show, and because somewhere deep down, Eros had craved to witness it. Gaia's methods were cleaner, albeit still somewhat of a mess to dispose of later.

The instant his incisors broke through Aphrodite's skin, she squealed, she squirmed. This was too much for her; Gaia heard her thoughts, jumbled and screaming on the inside, but there was nothing she could do, overpowered as she was. Lukus kept her in place, and in any case he took no note of her movement, too busy slurping up her juices. Not a single drop fell from his mouth—he'd let not even a slither of his mother's blood go to waste.

The rhythmic *slurp, slurp* was like ecstasy to Gaia. She couldn't contain her internal joy as she watched Lukus drink up, and Aphrodite writhe in disgust and fear beneath him.

"Enough," said Gaia, once more snapping at Lukus, who stood, straightened up, and wiped his mouth. A faint hint of blue had smeared over his lips, and he licked them for good measure, a twinkle in his eye as he absorbed the flavor. "Now go for Athena's upper arm."

To Gaia's surprise, Athena didn't draw back or attempt to resist him. Wise as she was, she knew resistance was futile, and he'd get what he wanted. It was almost as if she *gave* her arm to him, making it easier for him to dive into her skin. And yet her flinch when his teeth made contact and tore through showed she hadn't been quite ready for this. She'd allowed it because she, unlike her compatriots, knew better than to dispute a creature under Gaia's control.

But that didn't mean she liked the sensation of having her ichor sucked up and out of her. The growing disgust on her face—nostrils flaring, eyebrows drawing in, skin shifting to a pale, cream color— was invigorating to Gaia, who again watched with disturbing pleasure as Lukus drank, this time drizzling some blue ichor onto the mud.

Athena's blood was of lesser importance to him, it seemed; that, or didn't taste as good? Who knew; Gaia wouldn't ask questions, nor did she care about flavoring.

"Stop," said Gaia, seeing Lukus becoming a bit too enthusiastic, his slurping faster, the blood dribbling from his mouth now going to waste. "Move on to Hera. Her neck—the wound there is still fresh and won't be hard to re-open. Be quick about it."

Lukus obeyed, but instead of rising up this time, he crawled up to Hera, who'd huddled into a ball and tried to shield her neck with her shoulder. It was no use—he shoved her shoulder out of the way with such force, Gaia could have sworn she heard a *crack* that had dislocated the clavicle, followed by a muffled screech by Hera that seemed to confirm as much.

No matter—she'll mend. Bodily injuries are the least of my concerns right now.

Without hesitation, Lukus thrust his teeth in, fitting perfectly in the holes left behind by Rhea. Gaia peered at Rhea, briefly, to see if she was witnessing Lukus picking up where she'd left off. But she'd closed her eyes and was muttering under her breath—prayers, it sounded like, how cute—with no interest for the gruesome scene in front of Gaia.

Lukus guzzled down the ichor, and Hera had closed her eyes, too, likely reciting the same prayers as her mother, but in her head. Gaia was too ensconced in watching Lukus' feast to listen to whatever she was praying to. Every lap of his tongue, soaking up the sugary-flavored liquid, made Gaia delirious with satisfaction. As if *she* were drinking, too, vicariously, enjoying the blood as Lukus swallowed it. She could smell god's blood, but had never tasted it, and wondered if maybe *she* should drink, too, in the long run?

She shook off the very arousing thought of embedding her teeth into Zeus' upper thigh, and snapped at Lukus. "You're done."

He got to his feet, and stood before Gaia, again wiping his mouth, leaving a streak of blue on his arm where he'd rubbed. Blue and red blood stained around his lips, with a drop or two still sliding down his chin. Gaia swallowed, holding in her instinct to shove into him and lick his skin, drink up the residue of this godly blood and finally taste it for herself. But his eyes, fixing on her, flashed green. Green like her emerald gown, like the leafy vines she'd used to tie up the goddesses. She was taken aback by the seriousness of his stance, of his expression.

"What are your orders, my Queen?" His voice was low in his throat, near a growl, a sensual sound she'd rarely heard any human able to produce. But that wasn't what made her shiver in delight.

My Queen, he calls me—how deliciously perfect.

"Have a seat somewhere, my pet," said Gaia, narrowing her gaze on the three Olympian deities behind him, gawking at their respective wounds, hoping they'd seal up and that blood would stop pouring from their veins and onto their clothes and the mud.

Gaia waved a hand and healed them—she wouldn't have their precious life juice spoiled, as she might need more of it later, were things to go awry.

She then caressed Lukus' cheek, puckering her lips to blow him a kiss as she nudged him towards the altar. "Your next orders will come soon."

|| 12. MESSING WITH MEMORIES ||
PERSEPHONE

Persephone hadn't been escorted anywhere in Hades' chariot in many, many years. Not since their wedding night, which was eons ago. And what a night *that* had been—filled with the sorrow of leaving her mother for half the year, and the fear of living in a dark, dreary world under the earth where she'd never get to sniff at roses and roll about in fields of lavender like she used to.

She'd gotten used to the place by now, and even learned how to plant her favorite flowers and crops and cultivate herbs; but that didn't mean traveling by chariot didn't reanimate the memory of earlier, more difficult times for her.

Hades reserved this old-fashioned mode of transportation for matters of official business—meaning this excursion up to Olympus was serious stuff—and usually traveled upstairs with his teleportation skill. When her time in the Underworld was up, Persephone was normally taken to the edge of the realm by Thanatos, who then ensured she teleported up to Olympus. It was a new experience for her to take the longer, scenic route up to her mother's home.

The late winter sun bloomed over her face as the chariot rose up and out of the Underworld, swooshing out of Lake Avernus without a single drop of water smacking onto her. Up and up the vehicle flew, soaring over Italian landscapes of faded green, of crisp, untended fields of burnt yellow and orange, before disappearing behind a mask of thick clouds. The sky was blindingly blue, and Persephone had to cover her eyes, though she absorbed all the atmospheric energy as they whizzed across the horizon and on to Mount Olympus.

Through slitted eyes, she sighted the gleaming golden gates from afar, shimmering in and out of focus like a mirage. The wind whipped into her hair and sent a comforting breeze down her neck and into her thick tunic, allowing her to relax her grip on the railing. She hadn't realized she'd been holding on for dear life.

As the horses skidded to a halt on the slab of pavement before the gates, Persephone smelled it—*home*. The fresh, mountainous air, the warmth of Hestia's hearths, the baked goods with ambrosia filling. As much as she loved pomegranates, after a while she became sick of them, and craved the almond-like flavor of the god's favorite liquid; a flavor Hades rarely indulged in nor kept in abundance at the Underworld Palace.

Licking her lips at the notion of a warm cup of ambrosia-tinted hot chocolate, she watched as Hades alighted from the chariot, then offered his hand to help her down. The instant their feet touched the concrete, the horses and carriage evaporated, and Hades approached the gate.

With a few swirls of his hands, he fabricated one of his flaming letters—the same he used to send urgent messages from the Underworld—and threw it up towards the sky. It zoomed above the gates and vanished from view.

"You still have to request access, though Zeus knows we're coming?" Persephone squinted at the gates. She'd never been barred from entry before, and habitually teleported to the other side, right into the courtyard. Rare were the times she'd had to wait here, in the blistering breezes, shielding her eyes from the glowing gold gates.

"He has the palace on lock-down," said Hades, staring at the gates, awaiting their squeaky separation to grant him entrance. "Until further notice, anyone who leaves has to notify him when they return and need to come in."

Persephone flinched; in all her centuries of existence, the palace had been on lock-down three times. The Giant wars, the Titan wars, and, for a moment, the Trojan War.

If Zeus is being this cautious, then things are far worse than I anticipated.

The gates screeched as they parted, and Hades snagged Persephone's wrist to hurry her through. Almost as if he worried his brother would change his mind and keep them pondering outside while he figured out if he trusted them.

They stormed up the steps, dashed through the courtyard, swung through the entryway, and hastened into the throne-room without a word. Once past the threshold, Hades stopped and moved aside as someone hurdled right into Persephone, nearly knocking her to the marble floor.

A wad of golden blonde hair covered Persephone's eyes, but she knew that scent of hay and buttered corn and fresh-cut grass. She knew that tight squeeze, those bronze arms encircling her in a bone-crushing hug.

"Mother," Persephone whispered, returning her mother's embrace, sniffing in her outdoorsy essence with a smile.

Demeter pulled away, her steely eyes scanning Persephone's face as she kept her at arm's length. "You're too skinny," she said, pinching her lips. "And too pale. Paler than usual."

"Well," Persephone broke free from her mother's scrutiny, "you don't get to see me around this time, so now you know. My lifestyle is a bit different downstairs."

"I see," said Demeter, her stony gaze now resting on Hades, who'd remained behind them, distant.

"Never mind that," said another female voice—a raspy, recognizable tone that most found frightening, but Persephone knew as friendly. "Good to see you, my sweet."

Hecate—garbed in auburn skirts covered in vibrant blue stains—gently nudged Demeter aside and took Persephone in her arms, sniffing at her hair, rubbing her back. Persephone's tension—that she hadn't paid much attention to until now—seemed to lessen, as if enchanted by Hecate's otherworldly presence.

Once freed from her mother's and best friend's embraces, Persephone stepped farther into the throne-room. Nothing much changed here, between her departure at the end of summer and her return in early spring; and yet something smelled different, this time. An atmosphere of dread, of doubt, with a hint of violence and a lingering stench of blood—of ichor.

Much of it has been spilled up here lately, hm?

It smelled like the aftermath of the wars she'd lived through. The dried ichor on the walls, the metallic odor permeating, polluting the air. A residual sound of *clang clanging* of swords, the *swoosh* of arrows, the ripping of flesh as it was sliced into. The ghost of a battle, of a scream, of heavy torment. Olympus gave off an ominous odor of destruction, of upcoming death.

What in Tartarus had been happening up here while she was in the Underworld?

A figure moved before her, drawing her back to the present. As he approached, she curtsied, on instinct. *His* aroma joined the others in the room, a scent of wet dirt after a rainfall, of a woodsy cologne—Zeus, king of the gods, god of thunder, and…her father.

She kept her head down, avoiding his gaze, though she felt it burning over her hair, warming her scalp. "Majesty," she said through clenched teeth, preferring not to add anything else, lest she rouse his temper.

They'd never been close, and neither had attempted to sever the issues between them. Persephone would never forgive him for hauling her off to the Underworld—though she now thrived there. And Zeus would never be able to erase the image of his own brother demanding to *have* her to himself, and how easily he'd consented to it. Father and daughter hadn't hashed out their differences, nor had they gone through a proper argument to let out their woes to one another. Persephone had every right to, she knew that. If she were to raise her voice and declare her anger to Zeus, he'd listen; he'd have to. Her own father had sold her off to his brother—and every day he got to live remembering that fact, and witnessing his sister's depression when fall rolled along.

Yet she remained silent, opting instead to avoid confrontation.

There's no point confronting him over something he can't change.

"Very well, then," said Zeus, sidling past Persephone as she rose from her curtsy, still keeping her gaze fixed elsewhere. "Brother, I'll accompany you back to the gates, yes?"

Persephone turned around in time to see her father take her husband out of the throne-room, leaving her alone with her mother and Hecate.

The latter walked over and took Persephone's hands. "Good to have you here," she said, with a small smile. "But we have much to do and likely little time to do it."

A figment of nervousness flitted through Persephone at the idea of enacting their rituals *here,* at the palace. Most days they'd travel off to some deep, dark spot in some woods, far from humans and out of reach from other gods. Here they were exposed, their secrets on the verge of spilling out.

They hadn't initiated their mysteries in several years, meaning Persephone wasn't sure she remembered her role in them, nor what was expected of her. She didn't remember much at all—their rites were so secretive even *they* didn't recall all they'd conjured and sacrificed once they came out of their trances. Demeter and Hecate always led these events, starting with a potent tea laced with strong toxins that put them in an ethereal state of mind, as if drugged. Then, whatever happened next was often lost to the depths of their minds, distant memories they couldn't keep at bay.

"What *is* it that we have to do, exactly?" Persephone pulled out of Hecate's grasp and backed up until her shins met the dais. "What do our mysteries have to do with what's going on, whatever that is?"

Hecate didn't approach her, but clasped her hands in prayer and pressed them to her chest, closing her eyes. "The power, the trance that our rites put us in might give us more insight."

Demeter meandered up to her, mimicking her posture; this was how they began their sessions, with a prayer to the earth, a prayer to the sky, a prayer to the mysteries themselves. "Which might help us figure out who's behind everything."

Persephone, without meaning to, also joined her hands in prayer, but didn't close her eyes. "But *how?*"

"Our ritualistic power is tethered to the soil, hm?" Hecate's voice was remote, as if she'd disconnected from the throne-room already, seeping herself into their opening rituals. "Well, the soil can capture essences, presences, sensations, smells; things we might have missed or been unable to see in our everyday lives. If we speak to the soil, if we conjure those elements, we should be able to analyze them, and piece together a few suspects. Hopefully."

The word *suspects* prompted a memory to pull Persephone's hands apart as she fell onto her behind, hard on the platform. "Mnemosyne is being suspicious, so before we even proceed with our rites, we should keep that in mind."

Demeter frowned. "Mnemosyne?"

Hecate showed no surprise on her face, and instead gave a brief nod. "I'm not shocked to hear this, but do tell me why *you* think this, Persephone?"

Persephone gulped, reliving the sensations her daughter had given her—despair, panic, a sense of losing oneself, of not having any notion where one was, what one was doing, thinking. A constant state of terror; worse than what Melinoë usually lived through.

"Melinoë," she said, her voice trembling with a mix of fright and fury. "She's more drained and sluggish than normal, and Mnemosyne has supposedly been *consulting* with her in your absence. I put two and two together; Mnemosyne is evidently doing something to Melinoë, and I won't stand for it, whether or not it's linked to this situation."

"Zeus *did* notify us of this," said Demeter, setting a hand on Hecate's shoulder. "I recall it now. That poor girl."

"Of course she's tampering with Melinoë," said Hecate, followed by a snort that was most unlike her. She became more unleashed when in Olympus, it seemed. Closer to humanity, away from the darkness of her crypt, her savage side came unhinged, waking the vengeful, frenzy-like piece of her. "She's weak and defenseless, even when I'm around. I can't be monitoring her at all times, unfortunately. Mnemosyne's specialty is trifling with memories, so surely she's had a ball messing with Melinoë's—a goddess of nightmares? Oh, I imagine she had a field day with that."

Demeter gasped. "What an ominous thing to do, though…for no blatant reason. I'm little acquainted with Mnemosyne, but is this something unordinary for her? Going around fiddling with other gods' brains for simple enjoyment?"

Hecate answered, "no," just as Persephone answered, "yes." The two looked at one another, and Persephone shrugged; Hecate would be best to answer this question, she knew. She had more knowledge of Mnemosyne than any of them did.

"I think what Persephone means is yes, it's unordinary in the sense that she doesn't usually mess with *us*. But she does enjoy toying with memories of lost spirits, sometimes of visitors to the palace, if they wander too close to her hut." Hecate sucked in her lips, then opened her mouth once or twice before finding the right words to continue her train of thought. "But she's grown bolder, of late. I'm well aware she's gotten into *my* memories, too. My recollections have been all over the place lately, remember?"

"Are you not able to resist her?" Concern grew on Demeter's face as her light blond brows arched, then scrunched. "Are you not more powerful than her?"

"In fact, I'm two generations below her," said Hecate, the flimsiest of proud smirks sketching over her lips for the space of an instant. "We're of similar strength, if one measures out our levels of power and knowledge of spells. But if she catches me at the right time, when my attention is diverted, or I'm weakened…she could absolutely trifle with my mind. No doubt about it. I can't see anyone else responsible for my memory issues but her."

"Oh dear," Demeter clapped a hand over her mouth, "the potions…your cabinet…?"

Hecate's smirk wiped off her face immediately. "Do I think Mnemosyne has been stealing ingredients from me? Most definitely." She turned and raised her hand near Demeter's lips before she could speak. "And why didn't I mention this sooner? Because I needed more proof, and Persephone has delivered it. Once we're done with our rites, we'll inform Zeus of this at once. And I'll take the blame for not mentioning it sooner."

Persephone got up and sauntered over to them, shaking her head. "But I don't understand why Mnemosyne would do that. What motive would she have to mess with you, with my daughter? To steal potions and create poisons and harm the gods? Why would she participate in this?" All manners of questions clouded her mind, clogged up in her thoughts; and Hecate was the perfect person to ask them to. "Is she not a neutral titaness, who keeps to her hut and her charges and her strange roles?"

"Let us not forget frolicking with ghosts," added Hecate, with a scoff. "But yes, in regular times she doesn't bother meddling with the gods and their squabbles, nor does she care much about humans. As far as I'm aware."

"Her roles," Demeter cleared her throat, "are you aware of those, too?" She glanced at Persephone, eyebrows raised, hands on her hips. "What exactly is Mnemosyne's purpose? What is it she does down…there?" A slight wrinkle of her nostrils showed she disliked saying the word—*the Underworld*—but she fixed her grimace as quickly as she'd made it.

Persephone shrugged; rack her brain as she might, she couldn't recall what Mnemosyne's tasks were, if she had any. "I was under the impression she was more or less banished down there because of her tendencies, no?"

Hecate nodded. "But I don't know that she was ever *given* any roles to fulfill, any particular job to attend to while in the Underworld. She has her hut, she often wanders near *Lethe* and *Styx* and observes others in the realm, but…as far as roles go, I'm not sure she has any."

"Or perhaps she's had one this whole time. A particular agenda that she's been pushing, under the guise of being banished, pretending to spend her time doing…what was it you said? *Frolicking* with ghosts?" Demeter sneered and shook her head. "Anyway, is it possible she's been down there plotting for centuries, and no one knew because in truth no one really knew what she was supposed to be doing, if anything?"

The facts hit Persephone hard in the chest, sending her back to the dais to sit down. Hecate's eyes flashed violet—as they did when she was conflicted with multiple emotions—and Demeter fanned her face as her cheeks turned a vivid shade of tomato red.

Had they figured out the culprit behind the attacks without having enacted their rituals?

No, it can't be that easy. Mnemosyne is involved, but is she the brains behind the operation?

Persephone released a sigh, a heavyweight breath she'd been keeping in, hoping she'd been hallucinating, imagining things. That she'd seen issues where there were none, and her confinement in the Underworld had rendered her mad. But it appeared she hadn't been alone in sensing something amiss, and that feeling had grown in the seconds since she'd arrived in Olympus.

"You were right—very much to do and very little time."

|| 13. A MEETING OF BROTHERS ||
ZEUS

To see Persephone reuniting with her mother—before due time, but out of necessity—warmed Zeus' heart for an instant. But it was an instant of weakness he couldn't allow, not with the state of things at the palace.

As he exited the throne-room, under the guise of taking Hades to the gates, he turned and waved a protective hand over the threshold. A slight film of prismatic light shimmied over the area, stretching over the door-frame.

"Protection?" Hades watched his brother's work, head cocked.

"A small cloaking charm," said Zeus, leaning close to ensure his spell had worked—and sure enough, he couldn't hear anything escaping the throne-room. Not a word or a sound, not even a breath. "So they may enact their rituals in peace, with none of my nosy children getting in the way."

Hades gave a nod of agreement, and made for the corridor leading to the front door, but Zeus stopped him, hauling him down the other way, instead. Past bedrooms and courtyards and secret spaces until they reached one of the smaller ballrooms reserved for private events.

"I summoned Poseidon while you were on your way here," he

said, ushering Hades into the space—smelling of dusty disuse, with a flicker of light coming from behind the curtained windows. Zeus gestured at them to slide aside and let in some illumination, but regretted it as it showcased the layers of dust on windowsills and gathering in corners. "Confer with him and I, would you? We need to discuss this situation, as brothers…but also as kings."

Hades' low grunt indicated acknowledgment, and he wandered to the far end of the room, to the window overlooking the palace grounds. Verdant fields with mountains in the backdrop, glowing clouds encircling the property, a glistening sun basking them in heavenly light—all things Hades didn't often get to indulge in, stuck in his dark realm.

He hadn't chosen his lot, and yet, he'd accommodated. Hades had made a home out of his grungy dwelling, and had a host of staff-members and other deities who obeyed his every command. He inspired them, protected them, and drove them to do their tasks in timely manners and without protest.

This situation—gods getting out of hand, manipulated by an unknown culprit—went against Hades' flow, for sure. Disruption in his realm was rare, with all who were there to ensure its function. Zeus had no doubt the tension slowly seeping into the room wasn't only his own.

Adding to that tension was a fishy scent accompanied by strong human cologne—Poseidon had arrived, and his presence was felt even across the palace. Hades must have sensed it, too, for he looked away from the view and fixed his gaze on the open door, where Poseidon would show at any moment, likely swaying back and forth, inebriated to the point of slurring his words and making no sense.

Neither Zeus nor Hades had accepted Poseidon's deep dive into alcoholism, and they'd tried on many occasions to help him quit the behavior, and also his tendency to mingle with humans and play tricks on them. It was a Hermes-level attitude, and Zeus wasn't having it. But Poseidon always reminded him it wasn't his place to interfere, and that in any case, he stuck to port-towns and seasides where Zeus had no authority.

To Zeus' surprise—and probably to Hades', as he stiffened beside him—Poseidon showed up *sober*. No stench of liquor about him or his breath, no dizzying oscillation of his massive body as he walked. He'd even put on their godly attire of an over the shoulder tunic, held in place by a brooch showing one of his sigils—a trident over a fish, splashing out of water.

And—best of all—he didn't smell like he'd been frolicking with humans. As he entered the room and stormed over to his brothers, Poseidon was, all things considered, the god and king of the seas described in regular mythology; not the caricature he'd become in recent years due to stress and a lack of affection from his wife.

He gave a quick bow to his kingly siblings, then stood straight, one hand pumping to his chest. He deflated at the raised eyebrows and shocked faces of Zeus and Hades. "What? Did you not summon me?" His voice was gruff, lacking liquid, too dry for someone who dwelled ninety-nine percent of his life in a castle in the ocean.

Poseidon was the taller of the lot—his face not as smooth as Hades', but not as weathered as Zeus', still showing signs of his handsome youth, of the days when he'd seduce women into doing just about anything for him. Following in Zeus' footsteps—he had almost as many, if not more, illegitimate offspring as the king of the skies—and proud of it, he always stood rigid and puffed out his chiseled chest, though in recent years he'd slouched, overcome with drink, too tired and intoxicated to care about his posture.

"You're…*you*," said Hades, putting Zeus' thoughts into words.

"Of course I'm me, you moron," said Poseidon, his large nostrils wrinkling. He was akin to a giant, Zeus sometimes thought, with his regal figure and his bigger than normal face. *He* resembled most of the statues mortals had created of him, unlike many other gods Zeus oversaw. Poseidon was a sea god with a temper and unafraid to wield his power when he thought it necessary.

Zeus cleared his throat—Poseidon was staring Hades down as if considering whether or not he was offended by his comment. Zeus would rather he not start an argument now, amidst chaos at the palace.

"What he means, I think," he exchanged a quick side-glance with Hades, "is that you're sober, and cleaned up, and not smelling like a mortal you enticed into keeping you company."

Poseidon snorted and swung by them, headed for the dais where a single throne rested, cobwebs dangling from its armrests. "You told me to be on my guard. You told me this…this culprit, this insane, overpowered deity was targeting us all without rhyme or reason, and Amphitrite…well, she knocked some sense into me, too. So I…stopped drinking." He grunted. "For now, at least. Until we figure out what in Tartarus is going on."

"Good." Zeus snapped to summon three chairs below the dais— he didn't want them fighting over who got to sit on the dusty throne, though by rights it should have been him, since this was his home. "Having you sober is an advantage, because our situation has grown worse overnight. Sit, both of you."

Hades sat at once, moving his heavy black cloak about as he got comfortable. Poseidon snickered at the chair for a moment, then slowly lowered onto it, eyes narrowed on Zeus who parked himself in the middle.

"What happened?" Poseidon conjured a cup out of thin air; and when Zeus frowned, he leaned the cup close to show him it was only water.

"Aside from all the intelligence I've been sending you on what's going on up here? Disappearances." Zeus produced two more cups— one that he handed to Hades—filled with ambrosia water. "Several Olympians, titanesses, and the half-mortal Lukus."

Poseidon's grip on his own cup—bejeweled and sturdy— tightened, his fingers turning red, his knuckles white. "Who? When? Why?"

Hades set a hand on Zeus' arm, as if to signal he was able to help with relaying this information. Zeus took no offense—he was glad for a brother who'd ease his burden.

"Hera, Themis, Phoebe, and Dionysus, all of which may have been poisoned before being kidnapped." Hades took a swig of his drink, and swallowed. "Athena and Aphrodite, seemingly taken by force." He winced, watching Poseidon's cheeks swell and switch from a bronzy shade to a deep violet. "Lukus, as Zeus said, likely infected as well. And Mother, whose disappearance isn't quite…" He peered at Zeus, grimacing.

Hades still hadn't come to terms with the fact that Rhea might have been involved in all this. Would Poseidon be as loath to see the truth?

"Mother's scent and blood were found near where Hera's and Lukus' were, but…no trace of poison. More like the remains of a fight, a power struggle between her and…well, at this point, that's unclear. But she's not in the palace and she didn't say goodbye." Zeus rubbed his forehead, and regretted not slipping a bit of wine into his goblet.

Poseidon's cup dropped, clanging against the marble floor, water splashing over his sandaled feet. "And you waited this long to tell me?" He rose, and the ground shook beneath him, rattling the glass chandelier overhead, dislodging bits of dust particles to swirl around them like a tornado. The throne atop the dais shook side to side, and the curtain-rod looked ready to hop off and shatter onto the floor.

Zeus got up and grabbed Poseidon's shoulders, squeezing hard. "Stop. Control your temper. We can't have Olympus going to ruins before we figure out who's been sneaking about its halls to harm us."

Poseidon gritted his teeth and his arms turned rigid at his sides. "I…can't…stop." The shaking grew worse—the platform behind them began to move, and a few crystals from the chandelier smashed around them, like deadly arrows falling from the sky.

Zeus saw cracks forming in the ceiling, and snapped at Hades, who'd been gaping up in awe as well. "Help me."

Hades came to at once, and hurried behind Poseidon, embracing him from the back. Zeus tightened his grip on Poseidon's upper arms, cutting off circulation. Lightning zoomed up and down his arms, and he sensed his hair ends striking with electricity. A gloomy gray smoke swished around Hades, and his eyes shifted to a soulless, shiny black that signified a rising anger.

If Poseidon means to get riled up, we'll match his level to make him stop.

It was two against one, and Zeus knew he and Hades would prevail.

Poseidon fought them—a mental battle of wits and power, causing his earthquake to grow in intensity, to continue its progress in destroying the palace. But Zeus' thunder coursed in his veins and shot through his fingertips, shocking Poseidon once, twice, three times before Poseidon crumbled to his knees. A wash of black smoke then twirled around him and smacked him right in the chest, knocking him onto his back on the marble floor.

Hades snapped out of his dark trance, and Zeus took deep breaths to calm his erratic heartbeat, and to steady the electricity pulsing through him. He and Hades always had better control over their abilities and their tempers—Poseidon never learned to restrain himself, and had made it clear he never would.

Whatever had made him so angry, Zeus should have known that summoning him to the palace and telling him the news would be a risk to everyone. And yet he'd had no choice. It would take too long to travel to Poseidon's lair in the sea, or to figure a meeting point elsewhere for all three brothers to greet one another. He'd had no alternative, but wished his sibling would learn to control his emotions better.

Especially in times like these, when he's likely to get furious much more often before we see the end of this culprit.

"Mother," said Poseidon, still lying on the ground, his chest caving in and out with his heavy breaths. "You think her to be involved?"

Zeus fell onto his chair with a sigh. "I don't know what to think, that's why I summoned you. Hades thinks it impossible, but I can't ignore the facts. Rhea is gone, and something about her vanishing is off-putting and wrong."

Poseidon sat up and stretched. "Perhaps she's involved but not of her own volition? There's poison in this situation; a poison that seems to stir gods up, get them to become unhinged and act on crazy urges. These bitings you told me about…that's some serious, deep-level magic."

Hades retrieved the goblet that he hadn't let fall to the floor, unlike Zeus and Poseidon. "I can't see Mother wanting to harm any of us, so if she is indeed up to something…I agree, it wouldn't be of her own accord."

Zeus fingered his beard and gawked up at the cracked ceiling, wondering if he should leave it that way, or fetch Hephaestus to fix it at once. There'd likely be more cracks coming, if Poseidon's temper were to fire up again.

"Would you consult with your staff, your allies in the sea, for clues?" Zeus refilled Poseidon's discarded cup and made it float over until it nestled into the ocean god's grip. "Search the seas, ask your constituents and animal friends, the nymphs and mermaids in your realm. I know they pick up on things we cannot, and they might have overheard something that might help. We're certain whoever this culprit is, they have range. They have…access."

Poseidon nodded once, drained his cup, and got up. "I'd already started doing that, and I'll continue. But don't keep me out of the loop on such things anymore. If there are any more disappearances, I want you to notify me at once. I can't help, I can't protect our family if you leave out the essential details."

He was right, Zeus knew; but he'd had no idea how to put the news into words. *"Dear Brother, our family members are vanishing like smoke, and being poisoned. And also being taken to who-knows-where for who-knows-what reason, but don't worry, I'm working on it."*

It was the sort of news one said in person, but there'd been no time to convene with Poseidon until now. "Forgive me, brother," said Zeus, standing and reaching out a hand to shake Poseidon's. "The rising danger of this situation is becoming harder and harder to predict, and I'm afraid I'm…drowning."

The corners of Poseidon's lips twitched as their hands joined, squeezed, shook, then released. "Well, good thing I'm a sea god and can help you swim." He bowed, and exited the room at once, headed back to his realm to proceed with Zeus' requests.

Zeus cringed; his pride had taken quite the hit, admitting to Poseidon—and also to Hades, indirectly—that he was struggling to keep the situation under control. He'd barely blinked and several more gods had been poisoned, and they, along with others, were taken from their homes for this culprit's sick purposes. And he, the god of thunder, king of the skies, overseer of all living things—he hadn't been able to do a thing to stop it from happening.

"I see you're troubled," said Hades, a hint of smoke remaining around his figure, as if he, too, had difficulty containing himself for once. "Perhaps I should go to my own realm and proceed with similar interrogations?"

"Yes." Zeus had fallen onto his chair again, massaging his temples as he envisioned all the ways he'd grown weak and weary from his worsening predicament. A king unable to protect his family, his people—if there was to be a civil war, a rebellion, he doubted he'd be backed by many deities, who'd see him as flimsy and incapable. "Do that. Watch Mnemosyne in particular, and if you could speak with the judges and tell them to defer their usual duties if possible, patrol the area, be on alert for anything off." He scrubbed his face and groaned. "This contagion hasn't spared you and yours, so please, be cautious."

"I will. In fact, I've already begun ensuring my people are on alert," said Hades, depositing the now empty goblet on the floor. "Tartarus came to me earlier, informing me he's on edge and his mind is being trifled with, like Melinoë's."

"Tartarus—the primordial god who out-dates us all and whose power goes beyond anyone's knowledge?" Zeus' jaw was drawn to the floor, but he did his best to stop it from collapsing. "Someone…this culprit is messing with *him?* How in the…"

Hades' shoulders lifted, and his fingertips twitched near his pockets. "Would that I could tell you, but Tartarus himself is uncertain who'd have the gall and the power to do so. He's resisted thus far, but promised to keep Nyx apprised, as well. She's been traveling, but he hopes she'll come down to Tartarus for extra protection against whatever this is."

"Goddesses, titanesses, now primordials—who has this kind of ability? There cannot be one culprit, there's no way. It's a team, and Mnemosyne is a part of it, and…I'm sorry, Brother," Zeus pinched his lips at Hades' scowl, "but Mother is involved, too, she has to be. The sooner we find her, and hopefully corner Mnemosyne, the better."

"I'll speak with Thanatos and the Furies, too. Maybe the Erinyes." Hades bowed. "We won't let whoever or whatever this is instigate another war, Zeus. We will not." With that he swiveled, his cloak swooshing in his movement, his gentle footsteps growing quieter as he departed the room.

Though his brothers' presences often riled him up, they'd been a comfort today. Even Poseidon's tantrum had been familiar and somewhat predictable.

Predictable—that's the issue, here. I can't predict anything.

The Fates themselves hadn't been able to decipher this riddle, this monster spreading insanity amongst the gods. And if *they* couldn't figure this out…who could?

Zeus' hopes rested with Demeter, Hecate, and Persephone. Their mysteries were a last resort—one he hadn't wished to employ—and he prayed they'd prevail in getting some answers. Any answers, at this point, would be welcome.

He flopped over to the dust-ridden throne and slumped into its cushioned surface with a sneeze. He missed his wife—her capricious nature, though annoying, had its charm. He was worried for his favorite daughter, wishing he'd listened to her more often. And how was the luxurious Aphrodite coping with being kidnapped?

He was also fearful for Lukus, who hadn't yet come into any godly powers and who'd have no means to defend himself were this culprit to seek to truly harm him. He was nothing but an overpowered mortal, lost in the midst of Zeus' family drama. *If* this culprit was family—Zeus doubted someone of his own blood would stoop to such levels of cruelty.

Or perhaps I don't know my family at all.

|| 14. THE RITUAL ||
PERSEPHONE

After Zeus' departure, and despite his kind gesture of cloaking the room—a weak attempt, according to Hecate—the ladies of mystery started their rites...but something wasn't *right*.

"There isn't enough vegetation in here," said Hecate, with a quick glimpse of the balcony behind the thrones, sniffing in the scent of the rose bushes. "Those aren't enough of a source for the power we need to conjure. We need more plants, more variety."

"And it's too *open*," said Demeter, gesturing at the balcony, at the pillars behind the thrones—and hinting at the ease of being able to eavesdrop. "That breeze whooshing in...it's tainted. We need somewhere purer, or at least better contained."

"But we do need to be outside, don't we? For our spells to function properly?" Persephone scrunched her nose. "So, what...a courtyard?"

"A courtyard." Demeter peered at the throne-room's threshold. "*The* courtyard, the main one. It's dead-smack in the middle of the palace, and frequented by literally everyone, but...it's the airiest space that's still enclosed, and the most soil-rich spot aside from Hestia's basement garden. I'd have used that, but like you mentioned, daughter, we need to be outdoors."

So with little argument, they broke Zeus' cloaking charm and headed for the courtyard. On their way, they ensured that servants and other inhabitants were aware to steer clear of the area. Once there, Hecate insisted on protecting themselves, anyway. *She* did the cloaking herself, to be certain not a single trace of their powers could be detected by any passing courtiers.

She sprayed her spell all over the floor-to-ceiling windows, inside and outside. Then sprinkled detection charms over doors, with alarms to notify them if anyone hovered nearby for too long. She covered up any cracks in the walls that might permit one to press an ear against it to eavesdrop. And finally, she loaded the air with anti-vision enchantments to make the courtyard look empty and uninteresting, to prevent curious onlookers.

As she went about whispering archaic Greek-based incantations to further preserve their mysterious rites, Demeter got to work, too. She conjured an overhead ceiling of vines and leaves, to protect them should their magic stir up a storm in the skies. That had happened before, as the energy they summoned sometimes trifled with the atmosphere and the weather.

Persephone busied about materializing pomegranates—her specialty—along with golden bowls, glass vials, and all the herbs and spices they'd need to pour into a cauldron to start whisking up the mysteries. She'd thought of taking some from Hestia's garden, but didn't want to disturb Hestia in her tasks; and in any case, Persephone had no trouble conjuring her own healthy herbs.

Once done with her cloaking, Hecate summoned a cauldron—a large, weathered copper thing they'd used so much over the years it looked ready to shatter. But it was sturdier than it appeared, laden with runes and ancient magic that wouldn't allow it to burst, no matter *what* they put in it. And within their mysteries, they often had to use dangerous, potent poisons to obtain the accurate results they sought.

Once all items were set up on tables and the cauldron placed in the exact center of the courtyard, the goddesses clasped their hands in prayer and recited the opening notes of their ritual. A long-lost mix of ancient Greek and another language so dead and buried that not even the primordials remembered it, nor knew that these three deities had learned it and used it regularly. A dazzling tune of a tongue that could hypnotize anyone else listening to it—another reason no one was allowed to eavesdrop. Only initiates of the Eleusinian mysteries were able to use it, listen to it, and understand it without harm.

They held hands, exchanged cryptic glances of well-wishes, muttered a few more prayers under their breaths—then they began the bulk of the work, the most mysterious part of all rituals. Gathering and tossing of elements into the cauldron, in an order that made sense to them only. With muted mutterings of more incantations, and lightly chanted melodies that woke the benefits and properties of each herb they used.

They dropped in various items, one by one, watching the different effect every spice, every seed, every liquid caused within the cauldron. Some steamed up, coating their faces with moisture as they looked within. Some *blew* up—prompting fits of coughs and even a few giggles of relief once the ringing ceased in their ears. Several ingredients were known to *not* mix well...so they mixed them. They sought adverse effects, a deep, dark aura that might draw the negative energy the culprit had been leaving in her wake.

Quickly enough, Persephone caught on to what sort of spell they'd be working with today. She recalled one of the rites she'd memorized, and that was coming back to her as she observed Hecate and Demeter going about it, deciphering one another's thoughts, understanding gestures. Without speaking, without needing to explain themselves, they'd both had the same idea, and were dipping ingredients into the stew of liquids and bubbles below.

Make evil to draw evil to you.

It was a ritual to detect evil by creating evil. And so, they were slowly putting the pieces together to recreate Hecate's poison, the one that had been the base of what had been used to intoxicate the gods. She alone had the full recipe, but it didn't take long for Demeter to catch on, and for Persephone to start adding in liquids and seasonings she remembered tasting while she was poisoned.

"To make this stronger," Hecate magicked a dagger out of thin air, "we'll need to draw blood and drizzle a bit of it into the concoction. All three of us, for a heftier brew, and better chances of results."

Hecate sliced the tip of her thumb, and squeezed the skin to produce three drops of blue ichor that *plopped* into the mixture. Flames rose up, nearly charring Persephone's face, prompting her to skid backwards, away from the cauldron.

Demeter winced, but hurried to draw her own blood from her pinky finger. Its contact with the liquid created more flames, these ones of a yellower, brighter shade.

The elder goddesses stared at Persephone, waiting for her turn. Persephone hesitated, her heartbeat racing as the flames died down. Was this the appropriate solution? To recreate this noxious tincture and make it readily accessible to any Olympian resident? Sure, the area was secure, no one would enter now. But what if the culprit was lurking and had a means to sneak in and take a few droplets to further its goal of intoxicating all of Olympus? What if it was in the courtyard that very moment, having escaped all Hecate's spell-work and made itself invisible to spy on the ultra-secretive mysteries in action?

"No one is here," said Hecate, either reading Persephone's thoughts, or sensing the hesitation in her stiffened stance. "If the culprit is near, it can't enter, not with all the charms I set up, not without triggering the alarm."

"It's just blood, sweetheart," said Demeter, with a frail smile that showed she barely believed what she was saying. "A few drops, toss them in, then we can analyze the stuff, get answers, and we'll make it disappear. No one will have access to this brew, correct?" She glanced at Hecate and raised her eyebrows in question.

Hecate nodded. "No one will have access to this brew. Not on my watch."

Still debating with herself, Persephone took the dagger from Hecate and swept its tip over her middle finger. She hovered over the cauldron, letting her life-juice drop in, and shimmied out of the way in time for another burst of flames to shoot out; these tinted green and red.

A thick smoke swirled out of the cauldron now, and with a few waves of her hand, Hecate shifted its shape into a perfect circle.

"Show me," she said, pressing her hand towards the circle, touching it, igniting it. She motioned for Demeter and Persephone to do the same, and they did. "Tell it what to do, ladies. Tell this smoke to show us what we seek to see."

"Show me," said Demeter, then repeating the words again in their ancient ritualistic language.

"Show us," said Persephone, squinting at the screen-like circle of smoke, demanding that it shift again, that it begin displaying scenes on it, like a TV showing one of her favorite programs that she liked to watch in the Underworld. And she'd watch this with as much fervor, as much intensity—glaring at it for any clue of this monster's identity. Any clue for how to approach it and terminate it.

"Show us the start." Hecate shook her hand over the circle, causing it to shake with her, every fiber adjusting, searching for the right satellite to gather its energy from. "Show us the events." She drew around the exterior of the circle with her index, and in her finger's wake a golden glow took light, enhancing the smoke's heavy gray hue. The smoke within shimmied and shivered, with small, dark forms appearing inside—figures, people. Individuals that would become less blurry soon enough and reveal themselves as suspects, as gods. As witnesses, as victims. "Show us the mystery, the truth behind what is happening to Olympus."

They held their breaths as the smoke continued to alter, the silhouettes enclosed within the golden circle becoming clearer, easier to recognize, human-like.

Persephone narrowed her gaze on the sight, desperate to perceive something, someone—anything that'd give her an inkling of an idea of who was responsible for hurting her family.

But she saw nothing, and instead focused on her mother and the witch-goddess, praying they'd see whatever it was she didn't. Praying they'd discover the answers she hadn't.

Please, save us all.

|| 15. VISIONS OF VINES ||
ZEUS

A migraine of thunderous proportions spread from front to back, from side to side, sliding over his forehead like a snake squeezing into a tunnel it didn't fit in, its fangs snapping at the walls to chew them away to get through. Zeus' fingertips rubbing at his temples did nothing to soothe him, and as he returned to the throne-room—to see that the ladies had vacated it, opting for somewhere more appropriate for their rituals—the pain only grew worse.

He should have gone to his chambers, where he could order a cupbearer to guard his room while he attempted an hour or two of sleep. Closing his eyes would be the best solution to his raging headache, he knew. But he also knew that the instant he tried to hide in slumber, his dreams would turn to nightmares. And in any case, he needed to stay awake, should anyone come to him with news to analyze, rumors to confirm, or culprits to pursue.

Minutes after he'd settled onto his stone throne, a darkly cloaked individual snuck into the throne-room; one that might have caused alarm to anyone else, as their hunched posture and hurried steps set off triggers in Zeus' mind, which prompted him to sit up straight.

Only one hooded god had free range of Olympus no matter if Zeus blocked the gates or not—for he *had* to have access for his duties, and Zeus' powers rarely had a full effect on him.

"Thanatos," said Zeus, as the individual approached, bowed, then threw his hood back. He smelled of the outdoors—of a freshly wet forest after a rainfall, of mud thick with moisture.

"Majesty." Thanatos' eyes were black and bitter as ever, yet Zeus knew there was no true bitterness to him. He'd seen the nastiest things, the most gruesome deaths, had reaped souls from catastrophic events and terrifying places, some darker and more dreadful than the Underworld or Tartarus itself. So his eyes showed nothing but the reflection of the horror he'd envisioned. He, himself, was far from horrible, and Zeus often enjoyed his short-lived but intriguing visits. He loved to deliver rumors, and Zeus loved to hear them.

Today wouldn't be a pleasant visit, though, and Zeus had grasped that fact the instant he'd sensed Thanatos' entry. The god of death was nervous, his hands shaking as he stuffed them into the pockets of his cloak. Some might say he looked like Hades; a smaller, thinner version of him, with a shorter mane and more scruff along the chin. But it was when they spoke that one spotted the difference—Hades had a regal, reserved sort of tone, where Thanatos was icy, slippery, slightly punctuated with depression.

"I'm sorry to barge in," said Thanatos, as Zeus indicated a seat off to the side, which Thanatos wormed on over to sit on. He dropped onto the spot with a light sigh, setting his palms over his knees. "But Hades told me of your concerns, and I had to come at once to…add to them." He winced; lines crawled over his youthful appearing face, and his eyes slitted as he focused on the floor.

Another jolt of pain sliced across Zeus' forehead. "Naturally. Do tell me what you have to say. Any and all rumors are welcome at this point."

Thanatos breathed in and scratched the back of his neck. "The issue is, this isn't a rumor. It's a fact. A sighting. A *personal* sighting. Observations I have made myself and kept to myself and shouldn't have, and I—"

"—get to it, Thanatos." Zeus had never lost his patience with Thanatos—whose stories, though brief, tended to go on with details that were unnecessary and colorful words to describe atrocious crime scenes. In other times, Zeus enjoyed such rich tales; but he was pressed for time, what with his family members disappearing.

"Mnemosyne." Thanatos shivered, which caused a shiver to slither up Zeus' spine at the sight. "I've seen her creeping in and out of her hut more often than normal. Not that I observe her or anything, but she's so graceful, and I like to watch her between jobs." He tilted his head, and for the first time that Zeus could recall, his eyes *brightened,* twinkling as he fixed his gaze on something in the distance. As if picturing Mnemosyne there, on the throne-room balcony, her brown and orange tresses swooshing in the wind, the hem of her tunic flapping about her well-formed calves, lifting up and up her thighs—

Zeus snapped himself out of the trance. Thoughts of Mnemosyne were *never* good, and always got out of hand. One time—*one time* with her had been enough to set him off course for years.

Never again.

Thanatos cleared his throat. "She's coming and going more than most days, and there's a suspicious air about her. She goes into the palace, via Hecate's secret but not-so-secret-anymore entrance, peering left and right as she does…as if aware she's being surveilled."

Zeus groaned. "Hades and Persephone informed me of this. But you're saying you've seen her too? Why, *why* would a titaness of her level be so sneaky?" He pinched the bridge of his nose with both index fingers, sensing his sinuses compress and pulsate. "She's free to roam anywhere she pleases in the Underworld. And also—can she not go through the front door, like regular visitors to the palace?"

Thanatos crossed one leg over the other, getting visibly more comfortable in his seat. Yet his face remained contorted in discomfort, his voice laced with hesitation. Whatever he'd seen, heard, felt—it had affected him in ways Zeus hadn't expected for a neutral, distanced reaper such as Thanatos.

"She usually *would* go through the front, yes. Though it's rare that she has any business at the palace. Hades has no use for her, and she's not close with Persephone." He extracted something from his pocket—a flashy, silver flask with a reaper's scythe carved on its sleek surface. "But as of late, I've noticed some interesting markings on the exterior facade, barring entrance to those of ill-intent, I believe. Hard to read these engravings, as they're in an ancient language I'm not proficient with, but I got the jist of the words." He unscrewed the cap, slung the liquid into his mouth, and swallowed, eyes closed as whatever it was traveled down his throat, warming or soothing him.

"Ancient engravings?" Zeus fiddled with his beard. "Hecate, I presume?"

"I can see no one else capable of such a blockade that would make Mnemosyne have to employ other means to get whatever it is she wants." Thanatos lifted the flask and tipped it towards Zeus, who refused; liquor with such a headache was a bad idea.

"But *what* does Mnemosyne want in that palace? And why her?" Zeus shook his head. "I believe you, and Persephone, but this doesn't make sense. She's a neutral titaness, no? I know she was upset about being sent to the Underworld, but that was eons ago."

"Sire." Thanatos stood and set a hand to his chest as he approached the dais, angling forward, as if to tell a secret. "If she's a part of all this craziness, I doubt she's at it alone. I think she has company in that hut of hers."

Zeus snorted; he was well aware of Mnemosyne's activities, as Persephone had given Olympus all that gossip for centuries, whenever she returned from her stay in the Underworld. Mnemosyne's *company* was that of the ghosts awaiting trial—she'd steal them away from their camp and seduce them and have her way with them. She had no one else in the Underworld to play her mind tricks on—all avoided her because they knew what she wanted—so she'd resorted to flirting with spirits and drawing them away from the decision of their final resting place.

So many wandering souls, according to Hades. He can't contain them all, not if she keeps this up.

"We all know what kind of company she keeps, Thanatos. Thank Olympus I asked her to leave when I did. Who knows what she'd have done up here once she'd used and slept with the entire staff? Now she's gone to ghosts—that's her prerogative, not mine."

"No, majesty, this is something else." Thanatos gulped. "We know of her ways, of course, but…there are flashes of light in that hut, like spell-casting flashes. Colored smoke coming from the chimney—there's *never* smoke coming from that chimney, she doesn't use it. She doesn't have an actual hearth, it's only decoration. No, this is charm brewing…I smell ominous things whenever I pass by there. More ominous than usual; not the marshy, muddy scent that place usually gives off. And I," he cringed, "I could have sworn I heard voices occasionally, too. And not the spectral sounds of the spirits of the men and women she likes to entertain."

Zeus gripped the armrests and sensed his teeth grinding in his mouth, out of his control. Electricity shot up his spine, and his hairs stood on edge, the strands curling, coiling around his head like the snakes of Medusa herself.

"Continue to monitor her, but be careful, Thanatos." Zeus inclined his head, gesturing towards the door. "I have much thinking to do, decisions to make on how to approach this. Please, return to your realm and notify Hades that I will be sending him a message soon."

A message asking for entry to his realm.

If anyone had been able to read his thoughts—he still had them cloaked—they'd have gasped, they'd have clapped their hands to their mouths, they'd have thrown mythology books at his face to remind him that Zeus, king of the gods, god of the skies and thunder, *never went to the Underworld.*

He didn't want to, and he hadn't ever needed to, until now. Until finding out that the source of the evil infecting his family might lie in Mnemosyne's hut. He didn't believe Mnemosyne herself was responsible, but she might have been playing host to the vile creature who was. And Zeus needed to investigate this for himself. No more emissaries, no more favorite daughters playing detective, no more rumors given by favored reapers.

Thanatos left without another word, and Zeus summoned a cupbearer to bring him pen and paper as he formulated the message in his head.

"Dearest Brother, it is with regret that I must ask you, for the first time in history, to grant me access to your realm."

He flinched at the notion, worried he wouldn't even be able to write it. Should he simply appear there and bang at the gates until Hades let him in? He wouldn't refuse him entry, not now, not with all that was going on.

But Zeus didn't wish to leave Olympus unattended, either. What if this creature knew Zeus would react this way, and was seeking to trap him? It would float up to his palace while he visited his brother, it would intoxicate the remaining deities, turn them against him. Because that was what it all came down to; Zeus was no fool. Whoever this culprit was, it was Zeus' head they wanted on a pike. And causing a revolution among the deities was a great way to make it towards that final result. Three wars had tested him, two of which had been directly against *him*, to take his throne, to remove his authority. Could this be the third, possibly the last? The one that would finally dethrone him and send him off to rot in Tartarus with his father and grandfather, whose thrones had been stolen too?

With reason; they were chaotic, evil-hearted monsters. I am benevolent. I am good.

He had to go to the Underworld. He trusted those who'd reported to him, but he needed to see these events with his own eyes. To judge the situation himself, and determine how to fix it. Mnemosyne spell-crafting with someone in her hut, sneaking into places that were seemingly barred against her entry—this was a matter of grave importance, one that a king like him needed to address in person.

Who would he leave in charge of Olympus? Demeter, surely; and Hestia could be a back-up, though she'd decline to participate in any fighting should it come to that. Perhaps he'd summon Oceanus, the only male titan he'd ever trusted, to keep watch. Apollo and Artemis might be able to scout the perimeter, and Hephaestus could come up with some hefty traps in a pinch, no doubt about that.

Things will be fine. I'll make it a rapid trip, and once Hermes has escorted us, he can come right back up to further protect our home.

Zeus would need Poseidon with him and Hades in the Underworld, in case of confrontation. And Ares, too. He beckoned another cupbearer to fetch the latter—he was likely sulking about near Aphrodite's room praying for her to come back. As he started the procedure to call Poseidon, the three mystery-invoking goddesses stumbled past the threshold, all three running up to him as if competing to see who'd get there first.

In a rush of skirts and grunts and panting, it was Demeter who arrived first, flushed, her golden hair sticking to her forehead as she offered a quick curtsy. Hecate came next, her dress further stained and ruined than it had been earlier, smelling like an explosion of exotic spices and herbs. Persephone was wide-eyed, tongue-tied, her mouth opening and closing while she sought her words. All three had the airs of women scorned but still in shock from the impact.

"Ladies." Zeus got to his feet and raised a hand, begging them to calm down. "What happened?"

They proceeded to talk over one another, a mix of mumbled excuses and jumbled sentences that Zeus couldn't make light of.

"*Ladies,*" he repeated, snapping at Hecate—the one he thought might be best to speak to, as she tended to be the calmest. "Please, Hecate, take the floor, would you? While those two catch their breaths."

Demeter scowled at him, but Persephone seemed somewhat relieved and let out a large breath that sent her toppling forward, catching herself on the dais before she face-planted.

Hecate's eyebrows drew in and she took a step closer to the platform. "We did our rituals." She inhaled, exhaled, and joined her hands near her navel. Zeus noticed her fingers trembling. "We asked questions, and received answers in the form of images. Hearts thumping, dripping blood. Noxious purple smoke smearing a landscape of lavender fields. Puddles of blue ichor glistening on marble floors. Then…we got mixed visions of leaves, grass, earth, trees, blue skies, clouds. And flashes of," she swallowed, frowning, "curly, messy red hair entwined with vines. A malicious smile spreading over dark-colored lips, and a fire rising, consuming everything in its passage."

Something lodged in Zeus' throat; something large and agonizing, cutting off his steady breaths, blocking the saliva coming from his mouth. "What does it mean?"

"In our opinion," Hecate's eyes flared with scarlet and violet, before she bowed her head to avert her gaze, "these are signs. Signals pointing towards the person who might be behind all this. Indicators of its, of *her* identity, and possible predictions of what she might do. The hearts and smoke and ichor—those were reminders of what she *did* do."

Zeus grabbed at his throat, massaging it, hoping to make whatever the lump was go down, *down*, to stop constricting his breathing.

Signs, signals, indicators—of nature, of earthliness, of a mane of hair tangled with leaves, of fire devouring its victims.

Before Zeus could formulate the name out loud, before he could even *think* it, Demeter stepped forward, sliding her arm around Hecate's. "But it cannot be, can it?"

Hecate sucked her lips in, then shook her head. "Our mysteries are never wrong. *We* are never wrong. It is her, and we must acknowledge that fact quickly, before the fire spreads. That is the message *I* interpreted." She dared a glance at Zeus, turning stiff and suddenly solemn. "That someone with curly red hair is smiling at the damage she caused, and is ready to cause more."

Demeter tightened her grasp on Hecate's arm. "Yes, and that person is—"

"—don't say it. Do not even think it anymore." Zeus shrugged his fingers through his own messy mane and grimaced at the dampness—he'd been so on edge even his *hair* was sweating. "I can't fathom that she'd do this. Not now, not after all these years. Not after remaining neutral for so long. After claiming she tolerated me and my reign, after clarifying that she'd grown to accept that I'd imprisoned her sons, her monsters. No."

He heard her voice in his head as if she were there, remaining polite though her energy was sizzling with hatred. That slight twinge of disrespect, though she did all she could to conceal it. The narrowing of her muddy brown eyes as they bore into him, constantly reminding him what she truly thought—that he didn't deserve his throne, and that one day, *one day,* she'd take it from him.

But he never thought she'd act on those suppressed urges, the ones she thought she kept under control when she was around him. He thought she'd changed her mind, that he could trust her now, and that she'd given up seeking revenge for the children she claimed he'd wronged.

"Though our vision was clear," said Demeter, having appeared at Zeus' side as he'd blacked out, thinking of the potential identity of the culprit. "We can't be one hundred percent certain, Brother. We may need to re-do the ritual in a little while, to see if the result is the same." She stroked Zeus' arm in the loving way that had once drawn him to her, seeking comfort in her bed. The way that had led them to conceive Persephone—who was crouched by the dais, looking up at them with flaring nostrils.

He delicately removed Demeter's hand from his arm. "It's her. I should have known it. It should have been evident to me from the start, and I've been an idiot for not seeing it. But I have a way to be sure—we have witnesses." He motioned at Persephone—she'd been poisoned, too—and snapped, bringing one of his cupbearers to come skidding down the marble floors to prostrate at his feet. "Fetch me Eros and Psyche, at once."

|| 16. A THRONE THIEF ||

ZEUS

As he waited for Eros and Psyche to arrive—they'd likely taken refuge in their chambers, buried beneath heaps of blankets, having sex to ignore their rising anxiety—Zeus scribbled a hasty message to Hades and handed it over to Hermes, who'd popped up in the nick of time.

"Get this to my brother promptly, as your life and many others depend on it," he said to his mischievous son, who didn't ask questions—for once—and hastened off and out of the throne-room.

Demeter had taken up her throne, one leg crossed over the other, her dangling foot jittery. She grumbled, staring at the throne-room's threshold, awaiting the gods Zeus had summoned. Persephone sat on the dais at her mother's feet; she was equally stressed, but keeping her emotions under better control, not rocking back and forth as Zeus might have expected her to. How young and vulnerable she looked right now, her red-tinted curls framing her delicate face as she relived the tension of her childhood all over again. Kidnappings were traumatic to her, with reason; and to see her family members being picked off one by one? Zeus couldn't imagine her distress, and respected her command of it.

A true Queen of the Underworld, she is.

Hecate paced before Zeus, now and then stopped to raise a finger, to offer a formulation of a reason why the culprit had engaged in such cruel actions. Earlier, she'd sniffed out the remnants of Thanatos' spirit, and Zeus had reluctantly admitted he'd visited with rumors. When Zeus told Hecate those rumors—Mnemosyne's sneakiness and potentially hosting the culprit *in* her hut—Hecate's facade of calm had melted and she'd grown agitated, her eyes flickering with red and violet and a marblesque black that sent shivers down Zeus' spine.

At last, the god of love and his sweetling of a wife entered the room, hands behind their backs, their steps cautious as if approaching a giant who planned to put them on his plate for supper.

"Fear not," said Zeus, waving them forward, doing his damndest to appear solemn as a summer blue sky. Hera would have seen through his act in seconds, but Hera wasn't there. Half his court wasn't there. His family was in shambles, but he needed to keep up appearances—for now. "You're not in trouble. I seek your assistance with something that might make or break this case."

Eros bowed, Psyche curtsied, and they joined their hands as they glanced at Zeus. "Whatever you need, majesty," said Eros, a slight tremble in his tone.

"Tell me if you recognize this." Zeus lifted from his throne and weaved a hand through the air, grabbing at the particles, moving them, shifting them into a pattern. He snapped his fingers, and a voice broke through the eerie silence that had fallen on the occupants of the room as they watched him work his magic.

The voice was an herbal tea, a fresh field of grass; a soft whisper of wind with a hint of malice that only he detected, as that malice was always indirectly meant for him. It was that of a woman speaking; a conversation had recently in the throne-room, one where others weren't present, but Zeus had been there.

"Your court is restless because you have a secret culprit in your midst, you say? And what do you expect me to do about it?"

Zeus winced at the sound, bringing on the recollection of when he'd had this discussion with the owner of the voice. After he'd begged her to visit Olympus, to assist him in figuring out what was happening and why his family members were being infected.

Psyche squinted as the voice replayed over and over, as if coming from a recorder. "It's…oddly familiar, but I can't place it."

Eros, however, had frozen after letting go of her hand, his amber eyes widening as they zoomed in on Zeus. "Oh." He looked struck by lightning, an image paused on a screen, no longer breathing or able to speak.

"Oh?" Zeus snapped his fingers again and the recording ceased. "You recognize it?"

Eros, still caught in a trance, licked his lips. "It's…well, it's…" He cleared his throat. "It's Gaia, right?"

Before Zeus could confirm, Psyche gasped and grabbed the sides of her head, her eyes going as wide, if not wider, than Eros'. "Oh, no…*oh, no.* No, no, no…" She swiveled to Eros and pulled him to face her. She snatched his hands, connecting her gaze to his. "Please, tell me I'm hallucinating. Tell me you're not thinking as I am, that she…that that was…"

"The same voice we were hearing in our heads while we committed atrocious crimes against humanity?" Eros gulped, slowly spinning to Zeus. "It's not so much the voice itself, but the tonality, the measure of the words, the manner of saying them…"

"It's exactly the same," added Psyche, one hand over her forehead as her cheeks flushed five shades of pink. "The same resonance, the same rhythm…why, *why* didn't I piece it together until now?"

Another gasp came from Zeus' left; Persephone had gotten up and was swishing over, her palm clapped over her mouth, muffling her speech. "I heard it too, while I was poisoned. Faint, quite distant, but…hearing it over and over again prompted my memories." She set a hand on Psyche's shoulder. "We didn't recognize it because we had to hear *this* voice, time after time, to truly correlate the two voices." She peered at Zeus and flinched. "That was why you did that? Played it on repeat? Did you know it would trigger us? Mother and Hecate and I had no sounds coming to us during our rituals, so we…that's why we needed confirmation."

Zeus took a heavy sigh before collapsing back onto his throne, the motion slightly shaking the marble floors. "I had no idea what would happen if you listened to this. I actually hoped you'd recognize nothing. That you'd exonerate one of the most powerful goddesses in the universe from being a potential culprit seeking to dismantle my rule and harm my family."

"*Gaia?*" Eros' knees were visibly shaking and he held on to Psyche's forearm for balance. "How? Why? What would possess her to use some obscure magic voice to control us into…into killing? Poisoning? Destroying…why?"

Series of chills cruised all over Zeus' body as Eros laid out the facts, reminded of the gruesome acts he and his wife had committed against their will.

How to remain calm, how to remain kingly and responsible and mature when Zeus' own grandmother was likely conspiring at that very moment, desperate to rip him from his throne and sit herself on it in his place? Because that was what it was. Gaia had no other reason to harm *her own* family members if not to seize the crown for herself, and to liberate her children from their confinement.

"Gaia is a mystical goddess. An all-powerful primordial deity with many tricks up her sleeve and ancient powers we're unaware of. And motives that could surpass all our assumptions." He ignored the acidic saliva gathering in his mouth. "So *why* Gaia? I can't answer that. What I can answer is that we now have proof—Gaia is the one pulling the strings in this operation, that much is clear."

"Because she means to overthrow you, right?" Demeter had popped up beside Zeus without him noticing. Her arms were crossed, her eyes slitted, and a veil of fury rose over her face, transforming her usual bronzy skin to a glowing, fiery red. "She means to pick up where her children left off? Her despicable Giants, her monstrous Titans— she wishes to do what they couldn't?"

Zeus had no words to respond. Demeter had put all his thoughts into three sentences and smacked him in the face with them. The truth hurt, more so when said out loud—and now, containing his own rage and fear would be close to impossible.

But he tried, damn him, he tried. He gritted his teeth, he scraped his nails into his arm-rests, holding on for dear life, praying the electricity simmering within him would remain inside for a few more moments.

Let me get out of here, with my brothers—then I can unleash my anger away from these innocent souls.

"And *she* is the one in the Underworld with Mnemosyne," said Hecate, staring at Zeus, her eyes finally settling on a glossy shade of crimson. "You said Thanatos mentioned a guest in her hut—it's Gaia. It has to be."

Persephone's jaw dropped. "Gaia *in the Underworld?* Wouldn't we have sensed that? Wouldn't Hades have known? He always senses primordials. Tartarus and Nyx never sneak in unannounced because he detects the shift in the air, the growing energies…"

Hecate kept her body turned to Zeus, her gaze fixed on him, but addressed Persephone. "She has the power to cloak herself. So do the others, though they choose not to, because their intentions aren't malevolent like hers. She's in the Underworld…to free her children."

Zeus chewed on his lower lip to refrain from letting out a gasp of his own.

She'll let her kids out, team them up, and with all those powers combined…she'll throw me off my seat.

He'd fought the Giants, the Titans, even had a few battles of wits with Gaia—separately. But if they were to all get together and combine their strength…

"She has always wanted to let them out of Tartarus." Hecate's hands curled into fists at her sides, her veins shifting from blue, to purple, to black. "Her sons, her Giants, her monsters—those remaining from the wars, that is. She's always been angry with their imprisonment, complained about them having been locked up for long enough, they'd learned their lessons. I know; I've heard her saying it, heard her cursing you, Zeus." Hecate's neck cords were rigid, and Zeus worried she was a ticking time-bomb on the verge of exploding. "During my frenzies, I…bumped into her, I…"

Persephone hurried over to take hold of Hecate's hands, to squeeze them, drawing her friend away from the brewing storm of emotions she'd been stuck in. "You forgot about it," she said, swiping a few stray strands of black hair from Hecate's face. "She fucked with your memory, and so did Mnemosyne! They both had to work on you, to keep you quiet. You saw them, *you saw them* in whatever sort of business they were doing and they couldn't kill you, so they had to cover their tracks, somehow."

"But," Zeus cocked his head, narrowing his gaze on Hecate, "you haven't had frenzies for decades, no? I was under the impression you'd stopped them."

Hecate's eyebrows shot up so fast they might have flown off her forehead. "I *have* stopped. My last one was…give or take twenty-something years ago." She placed a hand near her throat as she swallowed. "They ceased after I saw her, or Mnemosyne, or whoever it is who's been messing with my mind."

"Twenty-something years." Zeus had to cover his mouth and pretend to yawn to not let out the furious screech he'd been holding in. "So she's been plotting for a long time, then. Longer than twenty years, I'd wager. Centuries, knowing her." He shook his head and tipped backwards to glare up at the ceiling, wishing it to crumble, to crash over him, hit him hard, and put him into a deep slumber that he'd awaken from to find out he'd been having a horrendous nightmare. "And here I'd thought she'd finally given up on demanding that I release her offspring. Instead, she's gone around getting goddesses impregnated without their knowledge, creating demi-gods that she hid amongst humans for some unknown motive. Turning innocent deities like Mother into poisonous fiends, and allying with a mind-warping titaness who thrives on high emotions and deceit."

"Mother?" Demeter, who'd dropped onto the closest throne—Hera's—sat up straight. "You're saying Mother is involved in all this? You're certain?"

"I'm not." Zeus' toes curled, and he twirled a finger in the air to magically lengthen his tunic to conceal his feet. He didn't want them seeing his distress; not now, not as all the answers were coming to them like missiles being fired into their chests. "But the blood she left behind, non-poisoned, and so close to two others who were clearly contaminated…that makes me doubt. And the fact that she's gone, like everyone else…it pains me to say it, but I think Rhea is in on this. Perhaps not willingly, mind you; but it's too obvious to ignore."

"But Themis and Phoebe?" Eros—who'd kept quiet as he watched everyone work out the reasons Gaia would turn so rebellious—cracked his knuckles. He was by nature a sweet-hearted being, but all of a sudden his earlier bloodlust swelled in his eyes, turning them a similar scarlet as Hecate's. As if he were possessed with a carnivorous craving again, but was directing it towards Gaia, instead. "They were poisoned, but they're daughters of Gaia, like Rhea and Mnemosyne. Is it possible they were decoys of some sort? That they're working with Gaia, too?"

"No," said Hecate, lips pursing as she rubbed her chin. "Phoebe is my direct grandmother, and I can assure you she wouldn't do this. Neither of them would ally with Gaia if they knew she planned to open up Tartarus and free their brothers. And potentially their father—oh, heavens. Zeus," she clasped her hands under her jaw, keeping it from tumbling to the floor, "if she gets Uranus out, or Cronus…if she succeeds—"

"—not while I'm alive." Zeus rose from his seat, his shadow taking the shape of an eagle, a phoenix aflame with loathing and revenge. "We can speculate all we want, but we can't come to any conclusions regarding anyone else at this time. Gaia and Mnemosyne—they are sure things. They are behind this, I feel it in my bones, and I don't like it."

"Brother?" A new arrival prompted everyone to spin towards the entrance. Hades had arrived, haggard and exhausted looking, grazing a hand over Persephone's arm as he joined the small crowd before Zeus' throne. He didn't even bow; this sort of summoning called for action, not formalities. "What news? Why in Tartarus are you asking to come to the Underworld?"

Multiple gasps resonated through the room. Zeus could have sworn a few came from *outside* the room, proving they'd had eavesdroppers for quite some time. But Zeus ignored them as he descended from the dais and planted before Hades.

"Because Mnemosyne is down there playing with fire—with Gaia."

Hades blinked once, twice, then angled forward, squinting at his brother. "Are you unwell? I'd know if Gaia were in my realm."

"She's there," said Hecate, gripping Hades' arm to pull him away from Zeus. Both men were snarling, though Zeus knew they weren't doing so *at* one another. "Our mysteries…we saw her in the smoke."

"Curly red hair, messy with vines, earth and sky and green grass—all signs point to her," added Persephone, taking up her husband's other side, sliding her hand into his.

"And her voice," said Psyche, who'd also opted to stay silent, like her spouse, but who'd had enough of not giving her opinion. "Zeus played a recording of Gaia's voice and it was…it was the same as the one we heard while we were intoxicated, going on a…a rampage." Her teeth clattered, and Eros took her by the shoulders, massaging them to soothe her.

He took a quick gander at Zeus, then nodded towards the doors. "May we leave, majesty? We provided what you needed, and Psyche and I are distraught. This is a lot for us."

"Go," said Zeus, not even looking at Eros or Psyche, but silently wishing them to heal, to recuperate—and to prepare for war.

Because it's coming. I smell it; blood and guts and burnt flesh. It's at our doorstep, and no one will be spared if we don't act fast.

"It's Gaia, and she'll stop at nothing until she's taken what's mine by birth. The seat I've sat on for eons, the one given to me, the one I've occupied with nothing but respect and cautious ruling. And," Zeus seized his brother's upper arm, "she'll come for yours and Poseidon's next, no doubt about it. If we resist—and we will—she'll continue plucking off our loved ones one after the other. I *must* go to the Underworld to find her, if she's indeed there—and then come home to plot how to bring her to justice."

It was a long time coming; centuries of dealing with Gaia's attitude towards him, her coldness, the nonchalant manner of speaking, the subtle comments whenever no one else was near. He'd never told anyone—his own grandmother, bullying him? No one would believe it—but it was all coming back to him now, and Zeus wouldn't have it. Not anymore.

Hades gulped, rolled up his sleeves, and backed away from those who'd gathered around him to convince him of the truth. "So it's all unfolding on *my* turf, then? She's occupying my realm, she's using my resources, she's sneaking into my home, stealing from my inhabitants?" He side-glanced at Hecate, who nodded. "Thanatos told you about what he'd noticed, I presume?"

"He did, and along with what Demeter and Hecate and Persephone figured out with their mysteries, and what Eros and Psyche remembered from their experience, and what Hecate is recollecting from her own…it's come down to this." Zeus extended a hand towards Hades, needing his authorization, his approval.

I need to go to the Underworld, now.

Hades slipped his hand into Zeus' and shook it. Firm, but with a shiver as his skin became clammy. "Then you, Poseidon, and Ares are granted temporary access to the Underworld. Hermes can provide you with directions, and I'll be waiting."

Without another word, Hades hastened out of the throne-room, a trail of black smoke in his wake.

The tension in the room didn't dissipate with his departure; it grew worse. For no one would say it, but all knew—for Zeus to travel to the realm he feared more than death itself meant a great deal.

"I need my family back," he said, turning to Demeter. "If your mysteries cannot reveal the locations of those kidnapped, then I'll need you to *physically* look for them. Hera is your sister; surely you can sniff her out, right?"

Demeter inclined her head. "I can. So if we find her…we may find the others?"

Zeus thought of his precious Athena, and the mighty Aphrodite, bound and gagged in some dingy dungeon somewhere, waiting for Gaia to decide what to do with them. He envisioned Lukus, chopped into, his organs tossed into a cauldron; and Dionysus overdosing on drugged wine, half-dead in a corner.

He peered at Hecate who, among those remaining in the room, had the most resources, the strongest nose, the best of abilities to track someone down. "Help Demeter find my family. And you," he motioned at Persephone, "you're Queen of the Underworld; I assume you can grant access to it, as well?"

Persephone opened her mouth, but said nothing, opting for a nod.

"I'm willing to bet they're all in the Underworld, where Gaia can keep an eye on them. Locate those who were kidnapped, and bring them to safety. I'll be leaving Olympus in Hestia's care, and Apollo, Artemis, and Hephaestus are to be on alert. And I'll inform Leto to call

all Titans to the palace—all those who *won't* side with their crazy mother and her ichor-spilling schemes."

Zeus stormed out of the room, calling out to all those he'd named as protectors of his realm in his absence.

I'm not letting another invasion happen, and I'm not going to lose my throne.

|| 17. POWERLESS ||
GAIA

As Mnemosyne took a bundle of freshly made poisons and hastened out of the hut, Gaia suppressed a shiver—one with a meaning that she couldn't identify, and wasn't sure she wanted to.

Things were taking a turn, and fast. The goddesses had given their blood—unwillingly, of course—the decoys had all served their purposes, Lukus was primed and ready to be deployed as necessary, and the overall atmosphere of both the Underworld and Olympus were dreary. Everyone was on alert—she could feel it, even down here. How they tiptoed about, afraid the slightest movement would get them attacked, their ichor drained from their neck. Worried the flimsiest of complaints would put a target on their backs.

Worry not, my dears—the only one with a giant target on him is Zeus.

It was a rarity for Mnemosyne to leave the Underworld, but she'd insisted it was best she check on the army of zombie-humans, and not Gaia. *"You shouldn't leave the protection of this space, for now,"* she'd said, as she opened the hut's door and slithered out into the Underworld's depths. *"Hades and Persephone are on edge, and I'd rather not risk you being seen. Not when we're so close to executing your carefully composed plans."*

In any case, Mnemosyne knew all the entrances to the Underworld better than Gaia did. She'd know where to herd the human-zombies, which parts of the world they'd need to concentrate in to better hear the signal. She and Gaia had decided it'd be best to draw the humans to them, as they'd have to be within Lukus' range, where he'd be able to control them, send them off to do the dirty work of biting, slicing into flesh—not animal flesh, this time—and poisoning anyone in his way.

She hadn't been able to explain it, but Gaia had insisted on preparing for an Underworld battle. *"A tingling image of Zeus and his brothers entering the darkness... and not getting out,"* she'd said, as she attempted to describe the ominous sensation in her gut, telling her there'd be a power struggle sooner than planned, and not *where* she'd planned. She'd hoped the big confrontation would take place in one of the forests poisoned Psyche had roamed about, setting up traps of toxins, leaving carcasses of rotting animals to distract the gods from the main purpose. And once she'd found a means to get the gods to gather there, she'd attack, throw her army of minions at them, led by Lukus, and destroy any deity preventing her from getting her claws into Zeus.

She didn't want the bloodshed, but she'd have no choice; they'd all stand up and defend their almighty king to the death, wouldn't they?

It's fine—we'll repopulate. I'll have Giants and Titans in the palace, and myself to oversee them.

She'd considered a straight-up invasion, but recalled how those had gone, eons ago. The Giants had wrecked parts of the Olympian palace that had taken decades to fix, and the Titans had left bloodstains on the walls that she still wasn't sure Hestia had been able to scrub completely clean. If one looked close enough, there were ichor prints on the back of Zeus' throne, where one of Gaia's sons—she couldn't remember which one—had attempted to pick up Zeus while seated on his throne and toss him from the balcony.

It had failed. All of those poorly plotted yet well-executed attacks *had failed.* Gaia would accept failure no more. It was time for change, and she'd have to get her hands dirty to make it happen; and this time, she wouldn't sit back and watch as others fought her battles. She'd fight *with* them.

She snapped at Lukus, indicating that he should stand up. He did so immediately, having been seated in a corner of the hut, waiting for further instruction. So tall, so stiff and obedient, his eyes glowing green with anticipation and hunger. Oh, the blood he'd taste, the bones he'd break, the glory he'd give Gaia on a platter. She'd conditioned him for this—for the role of a commander, a bloodthirsty leader who'd have no hesitation tearing and piercing through the blockade of deities to get to Zeus. For Lukus was the one who'd weaken Zeus—he would confront the king of the gods first, and then Gaia would take over once he was near the brink of exhaustion.

Magically conditioned, brainwashed by her poison, Lukus would deliver her victory. He'd command the army of poisoned humans into striking Zeus the instant they saw him. And it might be that the army would see Zeus *here*, in the Underworld.

"Zeus, in the Underworld?" Gaia chuckled. "Now *that* would be historical, defying all mythology, wouldn't it? A *new* mythology. We are rewriting it all."

She'd turned her back on Lukus, who stood rigid as stone by the altar. But as she switched back, she noticed Hera and Athena staring at him—and Aphrodite crawling *towards* him.

"Excuse me?" Gaia whipped out a few vines to smack Hera and

Athena backwards—they'd seemed ready to *help* Aphrodite, from how their bodies angled forward and their eyes were wide, cheering on the goddess of beauty as she pursued her path. Gaia stepped in front of Aphrodite. "What do you think you're doing?"

Aphrodite paused in her pursuit, and looked up at Gaia towering over her. She was gagged—all three of them were, as Gaia wasn't falling for their feigned breathlessness. They were breathing *just* fine, their heartbeats were *just* fine. But her thoughts were clear as day and penetrated into Gaia's head.

"I'm saving my son before you set him on a warpath he'll never recover from."

Gaia snickered, and kicked Aphrodite backwards, her foot lodging between the goddesses breasts. Aphrodite whimpered, and Gaia kicked again, harder this time, meaning to hurt her, meaning to frighten her.

Is physical violence the only way this generation of deities understands anything? Apparently so, since that's my only option to show how ruling is supposed to be done.

As Aphrodite began to sob—Gaia saw a reddening bruise developing on Aphrodite's once pristine skin—Gaia crossed her arms and tutted at her. "I gag you, I weaken you, I take your blood, I let you overhear all my plans and make it quite clear to you that you are *powerless* in my presence—yet still, you try to defy me? How old are you, girl? How *stupid* are you to seek to dismantle what I've set in motion?"

Aphrodite didn't reply; not with a sob, not even with her thoughts. She pulled her knees to her chest and lowered her head between them, as best as she could considering her bound wrists and ankles.

Athena nestled close to her, as if to comfort her—another shocking sight between goddesses who usually loathed one another. Hera scowled at Gaia without an ounce of remorse. She likely thought herself fearless, sticking up for her husband's constituents, attempting to protect her family. But Gaia saw her, and the others, as nothing but stubborn bugs she wanted to smash against a wall and be done with it. They weren't fearless—they were idiots.

But I can't kill them; not unless they get in the way of me approaching Zeus.

"You have no power over him," said Gaia, jutting her chin at the ever-still, statuesque Lukus. His green gaze was fixed on the walls ahead of him, unwavering. Not a bead of sweat slipped down from his temples, not a single muscle twitched on his body. He was, as Gaia had planned, a robot waiting for her to press the right button to get him going. "His role is set in stone, you see, and nothing you try will faze him. And besides," she snorted, looking at the state of the goddesses sprawled out before her, "you're all gagged, reduced to using your thoughts, and Lukus can't hear those. He can only hear mine."

She patted Lukus' muscular back and moved on to check on her other prisoners, who were fast asleep now, still exhausted from their rituals and chanting. Themis' head rested in Dionysus' lap. Dionysus was propped up against the wall, his head lolling down as he snored softly. Phoebe was curled up beside them, her breaths easy, steady.

Gaia pushed a few of Phoebe's midnight curls from her face, and placed a gentle kiss on her forehead. "Rest, darling. Your work is done." She smooched Themis' cheek, and took her out of Dionysus' reach, instead hauling her and Phoebe over to a different area, away from the Olympian. Once they were settled, peaceful as babies in slumber, Gaia returned to Dionysus and prodded at his thigh with her foot. "I've changed my mind about you. You'll never see Olympus again, you thirsty little mongrel. You'll stay in the Underworld, likely in Tartarus, where someone as affected and maddened as you belongs."

Dionysus the drunk, she'd called him more than once, even in Zeus' presence. Such a poor choice of a replacement for Hestia on the Olympian council; yet no one had listened to Gaia's opinion. What had Dionysus done to help the world? Aside from enticing its inhabitants into drinking, frolicking, doing drugs, and going on naked rampages through the forest. If his powers were harmless, if they were of no consequence to humans, she'd have left him be; but the multiplying accidents occurring on earth, the deaths due to alcohol and overdosing…she wouldn't tolerate those anymore.

Themis and Phoebe, as titanesses, would be restored to Olympus in due time, amongst their siblings. But Dionysus? He'd remain down here, where he belonged. Along with deformed monsters like Hephaestus—she had nothing against deformities or handicaps of any kind, just not *him*. He was a vile thing, a product of hatred—Hera's hatred towards Zeus and his escapades. And though he created gorgeous jewels and strong weapons for the gods, Gaia didn't want him in the forge anymore, not with the temper he'd harbored in the past, and the violent tendencies he'd had towards women who rejected him.

She had a few more ideas of where to *put* any Olympians who might survive this incursion. She'd keep Hestia in the kitchens because, truth be told, her food was amazing and she'd never raise arms against Gaia, anyway—

Her thoughts were interrupted by the door banging open, then closing again at the speed of lightning.

Mnemosyne hurried over to the cauldron, gripping its edges as she hunched over and stared deep within its depths. She was breathless—she seemed to do a lot of quick traveling that accelerated her heartbeats, lately—and gave a vague nod of acknowledgment to Gaia as she came closer.

"What happened?" Gaia felt the tension on Mnemosyne's skin without even touching her. She was warm, *hot*, and her pupils were dilated. The steam from the cauldron rose up and coated her orange-hued hair with moisture, making it grow more voluminous than it already was.

"My nymphs," said Mnemosyne, straightening up, cracking her back in the process with a grimace. "As I went up to ensure all the zombies were in place, my nymphs warned me…a surge of power is coming our way."

"Surge of power?" Gaia squinted at her daughter, doubting her small group of forest nymphs were able to detect *any* kind of power. They were woods-dwelling beauties whose only role was to seduce lost travelers into sharing a bed of leaves with them, then wailing into the night, prompting nearby human settlements to think the woods were haunted. Mnemosyne's idea of fun.

"Something foreign, something…that's never been here before." Mnemosyne's face drained of color. "You know how they lurk near the entrances; how they lust for my energy, for me to give them more powers. Well…they've detected *something* on its way. And for them, weakened as you know they are, to *feel* anything coming…it means something *big* is coming."

To Mnemosyne's obvious shock—her eyebrows slid up and her eyes grew round as saucers—Gaia smiled.

"Wait," the memory titaness backed away from the cauldron,

"you're *happy* about this energy coming towards us, whatever it is? Have you summoned someone else to our cause, someone who dwells in the sky and has agreed to lend a hand? Because we'll need one, we'll—"

Gaia set a hand on Mnemosyne's arm and squeezed, silencing her at once. "No. I'm not happy, but I'm smiling because I *knew* this would happen, and I am prepared for it. It will put things in motion a bit faster than planned, and might hasten our attack, but…I had a feeling about it. It's not an ally." Her smile widened as she envisioned shadows dancing in the Underworld's obscurity, figures fighting, hurling balls of energy at one another, tips of swords piercing into bellies, and heads being chopped off. "It's Zeus. Hades is letting Zeus into the Underworld, which is *exactly* where I want him to be."

|| 18. THE WORKS ||
PERSEPHONE

"Locate those who were kidnapped and bring them to safety."

Zeus' words resonated in Persephone's mind as she watched her mother and best friend pacing, their rhythms so different, their appearances so conflicting it rendered her too dizzy to join in. Demeter, a blur of blue skirts and golden hair; Hecate, a dark cloud flickering with red. Persephone loved them both, and wanted to help, but felt powerless.

Who was she but a second generation Olympian who dwelled underground for six months out of the year and took the six months she was above-ground to catch up on all the gossip and remember how to be a socially-skilled, smiling goddess who enjoyed the touch of the sun and the scent of fresh meadows despite the eerie recollections such places brought her?

Gaia. *Gaia?* She didn't have the power to confront such an ancient, incredibly powerful deity. No one did. When she'd sat back and watched her offspring attack Zeus, it had been one thing; but if *she* was now leading the assault, there was no hope. Persephone tried not to be a pessimistic goddess, but in such a situation, she didn't see the point in staying positive.

"Right, so," said Hecate, breaking the silent trance she'd been in as she swished to Persephone, who'd been sitting on the dais, legs dangling. "I agree with Zeus—those kidnapped by Gaia are no doubt in the Underworld, likely hiding out in Mnemosyne's hut under some sick enchantment that cloaks them. Between Gaia and Mnemosyne they could have ensured no regular inhabitant of the realm detected unusual activity."

"But you did, didn't you?" Persephone placed her hands on the platform, on either side of herself. The old wood would likely splinter her skin, but at this point, she no longer cared. "You sensed something amiss this whole time, but your memory was messed up. I should have listened, *Hades* should have listened, and we should have—"

"—darling," said Demeter, settling beside her daughter and moving a few threads of auburn hair from over Persephone's eyes. Auburn hair that was already switching to a deep scarlet—the shade her curls took on during spring and summer, nourished by sunlight and fed by her mother's affection. "It's too late to think of what *could* and *should* have been done. We must focus on taking action now."

"Action?" Persephone leaned away from her mother's kind gestures and shook her head. "Action against *Gaia?* There *is* no action against Gaia. There's nothing to do. Zeus can't fight her, *we* can't fight her—"

"—and *we* are not going to," interjected Hecate, eyebrows scrunched and eyes piercingly violet. "We were told to locate the kidnapped ones, not confront Gaia. And that's what we'll do; we'll head to the Underworld now and start our search, as discreetly as possible."

Demeter wiggled her nose. "But I've…never been down there," she said, shifting uncomfortably as her fingers twitched in her lap. "Am I allowed?"

Hecate scoffed. "You're allowed if I say so. Hades granted me special permission centuries ago. Should there be an emergency, I'm permitted to bring in any guest to the Underworld that I so choose, anyone who'd be of assistance to whatever emergency we're having. He won't say it out loud, but I'm sort of a bodyguard, a soldier who oversees the protection of his property, when I'm not busy brewing potions and being all…well, witchy." She smirked, and Persephone's heart filled with warmth at the sight.

Persephone got up. "And in any case, like Zeus said; *I* am the Queen of the Underworld, and if I wish for my mother to visit the Underworld, then she will. The gates won't stop you, and neither will Cerberus."

Hecate's lips twitched. "Ah, we…won't be going through the gates." She rolled up her sleeves and wagged her fingers, indicating that Demeter and Persephone should get close to her. "I have a particular charm that'll transport us directly to my lair," she winked, "another spell reserved for emergencies. I doubt Hades will bat an eyelash at my usage of all these spells during such trying times. After all, he's granted access to *Zeus,* of all people—a historic moment in the making, no? I don't think one more Olympian deity sliding in is going to make a big difference."

She whispered a few words in ancient Greek, swirled her arms overhead, drizzled a few pinches of a black powder that smelled like sulfur—and off they went in a *poof* of black fumes.

They landed in the middle of Hecate's witchcraft and potion room, down in the crypt. Demeter collapsed, gasping for air—she wasn't used to this atmosphere and it would take her a few moments to adjust. Hecate toppled forward and caught herself on her cauldron, and Persephone closed her eyes, wishing the dizziness away. She'd traveled by such magic once—Hecate had come to visit her in a dream and told her she was needed in the Underworld, during her spring and summer stay up in Olympus. Persephone had met her at the golden Olympian gates, and Hecate had whisked her off by these means—a quick but tumultuous teleportation through time and space that left one's insides jiggly and jelly-like, and definitely didn't feel like *regular* teleporting.

That uncomfortable feeling swelled in Persephone's gut as she reopened her eyes. It worsened and reached a peak when she sighted that they weren't alone in the room—someone was slumped on the other side of the cauldron. A bush of their black tresses was showing, as well as a pallid, thin arm covered in scratches and bruises.

Persephone's dizziness evaporated as adrenaline coursed through her. She marched around the cauldron to discover her own daughter, half-knocked out, crumbled against the sleek metal surface of the cauldron, and mumbling incoherently. More so than usual.

"What in Tartarus…?" Persephone fell to her knees before her offspring, and swept a hand over her forehead. It was hot. "Melinoë, what happened? What are you doing here?"

She'd been abed, sickly and exhausted, last Persephone had checked. So how and why had she ended up here, in Hecate's potion room? She had access to it, sure; but she had no energy and no need to come this far for…for what?

Persephone looked around to see if anything was amiss. Any bottles broken on the floor, any books out of place, any herbs scrunched in Melinoë's hands, as if she'd come to steal something. But nothing was wrong. There was no disturbance in the room aside from the growing negative energy coming from Persephone herself as her anger built inside her, brick after burning brick.

"What is it?" Demeter crawled over and clapped a hand over her mouth. She'd never met Melinoë—Persephone had refused to introduce them—but she knew who she was and appeared as astounded and angry as Persephone at the vision of her in a heap of stained skirts on the floor.

Hecate, who'd recovered from her instability, came around and instantly lowered to Melinoë's level, taking one of her hands in hers. "She's drained." When she let go of Melinoë's hand, it flopped down to the floor, as if dead. Melinoë was breathing, but barely; her lips were chapped and peeling, and her skin so pale she was ghostly. Ghastly. More so than her usual near-white skin tone.

Persephone gulped. "She…she was drawn out of bed, wasn't she?" She couldn't move, couldn't stand up or turn her head from the vision of her daughter in distress. The poor thing was terrifying to look at on any normal day, but here she was something straight out of a horror movie, with eyes bloodied and tears of blue ichor, with black veins creeping up her white, *very* white arms, and with pockmarked flesh that would disturb even the most avid gory novel fan.

She was a zombie—a powerless, pitiful creature who'd been trifled with one time too many, and who now had nothing left to give.

Strength grew in Persephone's limbs—fury and absolute disgust fueled her, allowing her to get to her feet at last and kick at the first thing she could; a stool, that her foot sent hurtling across the room to shatter against a wall.

"No." Her fists curled and a sizzling, seismic energy developed in her fingers, traveling to her fingertips. "This is…I can't…that *bitch* broke my daughter?" She spun and glared at Hecate, who'd been muttering an incantation to put Melinoë to sleep. "This was her, right? That two-faced memory-messing Mnemosyne?"

Hecate placed a gentle kiss on Melinoë's forehead as her head lolled to one side. She was passed out, peaceful. "I can't see who else would do this."

"That…that *thief* took advantage of my sweet girl's differences, of her weakness. She'll," she sniffled, and Demeter shot up from her kneeled position to take her hand, "she'll *pay* for this."

Titaness or not, Persephone wasn't afraid of Mnemosyne, and never would be again. No, she'd hunt the damned bitch down and would chop her head off and put it on a pike that she'd display at the entrance of the Underworld for all to see.

Don't fuck with Persephone, or else.

"Let us get her to her bed," said Hecate, motioning at Persephone to help her pick Melinoë up. "Demeter, would you start rummaging through my cabinet for supplies?" She flicked a finger towards said cabinet, unlocking it from a distance. The door sprang open, revealing shelves of sparkly toxins and dried herbs that Persephone didn't even know the names of. "We'll need the works. Spices, protection, healing—all that you can remember."

Persephone and Hecate dragged Melinoë to her chamber, in silence. There was nothing to say—Mnemosyne had tested them both beyond measure, and to speak would only further their rage. Persephone couldn't read Hecate's thoughts, but she had no doubt she was seeing blood, and lots of it.

Good—let that mind-warping titaness trash be ripped to pieces by Hades.

Because Hades, a temper-controlled deity who preferred to stay out of wars, *would* go to war for this. Melinoë wasn't his daughter, but Persephone was his beloved wife, and he'd do anything for her. Including break the neck of the evil titaness who'd dared to fuck up

Melinoë's already weakened mind.

They returned to the lair to find a mess of pouches and ingredients splayed over the floor as Demeter tried to get organized. They were pressed for time, so Hecate joined her, and together they concocted three bags of various sorceries meant to be used in a pinch.

Defensive spells to be thrown to the ground so they'd explode in a gush of smoke. Invisibility charms that would help them navigate around the realm undetected. Confusion brews—these were in vials, tucked into pouches, and meant as a last resort, as they were technically poisons that had all sorts of different effects: instant slumber, nausea, wobbly legs, numbness, clogged breathing.

As she manned the cauldron, stirring whenever Hecate told her to, Persephone recognized the spicy scents, the earthly aromas of all the herbs being crushed together in haste and tossed into sacks and tied tightly.

It pained her to remember how Hecate had done this before—when the Giants attacked, when the Titans attacked. She'd never had to use those spells, but Zeus had begged her to prepare; and prepare, she had. A plethora of incantations had been laid at Zeus' feet, hours before the threat had arrived at their door.

Persephone saw their stash now, and frowned. It was a meager amount compared to those wars. So many of Hecate's ingredients were missing—that pitiful Mnemosyne had stolen quite a bit, as it turned out—and she worried they'd not get far before needing to use those spells to evade whatever other minions Gaia had in her service. Because surely she'd enlisted plenty of gods and monsters who were upset with Zeus. The list was long, as much as it disturbed Persephone to admit it.

Let us pray she didn't manage to turn everyone against him.

"That's enough," said Hecate, handing Persephone one bag filled with enchantments, giving another to Demeter, then slinging one of her own—a smidgen heavier—over her shoulder. "Our goal isn't to get involved, it's to retrieve and save the kidnapped ones. We'll bring them here—the mansion is enchanted against those who wish us ill."

Persephone grimaced. "The front door is, but not your secret stairs. That's how Mnemosyne was getting down."

"Yes, well, I'm not sure how she was evading *that* spell," Hecate swallowed, gripping her bag, "because there was one. Perhaps because there's no actual door to weave a spell over…a bit of a loophole that she profited from. It doesn't matter now," she gestured towards one wall of her lair, "because we won't be using that, and I assume she's taken all she can from me. There's nothing left to take."

Demeter squinted at the wall she'd pointed towards. "Um, aren't we going *that* way?" She waved at the actual door to the potion room, wide open from when Hecate and Persephone had gone through it to take Melinoë to her bed.

Hecate grinned at them as she hastened to the wall, pressing a hand to its stony surface. "It's funny how everyone tends to underestimate me," she said, as a bright light glowed under her palm, burning into the wall. The stones suddenly shook and tumbled into a pile at Hecate's feet—revealing a tunnel-like passage out of the room. "You think I show all my cards and secrets at once? Never. You all think my *not-so-secret* exit is my only way to escape?" She urged them to hurry over and into the tunnel. "How else do you expect me to have crept out of the Underworld for my frenzies?"

Persephone couldn't help but smile at Hecate's evasion. Of course she'd have more than one secret means to get out of her lair without detection. Her *not-so-secret* exit was a decoy; a smart, Hecate-style diversion to ensure everyone misjudged her. She *wanted* everyone to misjudge her, so she'd be able to provide the element of surprise.

If they could provide that element now, perhaps they'd have a chance of surviving this new catastrophe.

They snuck down the damp, rotten-smelling tunnel, which led them under the palace and popped them out at the northern end of the Stygian Marsh, near where its waters ran into *Cocytus*. Before they exited from the ground itself—a mossy sewer-like cover had been camouflaged into the grass to keep the passage undetected—Hecate enchanted them with a stronger version of an invisibility charm. Persephone and Demeter both had that kind of power, but Hecate's version was more powerful and lasted longer. As a third generation titaness herself, she had a few extra skills and was definitely quite proud of them.

"If they smell us," said Hecate, reaching up to remove the cover from above them, so they'd be able to get out. "Then we'll have to deploy all we have and split up. I'll head towards the Elysian Fields. Demeter, you'll go back to the palace but *not* via any secret passages. And Persephone…you'll go towards Tartarus."

The notion of getting anywhere near the inflamed and highly dangerous fire river, *Pyriphlegethon,* that guided souls to Tartarus, made Persephone shudder with revulsion. But Hecate's plans usually had a meaning, so she nodded, praying they'd avoid detection and discover where the captives were being held.

And somehow save them from whatever torture Gaia has been putting them through.

|| 19. COME AND TRY ME ||
GAIA

"Your threats and insults no longer amuse me," said Gaia, snapping towards the Olympian goddesses who'd been thinking all sorts of demeaning things since Gaia had proclaimed that Zeus was on his way.

"He'll knock some sense into you with a dose of thunder," Athena had thought, her eyes morphing to a steely, metallic gray, a blockade of stone to conceal the anger growing in her gut.

Gaia sensed that anger, but it only made her laugh harder.

"My husband has won all wars brought to his doorstep. This one will be no different," Hera had thought, though she'd wisely opted to keep her gaze averted, focused on Aphrodite.

Through her gag of leaves and vines, Aphrodite had been mumbling in a high-pitched voice, rocking back and forth and wriggling as if unsure how to locate the true source of her pain. Internal? External? *Both?* Wherever that pain was, it was *annoying* and Gaia needed her, needed them *all*, to shut up so she could concentrate.

"Put them to sleep, would you?" She waved dismissively towards the goddesses as she glared at Mnemosyne. "They're giving me a migraine, and I *can't* have a migraine right now, not when I'm about to confront Zeus."

All three protested with squirms and fiery glowers at Mnemosyne, but the orange-haired titaness wasn't deterred by their muffled screeches. She sprinkled a bit of her brown sleeping dust over their messy manes, and within seconds, all three passed out, their heads lolled to the side.

"Thank Olympus," said Gaia, rubbing her fingertips hard into her temples, praying the pulsing pain away. "Way too much drama to handle. Why did I opt to keep them all captive together?"

Mnemosyne dusted herself off—she'd gotten some of the powder onto her gold-tinted dress—and shrugged. "There wasn't really anywhere else safe enough to hold them, Mother. I do think you should have kept them unconscious this whole time, though."

"Indeed." Gaia motioned at the door. "Are we ready? Do you have all the potions?"

Mnemosyne swept by the cauldron and picked up a bag from the floor, containing clinking glass vials and heaps of powder-filled pouches of spells and curses they might need in a pickle; if their regular powers failed to cause an effect on Zeus and his groupies.

"We're as ready as we can be on short notice," she said, with a slight sneer at the door.

Gaia's face twisted into a sneer, as well. She knew what Mnemosyne meant, but also knew that Mnemosyne had been working hard to craft as many charms as possible, and wouldn't say they were ready if they weren't.

"I *did* sense that Zeus might show up here in some sort of ambush…but not yet, not so soon." Gaia brushed her fingers through her hair, untangling a few vines stuck in the deep fiery tresses. A soothing scent of fresh dirt reached her nostrils, and she sucked it in, praying for energy, for the earth's support in her endeavors. "I thought we'd trap *him* before he passes the Diamond Gates and has Hades' full protection within the realm."

"Ah." Mnemosyne slung the bag over her shoulder and reached out a hand to help Rhea up from her curled position in a corner. "So you mean to shed blood *in front* of the Underworld, not quite in it?"

Gaia marched over to her precious half-human zombie army leader, walking around him as she dragged her fingertips over his silky, smooth, nearly hairless body. "If I shed blood *in* the realm, there will be harsher consequences if we were to fail. We won't." She sent a scathing side glare at Mnemosyne, who'd been about to gasp, she'd sensed it. "But *if* we do, the judges will instantly sentence me to Tartarus. I *will not* go to Tartarus, not for my attempt to save the world. Because they'll call this a crime against the gods; I'm sure they already do, hm?" She peeked at Rhea, who'd been up there mingling with deities during all the attacks. She'd *started* the attacks, and had had a chance to overhear what all the gods were saying, inconspicuous as she'd been.

Rhea nodded, without a word. She was still in a sort of an after-effect trance, still digesting the godly blood she'd drank from Hera, Athena, and Aphrodite. Gaia felt the power surging and growing inside her. Her jungle side, the lioness contained in her belly, was growling for action, demanding something to sink its teeth into.

Soon, my sweet; soon.

"I didn't want this," said Gaia, as she snapped at Lukus, somewhat awakening him from his rigid stance where he'd been staring at the muddy wall. "I didn't *want* to poison my kin and draw blood, but Zeus left me no choice. Nor do I want to kill him or any of those who oppose me; but anyone standing in my way *will* die, and that's the end of it. If they die outside of the Underworld, they'll roam as ghosts along the Diamond Gates for all eternity. If I were to murder them *inside*, however…" She nudged Mnemosyne and Rhea towards the door, her gaze resting a few seconds longer on Mnemosyne.

"They'd haunt the place and everyone would go mad." Mnemosyne sighed, taking Rhea's hand to help her walk with stability. "That wouldn't do."

Gaia had actually been thinking that if the ghosts of Olympian gods were to float about the Underworld, Mnemosyne would *sleep* with them all and sentence their souls to wander with even more wails. And if Gaia were to be tamed and stopped in her plots and also sentenced to live in the Underworld, she *didn't* want to have to endure any of that.

If she were to bring the war into the realm, she'd attract the attention of those she hadn't been able to coerce to her side—the other primordials, who'd denied her countless times. She'd had one last attempt at subduing Tartarus from a distance, but he was unresponsive to her seduction, no longer sensitive to her charms.

If we fight inside the official Underworld grounds, he'll rally to Zeus' side, not mine. I can't fight one of my own.

She snapped at Lukus again. "Come, my pet. We must get moving; your big moment is approaching at high speed."

Lukus' glowing green eyes glinted with a slash of sparkly black. "Yes, my queen." He turned and marched robotically to the door, having to bend to pass under the threshold.

Gaia followed, with one last glance at her beautiful daughters, sleeping soundly. At Dionysus snoring and drooling, isolated from the titanesses. And at the three Olympians huddled together, with no clue that their precious positions at court would soon be revoked.

She closed the door behind her and caught up to Mnemosyne,

Lukus, and Rhea as they crossed the bridge over the *Acheron*.

"And the humans?" Gaia sidled up to Mnemosyne and lowered her voice. "You said you spoke with your nymphs, but were you able to confirm that the humans are in place, that they're ready?"

Mnemosyne nodded. "They're all gathered at the various entrances to the realm, which I have conveniently opened for them. They will come running at Lukus' command, as planned. He'll need only say the word…whatever word it is you programmed him with, that is. They'll amass in hordes, blocking all exits, ensuring Zeus remains stuck down here. Then they'll come to us when needed."

They began their trek towards the gates, keeping as low of a profile as possible. Gaia sniffed the air and stopped the proceeding, raising a hand to pause their steps.

"Wait," she said, spinning to look towards the hut. "Something…is off."

Mnemosyne squinted at her, the hut, then at her again. "The negative energy caused by Zeus? Can *you* smell it already?" She sniffled once, twice; and her brown eyes gleamed with gold as she shook her head. "I don't detect anything yet, Mother."

Rhea prodded over to Gaia's other side. "What do you sense, Mother?" Her voice was strangled, as if two sides of her were waging a battle inside her throat, deciding which timbre would win, which would come out as hers. She was tired, aching in the pit of her stomach, sick of being poisoned to obey her mother's commands.

I'm sorry, my sweet daughter. Only a little longer.

Gaia grimaced. "Something foul, something…a sinister scent of scheming, that's what I sense." She took a step forward, envisioning the hut, but sensing that whatever was bugging her came from beyond it. Across the marsh, possibly close to the palace, if not inside of it. "Is

Hecate home?"

Mnemosyne cupped a hand over her forehead, peering out at the big black palace in the distance. "I can't tell. We're still warded from the palace, remember?"

"Maybe it's nothing." Gaia's shoulders were tense, her calves aching, and her veins pulsing with blood. It *wasn't* nothing, but she couldn't seem to find any means to explain what it was she was feeling, what was putting her off. A trail of mischief, of essences that didn't belong. A soupcon of dark magic—not necessarily evil, but *dark,* as in ominous energy that signified immense power. Power tethered by a leash and hidden under a tarp, awaiting the right moment to strike.

Such scents, such *odors* only evoked one memory to Gaia—the day she'd first started drugging Hecate, taking over after Rhea had become occupied with other things. Hecate's response to the poison injected into her was this; a certain need to ascertain dominance but being unable to fight the control the toxins had over her blood, over her abilities. Her eyes had rolled back, she'd curled her fists, and she'd had a thirst, a *hunger* to claw Gaia's face off; and yet she couldn't. The desire was there, but Hecate couldn't act on it.

That was what Gaia felt now. A repressed desire that was being hushed, contained. Concealed.

Someone was hiding within reach, watching them.

"We have to keep moving," said Gaia, twisting away from the sight of the hut and the palace, and ushering her group faster down the path, passing the camp for souls awaiting judgment. "I can't tell if it *is* Zeus I'm sensing, or something else. I worry others are coming with him. He brings allies."

"*We* have allies," said Mnemosyne, her focus straight ahead, on the glistening Diamond Gates, the surface littered with actual diamonds that shone in the gloomy Underworld light. "We have Lukus' army, we have ourselves, and the Tartarus guards need only one word from me to open the cages and let *them* out. If it's time…" Her head tipped to the left, slightly angling towards the smoky stream of fire otherwise known as *Pyriphlegethon,* the river leading to Tartarus. "Warn me. It'll take seconds, and you'll have your sons here, your beloved children, to fight alongside us."

Gaia allowed a slither of air to enter her lungs and expand within. A slither of hope to blossom in her heart, recalling that Mnemosyne had *finally* negotiated with the guards, had *finally* offered a compromise that pleased them. It had happened days ago, during the blur of events ongoing up in Olympus, but Gaia had received Mnemosyne's call. *"It's done, Mother. They'll do it. They'll open the gates and let your offspring out, when the time is right."*

Gaia had almost forgotten that it was a done deal; that if her children were unleashed and set upon Zeus, he'd never stand a chance. Not after their centuries of brewing in rage and stewing in hatred and waiting for the moment to take their revenge.

But there was *still* something amiss, something Gaia couldn't describe, and that didn't sit well with her. Zeus would never come here alone—he'd have Poseidon, probably Ares with him—but there was *someone else* down here that shouldn't have been. Someone she smelled but didn't recognize. Someone trying to conceal beneath a pungent invisibility spell—a spell she had no doubt belonged to Hecate.

Hecate is definitely here. And she *brought allies of her own?*

Gaia wouldn't voice this concern, not now. Hecate was strong, and would cause problems, for certain, but for now, Gaia needed to concentrate on the matter at hand—on Zeus coming to the Underworld to confront her. Did he know who he was up against? Had he managed to figure out the mystery without his witty favorite daughter at his side?

Gaia sniffed the air once more, winced, and sped up her pace. "We will hold off on summoning them for now. I created Lukus for this; all the bloodshed and diversions led to this moment. I must give him a chance to deter Zeus, as I intended. If he fails…" She gave a loving, motherly glance at her wondrous army general, her strong-backed, muscular, infallible warrior that she knew wouldn't disappoint her. "Then you can ring the bell for my children. They will be released, at some point, regardless; but I've not yet decided how involved I want them in Zeus' death, if I opt to kill him. Perhaps it should be me, their mother, who does the deed. I couldn't protect them all those years ago, so it may be that the vengeance is mine to take."

The image of Zeus bleeding out on the ground, all his immortality draining from his being, became more enticing than the notion of him rotting behind bars. Perhaps she *did* want him dead, after all; and perhaps she'd been suppressing that desire for so long that it now flashed before her with viscous vitality.

"And if there *is* someone else down here," she raised her voice, intending to be heard by whoever Hecate had dragged down with her, "well, let them come and try me, hm?"

|| 20. CONFIRMING THE CULPRITS ||
PERSEPHONE

"Well, let them come and try me, hm?"

Distance was no concern; at this vantage point, and even from behind a cluster of moisture-ridden bushes, Persephone had no trouble hearing the threats uttered by a mildly raspy feminine voice that still echoed in her mind. Nor did she have trouble recognizing the four individuals who'd exited the hut, including the one who'd spoken.

She'd shuddered at the vision of the flaming, vine-entwined hair of Gaia, primordial goddess of the earth, mother of all things. And the curly orange tresses of Mnemosyne, radiating with a golden glow— the one she used to draw in curious ghosts and to confuse deities and creatures into letting her fool around with their memories.

With them was a man Persephone didn't know, and Rhea— *Rhea?* Mother of Olympians, docile, sweet-natured former queen? It was true; Zeus had mentioned his mother might be involved, and here she was. So, his doubts concerning Rhea were more or less confirmed?

Last Persephone had heard, Rhea had taken a bit of a sabbatical in the jungle to study felines. So what in Tartarus was she doing there, with the two supposed culprits? Why, *why* had Zeus been right about this, and how had he known?

Persephone, Demeter, and Hecate remained huddled by the leafy, marshy shrubbery, cloaked under Hecate's waning invisibility spell. All three had trembled when Gaia stopped walking, after they'd gone over the bridge over the *Acheron*. She'd sniffed the air, spun towards the hut, her gaze so inflamed they could see it from their hiding spot. That gaze seemed to zoom *past* the hut, and straight onto them, kneeled and shaking and praying for the great goddess to not know they were there.

There was a malicious look to Gaia, a sense of something off, something disturbing in her straightened stance. Persephone would have once called her solemn, reverent, a gracious goddess akin to a wise and ancient tree abundant with vibrant green leaves and red poppies exploding with life from her lengthy branches. Here, she was a vicious, leafless, soulless clump of thick sticks with sharp ends, and flames of hair sticking out as if to ward off anything that might block their way.

"She smells something is up," said Hecate, speaking into Persephone's mind. Demeter nodded, which meant Hecate had established a three-way communication.

Persephone prayed to any god who might be intuitive to silent prayers that Gaia had no means to include herself in their privacy.

"She doesn't," said Demeter, proving she was listening in. *"This mind-reading is linked to our mysteries, to our recent experiments. I agree with Hecate; Gaia smells something, but she cannot hear or see us yet."*

"'Yet' being the key word, here," added Persephone, gritting her teeth as she watched Mnemosyne sniff and shrug, and Rhea scrunch her nose in concentration.

"It's me she's after, I guarantee it." Hecate shifted beside

Persephone, her skin cold and clammy, riddled with goosebumps. *"If she detects my presence, and she will, she'll be pissed. If she's been poisoning me this whole time...no doubt she'll explode if she knows I've been able to escape her clutches and am no longer fully under her spell."*

"And us?" Demeter's thoughts were troubled, and she couldn't seem to stay still. Persephone squeezed her hand, though she realized *she* wasn't reassured, either. *She* lived in the palace, this was her home six months out of the year; but Demeter didn't belong here, and the Underworld itself might reject her. Hecate had let her through, and Persephone had granted her passage—but a guest is only officially a guest if Hades says so.

And he has no idea we brought her here.

"I don't think she's detected you," said Hecate, leaning around Persephone to stroke Demeter's arm softly. *"She'll have sniffed me out; my scent is detracting, and can be strong for those not used to it. And since I haven't been down here for the past day, she'll have noticed the difference in the atmosphere. But that's okay, we...we can work around this."*

Gaia seemed to hesitate to move forward, to proceed in the direction of the gates. The fourth individual in her group was one Persephone didn't recognize. A man, bare-chested, tall, with a vague green glow about him. He had the airs of someone handsome, someone who knew how to carry himself, and a mop of black hair that gleamed almost blue in the fake starlight. But he walked in robotic strides, turning to look at Gaia, as if awaiting her command.

"That's Lukus," said Demeter, interpreting her daughter's thoughts at once. *"The half-human Zeus summoned to Olympus to investigate the case. Well, looks like he found the culprit, didn't he?"*

Hecate angled forward, almost falling on the other side of the bushes and into the murky water. *"He's not a captive, then? Why would he be out here, following them?"* She returned to her spot, but was fidgety. *"What does she want with him?"*

"I'm not sure, but she's got him under her spell, for certain." Demeter's mind showed a zoomed-in version of Lukus; as if she were sharing her own vision with Persephone and Hecate, and pinpointing the details of what she saw. *"That green glow around him? I think it means he's possessed. The voice... Gaia's voice... it's in him."*

"So he's poisoned?" Persephone hadn't stopped shaking since they'd lowered behind the bushes, but now her shakes were growing harder and harder to contain. She feared anyone in the vicinity would see the leaves trembling with her.

"He must be. Poor sod," said Hecate, reaching into her bag, but not communicating with Persephone and Demeter what she was looking for. *"I assisted him quite a bit while I was up there, and he's a good man. He doesn't deserve this sort of treatment."*

Persephone gulped. She had information on this Lukus, didn't she? Hades had told her of something Zeus had said, and perhaps it was important here—perhaps it meant something that might enlighten them.

"Hades told me he's Aphrodite's son. Zeus told him."

Demeter stumbled backwards, falling onto her ass. Hecate muffled a gasp that might have triggered Gaia were she an inch or two closer.

"What?" Hecate grabbed Persephone's wrist. *"Aphrodite's son? Does she know? Does he know? Because he certainly didn't when he and I spoke."*

"How in the heavens would Zeus know this?" Demeter seized

Persephone's other wrist, tighter, cutting off circulation. *"He had inklings that the man was half-god, but kept claiming he didn't know the parentage..."*

"Well, he does. Only a handful of people are aware, and yes, Aphrodite included. And...from what I understand, Gaia knew as well." Persephone swallowed again, this time finding her throat painful and dry. Why hadn't they brought something to drink on their little venture?

"This could be tremendous information," said Hecate, scratching her chin as she used her other hand to keep searching through her bag. *"Gaia taking control of a demi-god, a son of Aphrodite... he'll develop powers, strong ones, I'd bet. Aphrodite is not a regular Olympian. Her children are much more powerful than they let on."*

Persephone squinted at the four figures growing smaller as they continued their trek towards the gates. *"Does Gaia have a particular grudge against Aphrodite? Or is she taking advantage of that power? She* did *poison Eros, after all. And Psyche, his wife. Are those simple coincidences, or..."*

Demeter finally released Persephone's wrist and let out a lengthy but steady breath. *"We can only make guesses at this point. Getting inside Grandmother's head is impossible. It's never clear what she's thinking. A cryptic goddess if there ever was one."*

Another chill coursed through Persephone; one reminding her that there were other captives, one of which was closer to Gaia and Rhea than all of them—Hera.

"We have to find the others," she said, nudging Hecate, who'd been busy ruffling through her bag. *"Of all of us, Hera knows Gaia best, no? Even Zeus can't quite figure her out, he made that clear upstairs. If we find Hera, if she's unharmed...perhaps she'll be able to*

pinpoint weaknesses that we can use to stop Gaia."

Hecate stopped what she was doing and took hold of Persephone's wrist again, but this time turning her to face her. *"We are not doing anything that involves getting close to Gaia, do you understand? We're here to locate the captives and get them to safety. We will not get involved in this any further. Gaia..."* She shivered, and her fear was felt in the air itself, turning it to ice. *"She's not one to be messed with. Zeus has no choice, but we...we mustn't get in the way."*

She was right, and Persephone knew it; and yet she couldn't help thinking that a massive force was what Zeus needed to back him up. Gaia *wasn't* to be messed with, indeed—but Zeus couldn't win against her and whatever her sordid plans were on his own. He'd have Hades, he'd have Poseidon and Ares, and possibly the judges if they were nearby and scented the violence in the air. But Gaia was who-knew how many times stronger and wiser than them, and had who-knew how many other allies hidden in the folds of her sleeves.

"Let's go," said Hecate, out loud this time, apparently deciding Gaia and her crew were far enough that she couldn't hear them—or wouldn't care to. "The hut—they're likely in there."

Persephone and Demeter didn't hesitate to follow Hecate, who didn't walk, but dashed around the marsh, hopping over mushy spots and weaving through shrubs as if she'd taken this path a million times and could use it with her eyes closed. Demeter was agile, but more used to dry lands of sunflowers and corn. And Persephone was a more passive goddess who, though she'd explored the swamp occasionally, rarely ran around it.

They didn't use any of the bridges—there was a shallow spot over *Lethe* that Hecate hopped over, and they hastened after her, paying close attention to where she put her feet, to avoid falling in. Of all rivers to take a swim in—including the fiery *Pyriphlegethon*—*Lethe* was a dangerous one, as its waters had properties that screwed with one's memories.

We've had enough of that for several lifetimes.

At the door, Hecate dug through her bag, likely in search of something to dismantle whatever charms Mnemosyne might have set up to prevent them from entering. But she frowned, scrunched her eyebrows, and approached her hand to the door.

"Hm," she said, touching the door with a flinch, then blinking at her hand, as if expecting it to burst into flames. "No protection? No warding? That's odd. She's cautious to lock doors when she's doing questionable things, usually."

"Too distracted," said Persephone, pushing past Hecate and kicking the door open, sick of wasting time. They needed answers, they needed them *yesterday,* and it was clearer and clearer that everything they'd need was inside this hut. She felt it deep in her bones, and had been feeling it since she'd noticed Mnemosyne's treks into the palace via not-so-secret stairs. This titaness had secrets and they'd be found inside her hut. "Or a trap; but it's too late to care. We're going in."

Persephone had never been inside the hut. She'd wandered past, she'd heard the noises—cackling or love-making most often—she'd sniffed out the wretched odor of vile potions, similar to how Hecate's lair smelled.

The place was small, cramped, and reeked of wet dirt and grass. The walls *were* dirt; as if someone had clumped mud together in a bucket and attempted to make sandcastles of it. This was no castle—it was a dump, and underwhelming for someone of Mnemosyne's standing.

A copper cauldron sat in the middle, still steaming, its aroma enticing—*too* enticing. Persephone shook her head at the sight of it; it surely contained the source of all their troubles, the stolen poison from Hecate that Gaia had been dosing gods with to fulfill her dark plans.

There was no furniture, no windows, little *real* oxygen. Yet there were bodies clustered here and there in corners, all seemingly breathing fine. Three women humped together on one end—Persephone recognized Aphrodite's silky, sexy nightwear almost immediately—and two other women sleeping soundly on the other side, along with a half-naked man slumped in a corner, drooling. *He* didn't look well off, compared to the others. There was a weird rhythm to his breaths, and snorting sounds that one might have thought were snores, but Persephone didn't think they were.

Hecate flurried over to the two slumbering women, muttering about mistreatment of titanesses as she checked their vital signs. From her flustered thoughts, Persephone understood the women were Phoebe—Hecate's grandmother—and Themis.

Demeter went straight to the Olympians—Athena and Hera were with Aphrodite, holding hands in their slumber.

Persephone went to the man, identifying him and his cluster of dark hair and his mostly naked body as Dionysus.

She hurried to tip his head up and make sure he was positioned to not choke. With all his excessive drinking and drug-indulgences, Persephone was used to finding him passed out in corridors in Olympus, and she'd recognized that slump of a massive, muscular body upon entering. But she'd also recognized the symptoms of an overdose—and she wouldn't have him in such danger when they'd only just located him.

Once assured he was safe, she rushed to her mother and Hecate, who were both busy ungagging and unbinding the Olympian goddesses. The poor women were pallid, drained of energy, their bodies like mush. They were dirtied, bruised, and stained, and looking worse for the wear—but they were alive.

What had Gaia done to them? Dragged them down here so they could watch her brew her toxins? Had she injected them? Had she *used* their blood for her perilous poison?

Even as Demeter sat them up against the muddy wall, and Hecate removed the tight vines around their wrists, none of the three reacted. They were in such a deep state of slumber that they had no clue they were being touched, rescued.

Persephone, Hecate, and Demeter crouched before the captured goddesses and let out a communal sigh. They were silent, exchanging glances, analyzing the women before them as if their wishes alone would wake them.

Persephone broke the silence first. "What in Tartarus is going on?"

|| 21. GROWLS FROM THE UNDERWORLD ||

ZEUS

Unfamiliar with the Underworld realm, Zeus wasn't able to teleport there. Not only did he have no clue how to access it—Hades refused to tell him—but there was also an unwritten law, a special spell weaved into the Underworld's bones, a proclamation that held jurisdiction over every single god and goddess, no matter their power level or status.

The Underworld is only accessible to those who have been invited and who know the way.

Unless teleporting *with* someone who dwelled in the Underworld—which Zeus declined to do, as it would drain the god doing the teleporting, and he couldn't have that right now—he'd have to enter through the Diamond Gates, via the tunnel underneath Lake Avernus, passing by the Acherusian Lake, and by taking Charon's ferry down the *Acheron*. The *proper* way.

Upon meeting Zeus, Ares, and Hermes in front of the lake, Poseidon hadn't been keen on the idea. He'd insisted on bypassing the rules, *"to Tartarus with your proper ways,"* and had demanded that they summon Hades to lift the restrictions and transport them inside with haste.

"We can't," said Zeus, narrowing his gaze on his brother, who'd come prepared in his full battle regalia—gleaming trident pointed towards the sky, a scaled suit of armor reflecting with prismatic colors of the rainbow, and his unruly hair tied behind his neck.

"Hades didn't set up the restrictions, Uncle," reminded Hermes, as he begged his father, brother, and uncle to turn around so he could work his magic to open the lake up. "To teleport all of you within his realm for the first time would take tremendous power that I'm sure he doesn't want to use up. Especially considering you're…well…" he gulped, "going to war?"

Zeus snapped, imagining his trickster son's scrunched features, his internal plea to know what they were up to and why he was allowing them into the Underworld. "We're going for *reconnaissance,* that's all. I have no plans to draw blood at this time."

He winced as he spoke. The sight of Poseidon's well-sharpened trident, and Ares' enormous sword glinting in the faint afternoon light reminded him that in truth, they had no idea when or if blood would be drawn.

With Gaia at the reins of this plot, who knows?

He himself had taken a few shots of pure ambrosia to re-energize, and had reinforced his staff, that he'd chosen to keep out of sight, for now. Poseidon and Ares thrived on appearing fierce, on instilling fear—Zeus preferred the element of surprise, and striking when one wasn't expecting it.

But *was* she expecting it? Did Gaia know he knew it was her? Had she figured out that *he'd* figured her out?

Hermes indicated that the passage was ready, and Zeus spun to find a set of downward stairs, leading under the lake. The air turned cold and stale, and Zeus nodded at Hermes once as he moved aside.

But when the young god made a move to follow them down the steps, Zeus thrust his arm out and stopped him. "No, Hermes. You're not coming with us."

The god's eyes flared with gold, with a spark of envy and curiosity. "But I thought…don't you need a guide? You have no idea where you're going."

"I don't," said Zeus, refraining from gulping, which would reveal how afraid he truly was, deep down. He couldn't show weakness, couldn't show any hint of his real emotions. "But Hades will find us, I imagine. He won't let us navigate his realm without assistance. I need you in Olympus," he gestured towards the forest in the background, "to help your siblings. Artemis and Apollo will need your cunning if anyone were to attack while we're gone."

The golden-haired god of tricks bowed his head, unable to disobey his father; but Zeus had a hunch he *might* end up down there spying on them, anyway.

Which might be for the best if we need reinforcements.

Without a word, Zeus, Poseidon, and Ares descended into the gloomy tunnel. Once they were all at the bottom of the steps, the lake closed up over them, a ceiling of murky water that seemed stopped by an invisible wall. Zeus squinted, and led the way down the obscure corridor leading to the Acherusian; a body of water he'd never seen for himself but had always ominously sensed the presence of. He'd had nightmares of it, of his family members floating along its borders, hauntingly wailing for access, that was denied to them. Visions of those he loved in ghost-form, their bodies mangled and slashed into, endlessly begging for a reprieve, desperate to be at peace after fighting the current threat to their kingdom. Those who wouldn't survive whatever war this was—and Zeus prayed it *wasn't* a war and could be averted.

At the end of the tunnel, a large lake welcomed them, its color a deep, matte navy color, and impossible to see through. Zeus imagined the substance was like tar, and wrinkled his nostrils as they walked around it, headed for a small wooden pier on its other side.

Two individuals awaited them—the ghostly, cloaked silhouette Zeus vaguely recognized as Charon; and the armored Hades, wielding his staff in their direction as if to urge them closer, faster.

Hades in battle gear was a sight to behold, and one Zeus hadn't been privy to in many, many years. Instead of his loosened off-black tunic, he wore a sleek, metallic bodysuit, tailored to fit his form perfectly, and slightly bulgier in the sensitive areas of the crotch, elbows, knees, ankles, and wrists. He, like Poseidon, had tied his hair back—which Zeus didn't recall *ever* seeing before—and inclined his head as they approached. Zeus hadn't changed into battle clothing, himself; he'd adorned a thicker robe that covered chest and thighs, but wore no helmet and no extra padding. Even Ares had geared up—then again, he was *always* geared up, as a god of war—and Zeus felt naked compared to them.

What part of reconnaissance don't they understand? Dressed like this, Gaia will sense an immediate threat and attack us, if she is indeed down here.

Charon's lifeless face went paler at the vision of Zeus, and he turned to Hades with an *"is this possible?"* kind of expression.

Hades chuckled. "This is big," he said, addressing Charon but glimpsing his brothers, who'd arrived near his realm for the first time in their lives. "Zeus and Poseidon, kings of other realms, visiting me. And Ares..." Hades scrutinized the youthful deity, taking in his plated armor and his clunky shield. "A fierce god of war, come to investigate the claims that something is amiss in my home."

"Enough pleasantries," said Poseidon, impatience rendering his voice deep and guttural. "Let us get there before she attacks *your* inhabitants."

That thought pressed Hades into action, and he ushered everyone onto the still shocked Charon's ferry. "Maximum speed, Charon," said Hades, low-voiced, cringing at Zeus. "We must hurry, as I'm sure you're aware there is evil lurking in our midst."

Though expressionless, Charon's eyes seemed to shift to a darker shade of black as he nodded, and drove his stick into the opaque waters of the *Acheron*. The bark took life, jolting forward a little faster than Zeus had anticipated. He steadied himself, feet firmly planted on the wooden floor. He regretted not summoning a staff to use to balance himself, like Poseidon was doing with his trident, and Ares with his sword.

Down, down they went; past gloomy pillars covered in a rotted moss, with rusted sconces holding flickering gray flames that barely illuminated the way. Shadows loomed, spirits howled in the background and up ahead, and Zeus could have sworn someone, *something* was watching them.

Poseidon brooded, staring ahead with ferocity, as if already envisioning Gaia and her posse there. Already preparing to apprehend her and demand that she explain herself. He'd been furious enough when Zeus had explained to him their mother might have been involved; but he'd caused another earthquake when finding out that Gaia was likely leading this rebellion.

"Has she not done enough? Standing by as her children invaded us centuries ago? Now she's wanting to do it again, but by taking their side? No." He'd roared and raged, and Zeus had had to strike him with

a thunderbolt to calm him down, and send him off to his kingdom to warn his wife what they were doing.

Now he was calmer, but still slick with fury. The hairs on his body were on edge, and he thrummed his trident to the surface in a rhythm Zeus didn't recognize, but had no doubt was a war-tune he'd hummed to back in the days of Troy.

Ares was also calm, but his thoughts were clouded with rage and worry. Rage at his ancestors—he usually revered Gaia, as they all did—and concern for his beloved Aphrodite, who'd been taken by her for reasons unknown. Zeus had tried not to seep into anyone's head since they'd departed Olympus, but Ares' thoughts were so strong, so *loud* it was impossible to avoid them. He wanted heads cut off and blood spilled and answers drawn *in* that blood, and he'd not stop his furious frenzy of ripping off limbs and slicing into chests until Aphrodite was safe.

Zeus himself had trouble being the tranquil, solemn deity he tried his best to portray. He was sickened, maddened, becoming claustrophobic from the walls on either side of the river and the sinister sense of danger impending ahead of them. He fidgeted, still unable to remain steady on his feet as the bark slid forward, creating ripples of waves near his feet. He'd have expected a sort of mist to come from the water, a spray of fishy air, of fresh sea and salt. But all he smelled was death and decay, bones rotting at the bottom of the river, and the odor of Charon's cloak that reminded him of an ashtray.

Eons, Zeus had been alive for; and not once had he needed to come to the Underworld. Not once had he *wanted* to, not even out of curiosity. He'd been told it was a nightmarish place where many became depressed and missed the light so much they'd die again to see it. A place where monsters were real and guarded the gates and snapped their fangs at anyone unwelcome. Where Cerberus, the mythical three-headed dog, ruled and roared whenever offended or threatened, and the entire realm rattled with the sound of his massive paws pounding onto the ground.

So far, Zeus sensed that this place was the opposite of Olympus, with its warm hearths and golden thresholds and happy paintings on the walls. He wasn't even *in* the Underworld yet, not technically, and he could already tell he'd be deprived of warmth down here. Everything was cold, dead or dying, and curdled his blood like nothing else ever had.

He exchanged a glance with Hades, who was stiff-backed but trying for a smile. "I know it's not magnificent like your home, but it's *my* home, and you are welcome here."

Despite his kindness, Zeus grimaced. There was a hint of panic in Hades' timbre, a trace of uncertainty in the rigidity of his posture. Surely he was undergoing thousands of irrational thoughts at once— he'd cloaked his mind from Zeus, from everyone, to protect himself— and it showed as he winced and bit his lip and squinted into the darkness ahead of them.

The Underworld, nightmarish as it was, was supposed to be a safe place. Far from outside threats, impossible to access without invitation or directions, and never, *ever* attacked by anyone. But now someone had snuck into its depths and was attacking it *from the inside.* Someone had infiltrated Hades' carefully crafted kingdom, dismantling it, seducing its inhabitants into disobedience.

Zeus was the best placed of all to understand Hades' concern, the evident panic he was trying so hard to conceal.

My realm was attacked, and now I must confront the attacker.

Zeus felt the gates before he saw them. A gush of *blocking* energy hit him square in the face and nearly knocked him backward. After recovering—Poseidon grabbed his arm to keep him from falling to his knees—he took notice of the grand, black barrier before them, studded with diamonds, its pointed tips reaching heavenwards, towards a navy sky sprinkled with fake stars.

It was impressive, almost as impressive as his own entry gate made of pure gold. It invoked the same awe, the same slight cease of the heart when gazing upon its thick surface, imagining how impossible it would be to breach it.

How *had* Gaia breached it? Even she couldn't outdo the magic that protected the Underworld, right? Had Mnemosyne been able to smuggle her in somehow, unbeknownst to Hades? Or, because she was a primordial goddess that predated the realm itself, was she simply able to appear within it and disappear from it as she pleased?

As the bark slowed down, arriving at a narrow pier where it would anchor and Charon would let them off, Zeus opened his mouth, meaning to ask Hades about Gaia's breach. But a sudden surge of powerful energy blew onto them, shoving them all backwards before they were able to disembark from the boat. Even Charon, with his stick deep into the waters, couldn't resist this blow and stumbled onto his butt with a croak coming from behind his chapped lips.

It was a mighty, *angry* energy; one that swelled inside Zeus and seemed to prod at his organs, at his soul, as if to deflate it and destroy it. It *hurt*. A deep, pungent pain that ripped through his gut and grabbed his intestines and squeezed.

Evidently, his brothers were feeling the same, crouched forward and moaning in agony. Ares had pulled up his shield in protection, but it didn't seem to be helping him much.

A growl pierced through the air—one that made all three siblings, plus Ares, peer towards the right side of the gates, where an enormous three-headed creature barked and clawed at the ground. Its shape towered over the top of the Diamond Gates, its shadow twice as long and reaching towards the *Acheron* as if to dip its toes in. Three sets of dagger-like talons ripped into the dirt, as if pawing at something underneath, buried far below. The heads tipped back, glaring up at the fake sky, and globs of saliva dripped from the colossal fangs protruding from all three mouths. It let out another ear-piercing bark before zoning in on the boat—and its riders.

Zeus immobilized, his gaze meeting those of the heads—gigantic yellow eyes riddled with red veins, wide and fixed on them. On *him.*

Hades slid in front of him, one hand raised. "It's not us he's growling at," he whispered through gritted teeth. "He smells something amiss."

"Yeah, *us,* " said Ares, getting to his feet and dusting himself off. "*We* are amiss, because we shouldn't be here. Isn't he supposed to obey your command, or something, Hades?"

"No," said Poseidon, who'd been able to get upright faster with the help of his trident. He aimed said trident towards the gates—they were moving. Creaking, opening up without Hades having asked them to. "There's something fucked up in there, I smell it." He nudged Zeus' arm. "Don't you? That blast of air, that gross feeling in your gut—you know what that is, right?"

Zeus swallowed, and on a whim, detecting a negativity he'd need extra strength for, he summoned his staff. Holding its cold surface in his clammy hand helped settle him, prepare him—because indeed, like Poseidon said, he knew what that scent was.

Betrayal.

The gates whooshed open, and a heavy smoke lingered in the

area, only showing four blurry figures, at first. Zeus didn't need to see them—their odors were familiar to him, as much as he hated it. Grassy moss, a delicate honey, a moisture-ridden jungle, and *humanity*.

And yet when the smoke cleared and he did see them, his heart did five back-flips in his ribcage, and he had to pinch himself to ensure this wasn't one of his nightmares.

There she was, in the flesh. Garbed in green, gloating, a sneering smile spread across her lips. Her fiery hair like bonfire exploding *from* her head, and her skin glowing a serpentine shade of earthly green.

Gaia. Why, why must you do this?

Before even breaching the gates, she zapped a thread of green energy mixed with vines in Cerberus' direction. The shot blasted into the three-headed monster's chest, silencing his growls, immobilizing him. In seconds, the overgrown pup crumbled to the ground with a massive *thud.* He was asleep.

Hades gasped, Poseidon blinked, Ares' jaw dropped.

How is that possible? I thought only Hades could subdue Cerberus?

At Gaia's side was the curly haired Mnemosyne, her gracious titaness silhouette appealing as ever, a sheer gold gown over her olive skin. Her eyes twinkled in delight at the sight of Zeus. Oh, she'd always loved taunting him, and the joy in her aura was powerful enough to reach Zeus and wrap around him. But he'd known she'd be there, and he'd been ready for her; her spells and sorcery would have no effect on him, not this time.

Hecate left me special charms to ward myself from her wiles, thank Olympus.

The sight that wounded him most was that of his mother, hunched forward and her gaze on the ground, like an embarrassed child being scolded by her scathing parents. She was wearing what he'd last seen her in, but her tunic was sullied, covered in blue and red stains, and riddled with mud.

The fourth being caught Zeus by surprise, to the point of pinching himself once more, to be sure he was seeing this clearly. He'd not mistake this bare-chested, chiseled man for anyone else, because he'd smelled him; and yet to envision him there, clearly siding with Gaia, was a stab to the heart.

"Lukus?" He squinted, witnessing the half-mortal walking slowly beside Gaia, his strides mechanical, as if controlled remotely. His eyes glowed green, and there was a matching green aura forming around him, enclosing around his body as if he were in a green-tinted bubble.

He growled—and it was then that Zeus realized that the growls they'd heard hadn't been from Cerberus at all. Cerberus' complaints had been faint compared to *these*.

These growls had come from Lukus, the demi-god son of Aphrodite, roped up and stuck in Gaia's schemes.

|| 22. ENOUGH TALKING ||
GAIA

To see the three Olympian kings all decked out in their fighting gear was a *pleasure*. One that woke the grandest of laughs in Gaia's chest. She certainly wouldn't hold in that laughter because they'd showed up with pitchforks and a swirl of fury.

As she stopped herself at the border of the Underworld, she noticed Zeus *wasn't* in armor as Poseidon, Ares, and Hades were. No, he'd retained one of his regular tunics, drab and gray, with little to no protection should he engage in combat. Had he come down here thinking to *talk?* To negotiate? Did he believe there *was* anything to talk about?

Sensing his master's emotions boiling, Lukus growled again; an earth-shattering roar that she'd have expected from Rhea, and yet it was Lukus letting it out, expressing Gaia's rage, her torment, her disappointment all in one piercing sound.

"Now, now, my pet," she said near his ear. "At my signal. Calm yourself for now."

Zeus' voice boomed through the mist and broke through the temporarily still air in the wake of Lukus' roars. "Gaia, will you explain yourself? What is the meaning of this?"

With a mocking curtsy, Gaia narrowed her gaze on her grandson.

"Of Lukus growling? Why, he's been bred to hate you. Bred to order his precious human minions to take you down and weaken you so I can seize you and lock you up, like you did to my darling children."

She hadn't meant to be so revealing in one sentence, and yet the energy brewing in her was uncontainable. She'd kept it in for too long, *much* too long, and it needed to be let out, to be given attention, and to be hurled at the person responsible for creating it.

Poseidon and Hades exchanged a glance behind Zeus' back. Zeus, who'd been holding a staff for balance—had the ferry trip unsettled him that much?—took one step forward.

"So that's what this is about?" He wasn't harboring the fear Gaia had hoped for; the worry that yes, once more, a war was being brought to his door and he needed to do something about it. Why was there no panic in his timbre? Why wasn't he shaking in fury, attacking before speaking, showing his cards too soon? "*Again?* Did we not agree on this? *I* didn't lock up all your children, Gaia. Your delightful husband helped."

Another growl echoed out through the smoky space, but it wasn't from Lukus, this time. It was from Gaia, gripping and scratching through the air, sharp like thorns and meant to slice.

"Do *not* bring my ex-husband into this," she said, seething, sensing her breaths getting out of control.

"*Mother, take it easy,*" said Mnemosyne, speaking into Gaia's mind, her hand an inch away from Gaia's and loading with a warm, soothing energy. They hadn't discussed this; they hadn't planned for a conversational confrontation with Zeus, and Gaia hadn't wanted one. She'd been ready for action, for attack, not for tea-time to converse about who did what and why. And certainly not to bring up her dreaded ex-spouse who'd been the source of a whole other set of problems.

"Did I agree to have my children locked up? Never. *You* had the power to release them; you were crowned king! And yet you did nothing for my children. *Nothing.* " She inhaled, exhaled, and absorbed some of Mnemosyne's relaxed energy. "I had no choice, no matter my dominance and my powers that have always been beyond yours. But the throne ascended to a *male*, didn't it? As always. Uranus," she gritted her teeth, dreading having to say his name out loud, "Cronus, Zeus…you and your cocks think to rule the world, but I have other ideas. Time for a new era."

Again, the other two siblings exchanged a glance. Ares continued to glare at her as if he had a single shot at stabbing at her with his cute little sword.

"So this *isn't* about your children," said Zeus, scratching his beard, unfazed as ever. He resembled the same Zeus who sat on his throne and listened to his wife's moaning or his daughter's bickering, and considered taking a vacation from it all. If he was afraid, if Gaia's presence had done anything to destabilize him, he was hiding it well. *Too* well. "It's about you wanting the throne, after all these years? Thinking it's owed to you, because at some point your husband sat on it and it should have gone to you after he was imprisoned?"

"Why isn't he shaking in his boots, like the humans say?" She dug into Mnemosyne's mind, begging her to activate her own power over Zeus—her seductive skills that always got him to crumble.

"Because he's processing, Mother. He's not sure he believes this is happening. I know that look." Mnemosyne jutted her chin at Zeus, who'd cocked his head and was still stroking his beard like a grandfather taking interest in a grandchild's new toy. *"He's putting up a front, but in reality he has no clue what to do. Keep talking—the more you tell him, the more off guard he'll be, and the easier it'll be*

to attack him."

Fists tightening at her sides, Gaia swallowed her disappointment at Zeus not cowering before her. He would, eventually. He had to.

"It's owed to me because *I* can do a better job than you ever have, Zeus." Controlling her voice, erasing the hints of hesitation from it, she sounded more menacing, and she smiled. "I'm more powerful, wiser, better versed in how the world works; I helped *create* it. You? You sit on your throne and dish out rules and play at being a king, and then think to come here and confront *me,* a true competitor for your crown, with your little posse of kings and warriors?" She snorted. "Let's see," she pointed at Poseidon, "a toxic drunk who prefers humans over his own wife?" She switched her gaze to Ares and refrained from snorting again. "An uncontrolled war beast who thirsts for blood but drops his drawers in private and rolls over at the snap of Aphrodite's fingers? And," she giggled at Hades lurking in the background, a dog with his tail between his legs, "the ruler of *this* realm, who can't seem to figure out what approach to take to defend it? Face it, Zeus. You and your team don't stand a chance against the truth."

None spoke at first, but Ares grumbled, taking a brave stride forward and thumping the hilt of his sword to his armored chest. "You poisoned my son. Kidnapped my lover, the Aphrodite you claim I bend over backwards for. You threatened my family, and you think we'll stand by idly and wait for you to *take* Father's throne? No. It doesn't work that way."

Gaia snickered at him. "*My* family. *Our* family, boy. You come here all gussied up and ready to fight, but *we* are family. I don't want to harm any of you, trust me when I tell you this. But he," she indicated Zeus, her arm trembling with rage as she lifted it, "has divided us all, and we need a new leader. If you wish to back him up, protect him, then I indeed am threatening you, darling."

Poseidon thrust the bottom of his trident to the ground, creating a few cracks that made their way to Gaia's feet, stopping before reaching her. "We do *not* need a new leader. Not in the sky, not in the waters, not down here. You are delusional."

"Delusional?" Gaia's eyebrows rose, and she felt Mnemosyne's touch again, preventing her from spiraling into a fit of shouting and throwing sharpened vines at Poseidon's pretty face. He *did* have a pretty face; one he paraded about all the realms and used to entice all manners of creatures to his bed, to birth more illegitimate children who caused chaos on earth. "Zeus has ruined this world, refusing to interfere in matters he *should* be involved in. Letting his moronic humans think for themselves? Detrimental. He shaped them in his image, but his image is *wretched*."

"Moronic humans?" Zeus rolled his shoulders and finally ceased caressing his beard as he fixed a stern, fatherly gaze on Gaia. "Yet you mentioned something about Lukus being in charge of some of them, of inviting them to *attack* me? Interesting."

Gaia scrunched her nose. Her fingers were twitching with power, refusing to accept Mnemosyne's calming vibes. She wanted to slap him, punch him, claw into his chest and rip out the heart she knew was within, and blackened with envy and vice. Zeus *wasn't* a good king; he never had been, never would be, and he needed to be punished for it.

"They're expendable, this lot," she said, waving a hand towards Lukus. "Once they've served their purpose, they'll be rewarded, and we'll continue purging through the population. And then I'll make *new* humans, better ones. These ones," she snarled towards the distance behind her opponents, to the entrance the zombies would likely come from, "they've destroyed nature. Infected the atmosphere with cruelty. Allowed evil monsters to rule over them, and forsaken the gods and their worship. They have other beliefs, or *no* beliefs at all, and it's weakening us, rendering us futile. Why would you let that happen? Why wouldn't you say something, *do* something, to stop your cherished humans from forgetting about you?"

She pressed her lips together as the images she'd captured to memory over the years flashed through her mind. The bloody, unnecessary wars, the religious contradictions and battles in the name of gods who'd long since left the earth, abandoned their worshipers. The corrupt politicians who, to her, were all the same and all made promises they never kept, leaving their people in despair and fighting one another for nonsense reasons. And the pollution, *the pollution* that no one seemed to know how to or to even *want* to stop.

Pain seared across her forehead. She crushed her teeth together to avoid screaming out at the sensation, at how it burned, it exploded, it poked into her scalp and prodded her to need to move forward, to start tearing into Zeus' face and ripping it off until she no longer had to witness his smug *"I am the king by birth"* expression.

Zeus' silence—he appeared to be ruminating over her words, deciding how to address them—further worked Gaia up. "I will bring back our worship. I will re-install a proper way of this. My children and I will bring back order and fix the mess you made, once and for all."

Those words were enough to wake something in Zeus; a speck of anger, of actual emotion, breached through his cautious facade, and he frowned. A flicker of electricity shot down his arm and his veins flashed a deep, navy blue.

"Your *children* are what started all the messes, Gaia, not me. They are the reason I can't interfere! I did interfere once, remember? I tried to when they invaded my home." He took a breath, and it came out as a whirl of smoke from his nostrils. "I enlisted heroes and half-humans in the battle, and some prevailed, and some were lost, and I wouldn't lose anymore. To protect them, to defend *all* humans, it was best to not get them involved with anything godly. To preserve them from your *children,* who are volatile and dangerous."

Gaia's legs prepared to launch her forward, but again Mnemosyne prevailed in halting her physical progress. *"Not yet. A few more words, Mother. He's close to being too riled up to be a proper fighter."*

Gaia grumbled under her breath. "Volatile and dangerous? Look who's talking." *He* was the dangerous one, refusing to aid his humans yet bedding them on any occasion, the instant his wife's back was turned.

Granted, he has been good the past few centuries, but who's to say he won't go rogue again?

Zeus ignored her smite as he made his staff vanish and more pulses of electricity swerved up from his wrist to his shoulders. "You think to unleash a handful of pissed-off Titans, a few stir-crazy Giants, and several seriously delirious monsters and *controlling* them? Enlisting them into *fixing* this world I've supposedly destroyed?" He shook his head, his arms tensing at his sides. "What has gotten into you?"

"Revenge. Rage." Gaia didn't miss a beat; Mnemosyne was right, and now was the time to trigger Zeus, to get him so infuriated he had no command over himself. He'd shoot himself up with too much energy and use it poorly, and then Gaia could strike. "Pure, unadulterated rage, my dear grandson. It's been building up, and at this point none of you can stop me. I have allies waiting to be unleashed, I have an army of poisoned humans, and I have a direct descendant under my control." She patted Lukus' arm, and he startled out of his silent stupor, as if sensing she was about to activate him, his power.

Poseidon again thrummed his trident to the ground, harder this time. The cracks reached Gaia and traveled under her, provoking the earth into shaking, coming close to tearing apart. She bared her teeth at him—his temperamental earthquakes had been so destructive through time that she'd more than once considered invading *his* realm first, and taking him to the depths of Tartarus where his destruction would have no effect.

"Enough talking, Brother," he said, a puddle of water gathering at his feet, swirling around him to form a tornado of liquid, a barrier of waves that he'd launch onto Gaia at the earliest opportunity.

Ares' helmet took shape over his head and he raised his sword, angled at Gaia and her crew. "Uncle Poseidon is right, Father. Words will do nothing here."

Zeus pinched the bridge of his nose and looked down at his feet. "This isn't right. I didn't come here to fight, I came to *understand*. This shouldn't be happening." Despite the evident reluctance in his stance, in his voice, he let loose a few more jolts of electricity as he slowly raised his chin and glowered at Gaia. "Why must you do this?"

Gaia paid him no heed, her concentration on Hades; the brother she'd always secretly pegged as the smartest of the three. He'd kept out of their affairs, had remained loyal to his wife, and he *had* gotten involved with human issues occasionally, showing there was a chance that *someone* in the family might have some logic.

And yet to her detriment, he stopped sulking in the background and joined his brothers, sidling between Zeus and Ares. "I'm not keen on this either, but she's not going to concede with a simple discussion. She wants vengeance, Zeus. And she knows she'll only get it with your head on a platter." He summoned his own weapon. He had a few, but Gaia knew he preferred to take on bigger battles with his silver glaive, which he did now. He stood firm beside his siblings and nephew. "We will not let you cause more disruption in the realms, Gaia."

Though chagrined by Hades' decision to join in on the fight—she'd counted on him wishing to sit things out—Gaia let out a cackle and snapped her fingers near Lukus' ear. "It's time, my pet."

Lukus tipped his head back and howled up into the fake sky. His skin glowed greener, and vines wrapped around his arms and legs as if growing from within him, and infusing him with power. It was the call to his army. Soon, a horde of zombified, poisoned humans would spill into the Underworld and throw themselves onto Zeus and bite into his flesh until he conceded.

Or dies, whichever method he chooses to abdicate is fine by me.

Rhea released a growl of her own and barreled forward, while Mnemosyne enveloped herself in gold and violet vibrations that twinged from her fingertips and ignited the ends of her hair. She hovered a few inches off the ground and followed Rhea.

Gaia charged her own power, and green jets of sharp leaves and pointy twigs erupted from her hands, weaving around her arms and legs, whirling up around her like a barricade of branches to protect her from attacks.

They were ready, she was ready. It was time to take what was hers.

|| 23. DAUGHTER OF URANUS ||

PERSEPHONE

A heavy, negatively leaning energy swept into the hut as Persephone, Hecate, and Demeter worked to revive the Olympian goddesses from their comatose-like slumbers. A skin-chilling sensation that all three had no doubt was linked to rising tension and deepening anger.

Had Gaia reached the gates to be confronted by Zeus and his brothers?

Zeus and Poseidon, in the Underworld—how the world has changed.

While Persephone unfastened the binds of vines around the goddesses' wrists and ankles, Hecate was rummaging through her bag of potions and charms, grumbling to herself as she threw bottle after bottle onto the ground, never finding the right concoction to reanimate them. They'd all agreed that the Olympians were a priority, that these three women would need to awaken quickly, especially Athena; a goddess of wisdom and war who'd need to be at her father's side as he confronted Gaia.

The confrontation was nigh, Persephone could tell. The atmosphere had shifted in the minutes since Gaia had exited the hut with her group. An air thick with betrayal and distrust had settled over the already uncomfortable aura often felt in the Underworld. The aura of something crawling up and down one's spine, something tickling at the hairs on one's neck, a vague feeling that *someone* was following you. It had grown worse, and Persephone wished she'd stayed in the security of the palace. But she'd been given tasks by the king, her father, and her mother needed her.

Demeter was working to weave Eleusinian spells, hoping they'd help in waking the goddesses. But the three remained groggy, as those mysterious spells were mostly meant to *put* to sleep, not awaken. Demeter's combinations of words were well chosen, Persephone thought; but against whatever poisons Gaia and Mnemosyne had used, they weren't powerful enough.

Hecate had finally located what she was looking for—a large vial of something viscous and violet in shade—along with a smaller, half-filled vial of a clear liquid that she set onto the floor. The violet tincture she hurried to slide down the goddesses' throats, with Demeter's help in getting their mouths open. Persephone watched, unsure what more to do to assist, but as a slither of the purple potion trickled down Athena's chin, she rushed to wipe it off with her sleeve.

"It's not the best option, and it may take a moment for them to wake," said Hecate, sneering at the now empty vial that she'd tossed to the ground, joining the other concoctions she'd discarded. "I'm better at the darker spells. This is something more on Apollo's level, but I don't have time to teleport to Olympus and fetch him. This'll have to do for now."

"And that?" Persephone pointed at the other vial, with the transparent liquid. It smelled familiar, but its contents were sealed quite tight, and Persephone couldn't put a finger on what it might have contained.

Demeter took one look at it and frowned. "Ambrosia?"

"Pure and undiluted," said Hecate with a brief nod. "I usually have more on hand, because you never know when a god is going to need a supercharge, but…well, like most of the other ingredients, my reserves were taken. I luckily found this at the very back of the cabinet, gathering dust. It's a single dose."

Persephone glanced at the Olympian goddesses, slowly wriggling about, coming to their senses; then at her mother, whose frown deepened. Had she known, with one look, that the measure of ambrosia wouldn't be enough for the three of them?

"We could split it, but it'd do no good in this situation," said Demeter, rubbing the bridge of her nose, setting her gaze on her sister and nieces. "We could give the full dose to one of them, but who?"

Persephone crossed her arms, studying them all. Wasn't it obvious? "Athena, right?" Demeter and Hecate peered at her, eyebrows raising. "She'll need to hurry to Zeus, help him out. He's here, I can feel it. And Gaia is pissed, we can *all* feel that. The sooner Athena is up and on her feet and ready to fight, the better."

Hecate opened her mouth to reply, but it wasn't her voice that shocked through the room—it was Athena herself, sounding dazed, like a croak cracking through the semi-darkness.

"No," she said, lifting her arm as her audience turned to look at her. "Give it to Aphrodite."

Hecate's jaw dropped, and Demeter kneeled down to swipe a hand over Athena's forehead. "Are you all right?"

Hera, beside Athena, stirred awake as well, but kept her eyes closed. "Agreed. Aphrodite should get the dose."

Hecate now lowered to Hera's level, inspecting her clammy skin. "Is this some kind of joke? Are you two hallucinating?"

A side-glance at Aphrodite showed she'd not awoken yet—or was faking it, dramatic as usual, wishing to be the last to rise and stun them all with her beauty despite having been knocked out. Persephone chose instead to focus on Hera, whose eyes were now open— reddened, glossy, but concentrating on Demeter.

"Her demi-god son is under Gaia's control," she said, her voice not as raspy as Athena's, somehow more composed considering she'd been attacked, drunk from—Persephone noticed slight scars on her neck—and put to sleep. "Lukus—Gaia's got him working for her, and that cannot be, and Aphrodite has to be the one to fix that."

"Right." Demeter moved from Athena to her sister. "We heard that he's Aphrodite's son, indeed. I had no clue *you* knew, though."

"Gaia told us. Aphrodite and I… and I was the one who delivered the news to Lukus, and he panicked. Naturally. I'd have had a fit if I'd found out my whole life was a lie, and my mother was *her.*" Hera directed her gaze towards the supposedly still sleeping goddess of beauty. "So I get it."

"We assumed he was under Gaia's control, as they left the hut, and he was… green. Glowing green." Hecate gulped. Considering her age and all she'd seen in her lengthy life, to see her so uncomfortable made Persephone uncomfortable, too. "But why would she seek to control a half-human? Has he come into his powers? Does he have some ability she finds useful to taking down Zeus? As I presume that's what she wants, yes?"

Hera and Athena nodded, but it was Hera who spoke, as Athena cracked her neck and knuckles, regaining her mobility. "She gagged us, but kept us awake for enough time for us to listen to all her plans. Yes, she wants Zeus—alive and locked up, or dead and in a ditch, cut up to pieces, if she has it her way. She wants him gone, and wants her children released from Tartarus, and wants to repopulate the planet because Zeus did it wrong and Zeus is a *man* and—"

Demeter swore under her breath. "I knew it. She stood back and watched when the Titans and the Giants attacked, but this time she's actively participating."

"She's the commander-in-chief," said Athena, in a hoarse whisper. "The head of operations. She's been plotting this for *centuries*. Lukus is a pawn, but one she created via Aphrodite and set up on her chessboard as a general to an army of zombie humans. Those Psyche poisoned? They were never cured; they're lurking and waiting for Lukus' signal to attack Zeus."

Persephone clapped a hand over her mouth, and Hecate fell to the ground with a groan.

Athena scratched at her forehead. "She has so many fail safes in place that I doubt she hasn't anticipated every single move Zeus might plan. And of course, she'd expect me to somehow free myself and go to him, to help. Which is why I can't go."

"It must be Aphrodite." Hera nudged Athena, who nudged Aphrodite, who remained asleep, head lolling to the side.

She's faking it, isn't she? Waiting for us to sing her praises so she can wake and smile and go off to be a savior, for once?

Hera glanced at Hecate, then at the untouched vial on the floor. "As Lukus' mother, she has a direct blood bond. She can sway him, and he *needs* to be swayed, as he's a powerful weapon for Gaia. But he will be more powerful once out of her spell and used against her."

"And remember," said Athena, her normal, neutral voice returning to her. "Aphrodite is much stronger than she lets on, as a direct descendant of Uranus."

The name sent a cascade of chills down Persephone's back, and it apparently did something to Hecate, too. She leapt to her feet and clapped once.

"*Uranus,*" she snarled, "of course. Gaia is estranged from him, she hates him. Was she planning to let him out, too?"

Athena and Hera shook their heads violently. "Certainly not," said the former, blowing a lock of dark hair from her face. "She's enraged at him; she'd never release him. And has no plans to let out Cronus, either. Only her *good kids,*" Athena used air-quotes, "and whatever monsters survived past wars and are locked up in Tartarus purging for their crimes."

Hecate's snarl transformed into a smirk. "Aphrodite is Uranus' pure daughter. Made from him alone, crafted without a mother. Without Gaia." She tapped a finger to her chin. "If she were to be overpowered and to fight at Zeus' side, and to snatch Lukus from Gaia's control...oh, Gaia will be put off balance, for sure. You two," she pointed at Athena and Hera, "are brilliant."

"Nothing to do with brilliance," said Athena, with a weak smile. "We know that Aphrodite and her stubborn self can convince Lukus to use his powers for good. To snap him out of his trance and come to the light. He'll have immense power, I can tell. I could smell it on him, while he slept on *that* altar." She signaled towards a block of stone in the middle of the room. "And more so as he woke and began obeying Gaia's orders."

"He and my husband and my brothers are the only ones who can confront Gaia. She has more power than them, but with their cunning, their skills, and *two* descendants of Uranus up against her...it'll take her off guard, and she'll make mistakes. They'll be able to corner her, and hopefully, lock her up."

At long last, and in dramatic fashion, as Persephone had

predicted, Aphrodite woke with a yawn and a seductive stretch of her arms and legs. Like a feline awakening from a long nap and licking its lips in anticipation of a tasty breakfast.

"What—" she startled at the sight of Demeter, Persephone, and Hecate, who all stared at her in disbelief, "—we're *saved?*" She continued to stretch out, languorous, as if she hadn't been a captive of a rage-induced primordial goddess for most of the day.

Athena snorted. "*We* are saved—you have work to do."

Hecate fetched the vial and handed it to her, no preamble or explanations forthcoming. "Drink this."

Not one to deny a drink of any kind, Aphrodite took the vial, sniffing at it. "Is this what I think it is?"

Hera leaned over Athena and shoved the thing closer to Aphrodite's pouty mouth. "It is, and you need it, now. Gaia and Lukus—they must be stopped, and as Lukus' mother, you're the best placed to do so. You have to go save him from her wrath, Aphrodite. You have to go save *us.*"

Though she hesitated, Aphrodite uncorked the vial and took a deep breath. "I'm not allowed to drink this, per Zeus' orders. It'll make me more powerful than him." She peeked into the container, eyes sparkling with curiosity. "I haven't drank it in centuries."

Demeter lurched forward and pressed a fingertip to the bottom of the vial, shoving it closer to Aphrodite's lips. "He'll understand and forgive you for this, I swear it. Now *drink.*"

Time stopped as Aphrodite slurped up the magical liquid of the gods. At once, thick veins populated all over her exposed skin, flashing gold as the substance shot into every cavity of her being. Her muscles bulged, throbbing as they drank in the ambrosia. She shivered, absorbing the shock of the new energy infusing into her, then jumped to her feet with a force that knocked all those kneeled near her backwards, including Persephone, whose back slammed into the altar.

But she watched in awe as Aphrodite, goddess of beauty, daughter of Uranus, stood tall and spread her arms and wiggled her fingertips, showing how they radiated with energy and firepower.

Persephone had witnessed gods taking pure ambrosia before, and it was always an experience of wonder and envy, a vision of power and one's engorging of it. But this was different. There was something *more* about Aphrodite, an excess one might have attributed to her usual theatrics, and yet Persephone could tell she wasn't controlling it. There was a burst of strength, loaded with a fury that didn't match Aphrodite's aura. It jolted up from her feet to the tips of her hair, making the blond tresses seem to twitch with electricity.

"It's...*him,*" said Aphrodite, her voice strangely softer than how Persephone had anticipated it to be, now that she'd taken the ambrosia and charged up. "Uranus—his blood in my veins...makes me even stronger."

"I *told* you," whispered Athena, her chin lightly dipping towards the ground; she looked befuddled by Aphrodite's increasing power levels.

"She's basically primordial, at this point," suggested Hecate, her face illuminated by the glow emanating from Aphrodite's body. She grinned and rubbed her hands together. "This is even better than I expected. With her," she beamed at Persephone, then at Demeter, "we might have a chance of winning."

Persephone wanted to beam back, but a pit in her stomach told her to not hope. Gaia had Mnemosyne, a titaness, and Rhea, another titaness, at her side. Until Aphrodite could reach him, she had Lukus, too, and a butt-load of bloodthirsty humans, according to Hera. She likely had contacts in Tartarus, who'd open the gates to the prison and release her monstrous children if she felt she was losing the battle. And, knowing Gaia, there had to be more of her friends hiding in wait for the cue to come launch themselves on Zeus.

All Persephone and her team had was Zeus himself, Poseidon, Hades, Ares, and soon, a supercharged Aphrodite. Would it be enough? Would they be able to thwart Gaia's desires to overthrow her grandson and steal the throne reserved for him for eons?

"Go," said Athena, wobbly as she got to her feet, aided by Hera. "The king needs your help. I sense he's here, he's arrived, and Gaia will not wait long to start throwing her vines at him. We'll follow shortly."

With a cheeky grin and a nod, Aphrodite zoomed out of the hut, leaving the muddy walls to rattle in her wake. Persephone zipped her mouth shut and prayed to any benevolent god in the vicinity that *her* team might win.

|| 24. EXHAUSTED ||

ZEUS

Between dodging Gaia's jets of sharp leaves and plunging beneath Mnemosyne's strikes of purple electricity, Zeus was breathless—and they'd only been at it for ten minutes, possibly less.

It had dawned on him the instant everyone started charging up their powers; he was understaffed for this task. Poseidon's power of the ocean was strong, but Rhea, roaring like the lioness she contained inside, was infused with Gaia's extra-special poison, and it radiated off her in toxic waves that made the king of the sea struggle to concentrate. He jabbed at her with his trident, but was unable to hit his mark—and he was hesitant to do so as she was, of all things, his own mother.

Mnemosyne, who was facing off with Ares, had most definitely given herself some sort of boost, as she was electric, loaded with energy that even Ares' shield had difficulty blocking. He was unharmed, and had managed to slice a few scrapes into Mnemosyne's arms. But she was undeterred in her attempts to destabilize him, continuously shooting her rage at him in streaks of vicious violet.

Gaia hurled her vines at Zeus, who blocked them with his thunderbolts—but he sensed his strength depleting slowly with every usage of his heavenly ability. Every thunderbolt felt smaller, weaker as he conjured it, and his reflexes were so borderline compared to

Gaia's, he feared one of her thorns would soon find its target—his heart.

Or my neck, since she keeps staring at it as if she wants to tear through it.

He'd never known Gaia to be docile, but her demeanor in this battle was beyond anything he'd ever seen before. She was wrathful, a rabid dog with teeth so sharp and so stained with poison that he smelled her toxicity from the dozens of feet that separated them. She grew closer every few minutes, gaining on him. And the more he moved backwards, the nearer he was to falling into the *Acheron*, looming spookily behind him. The smoke wafting off its waters were like a veil he'd much rather be hiding behind instead of facing *this*.

Hades swept from opponent to opponent, attempting to offer his assistance; but Lukus followed him like a puppy, a monstrous one, out for his head. Gaia had ordered him to block the god of the Underworld, who was tackling the task of sealing off all entrances. Lukus wouldn't attack Zeus alone, and waited for his army—and it was coming, Zeus could hear it. Even through the grunts of Ares and the whoosh of his sword as he swung it through the air; even underneath Mnemosyne's out of place war cries and Poseidon's hefty earth-shakes, Zeus *could hear it*. The distant drumming of heavy footsteps, feet on pavement, marching. Soldiers coming to assist their leader, and to dismantle Zeus from limb to limb.

Zeus wasn't afraid of humans. He'd created them, knew every little fiber that composed them. Knew what made them tick, what made them happy, what prompted them into rebellion. But these weren't humans, not really; they were disastrous creatures loaded with raw animal flesh and inhaling waves of purple and green poison that continued to infest their lungs, their hearts, their brains. They were *zombies*—except their end goal wasn't to eat brains, but to devour Zeus in his entirety. Skin, bones, organs—they'd take it all until there was nothing left but an immortal soul, floating before them, waiting for entry into the Underworld.

But he wouldn't be granted entry. If he were to die, Gaia would make certain that he'd never gain access to any eternal resting place. Not the Elysian Fields, not Asphodel Meadows, not even the dreaded Mourning Fields. He'd be sentenced to wail and beg for mercy until the end of times.

If Gaia won this, it *would* be the end of times. He only wished she'd snap out of her voracious trance and understand that.

But there was no getting through to her, not when she was like this. He couldn't tell if it was the toxins in her veins—he smelled them more as she approached him—or if her fury with him had developed sooner, without the effects of whatever she'd ingested. She'd been angry with him for centuries, but he'd hoped, *prayed,* she'd calmed down. That she'd moved on to bigger things—such as all the pollution she was so furious about. Global warming, corrupt politicians, civilizations dying out; weren't those more important?

He'd never told her *not* to interfere with that; he'd only asked that his subjects not directly interfere with human's lives. Had she misinterpreted his meaning? Or had she found no means to solve the pollution problem without direct interference?

Why had she opted to plot behind his back for centuries, instead of coming to him to discuss things like rational gods? They might have taken tea in one of the courtyards, or settled in Zeus' private office with some ambrosia liquor and some biscuits, and conversed over what was irking Gaia, and how he might be able to fix it. He'd never release her children—that was and always would be out of the question—but he'd have considered offering her some guidance on how to approach the worldwide issues that mattered to her.

No, she'd chosen violence. She'd chosen to stew in her fury for eons and raise up an army in rebellion against her king, instead of requesting an audience with her grandson. *Her grandson.*

I'm her damn kin, and this is how she decides to confront me? With death?

He didn't want to fight, but he didn't want to die, either. Hopping left to right, steering clear of her attacks, he sensed pain flaring in his calf muscles and his heart started thumping out of control. Immortal and incredibly powerful as he was, he'd grown old, stiffer than he'd been during his last massive battle. His back was sore, and he'd worn the wrong kind of shoes. He grunted, realizing he should have followed his brothers' and son's lead by gearing up for war instead of a negotiation. His wrists were throbbing from incessantly flinging thunder at his grandmother.

Gaia, however, looked replenished, refreshed, not a hint of her true age showing on her face. She'd always opted for a youthful appearance, looking like a twenty-something maiden straight out of a jungle of vines, and not the billion-or-so-year-old primordial deity that she was inside. Her body was strong, firm, not seeming tired in the slightest or ready to give up.

Zeus gulped, bending down in time to avoid one of her whipping vines before it slashed across his forehead. That one might have ripped *off* his forehead, he thought, from the sound it made as she yanked it back to her, and wound it around, preparing to throw it at him once more.

His brothers weren't faring so well, either. Both were depleting, their weapons still gleaming under the fake stars, but their movements choppy, broken. Poseidon's grip on his trident was slipping, and his earthquakes were wearing off, no longer as hard to keep upright for. Hades' glaive couldn't stave off Lukus, who bared his green-glowing fangs, snapping at him, causing him to retreat farther every time.

Ares was the only one managing to keep up, but his shield looked worse for the wear, and Zeus wondered if he'd brought another one with him. Or if he'd be able to maybe summon one of Athena's? Hers were enchanted with the skin of some of Gaia's children, and Gaia would take that as a slight; but such a sight might also destabilize her.

Zeus shook his head as he swerved to avoid a vagrant jolt of Mnemosyne's electricity. Her streams of electric power were now laced with gold, and she continued to hover above the ground, whispering sinister incantations as she flew side to side to evade Ares' sword pointed at her.

If one side didn't cave soon, neither would, and they'd all be too exhausted. Gaia would take advantage of that exhaustion, wouldn't she? That'd be when she'd call her sons from Tartarus to strike, and Zeus wouldn't be able to wave a white flag—she'd cut off the hand he'd need to use for that.

The march was closer. Zeus caught the scent of human blood tinged with toxins, nearing their battlefield. He wasn't positive which entrance they'd come from—it was quite possible they'd been waiting in front of several of them—and didn't know where to look. But he also didn't *want* to look away because a single second of inattention would give Gaia an advantage.

He loved his throne, he loved his crown—but were they worth his death, and the death of those he loved? If he abdicated now, would that save them all? He couldn't imagine doing anything other than ruling over this planet and its inhabitants; a position he'd earned but had also been gifted, and one he'd fought to keep for eons. Every other invasion into his territory, he'd not only survived, but succeeded in repelling those who'd rebelled. But today, he wasn't *in* his territory, was he? He was somewhere in between—a place not quite belonging to any of them, though adjacent to Hades' realm. The gloomy pathway to the Underworld was, in truth, no man's land.

Which meant this place held power for Gaia. Any area on earth that wasn't his, or Poseidon's, or Hades', was hers, by right. She was a goddess of the earth, *the* goddess of the earth, and technically, everything belonged to her. She'd discarded a majority of her rights when her husband, Uranus, had been crowned king, then Cronus after him. Then Zeus.

Zeus was paying the price for both deities and their cruelty. He was being accused of acting *like* them, which caused him to grimace as he hurled two hefty thunderbolts right at Gaia's face, while she was rounding up her whip. He'd hoped to catch her unawares, but she slung the whip at both bolts, hacking them in half, sucking the energy from them. The vine-whip absorbed the thunder as if drinking it up, and electricity slithered up and down the thick brown branch, coating it.

Great, now she has electricity, too?

He was the longest reigning king of Olympus, but his reign was at an end, he felt it. He had the taste of failure on his tongue—bitter, copper like human blood, sourly sweet like ichor. Or perhaps his mouth was bleeding, he couldn't tell. Surely several of Gaia's attacks had breached through and hurt him, but he was so numb he wasn't sure he experienced physical pain.

I love my role. I love my humans. But I can't do this anymore.

He was breathless, nearly tripping over himself as he leapt up before another of Gaia's vines knocked him over. He panted, unsure how to protect those he loved if he was dead, and at this rate—with him heaving out heavy breaths and Gaia barely batting an eyelash—he had no doubt she could and would kill him at any moment.

If he were to surrender now, he'd not only save his brothers, his wife, his children, but he'd stay alive. She'd lock him up in Tartarus, of course; but he was *Zeus*, for Olympus' sake, and he'd find a way out, even if it took centuries. Granted, he was responsible for many of the creatures in there being locked up, too, but he had a way about him, a charm many couldn't resist. He'd find allies, and he'd get out and take back what was his.

But first, he needed to give up this fight.

He was seconds away from dropping to his knees and raising his arms in surrender, when a deadly, hoarse voice crept into his mind.

"You'd dare give up now, you coward?" It was Poseidon, who'd crept up to his side, snarling at him. Zeus had forgotten he'd deactivated the cloak on his mind to allow his siblings access to his thoughts. *"You'd throw your crown at her feet and move on as if she hadn't defied you one time too many? No, Brother. Absolutely not. You will not abdicate. And you will not die. She'll come for us, next, if you fall. Don't think that your surrender will cease any of this, it'll only make it worse."*

Zeus snorted at his brother's rare optimism. Poseidon was as exhausted, if not more, from thwarting Rhea's claws and wincing from her ear-piercing roars. She'd dug her talons deep into his arm, and he was bleeding profusely, but ignoring the blue liquid spilling from him. Rhea, meanwhile, had backed away to lick at those talons and guzzle up his blood—and smacked her lips in satisfaction.

"There's no way out of Tartarus," spoke Hades, his voice distant, and choked with breathlessness. Zeus caught him from the

corner of his eye, still running from the never-fatigued Lukus, whose eyes were wide and green with hunger. Why he was so focused on Hades, Zeus wasn't sure; a trick of some kind, likely to get Zeus to lower his guard. *"No one has ever escaped from there. Should you concede, you're as good as dead. Might as well keep going."*

"We do not give up!" Ares' thunderous timbre, if Zeus ever heard one, blasted into his mind, making him cringe. *"I will send for reinforcements right now. The Amazons can be here in minutes. And I have a few offspring living down here, in case you forgot. This battle isn't lost, Father."* He shot up in the air to dodge Mnemosyne's gold and violet flash of light, then landed, crouched, with such power that the ground shook beneath him. *"You're defeated, I understand, but we aren't done here. Gather yourselves, and get back to work!"*

Poseidon raced straight at Rhea, aiming the points of his trident at her belly. Zeus gasped, anticipating her skin to be torn into; but she slid sideways with precision and instead jammed an elbow hard into Poseidon's side, throwing him off balance.

Hades was still trying to shake off Lukus, who'd managed to hop onto his back and was seeking to bite at his neck.

The only one still actively on top of his own fight, with Mnemosyne, was Ares.

Zeus growled at Gaia. "Take your damn children, you senseless old crone," he said under his breath, though certain she had no trouble listening to his words. "Take them, and try to fix this world if you can. You think I failed?" He tossed more thunder at her, which she skillfully avoided, looking like a ballerina attempting the easiest of jumps across a light-ridden stage. "You have no idea how difficult this planet is to watch over!"

Gaia, sure enough, heard all of it, and though she slowed her attacks, she didn't lessen the animated rage in her aura. "Of course it's difficult for you; you're a *male*. You cannot multitask, you cannot think with anything other than your cock! Yes, you failed, and I *will* rectify your mistakes. You can thank me later."

Though his blood boiled at her taunts, and the urge to rip her apart tore through him, making him grit his teeth and hold in a scream of horror, he held his ground, summoned his staff, and aimed it at her.

"I've had enough of your nonsense, Gaia. I ask you now to cease this and discuss things with me like a loyal goddess, like a *female* with multitasking abilities and who doesn't have a cock." He snickered. "Would you consider pausing this insanity to at least *talk* to me?"

Gaia didn't talk—she cackled, and with a *whoosh*, hefted her vines into the air, directed at his forehead.

This time, Zeus didn't duck.

|| 25. A MOTHER & DAUGHTER ON A STROLL ||

PERSEPHONE

After Aphrodite had hurried out, it was agreed upon that Persephone and Demeter would follow her, to ensure she reached her destination—wherever the battle was taking place. Hecate believed Athena and Hera needed a bit more nurturing—which prompted Athena to wrinkle her nostrils and recoil, but Hecate insisted. She'd stay behind and join them as soon as the goddesses were up to par.

"But Zeus might need you." Hecate patted Demeter's arm. "And Hades will most certainly need *you.*" She caressed Persephone's cheek. "So go, both of you. We'll catch up."

Reluctantly—Persephone still smelled a tinge of betrayal in the air, and much too close for comfort—they left Hecate to tend to the queen of the skies and Zeus' favorite daughter while they went in pursuit of the overpowered Aphrodite.

Once outside, a chill that had nothing to do with the dramatic drop in temperature coursed along Persephone's arm, curling its hairs, populating goosebumps. Something was definitely amiss, but the dreary sensation of it wasn't coming from the hut, or the palace, or its environs—it was coming from behind the gates. Persephone and Demeter both looked toward them at the same time, sighting a large onrush of smoke and blares of colored lights, akin to energies and powers being hurled around in the near-dark.

A battle. It's happening, already.

"Hurry," said Persephone, swallowing a glob of fear for her husband, who was likely in the thick of it. He didn't like fighting, and less so with anyone he considered family. Gaia, despite her tantrums, *was* family. The matriarch, the creator, a revered figure of their genealogy—and she was in a rage, throwing a fit over a throne.

On the way, they didn't creep around. There was no need to be hidden or secretive, as Gaia and Mnemosyne were much too busy angling attacks at Zeus and his posse to care that Persephone and Hecate had brought a distraught but slightly curious Demeter to the Underworld.

Demeter's dress was soiled at the bottom, as she kept veering off the path and wading through weeds and dirt, kneeling down to check on crops that were, to her detriment, long dead. "Is *anything* alive down here?"

Persephone smiled—despite their urgency, despite the war being waged yards ahead of them, Demeter couldn't help but be entranced by anything plant or crop-related, and had to slow her pace to check on the status of a patch of wilting flowers. Persephone had gone through that phase, too, millennia ago when she'd first become a resident of the Underworld. The stale scent—sometimes a lack of a scent altogether—and the dreadful darkness soon became comforting, though. And even the fake stars overhead were lovely to look at, if one ignored the fact that they weren't real. Hades had enchanted them to appear as realistic as possible, but if one were to use a telescope and zoom in…one would see the truth.

"Mother," said Persephone, urging Demeter back onto the path.

"We must go. I promise, if we survive this, I'll see about organizing a tour for you, yes?"

Demeter's eyebrows raised and she shook her head. "Goodness, no. I'd lose my mind. Not a single crop is healthy in this place, I can smell it. Decay and…transformation?" She suppressed a shiver. "No, thank you, my sweet."

Persephone tried not to giggle at the word *transformation*. It was more like transmutation—some plants Hades had had planted down here had indeed grown into…something else. A few had teeth, others had developed legs and tended to scurry around and disturb the nymphs by the marsh…

"Nymphs," she said under her breath, turning to look at the swamp they'd hastened away from. "We could use them."

"Come again?" Demeter peered in the same direction, likely seeing nothing but the foggy marsh and its overgrown weed-like bushes. She scratched her arm; surely she still *felt* those bushes from when they'd hidden in them. "How can we use nymphs?"

"Well…" Persephone scrunched her nose. "Mnemosyne sometimes uses them to distract ghosts, to divert them to her hut. So *we* could use them to divert the ghosts over to the battle." She spun back to where the flaring lights continued to shoot back and forth, their intensity growing. She could have sworn she heard grunts and even *marching*—was that Lukus' human army? "And the zombified humans the goddesses mentioned—someone needs to keep those out of the way, no?"

Demeter scratched her head, ruffling her corn-colored curls. "And the nymphs could do that?"

"They don't abide by the regular Underworld rules, from what Hades told me. They're just…there, but they *can* come and go as they please." Persephone changed her direction and headed back towards the murky waters. "This will take but a few seconds, but it might give Zeus and the others minutes of an advantage. It's important."

She found a purple skin colored creature lounging on the bank, half her body concealed inside the shrubbery. A lithe, luscious thing she was, naked but for a small shift over her private parts. She was twirling her hair around a finger and smacked her lips in delight at the sight of Persephone.

Persephone normally wouldn't be insensitive to her charms, and would rush home to lounge in bed and think about that body while exploring her own. But they didn't have time for that.

She pressed the nymph to inform all her friends that an army of humans was coming to the realm—she didn't feel the need to specify that these were *zombies,* but didn't think these lustful ladies would care—and that Hades required them to not reach the gates.

The nymph got the hint immediately. "Anything for Hades," she said, with a twinkle in her eye that caused a slight burn in Persephone's stomach.

She clenched her fists, holding in a jealousy that wasn't warranted—Hades *hated* the swamp nymphs—and returned to her mother, so they could continue their journey towards the warring family members.

"I'll need to warn the judges, unless Hades has already done so," said Persephone, as the Judgment Palace became more visible, its black marble shape a smaller version of Hades' home. "They shouldn't take part in anything like this, but if our entire realm is at stake…"

"I'm sure Hades told them," said Demeter, peering at the building they were approaching, fascinated by its marbled veins and its sleek, shiny surface.

If she'd seen our Palace walls encrusted with jewels…she'd have been mesmerized.

Demeter always worried that Hades' realm was a dark dungeon of despair, with nothing beautiful to behold, no comforts, and no vegetation—she was mostly right on that last part. But today, Persephone was able to prove to her that there was so much more to this place. There was a beauty in the craftsmanship, a creativity in the touches of luxury spread throughout the area. The waters were gloomy and the atmosphere somewhat sinister, but Persephone *was* comfortable down here.

Perhaps now, Demeter would rest easier during fall and winter, while Persephone was away.

"The Erinyes," whispered Persephone, not wanting to say their name out loud, lest that bring them to her. She shuddered—these vengeance-ridden creatures were powerful and would be mighty allies on Hades' team, but they terrified Persephone. The simple notion of their massive wings and their bloodshot eyes—

"I'm sure they fight for Hades already, no?" Demeter had read Persephone's troubled thoughts, and took her hand as they neared the Judgment Palace.

Persephone squinted at the ongoing struggle, clearer now that they were closer. "I can't tell." Flashes of light continued to zoom through the smoke, and though she deciphered a few figures moving to and fro, and heard the clash of swords and the sizzle of electricity, she couldn't see well enough to figure out *who* was fighting. "But he needs them, if they're not. And the Harpies; they and the Erinyes live outside the gates. They must have been watching and will interfere…"

"They're loyal to Hades, yes?" Persephone nodded, and Demeter squeezed her hand. "Then they'll come when called, if Hades finds it necessary. He's fought many wars, darling. As much as I hate him most days, he *is* efficient."

"Eris!" Persephone cried out, then clapped a hand over her mouth. "*That's* who they need, and she also lives outside the gates, and she's strong—"

Demeter took Persephone's other hand and held both tightly, forcing her steely gaze on her. "Stop. I know you're thinking ahead, trying to help—but there's nothing you or I can do, not unless asked. We're back-up fighters, hm?" She released one hand to move a strand of Persephone's auburn tresses from her face. "I'm afraid, too. If Gaia wins, we…we all lose. Zeus," she cleared her throat with a flinch, "has been a horrible father to you, and a worse brother to me, but he *is* our king and he has been benevolent to his kingdom. If he were to fall…"

Sensing her mother's fear rising and growing worse than her own—she had much more to lose—Persephone pressed their foreheads together, wincing as the not-so-distant sounds of fighting continued. More sword clinking, the *whoosh* of vines being whipped out, the zap of powers being thrown at one another. Sounds that she and Demeter were both all too familiar with and not quite ready to witness close-up.

But they had to—from their vantage point, and despite how close the Judgment Palace was to the gates, they couldn't see a thing, still. The smoke—gathering from all the energies being hurled and the attacks hitting the dirt and creating whirls of dust—was thick, and all they were able to detect were the prismatic flashes: gold, violet, and green being dominant.

Those are Mnemosyne and Gaia's colors. This is bad.

They decided to slip out of the gates. Persephone felt they'd be safe if they were close to Cerberus, as Hades had trained him to recognize and accept Persephone many moons ago. But as they approached the wide open space where the gates were usually tightly sealed, they encountered another being lurking, its black cloak trailing over the dust-ridden pathway as it paced back and forth in front of the opening.

The being turned its head, revealing its charcoal-colored eyes and the neutral expression of Thanatos. He was holding his scythe—which prompted Persephone to gulp loudly as she acknowledged him. Thanatos lurking anywhere while keeping a tight grip on his weapon was bad, *bad* news.

"I can't interfere," he said, his voice low in his throat as he bowed to Demeter, not even questioning why she was there. Everything was topsy turvy and the barriers to all realms had likely been lifted, by this point. "But I fear there will be a reaping, and I fear whose soul I'll be taking tonight."

Demeter shivered beside Persephone as she stared out into the smoky fog. "And you're certain you *will* be taking someone? Someone out there?"

Thanatos nodded once, solemn as ever, though Persephone perceived the smallest of frowns on his usually expressionless face. "I do not know if it's *out there* or simply nearby, and it could be anyone or anything, but yes. I was drawn to reap a soul, possibly several, and there's no changing that."

His words, so to-the-point and delivered with such confidence, prompted Persephone and Demeter into action, both dreading their family members losing their battle against Gaia. It was possible Thanatos might reap Gaia's soul that night, but Persephone found it unlikely, and doubted Mnemosyne would fall, either. It was Hades she feared for the most; Hades who stayed out of his brother's issues and nourished his under-the-world realm and dealt with the trivial matters of ghosts disappearing and judges being overwhelmed with work.

They slipped out, and Persephone directed them to the left, past the Elm Tree—which she begged her mother not to touch, not to *look* at. They ventured to where Cerberus would be on guard, watching the fight and waiting to intervene. Why he *hadn't* already gotten involved caused concern; normally, he'd start slashing with his fangs if he sensed any threat to Hades or the realm.

But when Persephone found him, completely knocked out and barely breathing, an enormous mass of legs and furry bodies and lolling tongues, she gasped.

"How in the…who could…" He wasn't dead; he *was* breathing, his monstrous chests heaving in and out slowly.

Demeter took Persephone's wrist and, though she'd been trembling at the sight of the mighty three-headed dog collapsed on the ground, and had cursed internally while taking in the size of him, she took her daughter around him, to hide behind his giant form.

The smoke cleared a bit, as a breeze came from down the *Acheron*. Had someone opened the lake and gotten in? Was it Lukus' army, or had someone come to help Zeus? Persephone knew that breeze, recognized its freshness, its outdoorsy aroma, and breathed it in for the brief instants it lingered near her.

Now she witnessed what had been going on—the four against four battle she'd been listening to and dreading since she'd left the hut. Gaia towered over them all, whipping her vines at an evidently exhausted Zeus, who was thwarting her with thunderbolts—but they weren't as bright as Persephone knew them to be, and flickered with flailing energy. And they did nothing when tossed at Gaia, melting into her green bodice as she absorbed them into her core.

A bold half-lioness creature garbed in a stained tunic—was that Rhea?—was clawing at Poseidon, who was shoving her back with his trident. He was half-hunched, bleeding from his arm, and a few large scratches glowed blue on his cheeks. Nearby, Mnemosyne was hovering in the air and shooting violet jets of electricity at a shield, behind which Ares was crouched, cringing through her attack. He then hopped up and shot his own electric jolt at her—a deep, bloody red that reverberated with a *screech* but was deflected by Mnemosyne with a wave of her hand.

Then Persephone spotted Hades, at last, running backwards as he swung his glaive at a growling, green-glowing, bare-chested man who looked ready to dig his fingers into Hades' torso at the first opportunity. She assumed that was Lukus; but wasn't Lukus supposed to be after Zeus? Why was *Gaia* the one working on Zeus, and the little half-human minion she'd trained was instead pursuing Hades?

Persephone and Demeter held hands, standing behind Cerberus' inanimate body. He was so large that they didn't need to crouch to remain somewhat hidden—not that anyone fighting would have noticed them, with how busy they were trying to rip out each other's throats.

But where was Aphrodite? Wasn't she supposed to come straight here and help Zeus, and help Lukus fight his possession? Why had Persephone and Demeter gotten there first, though they'd made several stops on the way?

Persephone couldn't swallow the acidic taste in her mouth; the notion that something had gone badly wrong, and all she could do was stand back and watch it continue to go wrong.

|| 26. CENTURIES ||

ZEUS

Still deep in the throngs of the battle—his attempt at letting Gaia apprehend him had failed—Zeus swiped a hand over his sweat-riddled forehead. Between dodging Gaia's vine-whip and her shots of spiked leaves, he shrugged a hand through his curls, and found that not only were they damp and tangled, but some of them were *falling out*. Not that he paid more attention than most to his hair, but he only started losing it if he was weak—and he sure as hell knew how weak he was now.

He'd been ready to surrender, to let Gaia whip him hard in the forehead, to the point of slicing off the top half of his head; but Ares had interfered, tossing his shield in front of Zeus in the nick of time.

"Don't you dare, Father! I told you we will not give up, and that means you won't, either!"

His son, more intuitive and witty than he'd ever known him to be, had prevented Gaia's vine from slashing into Zeus, then summoned his shield right back to his hands to continue his own battle with Mnemosyne. A battle that he was, somehow, still fighting, despite having received a few blows to the legs and his helmet having been torched while protecting him from one of Mnemosyne's jets of energy. She was inclined to aim for the head—which meant Ares was the best placed to fight her, as he had the sturdiest headgear.

Zeus hadn't succumbed, not yet, but his knees were shaking from the constant bending and leaping and twisting to avoid Gaia's missiles. She was furious—red in the face, red in her eyes, red smeared all over her emerald-colored tunic. Red blood and blue ichor were *everywhere* on her, coming from the few wounds Zeus had managed to inflict on her with his thunder, and with a few throws of his staff that had done nothing but scrape near her neck or tear a slit into her dress.

Blood that didn't affect her in the slightest, as she kept going, tireless as a mother protecting her cubs, her attacks effortless as if she were throwing a frisbee in her backyard with her kids. Despite her redness, not a slither of perspiration had gathered over *her* forehead, and she wasn't panting, shaking, or close to crumbling to her knees in exhaustion.

Crumbling—Zeus heard a sound resembling that, seconds later, coming from his right side. He spun to the noise, while hopping up into the air to avoid Gaia's vines, and saw Poseidon fallen, his back having hit the ground with a colossal *thud* that cracked the earth around him. His trident fell too, and rolled out of his grasp, hitting a rock that stopped it from getting too far from Poseidon's fingertips. But those fingertips were inanimate, and Poseidon's eyes were closed.

"Fuck!" Zeus *never* cursed, not out loud, but the sight of his fallen brother ripped into his heart and destroyed any polite barriers he'd placed in his vocabulary.

Poseidon wasn't dead, no; he was breathing still, but couldn't move. Purple electricity shocked around him, circling him like ropes, keeping him tethered to the ground.

Zeus sneered at his attacker—Mnemosyne, hovering nearby with a satisfied smirk on her perfect face. "I was sick of smelling his blood gushing out from all his wounds," she said, as if she needed an explanation. This was war, and she'd done what any warrior would do—hurt the enemy.

She was right; Poseidon *was* bleeding profusely, though the gashes were insignificant and not as deep as they looked. Rhea had been launching herself at him with unparalleled ferocity. Never in his lifetime had Zeus seen his mother so wrathful, and though she was poisoned and not in control of her actions, he made a mental note to never, ever, make her mad. If this was how her warrior-self manifested—a lioness on the prowl and eager to sink her teeth into any exposed flesh she could find—then he'd prefer to keep his distance.

I do not want to fight with Mother.

Mnemosyne glared at Rhea, who'd calmed down briefly to catch her breath and lick her fingers, lapping up Poseidon's blood on her claws. "Stop playing with your food, would you? I don't want to have to keep *helping* you!"

Unfazed by the hint of insult in Mnemosyne's tone, Rhea shrugged and began to prowl over to sniff at Poseidon's inanimate body, and likely to take a few chomps out of him. She had that hunger in her expression, the slight snarl baring her lengthy fangs, a bit of drool gathering in the corners of her mouth.

I do not want to fight with Mother.

Zeus zapped a thunderbolt at Gaia, hoping to divert her for two seconds, while he charged up another to hurl at Rhea, against all the flashing signs in his mind telling him not to, but begging him to protect his frail brother. But it was Hades who blocked Rhea, inadvertently, while running backwards and dodging Lukus' attempts at jamming his fingers into his torso.

Mnemosyne saw it, and groaned as she kicked at one of Ares'

attacks—he'd hoped to distract her, too, it appeared—while hurling one of her own at Hades. With his constant movement, she missed, and instead her missile tripped Lukus, who fell smack onto the ground with an *oof* of surprise. He got right back up, shook his head, and continued his mission to rip into Hades.

"I'm growing dizzy from this nonsense," said Mnemosyne, again evading one of Ares' blasts of red light, and turning to her mother.

Gaia, if she'd been listening to the ongoing arguments, didn't show any interest in what Mnemosyne had said. She'd been too busy swirling her whip and aiming it at Zeus—who barely got out of the way before it slapped onto the dirt, digging a trench of several feet deep in its wake.

"*Mother.*" Mnemosyne's voice carried as much energy as her electricity did, striking through the air with such force that Zeus had to cover his ears. "Call your puppy back on to its original target, would you? Why in Tartarus is he pursuing Hades?"

Gaia spared Mnemosyne a quick and quite annoyed glance as she prepared for another firing at Zeus. "Because Hades threatened to stop his minions, and Lukus wants them here. As long as Hades keeps trying to seal the entrances—and he is, I can hear the incantations under his breath—then Lukus will attack *him.* In the meantime, *I* am handling Zeus, don't you see? Lukus is a *back-up.* Do you not listen to me when I speak, girl?"

Zeus concealed a smile.

Disruption in the ranks? This might be to our advantage.

He was still defeated, still on the verge of giving up—but there *was* hope if Gaia and Mnemosyne weren't quite on the same page regarding Lukus. It was odd, Zeus had to admit. The poor man was bred to attack and maim him, and yet he'd been chasing after Hades for the past thirty minutes, unrelenting no matter how many times Hades stabbed at him with his glaive. The sharpened edge had no effect on Lukus, who brushed away the pain as if it were nonexistent. He wasn't even bleeding, nor did he look ready to give up.

Mnemosyne swerved sideways to dodge Ares, who'd launched himself at her, sword aimed at her heart. "*Where* are his minions? His army? They should have been here ages ago!"

Gaia growled, teeth gritting as she spewed a horde of buzzing leaves towards Zeus, who smacked them away with a thunderbolt. "You ask me? I thought *you* said they were ready and waiting! Clearly, something has blocked their way!"

Zeus retaliated with a whoosh of lightning, its sizzle through the air making him flinch as he imagined being on the receiving end of it. Gaia moved out of its way, but the edge of it burned over her arm, and she hissed at the touch.

"Enough of *this*," said Mnemosyne, sending a shock of electricity into Ares' shield, at the same time as Rhea lurched into it, claws and fangs out to rip it to shreds. The shield exploded, leaving Ares exposed, with nothing but his sword and armor to protect him.

"Shit," he said, barely loud enough for Zeus to catch. He caught Zeus watching him, but waved him off. "I'm fine, focus on yourself— and on *them*." He pointed towards Hades, who'd kicked Lukus off long enough to go check on Poseidon. "I'll manage Rhea."

Mnemosyne's interests had shifted to Hades, as she left Ares and Rhea to a gruesome hand-to-hand—and sword—combat that Zeus was afraid of watching, wary of losing a mother or a son, or both. He instead focused one hand on Gaia, on blocking her oncoming attacks, and the other raised towards Mnemosyne, who was wiggling her fingers to prepare for a blast in Hades' direction.

Hades had been ready for her—as she flung her electricity, he diverted it with a swift swing of his glaive, sending the jolt swooshing on and over the Diamond Gates, illuminating the fake sky as it flew overhead. Zeus heard the *bang* of its implosion into something—he hoped, not *someone*—and Mnemosyne glowered at Poseidon defyingly.

"Ah, so you face your fears at last, my king?" Mnemosyne's orange hair shone purple from the jolts flickering from her skin, from the veins lighting up and down her arms.

"Fears?" Hades stood his ground, one eyebrow arching as he returned Mnemosyne's gaze without an ounce of apprehension. "Do you mean you and your powers? I've never been afraid of you, Mnemosyne. Why else do you think I'm the only brother who will let you live in his realm?"

Zeus figured Hades would hold his own. Though he abhorred wars and fighting, he *was* good at bickering and taunting, and would manage against Mnemosyne for a spell.

But not for too long.

Zeus realized all too late that Gaia's attacks had stopped, and as he twisted towards her to see what she was brewing up now, he saw that she'd gotten closer. *Too* close. She was feet away from him, her vines tucked into her dress, the menace in her stance and expression eerily died down.

"The best you can do is give up," she said, her voice soft, *too* soft. Like a lullaby, a sweet-natured tune tempting him into bending the knee to her, into surrendering his power, his throne, his crown, his *home* into her care.

"No," he said, sensing her energy rising and intensifying as she continued her approach. Her scent was of dirt and clumpy mud, of a forest after a deluge, of a fragrant but toxic flower blooming and spreading its poisoned pollen into the atmosphere. He wrinkled his nostrils and took a step back. "It's not the best, it's *your* best."

Lukus had stopped fighting. He was sniffing the air, looking towards the way Charon's ferry came from. The sounds of marching, Zeus noticed, had ceased. Or perhaps he'd grown so used to them, they'd become background noise? He couldn't quite tell, but last he'd heard them they hadn't gotten any closer. Were Lukus' minions blocked?

"Oh, but weren't you about to do it, moments ago?" Gaia cocked her head, showing the vines steadily crawling up her back, sliding up her neck like brown serpents spotted with sharp green spikes. She paid Lukus and his hesitation no heed, all her concentration on Zeus. "If Ares hadn't stepped in, you'd have let me harm you. That shot might have killed you. You *did* give up, so why the change of heart?"

He *hadn't* had a change of heart, and she knew it. Eons, they'd been a family. He'd tolerated her quiet quips and her discreet debate of his royal status. And she'd remained polite when others were near, pretending to revere him when in truth she loathed every fiber of him. He reminded her of her husband, of her corrupt son, Cronus, she'd once mentioned. Once, when he'd been so drunk she likely didn't think he'd remember her saying it. But he had remembered, and he should have remembered it sooner.

None of this would have happened if I'd listened to my gut when it told me you've never been on my side.

Centuries and centuries Gaia had sat back and watched wars unfold, had watched her offspring attack him, and had feigned acceptance at their imprisonment. Centuries and centuries she'd held in her emotions, bitten her tongue though her aura was always pungent with resentment towards him. But those centuries had done nothing to calm her down; they'd only riled her up further. Gaia, primordial goddess of the earth, wanted her planet back, and she wanted it now.

He imagined her slapping chains around his wrists and dragging him on to Tartarus. Was that the worst case scenario? True, he might not be able to escape, like Hades said; but he wouldn't know if he didn't try, right? If he surrendered now, if he gave Gaia what she wanted, would it save his siblings, his children, from sharing his fate? If he negotiated on their behalf, begging Gaia to let them live, that would be enough, wouldn't it?

All he cared about was their well-being. He was bad at showing it, as he spent more time sulking on his throne or hiding in his office than actually asking his family members how they were faring. But he *did* care. He'd spent eons frolicking about with women of all types, hurting his wife, wrecking his reputation, not giving a damn about consequences; but he'd stopped. He'd grown up, he'd matured into the role gifted to him by destiny. Now, Gaia wanted to take that away from him, and as much as he wanted to resist her, he was *too* tired, too overwhelmed to do so.

And too angry at his own mistake of not having noticed her plotting sooner. This—a raging civil war between siblings and parents and twice-removed cousins—needed to end. The only way to end it was with Zeus deserting his status and offering it up to Gaia on a silver platter. He knew it, they *all* knew it, and yet the words remained stuck to his tongue.

"You cannot win, Grandson." Gaia's grandmotherly voice struck through the air. It was the timbre she took with the grandchildren she *liked;* Hera, Athena, occasionally, or Hestia. Sometimes Demeter. Women, all of them. Gaia was so scorned by men that she didn't think twice about giving any of the *good* men a chance to redeem the entire male species. "But I'll give you this one last chance to end things peacefully, where no one has to die. Abdicate here and now, with me as your witness, and I'll spare your family. I'll even let them stay at the palace, in lesser upgraded rooms. But they'll be alive."

Zeus had decided, and this time neither of his brothers, nor his son, could interrupt him. Poseidon was knocked out, Hades was fighting Mnemosyne, Ares was exchanging dangerous blows with Rhea. No one could get in the way of him saving his people.

A giant blast of power fell and exploded at Zeus' feet. A blinding light shot from said power, forceful, making Zeus take a few steps back. He shielded his eyes, but did notice that Gaia had been thrown backwards, and the others in the vicinity had been temporarily weakened, too, all fallen to their knees and covering their faces to not look at the continuously bedazzling gleam before Zeus.

"No," it spoke, its voice strangely familiar. Feminine, with a dash of seduction and a pinch of sass, of spice. A whiff of the sea and heavily sugared perfume came from the mass of bright light, and a figure formed within it. A luscious, womanly silhouette with golden blonde hair, striking a pose with one hand on her hip, the other directed at Gaia, who was regaining her balance several feet away.

Zeus would recognize that tone, that attitude, that overall sense of perfection and sheer delight from miles away. He gulped as the light faded, and the ever-delicious shape of the goddess of beauty became clear to him as she turned to him with a sassy grin. As if she'd always meant to do this, to pop up at the opportune moment, to reveal her true self, her true powers and save his ass before it was handed to him in a bloody bag with the rest of his remains.

How? He had no clue, and he meant to interrogate her as soon as possible—once they weren't in the middle of a battlefield, that was. Hadn't she been kidnapped? Hadn't she been poisoned? What was she doing there?

"Aphrodite?"

|| 27. YOU ARE MINE ||

GAIA

It *was* Aphrodite; transformed, revitalized, and *awake?*

How the fuck did she get out of the hut?

Gaia had left Aphrodite and the others in a state of comatose slumber, and ensured they'd stay that way throughout her fight with Zeus. She hadn't wanted them involved. Athena was too cunning, Hera too distracting, and Aphrodite was…well, she was Aphrodite. One bat of her lashes and one blink of an eye and she'd attempt to turn all of Gaia's army against her.

But this Aphrodite, who'd popped in—*literally*, she'd landed in front of the about-to-surrender Zeus with a *pop*—wasn't in the state Gaia had left her. She was strong, flecks of forceful energy dazzling off her skin that glowed so gold she outshined even Mnemosyne.

Where *was* Mnemosyne? Gaia took a quick peek at the scene behind Aphrodite and Zeus. Everyone had been driven backwards from Aphrodite's arrival, and were still squabbling to get to their feet, rubbing their heads in confusion. Lukus was the only one who apparently hadn't fallen, and his gaze was fixed on the *Acheron*, watching, waiting for his zombies to show up.

Why *hadn't* they showed up yet?

Gaia hadn't crumbled, per se, but she'd sensed her knees

buckling as Aphrodite's energy had shoved her backwards. *No one shoved her backwards, ever.* What sort of power trip was this meager goddess on? The strength in her aura was blinding, even to Gaia. It was pungent, a putrefying stench of someone who'd recently acquired additional abilities and couldn't wait to show them off.

She straightened herself and dusted off the specks of gold on her gown, glaring at Aphrodite with a renewed rage. "I thought I'd taken care of you?"

Radiating with her spark of powerful purity, Aphrodite smiled in response; a taunting smirk that might have prompted Gaia into launching into her, under other circumstances. Aphrodite didn't care— there she stood, smug and thrilled because she'd had an element of surprise. She'd appeared where no one had expected her to, and for two seconds she had the upper hand.

Not for long, sweetheart.

"You made your point," said Gaia, snickering. "You have *some* power." She swallowed up the fact that this power was actually potent enough to rival hers. "And you want to help Zeus. Lovely. But you see, Zeus and I were having a conversation and you interrupted, and I'd appreciate it if you backed off." She sought to wave Aphrodite out of the way with a flick of her wrist; but Aphrodite didn't budge, not even a millimeter.

Gaia frowned. No, that wasn't possible. No one stood in her way, no one resisted her powers.

Her vines began to shoot out her fingertips and wrists and wound around her arms, engorging with her anger.

"Enough," said Aphrodite, her voice a clear and concise stream of controlled irritation. So calm, so *neutral* compared to the usual melodies she spewed out to draw attention and seduce anyone listening. "You will cease this attitude, Gaia."

Gaia chuckled, but deep down, she was still winded by the abrupt arrival, and her legs shook slightly beneath her skirts.

She cannot and will not best me. Caught off guard, that's all— I'll shake this off.

"And who are *you* to tell me what to do, child?" Gaia's intonation was raspy, sharp as a stake that she meant to drill into Aphrodite over and over until she understood her place. Hadn't she explained that place to her earlier, by kicking her backwards? Hadn't the goddess cowered at the brutality and learned something from it?

Aphrodite's eyes were prismatic, reflecting in vibrant shades of ocean blue, grassy green, lavender, with hints of scarlet. "Child?" She scoffed. "Yes, I *am* a child. *The* child of Uranus, in fact." Gaia flinched at the name, but Aphrodite ignored her. "The first one he fathered on his own, without meaning to. The one he inferred a plethora of powers on, also without meaning to. Uranus…your *husband,* remember?"

Gaia seethed, sensing her vines scratching along her arms as they doubled in size and started growing thorns. They whirled up and around her shoulders, surrounded her body in a barricade of bark and leaves. They grew, faster and faster, loading up for an attack. She couldn't stop them, she couldn't *control* them—there had been too many mentions of Uranus in the past few hours, and her soul didn't tolerate that. Her mind warped with ancient images of the creature in question—too tall, too fit, too perfect to be true; and he was, indeed, *not* true. He was a monster, and his direct descendent, the actual fruit of his loins, was here to remind Gaia of that fact.

But Aphrodite was playing, bringing up Uranus on purpose, wasn't she? Yes, she knew it'd throw Gaia off balance, rile her up, boil her blood. She wanted to catch Gaia unawares and seek a weakness she could exploit. But Gaia was bigger, better, stronger than that. If Aphrodite wanted her to attack, she'd have to be disappointed at the turn of things, because Gaia would hold back until Aphrodite was the one destabilized, not her.

Gaia jammed her teeth together and spoke through thinned lips, in a hissed voice she hoped Aphrodite would perceive as a threat, and move along and leave her to her business. "We're *estranged,* dammit! Divorced! He's my ex; why won't anyone address him as such?"

This *wasn't* part of the plan. Harming Aphrodite hadn't been included in Gaia's scheming. To take her blood, to weaken her, yes; but she'd wanted to keep her alive, use her and her charms into drawing more gods to her cause. Because even after she'd taken Zeus' crown, there'd still be others to convince, others who wouldn't grant her their worship right off the bat. And some might be persuaded with a show of Aphrodite's hefty breasts or a promise of a roll around in the sheets with her.

Aphrodite shook a few golden curls from her face. "Ex or not, I am your stepdaughter. Whether you like it or not. I've respected you for eons, and you owe me that same respect. And my powers?" She lifted her hand, showing a trail of golden veins shooting into every finger, a blast waiting to be delivered. "They've always been much bigger than I let on. I've been asked to gulp them down, *sit* on them," she sent a swift side-glare at Zeus, still cowering behind her, "pretend like they're not there, but they are." She focused on Gaia, her gaze a glare of suppressed rage. "I am, in truth, on a higher level than the precious Titan sons you so wish to release from their cages. I'm stronger than the Giants you want to set upon your own grandson. And more powerful than the monsters you think to let rip the heads off all the humans you dislike so much."

Such a speech would have made anyone else breathless—Gaia had been, listening to it—but Aphrodite was not. She took slow, steady breaths, her bosom rising and falling in a tranquil rhythm, as if she'd just addressed a few friends at a barbecue or toasted a boyfriend at a party.

The vines kept growing and covering Gaia's body. She was up to her neck, literally, in sharp bark that wouldn't stop encircling her, squeezing her, begging to be released. If Aphrodite cared, she didn't show it—her expression had returned to neutral, though peppered with a silent rage only directed at Gaia.

Gaia stomped a foot, causing dirty leaves to plummet from her and stab into the ground—they'd been sharp and stealthy, perfect weapons. "You're a *bug*, that's what you are, and I'm going to crush you." Gaia's words were leveled, surprisingly, despite the fury coursing through her, charging into her belly. "You may think yourself to be all powerful, but *I* am a primordial. I overpower you, on principle. You alone cannot overpower me and mine."

Where was Mnemosyne? Where were Rhea and Lukus? Gaia wanted to locate them, summon them to her side, but it seemed that all time had suspended since Aphrodite's arrival, and none of her allies had quite recuperated from the effects of her presence.

Was it time to call upon the guards of Tartarus to release her children? Should she give Zeus one last chance to free them himself, before she launched the signal?

"Ugh." Aphrodite groaned, finally showing some emotion—annoyance.

Gaia blinked at her, shocked by her defiance.

I tell her I'm going to end her life and she deflects the threat like an annoying mosquito?

"I *can* overpower you," said Aphrodite, rolling one shoulder back, then the other. "But who said I'd be doing it alone? I have help. Many allies, in fact, though you've beaten them down pretty badly, I see." She shrugged. "And you seem to forget I have my son."

They both turned to Lukus, who'd not moved an inch since Aphrodite's appearance. But now, instead of staring towards where his army should have been coming from, he was staring at Aphrodite. His head tilted slightly to the side, and he squinted, as if seeing his mother for the first time.

But he'd seen her earlier, he'd *drank* from her. Her appearance shouldn't have had any effect on him whatsoever. He was Gaia's, *her* leader, *her* precious half-mortal created to do her bidding among humans.

Something was wrong with him. Something in his aura was flickering, not quite switching off but no longer as intense as it had been. His hunger for blood, for someone to dig into, had diminished a tad—but enough to worry Gaia.

"Come to me, Lukus," said Aphrodite, spinning towards him and beckoning him with her hand. "Come to your *mother*. To your blood. Fight that nastiness inside you. It's not you. You're not a zombie commander, you're a *demi-god*, and you're my son. Remember who you are, remember whose side you should fight on."

Gaia tasted dirt and grass in her mouth. Her anger was so overpowering, it developed inside, swelling within her, demanding that she release it in the form of dagger-like leaves and harsh vines whipped at Aphrodite's beautiful face and voluptuous body. She wanted to tear her apart, yank the flesh from her bones, limb by limb, and watch her decompose at her feet.

I should have killed her, I should have known. But how *did she grow so powerful? How did she know how to tap into her ancient powers?*

Lukus glanced at Gaia, hesitant. Gaia grinned—oh, he was still on her team, if he was seeking her approval. He hadn't quite fallen to Aphrodite's tactics yet; the poison in him was intense, and his soul was, and had been, Gaia's from his birth. Aphrodite birthed him, but Gaia *made* him. He was hers.

He switched to Aphrodite again, a curious golden glow joining the glaring green in his eyes. A faint glow, but there, nonetheless.

He wasn't supposed to be curious. He wasn't supposed to have feelings, hesitation. His purpose was to be a wall of stone with one intention, and one only: to stop Zeus. Yes, he'd been distracted by Hades, allowing Gaia a shot at dethroning the king herself, but now she realized she'd been wrong to lust for glory so quickly. She'd been wrong to fight Zeus, and should have set Lukus upon him immediately. Should have thrown him off Hades and reminded him Zeus was his goal. And the zombies should have been there, *why* weren't they there...

A twinge of some foreign power came from Aphrodite, who was still gesturing Lukus closer. A magical pull of sorts, one that wasn't in her regular array of attributes; one that was *more* potent than when she used her girdle on innocent creatures hypnotized by her, or placed a swift and seductive spell with her pouty lips.

"No," said Gaia, marching over to block this new and frightening power from hitting its mark—Lukus. She grabbed Lukus by the tiny hairs on his neck and hauled him away. "No, my pet, you are mine. *You are mine.*"

|| 28. ENOUGH OF THIS ||

PERSEPHONE

From behind Cerberus' enormous but barely breathing body, Persephone and Demeter saw it all. Their team's struggle to maintain an advantage, Gaia approaching Zeus with twitchy fingers desperate to wrap around his neck and snap it. And then the surprise—but too long-awaited, in Persephone's opinion—arrival of Aphrodite, with a giant blast of light as she landed in front of Zeus, preventing him from, what Persephone believed, was his official surrender to Gaia.

Persephone and Demeter had shivered together as they watched Aphrodite and Gaia confront one another. A concentration of two very different powers pungent enough to cause a world apocalypse, contained within their bodies. Aphrodite, radiant with ambrosia and glowing a gold so bright it burned Persephone's eyes; and Gaia seemingly transforming into an actual tree, as vines weaved around her body and leaves spiked up on her elbows, around her fingers, and sprouted from her hair.

As they argued, they shifted their attention to Lukus, who'd grown abnormally still during the commotion, staring out at where Persephone assumed his army was supposed to come from. But the distant sound of marching had stopped approaching, remaining in one place. Did that mean the marsh nymphs had held the human zombies off? Had Persephone done *something* that would affect the outcome of this war?

Gaia stormed up to Lukus and snatched him by the hairs of his neck. Lukus grimaced, but didn't resist.

"You are mine," said Gaia, baring her teeth at Aphrodite as she hauled Lukus out of her reach.

Persephone had sensed Aphrodite's energy increasing with every breath she took. Now, she could *see* it, like two golden arms stretching out to take hold of Lukus and tug him into her embrace. She stood so still, so unfazed by Gaia's *also* growing energy, and was calmer than Persephone had ever seen her. Aphrodite was one to easily succumb to her temper, and so was Gaia; both were much too reserved and tranquil considering the circumstances.

One would likely blow, any moment now.

But there was nothing Persephone or Demeter could do. Demeter was right, earlier, when she'd said they were back-ups, that they needed to stick to the sidelines and wait to be summoned. So far, no one needed them—no one could *see* them, hidden behind the massive lump of Cerberus' body, in any case.

"*Exactly, my sweet,*" said Demeter, her voice soft and soothing in Persephone's mind. A breeze of fresh air amidst this stuffy, slightly muggy stench of confinement that the Underworld's entrance often took on. "*We wait here until we're needed.*"

Not that she had a quarrelsome nature—except to get a bit angry when Hades irritated her—but Persephone *wanted* to join the fight, by this point. She'd heard too many stories of how devastating the Titans were, of how gruesome the Giants were, of how terrifying the monsters were. She wanted to help stop them from rising up from their cages. Back then, she hadn't been permitted to be part of those wars—she'd been sentenced to sit back and wait to see if her family would prevail. This time, she had front row seats, but she wanted to be on the stage with her husband.

Hades was okay—she'd been keeping an eye on him, and as he started fighting with Mnemosyne, Lukus had *finally* lost interest. Like everyone else, he'd been knocked backwards by Aphrodite's arrival. But he was alive, breathing, brushing himself off as he slowly got to his feet to witness the goddess of beauty and the primordial goddess of the earth in their confrontation.

Aphrodite's power swarmed around her in a bubble of gold. A few ripples ran over its surface after Gaia's words of possession towards Lukus. "He belongs to no one, you grass-eating crone!"

Several gasps echoed from witnesses of the insult—including from Demeter, beside Persephone.

The largest gasp came from Gaia herself, as she set a vine-covered hand over her vine-covered chest. "The *nerve*. The audacity of someone so puny to speak to me like that!"

"*You* are puny," said Aphrodite, without missing a beat, taking a step towards where Gaia held on to Lukus, still. "Lukus is a free soul. A *good* soul, meant for *good* things. Not for your attempt at world domination!" She swiped through the air, sending jets of gold to sprinkle over the ground, lighting up a few of the sparse specks of grass that sometimes grew there. "He is meant for love, for peace. He came from *my* womb, and I am a peaceful goddess!"

Gaia snorted and spat on the ground where Aphrodite had ignited it. A smooth steam rose from the spot, tinted with green. "*You*, peaceful? Seriously, didn't you learn anything from your discussions with Eros, weeks ago? When he reminded you how *not* peaceful you are? How many idiots do I have to manipulate to make this evident to you?"

"*You* are the idiot for calling your own family members idiots," said Aphrodite, voice turning low and threatening, grating out from her throat as if waiting to be unleashed. "Stop changing the subject— let Lukus go. He's not yours. You may have *led* me to birth him, and created him for your sick schemes, but he is pure, he is kind. Can you not feel that in the smithereens of the heart you once had? He will not fulfill your despicable motives, not while I'm alive!" Her arms stretched out at her sides as she charged up more power, illuminating the space around her with a gold so intense Persephone and Demeter had to shield their eyes.

"Then I suppose we'll have to remedy that," said Gaia, using her free hand to snap her fingers twice.

Two lone figures approached Gaia—Rhea, growling, her claws elongating from her fingertips; and Mnemosyne, grounded at last, but still harboring flashes of her purple electricity.

Gaia had summoned her minions, preparing to take on Aphrodite. She wouldn't fight her herself? She'd have her daughters do her dirty work, again?

Zeus, Hades, Poseidon, and Ares were not ready for another round. Aphrodite would be on her own to confront two supercharged titanesses.

"Should we go? Now? Help her?" Persephone itched to join the battle, but mostly to protect her husband, who'd risen up to his full height but showed signs of exhaustion—labored breathing, pockets of black under his eyes, disheveled hair that he didn't bother to fix.

Demeter grabbed her wrist, sensing Persephone's motion. *"No; like I said, we wait. We'll know if we're being summoned, trust me."*

Mnemosyne gritted her teeth and came as close as possible to

Aphrodite before touching the extremity of her powerful aura. She didn't budge any closer, but showed a menacing glare that meant business. She wasn't afraid.

But Rhea stopped, having run into some sort of barricade, something stopping her progression. She shook her head, and blinked at the goddess before her, as if she'd just then materialized. As if Rhea's eyes had now opened, fully, and she saw, at last. Her expression changed from bloodthirsty lioness to worried mother, confused captive. As if she'd been snapped out of a trance and had no clue what she was doing there.

Persephone squinted at her, trying to zoom in and decipher what had caused the shift. Were Aphrodite's powers so immense that they'd rid the poison from Rhea's being and cleansed her?

"No…" Demeter had read Persephone's thoughts and spoke out loud. "No, she can't do that, no matter how much ambrosia she took."

"I…" Rhea looked at her hands and frowned. From her spot, Persephone couldn't be sure, but she imagined there was blood stained on Rhea's palms; her *family's* blood. She'd attacked one of her sons, made him bleed. "I can't do this, Gaia." She peered at Aphrodite and was somehow not blinded by the halo of light around her. "She's my sister, technically, isn't she? Daughter of Uranus? No." She spun to Gaia, and though Persephone could no longer see her face, she detected the negative energy coming from Rhea's body. "Enough of this, Mother. I've hurt too many gods, don't you think? I won't do this."

Mnemosyne had stopped, too, but she hadn't jerked out of her trance. She wasn't poisoned, and was operating as Gaia's right hand of her own volition. "Rhea, shut up. Obey."

"No," said Rhea, now twisting to Mnemosyne and shoving her

sideways, away from Aphrodite. "*You* shut up. Don't do this, not anymore!"

"*Get her,*" growled Gaia, whatever skin she was still showing turning green. Her eyes were so blazingly crimson that Persephone noticed them from afar and her heart skipped a beat. "Both of you. Immobilize Aphrodite and *finish* her. I don't give a shit what she is to you—*do it now.*"

Mnemosyne proceeded forward, but Rhea jammed into her, knocking her aside.

"I don't get it," whispered Persephone, realizing there was no point speaking into each other's minds—no one was paying attention to them. "How did Rhea overcome her toxins, then? She was deeply poisoned, Mother, I smelled it. How did she—"

A jet of charcoal smoke laced with red shot across the way, coming from the other side of the Diamond Gate. It smacked right into Gaia, who'd begun stomping up to Aphrodite to take matters into her own hands.

The missile didn't hurt her, not quite; but it did cease her steps and knock her slightly off balance.

The answer to all Persephone's questions came running forward, from the gates. A black-haired woman with streaks of red and purple in her locks, with a worn dress of deep brown garbing her figure, and fire flickering from her fingertips.

"*Hecate?*" said Persephone and Demeter in unison, witnessing the witch-goddess raise her hand and threaten to send another swirl of smoke at Gaia, should she opt to continue towards Aphrodite.

Behind her were the two limping forms of Hera and Athena, still not entirely up to par, but both wielding weapons and aiming them at Gaia and Mnemosyne. It was quite the sight—both of them in their nightwear, yet Athena pointing a well-used trident and Hera brandishing a rusty bow with its equally rusty arrow nocked and ready to loose into Gaia's torso.

Persephone had *never* seen Hera hold any sort of weapon. She normally fought with her hands, hurling energy balls at her enemies; but she must have been too tired for that. Persephone recognized their weapons—these were confiscated from errant spirits who'd somehow smuggled them down with them as they waited for judgment. Hecate must have grabbed them in haste to equip Athena and Hera before hurrying over.

Just in case. Smart move, Hecate.

"I knew I smelled your stench," said Gaia, snarling as Hecate came closer, though maintaining a safe enough distance. She'd thrown a hefty dose of magic at Gaia, but she was no match for her, and she knew it. "I knew you were up to something, you filthy little witch."

"Stop this, Gaia." Hecate's voice was trembling. She, unlike her peers who'd confronted Gaia before, couldn't keep her emotion from her timbre, and couldn't feign confidence like them. She was afraid, and had every right to be.

"Mother, please—we must go be by Hecate's side, no?" Persephone bounced on the balls of her feet, anxious.

Still, Demeter held her back. *"I swear by Zeus if you don't stop fidgeting I will slap you, and I don't care that you're a goddess grown and married and have had a child. I'm your mother, and I demand that you listen to me, for fucks' sake!"*

Demeter rarely swore like this—Persephone gulped and shoved all her urges deep inside.

"I'm not as old and wise as you, nor as powerful, but we both know I've seen a lot. I've *done* a lot, what with all my frenzies and the messes I've left in my wake. This," Hecate gestured at the wounded gods, at the ominous smoke still looming around them, and at Lukus, still held back by Gaia, "is insane. Chaos wouldn't want this. Tartarus wouldn't want this. My grandmother, your *daughter,* wouldn't want this. Yes," Hecate nodded at Gaia's sudden pang of shock, "Phoebe, remember her? The one you made someone bite and poison and then dragged down here to be a part of your plots? No." Hecate's lower lip trembled; Persephone saw it, sensed it. "Enough. Stop this. You are out of control and it has gone too far."

Gaia's vines continued to multiply, growing so thick her body was like a tree-trunk, almost as large as the Elm Tree looming nearby. She needed to unleash those vines soon, lest they consume her; or someone needed to slice through them to break the fury she was harboring. Only her face remained the same, though laced with a rage the likes of which Persephone had never seen on anyone's face before.

Gaia lifted a heavy arm and aimed her fingers towards Hecate, with Athena and Hera standing behind her. The vines shot off her and zoomed towards Hecate—but with a swift slice of her hand through the air, Hecate cut through the vines, chopping them to pieces before they'd come close enough to harm her.

Persephone had heard of Hecate's prowess in battle, but never witnessed it for herself. And with how fearful she'd been, how on edge, Persephone had no inkling how Hecate had managed to hone in her skills long enough to deflect Gaia's attack. Nor did she know if she'd be able to do it again.

"No," said Hecate, brushing off the remains of leaves and bark that had exploded onto her tunic. "I said *enough.* We will not stand down, Gaia. None of us will."

Athena and Hera echoed her, and so did Hades and Ares, in the background. Poseidon was still passed out, but Persephone could have sworn she heard his thoughts, repeating the words, as well.

Mnemosyne ripped from Rhea's grasp and kicked her down, spitting on her. "You disgrace me, you low-level titaness." She marched up to Gaia and cracked her knuckles. "Let's finish this, Mother. Give me the signal, and I'll get Tartarus to open up, I swear it."

Aphrodite stepped forward, but Hecate hastened over to stop her. "No," she said, indicating Lukus, that Gaia had let go so she could throw her attack at Hecate. "Go to him, persuade him, rid him of his mind-warping. It can be done, but only *you* can do it, as his mother."

With a nod, Aphrodite strode up to Lukus, sending a brief *zap* at Gaia on her way, to push her out of range of him.

Zeus straightened up, finding his voice at last. "We'll take care of her," he said to Aphrodite, shooing her off. He sidled by Hecate and found the strength to summon a few thunderbolts into his hands. "I've changed my mind; I no longer wish to abdicate."

Athena and Hera shimmied past them, on to help Aphrodite with Lukus. Perhaps this had been agreed upon while Hecate brought them here, or they'd decided to stick together, as fellow captives of Gaia.

Persephone pulled herself out of her mother's grasp. "*Now* can we go, please?"

Demeter grabbed Persephone's cheeks to spin *her* head back in the direction of the battle. "Watch and learn, for you're about to witness history."

|| 29. THE MOTHER OF ALL THINGS ||

ZEUS

The lightning ignited in his hand looked more menacing than it felt. Even he knew it'd do little to no damage, *if* it reached its target. But still, Zeus stood strong and proud beside Hecate, doing whatever he could to divert Gaia's attention away from Lukus.

He needed time, and additional ambrosia, if he could find any. But he didn't recall bringing any with him, as he hadn't come with the intention of fighting, not yet. Had Ares come better prepared, perhaps? Or Poseidon?

The latter was still out cold, with Ares kneeling by him to keep an eye over him. But Ares' gaze kept going to Aphrodite. His beloved, transformed, having unleashed the true power that she carried hidden inside. She'd never let it out before—though Zeus had no doubt Ares had felt it—and it must have been impressive from the point of view of a lover to see one's girlfriend shift into one of the most powerful deities of all time.

Gaia's gaze kept twitching over to Aphrodite, as well, who was circling Lukus. He was growling at her. "You can't cure him," she said, her nostrils flaring as she spoke, her words addressed at Hecate. "You can't cure *everything,* darling, I'm sure you're aware of that."

Hecate's fingertips jittered at her sides, and black smoke started to rise all around her, concealing her within its thick mist. "I can certainly try, and I'm going to start with *you.*"

Immediately following Hecate's last word, Gaia lashed out two sharpened vines and whipped them at Hecate, who shoved Zeus sideways, then hopped out of the way so they'd both avoid the blow. Zeus landed hard on his side, but was close to Aphrodite, Hera, and Athena, and opted to remain on the ground and regain some strength.

Hecate can take Gaia for a while. She's powerful enough to distract her without me.

He glanced around to check on the other foe, Mnemosyne. She'd resumed her own battles with Hades, and those seemed personal. She was lashing out at him, but he was swift and smirking as he barred her attacks with minimal effort.

Well, at least one of us is holding his own.

Ares remained out of commission, but Zeus communicated with him as discreetly as possible, via the mind. *"Are you equipped with ambrosia?"*

Ares' head whirled in his direction, and he squinted at his father. *"Hephaestus spared me a few doses. I wasn't sure when or if we should use any, since we already dosed up."*

Zeus shook his head. *"Not this instant, but we should be ready. If Aphrodite breaks the spell on Lukus, Gaia's rage will grow worse, and we must all brace for her wrath."*

Ares, with such speed and grace he might have been wearing Hermes' winged sandals, hastened over and deposited a tiny vial into Zeus' open palm. He then danced over to Hades and snuck another vial into his pocket, and retreated to guard Poseidon's comatose body. Zeus caught him opening the sea god's mouth and pouring the contents of one more vial within.

"This'll wake him up, I hope," said Ares, guessing correctly that Zeus had been watching him and wondering what he was up to.

Ares had been in enough wars to know how to time attacks and coordinate. He'd made it seem like he was focused on Poseidon, but in truth, he had eyes on the entire scene unfolding before them. Zeus trusted him to let him know if anything was amiss, so he chose instead to focus on Aphrodite's efforts to subdue her son.

She'd gotten Lukus to stop growling, but no one could approach him. Athena and Hera remained at the ready, their weapons aimed towards Lukus. Aphrodite had her arms spread apart as if to welcome him into a hug.

But it was Rhea, stomping over from who-knew-where, who took the reins of this attempt to save Lukus. She trudged past Athena and Hera, past Aphrodite, and strolled right up to Lukus, fending off his clawing at her.

She grabbed him by the shoulders, overpowering him somehow, and shook him violently. *"Stop."* He growled, but she replied with a growl of her own, ear-piercing and deadly, a lioness protecting her children. "Fight it, kid. Fight it. You're the grandson of Uranus, and deep down, you know you're the sworn enemy of Gaia. Our best chance at stopping her from this madness. So *wake the hell up!"*

"Wake up," said Hera, having slid over to her mother to seize Lukus' left hand in hers. She'd dropped her borrowed weapon and now concentrated on holding Lukus' hand, squeezing it. "Come to us, to your family. Do not let that poison inside control you." She'd been carrying something in her other hand, and now Zeus saw what it was— a vial of some cloudy-looking liquid, that she hurried to uncork and toss into his mouth as he exchanged growls with Rhea.

Zeus' heart warmed to see his wife's kindness showing through her usually sturdy barrier of coldness. A rare thing; he was certain she'd pretend all this had never happened when they got a chance to speak later. *If* they got a chance.

Athena did the same as Hera, though she didn't speak and didn't try to touch Lukus. She ditched her trident and dashed over to slip some other liquid into Lukus' mouth, then moved away in case he reacted badly.

Athena and Hera had showed up with Hecate. Had she given them doses of some anti-venom to feed to Lukus if they managed to get close enough? Would this anti-venom be strong enough to cleanse Lukus of what might have been the deepest, most powerful poison Gaia could come up with? It had taken all of Hecate's energy and skill to cure Eros and Psyche. Zeus worried two vials of liquid and three women yelling at him to *snap out of it* wouldn't be enough for Lukus.

Aphrodite, still glowing in a golden halo, approached, moving Rhea aside. She took both Lukus' hands in hers, and her golden warmth transferred into him, coursing up his arms, shoulders, and neck. A warmth Zeus felt from where he remained on the ground, ready to shoot up and help should Aphrodite's powers backfire. Or to protect the group should Gaia notice what was going on.

This warmth was so pure, but so heavy, it caused Zeus to clench his jaw and look away for a moment. Like shockwaves of pulsing electricity, he sensed it whooshing through his own veins, as if it had filled the entire area with its power. Aphrodite was like a lightbulb sizzling, absorbing energy, growing so bright she was impossible to look at. All that brightness was what she was trying to send *into* Lukus, to combat the darkness swirling inside his heart, his soul.

"Fight it, son." Aphrodite's voice was soft, yet it resonated in

Zeus' head as if she'd screamed it, burning his eardrums. "Fight this hold and turn on Gaia and help us stop her. You're *my* son, no matter what she says she did to make you come into being. *My* son, the blood of Uranus. She cannot control you."

Zeus checked on Hecate, who was taking bad, blunt blows from Gaia's vines, bleeding blue ichor all over the dirt. Yet she persisted, still hurling her own sharp attacks at the deity, and doing some slight damage. Gaia's face was red and she had a few scrapes on her arms—wherever there were no leaves or vines to protect her skin, that was. But she was smirking, enjoying herself—Zeus caught her licking her lips as one of her vines slashed into Hecate's leg, slicing through her dress and sending sprays of ichor to splash all around her.

Hecate seethed, bent her head to take a large breath, absorbing and accepting the pain. But she refocused on Gaia and shot several jets of black energy balls right at Gaia's chest, knocking her backwards.

Zeus returned to Lukus and Aphrodite.

Come on, Lukus. We need you.

He wondered if he should join his forces with the women striving to revive Lukus, but he sensed his presence would be unwanted. In any case, whatever Aphrodite had done with her powers seemed to be working, because Lukus struggled out of her grasp, hissing, wincing, wriggling about as if fighting something deep within him.

He convulsed as he closed his eyes, then held his head between his hands and angled forward, unleashing a lengthy, ghostly moan that Zeus knew would haunt him forever. His body twisted and contorted in ways that would usually cause irreparable damage to a human's body. But Lukus was no regular human, and the movements didn't seem to harm him much. The *crack* of his bones made Zeus flinch several times as he observed this eerie transformation from Gaia's minion to…what? What *was* happening?

Zeus had never seen anything like this, and had nothing to compare this situation to. A poisonous mind-control? Voices in one's head telling one to shoot arrows into soulmates, to feast on animal flesh, to bite into a fellow deity's neck? A mysterious son of a goddess being pulled into a family drama and warped into doing the culprit's bidding, though he was only half-god? And then a daughter of Uranus with dormant powers and the ability to ward off the toxins causing the mind-control? In all his eons of reigning, Zeus hadn't thought something so insane would occur to him and his family.

Was it working? *Was* Aphrodite powerful enough to remove Lukus' mind-warped intentions of destroying Zeus? Something was happening inside Lukus, for sure; he struggled, writhing about while standing up, not quite losing his balance. He was shivering, gritting his teeth, still holding his head as he shook it, slowly at first, then violently. After another heavy convulsion, he toppled to his knees and proceeded to throw up blood—red blood, and blue ichor, from what Zeus could smell. The blood spilled all over the Underworld's dirt, smoke rising from it. There was something else in whatever he was regurgitating—a tint of bubbly green, its odor so toxic Zeus had to pinch his nose, and he noticed the other goddesses doing the same.

But not Aphrodite—she was still as a statue, watching her son go through whatever process this was. Either reinforcing Gaia's hold on him, or finally ridding himself of it, Zeus couldn't tell.

As quickly as it had started, it stopped. Lukus, on all fours now, stopped throwing up and his limbs stopped quaking. He lifted his head to view Aphrodite, and his eyes wrenched open—blue, as Zeus had first seen them. Their original color.

"What," said Lukus, spitting out a bit more blood, then wiping his mouth, "the *fuck,*" he swiped some matted hair from his forehead, "is going on?"

The green gleam about his body had vanished, and he'd regained his vocabulary, foul as it was. His overall demeanor wasn't of someone possessed, robotic and ready to obey commands. It was him, the grumpy detective Athena had fetched from earth and brought up to Olympus.

I never should have summoned him to me. Maybe this wouldn't have happened if I'd ignored who he was and kept him anonymous.

"A battle, son." Aphrodite helped him up, her glow lessening a little; enough for him to see she was the one speaking to him. He winced at the word *son,* but allowed her to assist him. "You need to be ready, because you'll likely need to challenge her."

She jutted her chin towards Gaia, who'd become mad with power. Green electricity shot from the top of her head and all extremities, but she had no regard for the group with Lukus. She hungered for Hecate, who was clearly suffering, but doing her best to hold her own. Gaia was hovering in the air, vines surrounding her, covering almost her entire body, and empowering her as she struck Hecate left and right. Her hair was the shade of a wildfire and her eyes were bloody, so piercing they could be seen from miles away. And the *stench* of her; a sour rage covered in copper and rolled about in mud. Blood, blood, *blood.*

Lukus gulped. "H-her?" He blinked. "*That?*"

Zeus heard Hecate's panting from where he stood, and feared their time was running out. She'd soon collapse in exhaustion—or worse—and he and his brothers needed to interfere before it was too late. He exchanged a glance with Ares—who'd been observing the whole thing from afar—and at the same time, they both retrieved their vials of ambrosia, uncorked them, and guzzled down the magical, godly substance.

A pleasurable sensation tingled through Zeus, as if all his muscles were bulging, his bones solidifying, and the essence of his powers replenishing at last. Could he take on Gaia alone? No; but with his brothers, and with Lukus, if he agreed to do it, there was a possibility they'd contain her.

A small, truly minuscule chance.

Lukus gulped again. "Gaia. The mother of all things, isn't she? She…" He paused as he stared at Gaia, then returned to Aphrodite with scrunched brows. The fear Zeus had sensed in his aura was depleting, as Lukus discovered what Gaia was doing and what she was capable of. Anger was now swelling within him, and growing stronger by the second. "She did all this, didn't she? I remember now." He massaged his temples, and dragged his hands down his face. "She lulled me into the courtyard, made Rhea drink from me. I saw her, but I…I didn't recognize her right away."

"It's not your fault," said Aphrodite, sending a quick glance of her own towards Gaia, who'd gone so beyond madness that it was frightening to witness. She was a woman-possessed, battering Hecate who could barely stand upright, and who did her damndest to shield herself with her black smoke. "She's on a mission and she'll stop at nothing."

"Yeah, I heard." Lukus took notice of Athena and Hera, as if realizing for the first time that they were there, too. "She had me all fucked up and kept making that memory bitch put me to sleep."

The *memory bitch* in question was still having it out with Hades, but she'd gained the upper hand, now. Hades' armor was ripped into, and there were singe marks on his arms and neck.

"She thought I wouldn't hear…but I did. I heard *everything* she said in that…cave? Hut? Whatever the fuck it was." After a heavy breath, he stiffened, his gaze finding Zeus'. "It was her. She wasn't in my line-up, but *she* did it. Poisoned Persephone, Eros, Psyche, Rhea. And who knows who else. Right?"

Zeus inclined his head, accepting Lukus' detective-like tone, his formal accusation. And Rhea, who'd stayed nearby, nodded.

"Rhea was biting and poisoning the titanesses in Olympus. And then Dionysus—" he gasped, eyebrows sliding up, "—he was in the cave, I remember seeing him. Is he—" he inhaled, exhaled, shook himself, "—no, not my problem. Not now."

Zeus smiled at him.

Good boy, realizing he has other priorities.

"Gaia," Lukus scrunched his nose, "hurt so many people and gods, to let out her crazy kids and take Zeus' throne? Fuck this." He banged a fist to his chest and bent the knee…to Aphrodite. "What do you need from me…Mother?"

|| 30. FEAR ||

GAIA

Nothing was going according to plan. And, spontaneous as Gaia liked to claim she was, this *wasn't* her idea of fun.

Though she *was* having fun fucking up Hecate, for sure. How long she'd wanted to injure her, the untouchable witch-goddess, protected by everyone for no damn reason at all. The one whose magical cabinet was guarded at all times because of all the nefarious materials she kept there. *Why* was she allowed to keep such things with her? Who'd decided she was trustworthy enough to hold such valuable poisons at her disposal? Mere years ago she'd been going about her dangerous frenzies on earth, rattling human emotions, causing discord. Now all of the godly world revered her and her precious cures as if she were a queen amongst deities?

Gaia loathed her. Granted, she was her direct granddaughter, as a daughter of her own daughter Phoebe, but she *couldn't stand her*. The way she *used* Gaia's darling earthly plants, tossed them without care into cauldrons without the proper blessings, tore them into shreds to grind them into pungent pastes to use for medicinal purposes. Or the utter disrespect she'd harbored towards nature during her maddened frenzies, running amok in forests and scratching up trees and ripping out shrubs and flowers to eat them or transform them into who-knew-what as she danced under the moonlight. And did she clean up after herself once she was done? *No.*

Gaia despised her and her witchy presence, and was ready to tear her apart, limb from limb, to slice into that pretty chest of hers now, since she'd so willingly presented herself to fight.

Unleashing a cackle that she hoped would curdle the blood of all those who dared oppose her, Gaia stretched out her arms, elongating her vines. They escaped from her flesh, weaved around her tightly, shivering with the anxious need to be released, to shoot out and wrap around someone's neck and squeeze until their godly life left them. Oh, she'd wanted to choke Zeus out, but he'd weaseled his way out of death thanks to Aphrodite. Hecate wouldn't be so lucky. She was on her own, with everyone else busy trying to free Lukus from Gaia's hold.

A pinch of fear had fluttered into her belly as she'd sighted the group of goddesses hovering around Lukus, shaking him, yelling at him. As he'd bent the knee to his *mother*, to swear *her* fealty.

Idiots. He's not yours yet, he never will be.

Energies were shifting, and she did sense him slipping away slightly from her control; but he wouldn't fully escape. There was no way. She'd dosed him with so many toxins, made him drink from not one but *three* goddesses, and her minions had chanted the ancient ways of the primordials into his mind. He was possessed, and would remain as such even if they all thought they could save him. With all the transformations she'd forced into his body, he was impenetrable. One of her consciousnesses, that she'd implanted in him, was still actively chanting to keep his focus on the task—disarming, maiming, and dismantling Zeus from his throne.

She returned to Hecate, who'd been lashed on all sides from

Gaia's vines. She was bleeding blue ichor all over the place—wounds to her thigh, her ankle, both arms, a gash down her neck, and another down her cheek. Several of her hairs had been ripped out, clustered at her feet, and she was red with exhaustion, puffy with power that poured out of her unevenly. She had little command over her outbursts of energy, so busy trying to thwart Gaia's attacks, unable to hurl any of her own.

Still, she didn't crumble. She hadn't yet fallen to her knees or even lost her balance. The witch-goddess was either suicidal, or stubborn, or both, for she hadn't shown any sign of giving up her fight. She'd managed to nick Gaia's skin in a few places, but Gaia felt nothing of what Hecate likely hoped to sting her, burn her. Gaia's body was numb, surrounded by vines, squeezed by them. Nothing could harm her.

A sudden surge of pain grew in Gaia's stomach, and she bent over, sensing herself falling from her heightened position. She landed on the ground, on her feet, thankfully, but the agony was such that she couldn't stand straight, needing to bend in half to contain the swelling in her gut. A scream exploded inside, resonating in her eardrums—an *internal* scream, one only she could hear, she realized, as no one was reacting to it.

Oh, shit. The consciousness planted inside Lukus...

It was like feeling a piece of herself dying. A muscle no longer filling with oxygen and blood, a bone shattering, its remnants scattered all over the dirt. A heart ceasing to beat, to load up with ichor. Lungs constricting and refusing to take in any more air, refusing to function properly.

Something, *someone* had yanked out the piece of her that had been inside Lukus' mind, and destroyed it, and thus weakening her.

That was why she'd fallen, why she'd felt such intense pain in her belly. Like someone had sliced it open and removed her womb, then stomped on it right in front of her.

Shit, shit, shit.

Severed from that power, she'd need a few moments to recuperate, but she was still working on Hecate and couldn't afford to waste any time. After shooting a stream of serrated leaves at the witch—and hearing her squeak as they hit home, on her face—Gaia took a peek at her beloved Lukus, and gasped. He wasn't slipping away—he *had* slipped, completely, into the other team's grasp. He no longer glowed the green of Gaia's control, no longer stood like a centuries' old statue guarding an ancient temple, and no longer struggled with the eerie thoughts Gaia had been putting in him. Thoughts of heads being ripped off, of teeth being dug into necks and shredding into arteries and spraying blood everywhere, of limbs being cut off and tossed into the *Pyriphlegethon,* where they'd burn to a crisp.

He was no longer hers, and she'd been too busy play-fighting with her dinner—Hecate—instead of finishing her off as she should have eons ago.

The thrill of the battle had gotten the best of her. She'd claimed to be a queen of multitasking, right? How could this have happened? And *how* did Aphrodite break through the unbreakable hold Gaia had on Lukus' mind?

It wasn't possible. Mnemosyne messed something up in the ritual, in the potion. Something was wrong with the blood they'd collected, the ingredients they'd stolen from Hecate.

Gaia heard Hecate running towards her, and without even looking, sent a thick vine to trip her, promptly causing the witch-goddess to smack onto her face with an *oof* of pain.

Good, that'll give me a few seconds to reassess the situation.

Lukus had indeed snapped out of her possession, and was studying his hands. His arms were stuck to his sides. He squinted as something began to form near both sets of fingers—a slight smoke, brightened by a faint yellow light. A smoke that *shivered*, morphing into various forms, shifting, *shifting*.

"No," whispered Gaia, recognizing that smoke, that light, that constant changing of its shape. "No, *no*, this wasn't supposed to happen yet!"

As Hecate snuck up behind her—*oh, the daft girl, did she think I wouldn't sense her?*—she twisted and threw a bundle of vines at her, blocking her from moving forward.

"Is that…" Athena spoke in hushed tones, while watching the vapor surrounding Lukus' hands. "Is that what I think it is?"

Gaia flipped back around to watch the scene.

Hera's jaw had dropped, and Aphrodite beamed at Lukus, clasping her hands together under her chin. "It is. *It is!* My son is about to get his first godly weapon!"

The words pierced into Gaia's heart as if someone had stabbed her seventy times with the thickest of needles, and injected a suffocating poison into her bloodstream.

No, this isn't right!

Demi-gods were rarely accorded such a privilege, but Lukus was different; Gaia had made it so. So of course she'd *wanted* him to obtain that weapon, to come into his godly powers and figure out who he was, how he'd fight, what he'd stand for. But while he was under *her* control, not Aphrodite's. He was supposed to be her ultimate minion, her final card that would be the winning hand to defeat Zeus and his moronic brothers. The weapon that was about to take shape was supposed to be used against Zeus, not against her.

"Mnemosyne!" Gaia's mind-voice was riddled with angst and anger as she reached out to her daughter, who'd been occupied with getting some strange personal revenge on Hades. *"Enough of your nonsense and come help me! They've taken Lukus back, he's about to get his weapon. I need you to take out Aphrodite, immediately!"*

Mnemosyne's voice—not in her thoughts—flowed through the air at the same time as she approached Gaia and lent her a hand to help her stand up straight. "What?" She gawked at the scene, having had no notion of what had been going on while she swiped at Hades and stained his tunic with blood. "I'll get her."

She lunged at Aphrodite's back, but Aphrodite had been anticipating her and dodged to the side in time to avoid collision. Once Mnemosyne re-balanced herself from the failed attack, the two launched into a whirl of gold and purple electricity, thrusting their powers at one another, equally matched in their strength.

Mnemosyne will get the upper hand. She's an official titaness, not some bastard sea-foam replica like Aphrodite.

Gaia replaced her gaze on Lukus, cringing as he peered down at the smoke surrounding his hands, confused at what was about to unfold.

"He was *mine,*" Gaia said under her breath, sensing a growl growing in her throat. "Aphrodite birthed him, but *I* am his real ancestor, not Uranus. Ugh!" She unleashed a vine that whooshed into Hecate, who'd again thought to sneak up and attack her from behind. "I should have *made* him on my own, like I did Pontus. Why did I choose a damned descendant of my piece of trash ex-husband to do this?"

At the time of her plotting, she'd believed Aphrodite would be the perfect host for Lukus. She *was* more powerful than she let on, and *did* have the blood of Uranus in her veins, which Gaia had hoped would strengthen Lukus and make him a worthy opponent for Zeus. Half-human, yes; but once he'd come into his powers, he'd have all of Aphrodite's essence within him. And Aphrodite was more powerful than Zeus, though she wasn't allowed to tell anyone about it or prove it.

Gaia had banked on Lukus playing for *her* team when his full capacities came upon him. Not this; not them.

Hecate didn't try another attack. Gaia spun to find her crouched to the ground, taking deep, labored breaths, her witchy smoke frail and nearly transparent. Gaia didn't have much time to dwell on her success at overpowering Hecate—a lioness-like monster was storming up to her now, claws and fangs out.

"Rhea," said Gaia, snickering at her daughter, who'd halfway transformed *into* a lioness, with a mane of frizzy hair surrounding her head, and her hands resembling the giant paws of a feline. "Don't make me laugh. Have you not seen what I can do? Have you forgotten? I don't want to hurt you."

"I don't care," said Rhea, her voice more of a roar than her regular sweet-tinted, motherly timbre. "You've already hurt me by turning my family members against each other and creating this chaos." She gestured at Aphrodite and Mnemosyne, locked in their swirling, swaying battle—they were both floating as they sent their energies at one another. Then she pointed at the spot where Poseidon had been laying.

Poseidon *wasn't* laying there anymore, but Gaia didn't think Rhea knew that. Whatever else Rhea said was muffled, as Gaia searched the area for the once comatose god of the sea. How had he gotten up, revived himself? Ares had been hovering over him, but Ares had no curing powers, and no knowledge of how to revive a fallen god. He was a warrior; *he* did the killing, not the reanimating.

Now that Gaia thought of it, Hades had disappeared, too. When Mnemosyne had grown bored with him and concentrated on Aphrodite, he'd somehow escaped the battle. Where had he gone? Inside the Underworld, to nurse his wounds with his stolen bride? Or was he with Poseidon, hiding somewhere to plot how to bring Gaia down?

No...no, they cannot, they will not.

Her heart skipped a beat as she realized Ares was gone, too. Had they fled in fear? No—she sighted Zeus, hanging out near Lukus; no one would have left without his say-so.

As she focused on Zeus, she smelled him—a violent thunderstorm, an icy deluge about to unleash and smash into her. He'd regained some strength, and if she wasn't mistaken, he reeked of ambrosia.

Dammit. If he took ambrosia, it's safe to assume the others did, too.

She'd thought she'd depleted all the reserves of the godly substance from upstairs. She'd gone through all of Hestia's kitchen cabinets, ripped into all the coveted gardens where the ambrosia was cultivated, and had even snuck into Hephaestus' underground workshop to snatch up all his vials. Had she missed some? Or had Poseidon harbored his own stash in his kingdom, and he'd been the one to provide for his brothers?

No, no, no...this will not do.

For the first time in eons, perhaps in her entire existence as a primordial goddess, Gaia not only felt fear, but she succumbed to it. She stopped pretending it wasn't there, stopped fighting it. Now, as things stood, her chances of success had diminished, and she needed a new plan. Fast.

|| 31. YOU WILL NOT BE TAKEN ||

PERSEPHONE

"She's insane," said Poseidon, still recovering from his wounds that were slowly healing under Demeter's cautious watch.

It was eerie to see her working with him, easing his pain. Demeter and Poseidon often had explosive arguments that they thought no one overheard, but Persephone did. For them to set aside their differences in such a trying time was a good sign—her family wasn't *completely* broken.

"Yes, but I think we do have the advantage now," said Demeter, sending a side glance at the blur of gold and purple that was Aphrodite and Mnemosyne's confrontation. They were surrounded in smoke. It was impossible to see which of them had the upper hand, though Persephone prayed with all her might that it was Aphrodite.

Ares and Hades had dragged Poseidon over to Demeter and Persephone's hiding spot, behind the inanimate giant body of Cerberus, where no one had detected them so far. They'd noticed Gaia looking around, but Hecate had been keeping her occupied. Until moments ago, that was, when she'd crumbled from a too severe injury and couldn't find the strength to continue the battle.

Persephone had nearly rushed out of her concealed spot to grab her, haul her over to be protected. Within their trio of mystery users, they'd be able to disconnect from Gaia's insanity. But Demeter had held her back, warning her that Hecate, though *looking* finished, was far from that. *"Sense her energy, daughter? She's still powerful, but she's deciding to hold back for a reason, and we must give her the benefit of the doubt. If she needs us, she'll reach out."*

Persephone was getting a bit tired of having to stand aside and watch as others fought for their family's freedom. How she'd have helped, she wasn't positive—most of her powers revolved around flowers and plants. But she knew how to fight, how to throw punches. She'd *punch* Gaia in the stomach repeatedly until those damn vines spewed out her mouth, pricking along her throat on their way.

Only Poseidon had required more attention than the others, and Demeter seemed thankful for that. Though she *could* heal, it wasn't her specialty outside of the mystery rites. Most of the powers she had during their Eleusinian trances were sacred *to* those trances, and couldn't be used outside of them. But in any case, Ares assured Demeter that they'd all taken ambrosia and were healing from within, and would soon be able to re-enter the fight.

"Oh, look, it's happening," said Ares in a whisper—an oddity, as he usually spoke loud enough for nearby planets to eavesdrop. "Lukus—his weapon."

Sure enough, Persephone zoomed in on the blurry form of Lukus. His gaze was directed on the mist around his hands. He'd been staring at it for what felt like ages, while Zeus, Athena, and Hera semi-protected him from Gaia's wrath. Now, the mist was taking a defined shape, the smoke dissipating to be replaced by a device of cherry wood. A device fashioned into a lengthy, brand-new bow. In his other hand, a cluster of arrows appeared, their tips black and sharp, shining under the fake Underworld sky as if threatening to slice through a neck or two.

Ah, so he'll be a bowman, will he?

The bow was similar to Eros' weapon, but it gave an edge of power, of war. Eros' bow was supposed to find love and unite it, but it turned out Lukus' was supposed to hit its target and shred through it. Persephone shivered sensing the power surging from him, from the arrows, their pointy ends eerily already aimed towards Gaia.

She'd never received a godly weapon herself. One only received such a gift when in the act of battle and in need of something to use as an offensive against one's enemies. And as a goddess who'd steered clear of fights, Persephone had never gotten a chance to see what her essence, what her soul would have summoned for her.

A tinge of jealousy slithered through her as she watched Lukus, a *demi-god,* lift the arrows, sniff at them, then the bow that he admired with a growing lust in his eyes.

"That's the signal," said Poseidon, setting his trident's bottom to the ground and straightening his back as he glanced at the scene. "Aphrodite's got Mnemosyne under control, somewhat. And Rhea is approaching Gaia," he pointed his trident towards the lioness goddess in her slow trek towards her mother, "so it's our time to intervene."

Persephone's gaze found Hades, who'd been kneeling in front of her, catching his breath, replenishing his resources of energy. She lowered to his level and set a finger under his chin, pressing her lips to his in a swift kiss.

"Go," she said, helping him up and nudging him towards Poseidon and Ares. "Join Zeus and Lukus, and get Gaia while she's weak. She's distracted by Rhea right now, and none of her other allies are available anymore."

Ares nodded at Persephone's strategy—likely a smidgen

impressed at a goddess who had no knowledge of war-planning and who was revealing the correct path for them to take. He raised his sword and mouthed, *"time for war."* His shield had shattered earlier, but he no longer needed it; this blade radiated with a red electricity that sparked in the air, shocking Persephone's arm hairs into sticking up, and goosebumps to scatter up and down her arms.

Demeter took her shoulders and pulled her back, further behind Cerberus. "They have a chance, but just in case—if things go awry, you run back into the Underworld, you hear me? *Run.* Don't look back. Close the gates, warn the judges, and get to your palace. Do not go anywhere else; maybe in Hecate's crypt?"

"Mother," Persephone spun to Demeter, "what are you talking about? I won't abandon them, or you. My husband—"

"—if Zeus is wounded, or…" Demeter gulped, "*killed,* Gaia will go for Poseidon and Hades next. As Hades' wife, that puts you in danger. And if there's any way I can keep you *out* of danger, I will try. I wasn't able to prevent it earlier in your life, but I'll be damned if I let it happen again. You will not be taken."

A tear tickled at Persephone's lash-line as she and her mother returned their gazes to the battle. The discussion was over—Demeter had decided, and Persephone would have to abide by her rules. But she prayed she wouldn't have to go anywhere. Prayed Cerberus would wake up and bite Gaia's head off. Prayed that some magical army of allies would zoom down from the Acherusian Lake and sweep in to assist Zeus.

The fog around Aphrodite and Mnemosyne's tug-of-war had dissipated. They were both on the ground now, tossing balls of bright electric energy at one another. Mnemosyne's gold gown was torn, her usually frizzy hair on fire. She was panting, shrugging forward, struggling to hop from foot to foot to dodge Aphrodite's attacks. Aphrodite, on the other hand, looked like a glowing goddess from an ethereal dream, untouched and unsoiled by Mnemosyne's attempts to maim her. She stood straight, her balance impeccable, and her attacks timed as if she'd choreographed this entire battle ahead of time.

The brothers and Ares zoomed over to Zeus, whose color had gone from pallid to its normally somewhat tanned hue. He was *almost* healthy and radiant as a king of the skies should be.

He took ambrosia too? Good for him. Good for us.

Together, the siblings and the god of war approached Gaia from all angles, taking example from Rhea, who was still getting closer to Gaia. She had no weapons but her claws, but the kings and Ares had their own weapons thrust out and pointed at Gaia, ready to jam them into her if she were to make any menacing motion. She was focused on Rhea, and they were speaking, but Persephone couldn't hear what they were saying.

Suddenly, Gaia's voice grew louder, piercing through the area, causing Demeter to cover her ears and Persephone to wince.

"*No,* this is not how this goes!" Gaia arched her spine, lifted a few inches off the ground, a halo of green light swarming around her. Her vines swirled and swirled around her arms, shooting out in all directions but still aimed at the gods seeking to dominate her. They all moved before the vines could break through them. Persephone could tell the intent here was for those vines to *pierce* and destroy anything in their passage. The gods' confidence was tested, their plans put in suspense. "Mnemosyne—*let them out!*"

Mnemosyne, if she heard her mother's request, did nothing, still absorbed in her fight with Aphrodite.

Gaia was alone. And Zeus and his siblings had a few more

weapons in their arsenal. They had Hecate, who'd gotten back up and who, as Demeter had claimed, still had some reserves of energy. With her bare hands, she seized one of Gaia's vines and tugged on it, forcing Gaia to fall back onto her feet. Taking her cue, Athena and Hera also snatched up a few vines and yanked at them, now sending Gaia to her knees. She didn't stay down for too long, but as the goddesses had hold of her vines, she bared her teeth at them, unsure which to attack first.

Persephone saw Hecate, Athena, and Hera exchange brief glances that seemed to mean something to them. On a count of three, they rushed forward and proceeded to spin around Gaia in different directions, twisting the vines around her, binding her arms and legs. They pulled tight, ensuring the vines crushed into her, squeezing her into immobility, and stopping short of her neck, not wanting to choke her out.

They don't want to kill her... and I'm sure they know that's not possible, anyway.

Lukus stomped up to her, his weapon at the ready. He'd prepared his bow, and pointed a deadly arrow at her vine-covered chest, with the confidence of an archer who'd been groomed since birth to wield a bow with perfect precision.

"You're done," he said, his voice clear and concise; not the shaking timbre Persephone had heard before, when he and Aphrodite were talking.

Poseidon marched up and set the tips of his trident's forks under Gaia's chin, to make sure she didn't look down. He likely wanted to keep sight of her lips, were she to start muttering some incantation to free herself of the mess of vines.

With a gasp, Persephone watched Hades hasten up and aim his glaive at Gaia's head, where sharpened sticks seemed to crawl within her hair, preparing to pounce onto their victims. They stopped at once when Hades threatened them. Ares arrived and thrust his sword within millimeters of her Achilles tendons, making it clear that should she try anything now, he'd not hesitate to cut her there.

The three goddesses fought to keep hold of the vines—they were covered in thorns, which made the deities bleed from their palms, but they kept on, gritting their teeth through the pain.

Zeus finally ended the procession of gods by taking a few steps towards Gaia, then stopping. He peered up at the fake star-sprinkled sky, closed his eyes, and lifted his arms.

Within a few instants, he re-opened his eyes, which had turned an ethereal, electric blue. He lowered his arms abruptly. Lightning rained down on Gaia, who had no choice but to take the brunt of the shock, since she'd been immobilized and guarded.

The others scattered in time to be protected from Zeus' blows, leaving Gaia alone to face the deluge of electric light. It seared into her cheeks, singed her hair, burned her fingertips, and knocked her over, as she had no strength or ability to block each strike from harming her.

The vines loosened, withered, ripping from Hera's, Athena's, and Hecate's grips and straight back into Gaia's body, as she curled on the ground, writhing. She convulsed once, twice; then passed out from the agony and the aftershock of Zeus' power.

Taking a moment to steady his breath—summoning that much lightning had consumed all the ambrosia he'd ingested, no doubt— Zeus released a tremendous sigh and turned to Hades, who'd come to stand beside him.

"We need to get her to Tartarus and lock her up, under the tightest security you can think of," he said, as Hades patted his back in a *job well-done* manner.

"Tartarus himself will assist with that. And I'm sure he'll beckon the energy from Chaos itself for assistance. I will speak with Nyx, as well. Fear not, Brother." Hades wrinkled his nostrils as he shifted his view to the now inanimate and temporarily weakened Gaia. "She won't do this again, not under my watch."

Zeus nodded. "However the system works, I want her locked up for all eternity. No chance for escape. No pardon possible. Enough is enough." He welcomed Hera into his arms for a brief hug of reunion, before looking at Hades once more. "Seal her in there with her monstrous children and her dreadful husband. Make sure they remember that this is what happens when you test Olympus."

|| 32. THUMP, THUMP ||

EROS

The flicker of fireflies caught his eye as he sat and stretched on one of the stone benches in the courtyard. Fireflies—there hadn't been any of those in Olympus in months, and no one had stopped to notice that. No one had stopped to notice that the spark of joy that usually spread down the hallways, the sound of glasses clinking and harps playing magnificent melodies, and the aroma of lusty lovemaking had faded, lost beneath the waves of evil energy that had crept into the palace.

But those negative waves were no more. Finally, Olympus was restored to its usual lightheartedness. Its portraits no longer stared in accusation at anyone walking down the corridors. Every hearth radiated a real warmth—Hestia was *humming* when she walked to the kitchens. Parties and frivolities had resumed, and curfews were lifted.

The big boss himself, however, remained cryptic and scarce. It had been a week since the confrontation in the Underworld, and Zeus had not shown his face more than once, to warn all his constituents that they were now safe. That Olympus would no longer have to cower under the command of a culprit with sickening schemes of revenge.

Gaia. All this time, all these centuries, she'd been plotting to overthrow Zeus and take what she thought was hers. She'd been scheming to release her children from Tartarus, and setting up a civil war to see who among the Olympians could be trusted to help her pursue her goals. And who she'd have to put to the torch.

Eros shifted in his seat, his fingertips twitching with the need to choke something, someone. A rare violence that still sometimes grew in him when he was upset. A vague haunting feeling of all the horrific things he'd done when under the culprit's control. Under *Gaia's* control.

He shuddered, remembering when Zeus had made the brief announcement before disappearing into his chambers.

"It was Gaia, and she's paying the full price for her crimes." His voice had been a blurry breeze, hard to decipher. The thumping of his heart had been uneven, startling Eros into wondering how long it would take him to recover from such a battle. He'd dove into the Underworld—a first for the king of the skies—confronted his grandmother, and ended up shackling her wrists and ankles and sending her off to Tartarus. Or so Eros had been told.

"So this is what it's supposed to feel like up here?" A masculine voice came from the doorway; a figure stood cloaked in the shadows of the night, but as he stepped forward, arms crossed, Eros smiled.

Lukus—the wild card, the half-human who'd proved to be much, *much* more than what Gaia had had planned for him. Lukus—Eros' half-brother.

Eros shivered, still seeking to stuff down the atrocious memories of all *he'd* done to Lukus while under Gaia's spell. Lukus forgave him—and more so now that he knew they were direct kin—but Eros would never forgive himself. He'd never get over the spilled blood, the clash of Lukus' teeth on their mother's bones, the chewed flesh flying from his mouth and splattering on the ground. . .

Eros' stomach rumbled as he patted the bench, offering Lukus a space beside him. "Indeed," he said, taking a whiff of the fresh, untainted Olympus nighttime air—mountainous and fulfilling. A scent he'd longed for during his stint on earth, and worried he'd never smell again.

Lukus walked over and sat, wincing at the coldness of the stone. He wore one of Zeus' old short-sleeved tunics, and it was a bit big for him, but it still showed his perfect figure, accentuated his muscular arms. The drab gray color brought out the bright blues in his eyes. How had Eros *not* noticed the godliness about him before? He was handsome, gracious in his movements, and despite his foul, *very* foul vocabulary, he had all the makings of a god.

Demi-god, let us not forget. But Zeus wants us to treat him like one of our own.

"How were things on earth?" Eros took a swig of the ambrosia wine he'd brought outside with him. The party indoors was still raging on. He heard the laughter and the music filtering in from where Lukus had arrived in the courtyard, leaving the door open.

Lukus had asked to return home, to Washington D.C., to formally resign from his job and put his affairs in order. There was nothing left in America for him, he'd said, after Aphrodite extended an invitation for him to dwell in Olympus with her and his *true* family. To everyone's surprise—many had expected him to storm off and swear about being possessed by a primordial goddess and used for her perilous purposes—he hadn't hesitated. He'd accepted the offer.

Aphrodite had beamed at the prospect of having another of her children in Olympus. But there was something different about her emotions towards Lukus, and Eros was the only one who'd caught it. He knew his mother well; her heartbeat had switched its rhythm when she'd spoken to Lukus. A softer pitter-patter, not the urging thudding of when she encountered Ares, or the vibration of responding to a summons from Zeus, or the erratic pulsating of exchanging fake words of politeness with Hera or any other god she disliked.

With Lukus, she was calm, serene. Now that Eros thought about it, Lukus had been the one to change her attitude before, after her own adventures on earth. It was after returning from posing as a human, alongside Lukus, that she'd redecorated her entire room and rid herself of things she'd once called prized possessions, and had learned to better control her temper.

Eros wasn't sure exactly *what* had happened in the Underworld, between Aphrodite and Lukus. How she'd conjured the power to fix him, to dispel Gaia's negative forces from clogging inside his mind. Zeus had been tight-lipped about Aphrodite's role in all this, but other gods present during the events—Demeter, Poseidon, and Ares—had let slip bits and pieces of how she'd let loose her *true* power, her *true* self. *Daughter of Uranus* was an expression a few of them had whispered. Eros, stealthily sneaking around one evening, had heard them discussing how she'd glowed gold and emitted a surging essence the likes of which none of them had ever experienced before.

Aphrodite herself had been discreet, too, since coming home. She'd been by Zeus while he stood on the dais and addressed his Olympians, but once he'd scattered off to his hiding spot, so had she. She'd spent some well-earned alone time with Ares, and had spoken with Eros occasionally, one of those times being to advise him officially that Lukus was his brother, and he was to treat him with the same respect as he would any full-blooded godly sibling.

"It was…weird," said Lukus, peering at Eros' goblet in curiosity. Eros handed it to him, and he drank, only trembling slightly when the ambrosia hit his tongue. It would take some time for his taste buds to adjust to Olympus delicacies, but he'd get there. "When you find out your purpose, when you realize what you've been doing all these years was a front…it's just weird."

Weird. What an interesting word.

Despite the positivity reanimating in Olympus, there was indeed a *weirdness* to the place, too. With Zeus in hibernation, Hera oversaw most of the royal matters, but she was more reserved and less stern than was her habit. She sat on her luxurious throne with the same poise, the same stiffness as before, yet it was evident she'd been through trauma and had gained much knowledge from that experience. The most shocking of all was when she let Athena attend her meetings, or when she held court, allowing her to use her official role of advisor to the king. *"But today, you are advisor to the queen,"* Hera had said, causing a ripple of confusion in the audience in the throne-room. Whatever had occurred down in Mnemosyne's hut—Eros had heard rumors that they'd been captive there, with Aphrodite—it had changed their lives and their relationship forever.

Hades had swung by the day before, at Hera's invitation. He spoke to a small gathering of Olympians—Zeus wasn't there—to explain how Gaia was sealed in a super secure and secret section of Tartarus, where she couldn't receive visitors.

"She's to remain locked up for eternity, unless Zeus revisits the idea of releasing her after he's done stewing in his anger." The King of the Underworld looked rested and serene for what Eros believed was the first time in his life.

Whatever his reasons for keeping to himself, Zeus was *pissed.* Eros wasn't the only one who'd felt his rage rattling the walls and skidding down the marble floors. Whenever he passed the area where the king's chambers were, the air grew hot, thick with fury, and a cluster of goosebumps gathered on Eros' arm. And his heart was unsettled, too. It was beating, stopping, beating faster, stopping again, then taking off as fast as a racehorse and not quitting until Eros himself was out of breath from listening.

Hades had come with more news of the Underworld. A decision he and Hera had come to, apparently, was that he'd visit more often and offer more information about how his realm worked. She'd sought a similar accord with Poseidon, but he, contrary to everyone else who'd been in the battle, hadn't changed his ways and had resumed his drunken debauchery amongst humans.

"About Mnemosyne," Hades had said, turning a few heads, garnering a few frowns. Eros didn't know the extent of her involvement, but her name had been cursed by those who'd returned to Olympus after the fight, and he'd not dared ask why. "She was put on trial by the judges and Athena." Hades sent a quick glance at the goddess in question, who inclined her head in confirmation. "She was stripped of most of her powers. Forced to renounce her status as a titaness, and sentenced to be Melinoë's personal assistant—bathe her, feed her, tend to her needs. Persephone agreed to supervise this." A twinkle in Hades' eye had caught Eros' attention. He felt the King of the Underworld's heart pounding for his beloved wife and her own attempt to deal with the trauma.

Few knew who Melinoë was, but Eros and Persephone had spoken often, and she'd confided in him centuries ago about the child she had, whose father she refused to speak of. Eros had consoled her, and promised her secret was safe with him—it would remain so.

Two deities ran through the courtyard, breaking Eros and Lukus' quiet contemplation. They laughed, spilling their drinks as they flurried across the way, headed to who-knew-where. When Eros sighted *who* they were, he had no doubt they were hurrying to the casual courtyard, where some secret event was happening. Rhea, in a silk dress of fiery orange, nearly tripped over her own feet, and her companion—none other than the overly tipsy Dionysus—helped her stabilize. They both noticed Eros and Lukus and nodded in acknowledgment, feigning sobriety with such effort that Eros had to hold in a laugh, and he sensed Lukus doing the same.

Eros knew what the secret event was. A celebratory orgy of some kind, organized by Dionysus, and attended by so many deities that Eros pretended not to know that his daughter was on the guest-list. But so was Rhea, who'd spent centuries spying on such parties and never daring to join in. Well, seeing how close she'd gotten to killing half her family, she'd realized it was now or never, and even as a titaness, her days were counted.

She was pardoned for her role in the battle, of course, since she hadn't been in control of her biting habits. In her spare time, she'd chosen to take on a new godly role of overseeing humans with addictions, to help them heal.

"I'm so pleased to see them all so happy," said Eros, setting a hand to his heart, watching as Rhea and Dionysus stumbled through another door, back into the palace.

"Yeah, but," Lukus swallowed, "there will always be someone who wants to disrupt the gods, change the world, right? Maybe not Gaia, but I'll bet there are others with a rebellious nature."

Eros winced, disliking the sudden doubt, the sprinkle of negativity. "You're correct," he said, patting Lukus' arm. "But I have a new brother now, a powerful new member of the family who will be on our side when the next war comes. And," Eros sensed his lips spreading into a genuine smile, "an ally who will assist me with my charges on earth. A Cupid-in-training, hm? Is that what Mother and Zeus decided for you?"

In the faint candlelight from an overhead sconce, Eros saw Lukus flush as he gave a brief nod of his head.

"Perfect." Eros drained the rest of his drink and stood up. "Because I need to concentrate on *my* charge—my lovely Psyche."

By some magic, Psyche entered the courtyard, as if sensing Eros' need for her. He smelled her sweetness, detected her sexual presence before he saw her. He spun to her as she ran to his arms and pressed her liquored lips to his, animating an animalistic urge within him—*not* one of blood, but one of pure desire. Of naked flesh rubbing on naked flesh, of tongues twisting, hair tangling, spine tingling—

"Ew," said Lukus, who'd gotten up and begun to exit the courtyard. He couldn't read minds yet—Eros wasn't sure if he'd develop that power—but there was no escaping the lustful tension Psyche had brought outside with her. Eros imagined Lukus had grown a bit disgusted with their slobbery kisses.

He left, and Eros pulled the drunken Psyche from his mouth, holding her at arm's length. He tucked a blonde curl away from her flushed face, then kneeled and pressed his ear to her chest, right between her bulging breasts that he couldn't wait to massage and play with.

Thump, thump. Thump, thump.

All was right in the world—for now.

To be continued in:

THERE WILL BE SPIN-OFFS AND SEQUELS IN THE NEAR

FUTURE!

AUTHOR'S NOTE
&
ACKNOWLEDGMENTS

To this day, I still can't believe "GLORIOUS GAIA" made its way onto paper. For the longest time, it was nothing but a title, staring at me, expecting its story to be written. For the longest time, I *knew* Gaia was THE culprit in this series, but I just couldn't figure out how to get there.

Well, we got there. And I can't forget the glorious help of my beta readers, **Selena, Kat, Danielle, Emily, and Viviana**, some of which have been with me on this journey since book two, and all of which lift me up and remind me why I write.

To my boyfriend, Matt, for listening to my rambling about my five thousand different story ideas and believing in every single one of them.

To my family, who spread the news of my success and have made me famous in their small town of Venice, Florida!

And I have to set up a special dedication to a cat—*yes*, a cat. To Onyx, the first pet I ever had as an adult, and who was my everything for nearly twelve years. My companion, my best buddy, my cuddler, my butthead, my anxiety reliever, my baby. He passed away in August of 2022 at the age of twelve, and it was much, much too soon. This book is for him—for all those nights when he stared at me as I stared at the screen, probably thinking there was something tremendously wrong with me. There was, but hey—it translated to this awesome book series.

ABOUT THE AUTHOR

Stephanie Rose is an author based in Nevada, but her heart lives in Paris, France, where she resided for almost twelve years. When she's not writing, she spends her time going on adventures with her boyfriend, catching up on TV-shows, or snuggling her tuxedo kitten, Crowley.

"GLORIOUS GAIA" is the fourth in a four-book series, inspired by her obsession with Greek mythology. For updates on upcoming works and exclusive content about the Angry Greek Gods world, visit her website: www.stephanierose.online